O9-AID-319

Chapter 1

Scotland
Summer 1480

"Ye dinnae look dead; though I think ye might be trying to smell like ye are."

Angus MacReith scowled at the young man towering over his bed. Artan Murray was big, strongly built, and handsome. His cousin had done well, he thought. Far better than all his nearer kin who had borne no children at all or left him with ones like young Malcolm. Angus scowled even more fiercely as he thought about that man—untrustworthy, greedy, and cowardly. Artan had the blood of the MacReiths in him and it showed, just as it did in his twin, Lucas. It was only then that Angus realized Artan stood there alone.

"Where is the other one?" he asked.

"Lucas had his leg broken," Artan replied.

"Bad?"

"Could be. I was looking for the ones who did it when ye sent word."

"Ye dinnae ken who did it?"

"I have a good idea who did it. A verra good idea." Artan shrugged. "I will find them."

Angus nodded, "Aye, ye will, lad. Suspicion they will be hiding now, eh?"

"Aye, as time passes and I dinnae come to take my reckoning they will begin to feel themselves safe. 'Twill be most enjoyable to show them how mistaken they are."

"Ye have a devious mind, Artan," Angus said in obvious admiration.

"Thank ye." Artan moved to lean against the bed-post at the head of the bed. "I dinnae think ye are dying, Angus."

"I am nay weel!"

"Och, nay, ye arenae, but ye arenae dying."

"What do ye ken about it?" grumbled Angus, pushing himself upright enough to collapse against the pillows Artan quickly set behind him.

"Dinnae ye recall that I am a Murray? I have spent near all my life surrounded by healers. Aye, ye are ailing; but I dinnae think ye will die if ye are careful. Ye dinnae have the odor of a mon with one foot in the grave. And, for all ye do stink some, 'tisnae really the smell of death."

"Death has a smell ere it e'en takes hold of a mon's soul?"

"Aye, I think it does. And since ye are nay dying, I will return to hunting the men who hurt Lucas."

Angus grabbed Artan by the arm, halting the younger man as he started to move away. "Nay! I could die and ye ken it weel. I hold three score years. E'en the smallest chill could set me firm in the grave."

That was true enough, Artan thought as he stud-ied the man who had fostered him and Lucas for

HANNAH HOWELL

HIGHLAND BARBARIAN

ZEBRA BOOKS
KENSINGTON PUBLISHING CORP.

http://www.kensingtonbooks.com

ZEBRA BOOKS are published by

Kensington Publishing Corp.
119 West 40th Street
New York, NY 10018

Copyright © 2006 by Hannah Howell

All rights reserved. No part of this book may be reproduced
in any form or by any means without the prior written con-
sent of the Publisher, excepting brief quotes used in reviews.

To the extent that the image or images on the cover of this
book depict a person or persons, such person or persons
are merely models, and are not intended to portray any
character or characters featured in the book.

If you purchased this book without a cover you should be
aware that this book is stolen property. It was reported as
"unsold and destroyed" to the Publisher and neither the
Author nor the Publisher has received any payment for this
"stripped book."

All Kensington titles, imprints, and distributed lines are
available at special quantity discounts for bulk purchases for
sales promotion, premiums, fund-raising, educational, or
institutional use.

Special book excerpts or customized printings can also be
created to fit specific needs. For details, write or phone
the office of the Kensington Sales Manager: Attn.: Sales
Department. Kensington Publishing Corp., 119 West 40th
Street, New York, NY 10018. Phone: 1-800-221-2647.

Zebra and the Z logo Reg. U.S. Pat. & TM Off.

First Printing: December 2006
ISBN-13: 978-1-4201-4265-5
ISBN-10: 1-4201-4265-8

20 19 18 17 16 15 14 13 12 11

Printed in the United States of America

KISSING THE BARBARIAN

At the door to her bedchamber, Cecily turned to wish Sir Artan a good sleep, only to catch him staring at her in a very intense manner. "I thank ye for your escort, Sir Artan. 'Twas nay necessary, but it was most appreciated."

Artan looked into her lovely eyes, saw her uncertainty, and decided he needed to do one more thing before he was absolutely sure of his next step. Placing his hands on the door on either side of her, he took a step closer until their bodies almost touched. He took the sound of a slight hitch in her breathing and the widening of her eyes as a good sign. As he slowly lowered his head, he watched her face, her rapidly changing expressions telling him that she knew what he was about to do. The fact that she made no move to halt him or flee encouraged him.

The moment Sir Artan's lips brushed over hers, Cecily felt a warmth flood through her body with such speed and fury she felt dizzy. Sir Fergus's lips had never felt so warm or soft, or so gentle. At first, the gentle prodding of his tongue against her lips puzzled her. Then he sucked on her bottom lip and she gasped over the flurry of feelings that raced through her. The moment her lips parted, he thrust his tongue into her mouth, and in but a heartbeat, she felt herself shudder beneath the strength of what his stroking tongue was making her feel.

When he started to pull away, she grasped him by the front of his shirt and tried to pull him back. His soft chuckle brought her to her senses and she quickly released him. Even as she stared at him in astonishment, he opened the door to her bedchamber and gently nudged her into her room. . . .

Books by Hannah Howell

THE MURRAYS

Highland Destiny
Highland Honor
Highland Promise
Highland Vow
Highland Knight
Highland Bride
Highland Angel
Highland Groom
Highland Warrior
Highland Conqueror
Highland Champion
Highland Lover
Highland Barbarian
Highland Savage
Highland Wolf
Highland Sinner
Highland Protector
Highland Avenger
Highland Master
Highland Guard
Highland Chieftain

THE WHERLOCKES

If He's Wicked
If He's Sinful
If He's Wild
If He's Dangerous
If He's Tempted
If He's Daring
If He's Noble

VAMPIRE ROMANCE

Highland Vampire
The Eternal Highlander
My Immortal Highlander
Highland Thirst
Nature of the Beast
Yours for Eternity
Highland Hunger
Born to Bite

STAND-ALONE NOVELS

Only for You
My Valiant Knight
Unconquered
Wild Roses
A Taste of Fire
A Stockingful of Joy
Highland Hearts
Reckless
Conqueror's Kiss
Beauty and the Beast
Highland Wedding
Silver Flame
Highland Fire
Highland Captive
My Lady Captor
Wild Conquest
Kentucky Bride
Compromised Hearts
Stolen Ecstasy
Highland Hero
His Bonnie Bride

Published by Kensington Publishing Corporation

nearly ten years. Angus was still a big, strong man, but age sometimes weakened a body in ways one could not see. The fact that Angus was in bed in the middle of the day was proof enough that whatever ailed him was serious. Artan wondered if he was just refusing to accept the fact that Angus was old and would die soon.

"So, ye have brought me here to stand watch o'er your deathbed?" Artan asked, frowning, for he doubted Angus would ask such a thing of him.

"Nay, I need ye to do something for me. This ague, or whate'er it is that ails me, has made me face the hard fact that, e'en if I recover from this, I dinnae have many years left to me. 'Tis past time I start thinking on what must be done to ensure the well-being of Glascreag and the clan when I am nay longer here."

"Then ye should be speaking with Malcolm."

"Bah, that craven whelp is naught but a stain upon the name MacReith. Sly, whining little wretch. I wouldnae trust him to care for my dogs, let alone these lands and the people living here. He couldnae hold fast to this place for a fortnight. Nay, I willnae have him as my heir."

"Ye dinnae have another one that I ken of."

"Aye, I do, although I have kept it quiet. Glad of that now. My youngest sister bore a child two-and-twenty years ago. Poor Moira died a few years later bearing another child," he murmured, the shadow of old memories briefly darkening his eyes.

"Then where is he? Why wasnae he sent here to train to be the laird? Why isnae he kicking that wee timid mousie named Malcolm out of Glascreag?"

"'Tis a lass."

Artan opened his mouth to loudly decry naming

a lass the heir to Glascreag, and then quickly shut it. He resisted the temptation to look behind him to see if his kinswomen were bearing down on him, well armed and ready to beat some sense into him. They would all be sorely aggrieved if they knew what thoughts were whirling about in his head. Words like too weak, too sentimental, too trusting, and made to have bairns not lead armies were the sort of thoughts that would have his kinswomen grinding their teeth in fury.

But Glascreag was no Donncoill, he thought. Deep in the Highlands, it was surrounded by rough lands and even rougher men. In the years he and Lucas had trained with Angus, they had fought reivers, other clans, and some who had wanted Angus's lands. Glascreag required constant vigilance and a strong sword arm. Murray women were strong and clever, but they were healers not warriors, not deep in their hearts. Artan also considered his kinswomen unique and doubted Angus's niece was of their ilk.

"If ye name a lass as your heir, Angus, every mon who has e'er coveted your lands will come kicking down your gates." Artan crossed his arms over his chest and scowled at the man. "Malcolm is a spineless weasel, but a mon, more or less. Naming him your heir would at least make men pause as they girded themselves for battle. Aye, and your men would heed his orders far more quickly than they would those of a lass, and ye ken it weel."

Angus nodded and ran one scarred hand through his black hair, which was still thick and long, but was now well threaded with white. "I ken it, but I have a plan."

A tickle of unease passed through Artan. Angus's

plans could often mean trouble. At the very least, they meant hard work for him. The way the man's eyes, a silvery blue like his own, were shielded by his half-lowered lids warned Artan that even Angus knew he was not going to like this particular plan.

"I want ye to go and fetch my niece for me and bring her here to Glascreag, where she belongs. I wish to see her once more before I die." Angus sighed, slumped heavily against the pillows, and closed his eyes.

Artan grunted, making his disgust with such a pitiful play for sympathy very clear. "Then send word and have her people bring her here."

Sitting up straight, Angus glared at him. "I did. I have been writing to the lass for years, e'en sent for her when her father and brother died ten, nay, twelve years ago. Her father's kinsmen refused to give her into my care e'en though nary a one of them is as close in blood to her as I am."

"Why didnae ye just go and get her? Ye are a laird. Ye could have claimed her as your legal heir and taken her. 'Tis easy to refuse letters and emissaries, but nay so easy to refuse a mon to his face. Ye could have saved yourself the misery of dealing with Malcolm."

"I wanted the lass to want to come to Glascreag, didnae I?"

"'Tis past time ye ceased trying to coax her or her father's kinsmen."

"Exactly! That is why I want *ye* to go and fetch her here. Ach, laddie, I am sure ye can do it. Ye can charm and threaten with equal skill. Aye, and ye can do it without making them all hot for your blood. I would surely start a feud I dinnae need. Ye have a way with folk that I dinnae, that ye do."

Artan listened to Angus's flattery and grew even
more uneasy. Angus was not only a little desperate
to have his niece brought home to Glascreag, but he
also knew Artan would probably refuse to do him
this favor. The question was, why would Angus think
Artan would refuse to go and get the woman. It
could not be because it was dangerous, for the man
knew well that only something foolishly suicidal
would cause Artan to, perhaps, hesitate. Although
his mind was quickly crowded with possibilities rang-
ing from illegal to just plain disgusting, Artan decided he had played this game long enough.

"Shut it, Angus," he said, standing up straighter
and putting his hands on his hips. "*Why* havenae ye
gone after the woman yourself, and *why* do ye think
I will refuse to go?"

"Ye would refuse to help a mon on his deathbed?"

"Just spit it out, Angus, or I will leave right now
and ye will ne'er ken which I might have said, aye
or nay."

"Och, ye will say nay," Angus mumbled. "Cecily
lives at Dunburn near Kirkfalls."

"Near Kirkfalls? Kirkfalls?" Artan muttered; then
he swore. "That is in the Lowlands." Artan's voice
was soft yet sharp with loathing.

"Weel, just a few miles into the Lowlands."

"Now I ken why ye ne'er went after the lass yourself. Ye couldnae stomach the thought of going
there. Yet ye would send *me* into that hellhole?"

"'Tisnae as bad as all that."

"'Tis as bad as if ye wanted me to ride to London.
I willnae do it," Artan said, and started to leave.

"I need an heir of my own blood!"

"Then ye should ne'er have let your sister marry
a Lowlander. 'Tis near as bad as if ye had let her

run off with a Sassanach. Best ye leave the lass where she is. She is weel ruined by now."

"Wait! Ye havenae heard the whole of my plan!"

Artan opened the door and stared at Malcolm, who was crouched on the floor, obviously having had his large ear pressed against the door. The thin, pale young man grew even paler and stood up. He staggered back a few steps, and then bolted down the hall. Artan sighed. He did not need such a stark reminder of the pathetic choice Angus had for an heir now.

Curiosity also halted him at the door. Every instinct he had told him to keep on moving, that he would be a fool to listen to anything else Angus had to say. A voice in his head whispered that his next step could change his life forever. Artan wished that voice would tell him if that change would be for the better. Praying he was not about to make a very bad choice, he slowly turned to look at Angus, but he did not move away from the door.

Angus looked a little smug, and Artan inwardly cursed. The old man had judged his victim well. Curiosity had always been Artan's weakness. It had caused him trouble and several injuries more times than he cared to recall. He wished Lucas were with him, for his brother was the cautious one. Then Artan quickly shook that thought aside. He was a grown man now, not a reckless child, and he had wit enough to make his own decisions with care and wisdom.

"What is the rest of your plan?" he asked Angus.

"Weel, 'tis verra simple. I need a strong mon to take my place as laird once I die or decide 'tis time I rested. Malcolm isnae it, and neither is Cecily. Howbeit, there has to be someone of MacReith blood to step into my place, the closer to me the better."

"Aye, 'tis the way it should be."

"So, e'en though ye have MacReith blood, 'tis but from a distant cousin. Howbeit, if ye marry Cecily—"

"Marry?!"

"Wheesht, what are ye looking so horrified about, eh? Ye arenae getting any younger, laddie. Past time ye were wed."

"I have naught against marriage. I fully intend to *choose* a bride some day."

Angus grunted. *"Some day* can sneak up on a body, laddie. I ken it weel. Now, cease your fretting for a moment and let me finish. If ye were to marry my niece, ye could be laird here. I would name ye my heir and nary a one of my men would protest it. E'en better, Malcolm couldnae get anyone to heed him if he cried foul. Cecily is my closest blood kin, and ye are nearly as close to me as Malcolm is. So, ye marry the lass and, one day, Glascreag is yours."

Artan stepped back into the room and slowly closed the door. Angus was offering him something he had never thought to have—the chance to be a laird, to hold lands of his own. As the secondborn of the twins, his future had always been as Lucas's second, or as the next in line to be the laird of Donncoill if anything happened to Lucas, something he never cared to think about. There had always been only one possibility of changing that future— marriage to a woman with lands as part of her dowry.

Which was exactly what Angus was offering him, he mused, and felt temptation tease at his mind and heart. Marry Cecily and become heir to Glascreag, a place he truly loved as much as he did his own homelands. Any man with wit enough to recall his own name would grab at this chance with both hands; yet despite the strong temptation of it all, he hesitated. Since Artan considered his wits sound and sharp, he had to wonder why.

Because he wanted a marriage like his parents had, like his grandparents had, and like so many of his clan had, he realized. He wanted a marriage of choice, of passion, of a bonding that held firm for life. When it was land, coin, or alliances that tied a couple together, the chances of such a good marriage were sadly dimmed. He had been offered the favors of too many unhappy wives to doubt that conclusion. If the thought of taking part in committing adultery did not trouble him so much, he would now be a very experienced lover, he mused and hastily shook aside a pinch of regret. He certainly did not want his wife to become one of those women, and he did not want to be one of those men who felt so little a bond with his wife that he repeatedly broke his vows; or worse, find himself trapped in a cold marriage and, bound tightly by his own beliefs, unable to find passion elsewhere.

He looked at Angus, who was waiting for an answer with an ill-concealed impatience. Although he could not agree to marry a woman he had never met, no matter how tempting her dowry, there was no harm in agreeing to consider it. He could go and get the woman and decide on marrying her once he saw her. As they traveled back to Glascreag together, he would have ample time to decide if she was a woman he could share the rest of his life with.

Then he recalled where she lived and how long she had lived there. "She is a Lowlander."

"She is a MacReith," Angus snapped.

Angus was looking smug again. Artan ignored it,

for the man was right in thinking he might get what he wanted. In many ways, it was what Artan wanted as well. It all depended upon what this woman Cecily was like.

"Cecily," he murmured. "Sounds like a Sassanach name." He almost smiled when Angus glared at him, the old man's pale cheeks now flushed with anger.

"'Tis no an English name! 'Tis the name of a martyr, ye great heathen, and weel ye ken it. My sister was a pious lass. She didnae change the child's christening name as some folk do. Kept the saint's name. I call the lass Sile. Use the Gaelic, ye ken."

"Because ye think Cecily sounds English." Artan ignored Angus's stuttering denial. "When did ye last see this lass?"

"Her father brought her and her wee brother here just before he and the lad died."

"How did they die?"

"Killed whilst traveling back home from visiting me. Thieves. Poor wee lass saw it all. Old Meg, her maid, got her to safety, though. Some of their escort survived, chased away the thieves, and then got Cecily, Old Meg, and the dead back to their home. The moment I heard I sent for the lass, but the cousins had already taken hold of her and wouldnae let go."

"Was her father a mon of wealth or property?"

"Aye, he was. He had both, and the cousins now control it all. For the lass's sake, they say. And, aye, I wonder on the killing. His kinsmen could have had a hand in it."

"Yet they havenae rid themselves of the lass."

"She made it home and has ne'er left there again. They also have control of all that she has since she is a woman, aye?"

"Aye, and it probably helps muzzle any suspicions about the other deaths."

Angus nodded. "'Tis what I think. So, will ye go to Kirkfalls and fetch my niece?"

"Aye, I will fetch her, but I make no promises about marrying her."

"Not e'en to become my heir?"

"Nay, not e'en for that, tempting as it is. I will-nae tie myself to a woman for that alone. There has to be more."

"She is a bonnie wee lass with dark red hair and big green eyes."

That sounded promising, but Artan fixed a stern gaze upon the old man. "Ye havenae set eyes on her since she was a child, and ye dinnae ken what sort of woman she has become. A lass can be so bonnie on the outside she makes a mon's innards clench. But then the blind lust clears away, and he finds himself with a bonnie lass who is as cold as ice, or mean of spirit, or any of a dozen things that would make living with her a pure misery. Nay, I willnae promise to wed your niece now. I will only promise to consider it. There will be time to come to know the lass as we travel here from Kirkfalls."

"Fair enough, but ye will see. Ye will be wanting to marry her. She is a sweet, gentle, biddable lass. A true lady raised to be a mon's comfort."

Artan wondered just how much of that effusive praise was true, then shrugged and began to plan his journey.

Chapter 2

"A rotting piece of refuse, a slimy, wart-infested toad, a—a—" Cecily frowned and stopped pacing her bedchamber as she tried to think of some more ways to adequately describe the man she was about to be married to, but words failed her.

"M'lady?"

Cecily looked toward where her very young maid peered nervously into the room and she tried to smile. Although Joan entered the room, she did not look very reassured, and Cecily decided her attempt to look pleasant had failed. She was not surprised. She did not feel the least bit pleasant.

"I have come to help ye dress for the start of the celebration," Joan said as she began to collect the clothes she had obviously been told to dress Cecily in.

Sighing heavily, Cecily removed her robe and allowed the girl to help her dress for the meal in the great hall. She needed to calm herself before she faced her family, all their friends, and her newly betrothed again. Her cousins felt they were doing well by her, arranging an excellent marriage, and by most people's reckoning, they were. Sir Fergus

Ogilvey was a man of power and wealth by all accounts, was not too old, and had gained his knighthood in service to the king. She was the orphaned daughter of a scholar and a Highland woman. She was also a woman of two-and-twenty with unruly red hair, very few curves, and freckles.

She had long been a sore trial to her cousins, repaying their care with embarrassment and disobedience. It was why they were increasingly cold toward her. Cecily had tried, time and time again, to win their love and approval, but she had consistently failed. This was her last chance, and despite her distaste for the man she was soon to marry, she would stiffen her spine and accept him as her husband.

"A pustule on the arse of the devil," she murmured.

"M'lady?" squeaked Joan.

The way Joan stared at her told Cecily that she had spoken that last unkind thought aloud and she sighed again. A part of her mind had obviously continued to think of more insults to fling at Sir Fergus Ogilvey, and her mouth had unfortunately joined in the game. The very last thing she needed was to have such remarks make their way to her cousins' ears. She would lose all chance of gaining their affection and approval then.

"My pardon, Joan," she said, and forced herself to look suitably contrite and just a little embarrassed. "I was practicing the saying of insults when ye entered the room and that one just suddenly occurred to me."

"Practicing insults? Whate'er for, m'lady?"

"Why, to spit out at an enemy if one should attack. I cannae use a sword or a dagger and I am much too small to put up much of a successful

fight, so I thought it might be useful to be able to
flay my foe with sharp words."

Wonderful, Cecily thought as Joan very gently
urged her to sit upon a stool so that she could dress
her hair, now Joan obviously thought her mistress
had gone mad. Perhaps she had. It had to be some
sort of lunacy to try unendingly for so many years
to win the approval and affection of someone, yet
she could not seem to help herself. Each failure to
win the approval, the respect, and caring of her
guardians seemed to just drive her to try even
harder. She felt she owed them so much, yet she
continuously failed in all of her attempts to repay
them. This time she would not fail.

"Here now, wee Joan, I will do that."

Cecily felt her dark mood lighten a little when Old
Meg hurried into the room. Sharp of tongue though
Old Meg was, Cecily had absolutely no doubt that
the woman cared for her. Her cousins detested the
woman and had almost completely banished her
from the manor, although Cecily had never been
able to find out why. To have the woman here now,
at her time of need, was an unexpected blessing, and
Cecily rose to hug the tall, buxom woman.

"'Tis so good to see ye, Old Meg," Cecily said, not
surprised to hear the rasp of choked-back tears in
her voice.

Old Meg patted her on the back. "And where else
should I be when my wee Cecily is soon to be wed,
eh?" She urged Cecily back down onto the stool and
smiled at Joan. "Go on, lassie. I will do this. I suspicion ye have a lot of other things ye must see to."

"I hope ye havenae hurt her feelings," Cecily
murmured as soon as Joan was gone and Old Meg
shut the door.

"Nay, poor lass is being worked to the bone, she is, and is glad to be relieved of at least one chore. Your cousins are twisting themselves into knots trying to impress Ogilvey and his kin. They dinnae seem to ken that he is naught but a grasper who thinks himself so high and mighty he wouldst probably look down his long nose at one of God's angels."

Cecily laughed briefly, but then frowned. "He does seem to be verra fond of himself."

Old Meg harrumphed as she began to vigorously brush Cecily's hair. "He is so full of himself he ought to be gagging. The mon is acting as if he does ye some grand favor by agreeing to wed with ye. Ye come from far better stock than that prancing mongrel."

"He was knighted in the service of the king," Cecily felt moved to say even though she felt no real compulsion to defend the man.

"The fool stumbled into the way of a sword that would have struck our king, nay more than that. It wasnae until Ogilvey paused a wee moment in cursing and whining—after he had recovered from his swoon, mind ye—that he realized everyone thought he had done it apurpose. The sly cur did have the wit to play the humble savior of our sire, I will give ye that, although he did a right poor job of it."

"How do ye ken so much about it?"

"I was there, wasnae I? I was visiting my sister. We were watching all the lairds and the king. Some foolish argument began between a few of the lairds, swords were drawn, and the king nearly walked into one save that Ogilvey was so busy brushing a wee speck of dirt off his cloak he wasnae watching where he was going. Tripped o'er his own feet and stumbled into glory, aye."

Cecily frowned. "He has only e'er said that he did our king a great service. Verra humble about it all he is."

"Weel, he cannae tell the truth about it, can he? Nay when he let the mistake stand and got himself knighted and all."

So she was soon to marry a liar, Cecily thought, and inwardly sighed. That might be an unfair judgment. It could well have been impossible for Sir Fergus to untangle himself from the misconception. After all, who would dare argue with a king? And why was she wearying her mind making excuses for the man, she asked herself.

Because she had to was the answer. This was her last chance to become a part of this family, to be more than a burden and an object of charity. Although she would have to leave to abide in her husband's home, at least she could leave her cousins thinking well of her and ready to finally consider her a true and helpful part of their family. She would be welcome in their hearts and their home at last. Sir Fergus was not a man she would have chosen for the father of her children, but few women got to choose their husbands. Poor though she felt the choice was, however, she could take comfort in the fact that she had finally done something to please her kinsmen.

"Ye dinnae look to be too happy about this, lass," said Old Meg as she decorated Cecily's thick hair with blue ribbons to match her gown.

"I will be," Cecily murmured.

"And just what does that mean, eh? *I will be.*"

"It means I will be content in my marriage. And, aye, I shall have to work to be so, but it will suffice. I am nearly two-and-twenty. 'Tis past time I was married and bred a few bairns. I but pray they dinnae get his chin," she muttered, then grimaced when Old Meg laughed. "That was unkind of me."

"Mayhap, but 'twas the hard, cold truth. The mon has no chin at all, does he."

"Nay, I fear not. I have ne'er seen such a weak one. 'Tis as if his neck starts at his mouth." Cecily shook her head, earning a sharp reprimand from Old Meg.

"If ye dinnae wish to be wed to the fool, why have ye agreed to this?"

"Because Anabel and Edmund want this."

When Old Meg stepped back to put her hands on her ample hips and scowl at her, Cecily stood up and moved to the looking glass to see if she was presentable. The looking glass was one of the few richer items in her small bedchamber, and if Cecily stood a little to the side, she could see herself quite well despite the large crack in it. She felt that small worm of resentment in her heart twitch over being given only the things Anabel or her daughters no longer wanted or that were marred in some way, but she smothered it. Anabel could have just thrown the cracked looking glass away as she had so much else that had belonged to Cecily's mother.

Cecily frowned as she realized she would have to plot some way to slyly retrieve a few things from hiding. She glanced toward a still scowling Old Meg. One of the woman's most often voiced complaints was about how Anabel had tossed away so many of Moira Donaldson's belongings. It was, perhaps, time to let the woman know that not everything was lost. At first, it had just been a child's grief that had caused Cecily to retrieve her mother's things and hide them away. Over the years, it had slowly become a ritual and, she ruefully admitted to herself, a form of rebellion.

The same could be said for her other great secret, she mused, glancing toward the small ornately carved chest holding her ribbons and the meager collection of jewelry allotted to her. Anabel had rapidly claimed all the jewelry that had once been Moira's, or so the woman believed. Hidden away beneath the ribbons and trinkets in that chest were several rich pieces of jewelry that Cecily refused to give up, pieces her father had given her after her mother had died. He had intended her to have the rest when she grew older, but Cecily had mentioned that to her guardians only once. Anabel's fury had been chilling. In truth, Cecily suspected it was one reason Anabel made such a display of it when she threw away yet another thing that had once belonged to Cecily's mother or father. Holding fast to those few pieces of jewelry had been enough to keep Cecily quiet when she saw Anabel or her daughters wearing the jewelry that had once adorned Moira Donaldson.

The woman deserved something for caring for a penniless orphan, Cecily told herself, firmly pushing aside the resentment she could not seem to fully conquer; then she turned to face Old Meg. That woman looked an odd mix of annoyed and concerned. Even though Cecily had taken only a fleeting note of her own appearance, deeming it neat and presentable, she smiled at Old Meg and lightly touched her beribboned hair.

"It looks verra bonnie, Meg," she said.

Old Meg snorted and crossed her arms. "Ye barely glanced at yourself, lass. Ye got all somber and looked to be verra far away. What were ye thinking on?"

"Ah, weel, a secret I have kept for a verra long time," Cecily replied, speaking softly as she quickly moved to Old Meg's side. "Do ye recall my favorite hiding place?"

"Aye," Old Meg replied, speaking as softly as Cecily was. "In the dungeon. That wee hidden room. I ne'er told anyone, though I should have. Ye could have gotten yourself locked in there and, if I wasnae about, been stuck in there good and tight."

"Weel, ye were about and I was e'er safe. But heed me, please, for I may yet need your help. I have hidden some things in there, things Anabel threw away, things that Maman and Papa and e'en Colin loved." She laughed a little when Old Meg hugged her.

"And ye want me to be sure they go with ye when ye marry."

"Aye." Cecily pointed to the small chest that hid her other treasures. "And that wee chest."

Old Meg sighed. "Your da gave ye that. Ye were so pleased with the gift. It has a wee hidey-hole in it, and ye loved to put your special things inside it. What have ye hidden in it now?"

"After Maman died, my father gave me a few pieces of her jewelry. I was to get the rest when I got older, but Anabel," Cecily ignored Old Meg's softly muttered and rather crude opinion of Anabel, "kept everything. She said all of Maman's jewels and other fine things were now hers. So I kept the ones Papa had given me a secret from Anabel. 'Twas wrong of me, I ken it, but—"

"'Tis nay wrong for a child to hold fast to something that reminds her of her parents."

"That is what I tell myself whene'er I begin to feel guilty."

"Ye have naught to feel guilty about."

Cecily gently touched her fingers to Old Meg's mouth, silencing what she knew could easily become a long rant about how poorly she had been treated by her guardians. "It matters not. Anabel and Edmund are my family, and I have been a sore disappointment to them. This time I mean to please them. Howbeit, I willnae lose what little I have left of my brother, father, and mother. I need ye to ken where I have hidden what few things I could hold tight to."

Old Meg sighed and nodded. "If ye cannae get them away yourself, I will see that they come to ye."

"Thank ye, Meggie. 'Twill be a comfort to me to have them close at hand."

"Ye are really going to marry that chinless fool, arenae ye?"

"Aye, 'tis what they want, and this time I mean to please them. And as I said, I *am* almost two-and-twenty and have ne'er e'en been wooed. Or properly kissed." Cecily quickly banished the thought of Sir Fergus kissing her, for it made her feel slightly nauseous. "I want bairns and one needs a husband for that. I am sure it will be fine."

Old Meg gave her a look that said she was daft, but only muttered, "Let us now pray that those bairns ye want dinnae get that fool's chin."

"Weel, at least ye look presentable."

Cecily smiled faintly at Anabel, deciding to accept those sharp words as a compliment. She forced herself to stop staring at the intricate gold and garnet necklace Anabel wore, one that had been a gift her father had given her mother upon their marriage. It was painful to be reminded of times past, of the love her mother and father had shared, especially when she would soon be married to a man she was not sure she could ever love.

She looked around the great hall, taking careful note of all the people attending the feast. It was the start of two weeks of festivities, which would end with her marriage to Sir Fergus Ogilvey. Cecily knew very few of the people since she had rarely been allowed to join in any feasts or even go with her kinsmen on any visits. She suspected these people came to this wedding celebration to eat, drink, and hunt all at someone else's expense.

When she finally espied her betrothed, she sighed. He stood with two other men, all three looking very self-important as they talked. Cecily realized she was not even faintly curious about their conversation and suspected that was a very bad omen concerning her future. Surely a wife should be interested in all her husband was interested in, she thought.

As Anabel began to tell her all about each and every guest—who they were, where they were from, and why it was important to cater to their every whim—Cecily tried to find something about her betrothed that she could like or simply appreciate. He was not ugly, but neither was he handsome. He definitely had a very weak chin and a somewhat long, thin nose. His brown hair was rather dull in color, and it already showed signs of retreating from his head. She recalled that he had eyes of a greenish hazel shade, a nice color. Unfortunately, his eyes were rather small, his lashes thin and very short. He had good posture and he dressed well, she decided, and felt relieved that she could find something to compliment him on if the need arose.

"Are ye e'en listening?" hissed Anabel. "This is important. Ye will soon be mixing freely with these people."

Cecily looked at Anabel and tensed. Something had angered the woman again, and Cecily felt her heart sink into her stomach. She hastily tried to recall something, anything, the woman had just said, only to watch Anabel visibly control her temper. Cecily was surprised to discover that she found that even more alarming. Anabel very clearly wanted this marriage—desperately. Even if she was not determined to do this to please Edmund and Anabel, to try to finally gain some place in this family, Cecily realized there really was no choice for her. If she did not marry Sir Fergus Ogilvey willingly, she would undoubtedly be forced to do it.

"I was looking at Sir Fergus," Cecily said.

"Ah, aye, a fine figure of a mon. He will do ye proud."

Cecily very much doubted it but just nodded.

"And I expect ye to be a good wife to the mon. I ken I have told ye this before, but it bears repeating, especially since ye have always shown a tendency to forget things and e'en behave most poorly. A good wife heeds her husband's commands. 'Tis her duty to please her husband in all things, to be submissive, genteel, and gracious."

Marriage was going to be a pure torment, Cecily mused.

"Ye must run his household efficiently, keeping all in the best of order. Meals on time and weel prepared, linens clean and fresh, and servants weel trained and obedient."

That could prove difficult, for Anabel had never trained her to run a household, but Cecily bit the inside of her cheek to stop those words from escaping her mouth. Through punishments and long observation, she actually had a very good idea of what was needed to run a household. In truth, the many punishments she had endured had given her some housekeeping skills she doubted any other fine lady could lay claim to. Cecily inwardly frowned as she glanced at Sir Fergus. Instinct told her that the man was not one who would appreciate such skills, would actually be appalled to discover that his new wife knew how to scrub linens and muck out stalls.

"A good wife tolerates her husband's weaknesses," continued Anabel.

Cecily suspected Sir Fergus had a lot of weaknesses, then scolded herself for such unkind thoughts. She would be married to the man soon. It was time to find something good about her betrothed. There had to be something. She had probably just been too busy feeling sorry for herself and convincing herself to meekly accept her fate to notice.

"A good wife ignores her husband's wanderings, his other women—"

"Other women? What other women?" Cecily was startled into asking. This was a new twist in this oft-repeated lecture that she did not like the sound of at all.

Anabel sighed and rolled her eyes, big blue eyes that she was extremely vain about. "Men are lusty beasts, child. 'Tis their way to rut with any woman who catches their eye. A wife must learn to ignore such things."

"I dinnae see why she should. Her husband took

a vow before God just as she did. 'Tis his duty to honor vows spoken."

After looking around to make sure they were alone, Anabel grabbed Cecily by the arm and tugged her backward, a little closer to the wall and even farther away from the others gathered in the great hall. "Dinnae be such a fool. Men care naught for such things. They consider it their right to bed whomever they wish to."

"My father was faithful to my mother."

"How would ye ken that, eh? Ye were naught but a bairn. Trust me in this, ye will be glad the mon slakes his lust elsewhere and troubles ye with it only rarely. 'Tis a disgusting business that only men get any pleasure out of. Let the peasant lasses deal with it. Since men feel they must have a quiverful of sons, ye will be burdened with the chore of taking him into your bed often enough to heartily welcome such respites."

"Take him into my bed? Willnae he be sleeping there every night anyway?"

"Where did ye get such a strange idea?"

"My mother and father shared a bed. And, aye, I was just a wee child, but I *do* ken that."

"How verra odd," Anabel murmured, then shrugged. "Probably some strange practice from the Highlands. They are all barbarians up there, ye ken. Ye, however, have been raised amongst civilized people and 'tis past time ye cast aside such thoughts and beliefs."

Cecily hastily swallowed her instinctive urge to defend her mother's people. She had learned long ago that it did no good. All such defense accomplished was to anger Anabel and get Cecily sentenced to some menial, exhausting, and often filthy chore as a penance for speaking out. She had the feeling Anabel said such things to her on purpose. At times it almost seemed that Anabel hated the long-dead Moira Donaldson, although Cecily had no idea why the woman should do so or what her sweet mother could have done to earn such enmity. The woman often derided her father as well. Cecily did not understand Anabel's apparent animosity for her late parents and, sadly, did not think she would ever get Anabel to explain it.

The thought of her lost family brought on a wave of grief and Cecily stared at her feet as she fought back her tears. It would soon be her wedding day, the most important day for a woman, and she was surrounded by strangers and people who did not truly care for her. If Old Meg managed to slip inside the chapel or a few of the gatherings, Cecily would at least know that one person who loved her was close at hand, but she could not be sure Old Meg could do so. If Anabel even glimpsed the woman in the room, she would swiftly send Old Meg away, far away. She knew her family was with her in spirit, in her heart, and in her memories, but she dearly wished she had them at her side.

"Will ye smile?" hissed Anabel. "Wheesht, ye look ready to weep. Best not let Sir Fergus catch that look upon your face. He will think ye arenae pleased to have him as your husband."

There was a tone to Anabel's voice that told Cecily that that was the very last thing the woman wanted. If it happened, punishment would be swift and harsh. Although Cecily doubted she could produce a credible smile, she did her best to hide her sorrow. When she felt she had accomplished that, she looked at Anabel, only to find the woman was gaping at the doorway to the great hall. A quick glance around revealed that everyone else was doing the same thing, and Cecily became sharply aware of how quiet it had become in the hall.

Although the sight of so many silent, wide-eyed, open-mouthed people was fascinating, curiosity forced Cecily to look toward the doorway of the great hall as well. It was only a sudden attack of pride that kept her from mimicking the others when she saw the man standing there. He was very tall and leanly muscular. His long black hair hung down past his broad shoulders, a thin braid on either side of his stunningly handsome face. He wore a plaid, the dark green crossed with black and yellow lines. He also wore deerskin boots and a white linen shirt, both dusty from travel. From behind his head she could see the hilt of a broadsword. He wore another sword at his side, and she could see a dagger sheathed inside his left boot.

Cecily was rather glad she had not been in the midst of a hearty defense of Highlanders at that precise moment. This man did look gloriously barbaric. That appearance was only enhanced by what he held. Grasped by the front of their jupons and dangling several inches off the floor, the Highlander held two of her cousins' men-at-arms. The men did not seem to be struggling much, she thought with a touch of amusement, nor did their captor seem overly burdened by the weight he held in each hand. Deciding that someone had to do something, Cecily took a deep breath to steady herself and began to walk toward the man.

Chapter 3

Artan scowled at the people in the great hall, all of whom were gaping at him. He struggled to rein in his temper, but it was difficult. From the moment he had crossed into the Lowlands, his journey had become arduous. He had been watched, sneered at, fled from, and insulted every step of the way. Even knocking a few heads together here and there along the way had done little to soften his bad humor. Being refused entry into the Donaldson manor had been the last straw, or so he had thought. Being gaped at by all the people he now faced was rapidly surpassing that.

Out of the corner of his eye he saw someone move and he tensed. Glancing more fully in that direction, he watched a small, slender woman with dark red hair walk toward him. He felt an odd quickening in his heart as he studied her. She moved with an easy grace, her slim hips swaying gently with each step. The blue gown she wore was cut low enough to reveal the softly rounded tops of her breasts. Those breasts were not the heavy, bountiful sort he usually lusted after, but they were full enough to catch his eye.

When she was only a few steps away, he saw that her wide, heavily lashed eyes were a deep, rich green and he felt his pulse increase. She had an oval face, her skin clear and pale. Her lips were full enough to invite kisses, her small nose was straight and lightly freckled, and her chin held a distinct hint of a stubborn nature. If this was Angus's niece, Artan thus far had no objection at all to marrying her.

"Sir? Mayhap ye should release those men. I think they are having trouble breathing."

Such was the enticement of her low, husky voice it took Artan a moment to understand what she said. He looked at the two men he held and grunted softly. They did appear to be choking. He shrugged and tossed them aside, then scowled at the people who gasped and moved farther away from him.

"Thank ye, sir," Cecily said, struggling not to laugh. "May we ken who ye are and why ye have come to our home?" When he looked at her with his silvery blue eyes Cecily felt oddly lightheaded and quickly stiffened her spine. She was not sure what he was doing to her or how he could make her feel so breathless with just a glance, but she would reveal to him only a calm civility.

"I am Sir Artan Murray," he replied and bowed slightly. "I have come on behalf of Sir Angus MacReith of Glascreag."

"Uncle Angus sent ye?" Cecily wondered why the sudden thought that this man could be a close relative should upset her so.

"Ah, so ye are Lady Cecily Donaldson?" Artan

had to strongly resist the urge to rub his hands together in glee.

Cecily nodded and curtsied almost absently as she asked, "What does my uncle want?"

"He wants ye to come to Glascreag. The mon is ill and wishes to see ye before he dies." Artan did not really believe Angus was in danger of dying, but if the slight exaggeration got this woman to come to Glascreag with him, he saw no real harm in it.

"Nay!" screeched Anabel, suddenly shaking free of her shock and rushing to Cecily's side.

Wincing when Anabel grabbed her tightly by the arm, Cecily said, "But if my uncle is dying—"

"Ye can go to see him *after* the wedding," said Anabel.

"Wedding? What wedding?" Artan demanded.

"Cecily's wedding," replied Anabel.

"Angus wasnae told about any wedding."

"Why should he be told?"

"Because he is her closest living kin."

"Weel, we are her family, too, her guardians. I am Lady Anabel Donaldson and there is my husband, Sir Edmund, coming toward us. It was our decision to make, nay his."

Artan studied the woman clutching Cecily's arm in what looked to be a painful hold. The woman was pleasing to look at with her fair hair and blue eyes, but those eyes were cold. Her voluptuous body was well displayed in a deep red gown, but he suspected such bounty was wasted on this woman, her blood being as cold as her eyes. There was the hint of desperation in her stance and her voice. Artan immediately wondered what she gained from Cecily's marriage.

He looked at Cecily next. There was a faint pinch

of pain her expression, and Artan had to fight the urge to pry Lady Anabel's heavily ringed hand off Cecily's slender arm. There was also no hint of joy or anticipation in Cecily's expression, no sign of a bride's pleasure. He hoped he was not fooling himself, but he could not shake the feeling that this marriage was not of her choosing.

"Who are ye marrying, Sile?" he asked, using the Gaelic form of her name.

"Me."

One look was all it took for Artan to decide that he neither liked nor trusted the man who stepped up on the other side of Lady Anabel and laid claim to Cecily. Artan made a great show of looking down at the man who was nearly a head shorter and enjoyed the light flush of anger that flared upon the man's pale cheeks. He looked like one of those whining, grasping bootlickers who constantly danced around the king. Artan sniffed. Smelled like one, too. All heavy perfume spread over an unclean body.

"And who might ye be?" he demanded.

"I, sir, am Sir Fergus Ogilvey," the man replied, lifting his weak chin enough to glare up at Artan.

"Never heard of ye." Ignoring Fergus's soft curse, Artan looked to where Anabel's hand still clutched Cecily's arm and scowled at the dark spots slowly spreading beneath those sharp nails. "Let her go. Ye have pierced the skin."

Cecily breathed a sigh of relief when Anabel abruptly released her. She lightly rubbed her hand over the wounds she could feel beneath the sleeve of her gown. There would be a colorful array of bruises and scabs come the morning, she thought and hoped the bleeding would stop soon before it completely ruined the first new gown she had had in years. She looked from Fergus to Sir Artan and sighed, all too painfully aware of the marked difference between the two men. Sir Artan made Fergus look even smaller and paler than he actually was.

"When is this wedding?" Artan asked.

"In a fortnight," replied Fergus, crossing his arms over his narrow chest. "Today is the first day of the festivities."

"Then 'tis best if ye show me to my chambers so that I may wash away this dust and join ye."

"I dinnae believe ye were invited," snapped Anabel.

"I did note that rudeness, but I forgive ye." Artan smiled at Cecily when she released a surprised laugh, but noticed that she hastily silenced it at one hard glance from Lady Anabel.

"Of course he must stay, m'dear," said Sir Edmund as he joined them and looked at his wife. "The mon has been sent here by Cecily's maternal uncle. We must nay offend the mon by treating his emissary so rudely, eh?" He smiled at Artan. "Ye can stand in the laird's stead, aye, and then return to Glascreag with a full report of his niece's marriage to this fine mon." He clapped Sir Fergus on the back. "Now"—he waved over a buxom, fair-haired maid—"Davida here will see to ye. The meal will be set out in an hour."

"I will be here," said Artan. He turned to Cecily, took her hand in his, and lightly brushed a kiss over the back of it. "When I return we must needs discuss your uncle, lass."

As Cecily watched Artan leave with Davida, she quickly clasped her hands together behind her back so that she could surreptitiously touch the spot he had kissed. She had never had her hand kissed before. She had certainly never felt so abruptly warm and weak-kneed just because a man had touched her hand. Then again, she had never seen a man like Sir Artan Murray either.

She sighed as she thought of him being *seen* to by the buxom Davida. A sharp pinch of jealousy seized her, for she knew the very wanton Davida would soon be in his bed. Cecily could not really blame the woman. Davida had probably never seen such a lovely man either and was undoubtedly thinking herself blessed. Understanding did not dim her resentment by much, however. If nothing else, it seemed grossly unfair that the wanton Davida would have Sir Artan while she was left with only Sir Fergus.

"Edmund, how could ye ask that savage to stay here?" demanded Anabel.

"And what choice was there, wife?" Edmund grimaced. "Angus is Cecily's closest blood kin, and that mon said the laird is ill, mayhap e'en dying."

"Mayhap I should go to him then," said Cecily, then nearly flinched when Fergus, Edmund, and Anabel all glared at her.

"Ye are going nowhere," said Anabel. "That mon hasnae had aught to do with ye until now, has he?"

That was sadly true, although Cecily had always thought that a little odd. She could recall her uncle as a big, rough-speaking man, but one who had been unceasingly kind to her. Even though that last ill-fated visit had been made so that the man could meet her brother, Colin, who was his heir, her uncle had spent time with her, too. As always, she shrugged that puzzle aside and gathered up the courage to argue with Anabel, at least just a little bit.

"That doesnae matter," Cecily said. "What *does*

matter is that my uncle may soon die. Since he is my closest kinsmon, isnae it my duty to go to his side?" She tensed when Sir Fergus stepped up beside her and put his arm around her shoulders, for she sensed no affection in the gesture.

"Aye, 'tis indeed your duty," he agreed. "But 'tis also your duty to stay here and marry me. Your guardians have gone to a great deal of trouble and expense to arrange these festivities. And now that we are betrothed, your first duty is to me, aye? I shall take ye to see the mon after the wedding."

Cecily nearly ached to argue that and knew she had some very good arguments to make. The best being that her uncle carried some three score years. At such an age even a very mild illness could kill the man. Waiting until after the wedding could easily mean that all she got to visit was Uncle Angus's grave. She looked at Fergus, Anabel, and Edmund and could tell by their expressions that even sound arguments would not sway them, however.

"And since ye truly are his nearest kin, there may e'en be a chance that ye are the heir to something, so, of course, we should go and see how matters stand at Glascreag," Fergus continued.

"Quite right, Sir Fergus," agreed Edmund. "'Tis a long, hard journey, but there may be some benefit to it."

As she listened to her guardians and Sir Fergus discuss what her uncle might leave her when he died, Cecily fought to remain silent. She also tried very hard to convince herself that they were not really as cold and mercenary as they sounded. The way they spoke, as if it were Sir Fergus who would benefit, irritated her as well. She did not care if her uncle made her any bequest, but if he did, it should be hers and no one else's.

Then she recalled that Fergus would soon be her husband, and the law said that what was hers would become his. Cecily doubted her uncle would want the man to have anything for the simple fact that Sir Fergus was a Lowlander, but her uncle had no idea that she was about to be married. She had written to him to tell him of her marriage, but there was a very good chance that he had not received her missive before he had sent Sir Artan to her. If her uncle died before she reached him and Sir Fergus benefited from his death in even the smallest way, Cecily suspected Uncle Angus would be spinning in his grave. He had often made his low opinion of Lowlanders very clear, seemingly forgetting that her father had been one.

Her thoughts fixed upon the last time she, her father, and her brother were together, Cecily was startled when Anabel pinched her on the arm. Rubbing the sore spot those vicious fingers had left behind, she looked at the woman. She was not exactly surprised to find Anabel scowling at her. Sadly, Cecily almost always found Anabel scowling at her.

"Go and tidy yourself," Anabel ordered, nodding toward the small bloodstains on the sleeve of Cecily's gown. "Clean off those stains quickly ere they set firm. Ye had best nay ruin that gown. And hurry back. I will be verra displeased if ye are late to the feast."

As Cecily hurried away to her bedchamber, she wondered crossly if Anabel expected her to apologize for bleeding when her skin was pierced. It would not surprise her. Anabel always seemed to think Cecily should apologize for the times Anabel had to beat her until the blood flowed. Cecily had always been more than ready to accept punishment for any wrong she had done, but she realized she had never fully accepted that she deserved the very harsh punishments Anabel doled out.

Just as Cecily was thinking she needed to work harder on her humility and obedience, she heard Davida's very distinctive laugh. She frowned at the door she was near and wondered why she felt a very strong urge to burst into that room and stop Davida and Sir Artan from doing whatever was making Davida laugh like that. Since Davida had a well-earned reputation as a wanton, there was little doubt in Cecily's mind as to what those two were doing. She just did not understand why it should trouble her so much. Forcing herself to move, she hurried on to her bedchamber to do as Anabel had told her to do.

Artan scowled at the buxom Davida and pushed aside her hands. The maid was obviously eager and ready, but despite it having been a very long time since he had enjoyed a woman's favors, Artan found that he did not want to oblige her. His mind and, apparently, the rest of him had obviously decided he was soon to be a married man. He liked how Cecily looked, and he liked the sound of her voice. There was a glimpse of spirit in the way she was the only one who had moved to greet him. He had to learn more about her, and he felt sure that would be difficult to do if Cecily thought he was bedding Davida. Instinct told him Davida was not a woman who could keep silent about her lovers.

"If ye cannae simply help me with my bath, it might be best if ye were to leave," he said.

Davida stared at him in surprise. "Ye mean ye dinnae want—"

"Nay, I dinnae. Ye are a bonnie lass, but I have it in mind to become a married mon soon."

"Oh." Davida smiled and began to slide her hand down his belly again. "Weel, I willnae tell, and what the lass doesnae ken—"

"*I* will ken it," he said firmly as he pushed her hand away, annoyed at how his body was responding to her touch and the anticipation of even greater intimacies.

"Ye dinnae look reluctant."

"We both ken that that part of a mon has no mind and no morals. I dinnae think your master sent ye with me for that sort of play, aye?"

"Oh, aye, he did. And if he hadnae, Lady Anabel would have. I think they hope I will make ye miss out on the feasting."

Artan hid his shock over that even though he knew some keeps had such women within their walls, ones freely offered to the guests. It was the reason Davida believed the courtesy was offered this time that stunned him. "Will ye get in trouble for failing?" He scowled at the look of cunning that briefly passed over her pretty round face. "The truth now, lass."

Davida sighed. "Nay, Sir Edmund and, aye, e'en Lady Anabel will just think ye are a fast rider like Sir Edmund and Sir Fergus."

Although his pride pinched at being thought of as such a poor lover, Artan concentrated on what Davida had just revealed. "Ye have bedded them both, have ye?" he asked as she began to scrub his hair.

"I have, though I cannae say they were much worth the effort. S'truth, Sir Fergus is one who enjoys a bit of rough play, if ye ken what I mean."

"Aye, I do. Yet he cannae be sharing your bed now, nay at his own wedding celebration."

Davida laughed. "Ye jest. Of course he is. The mon has dragged near every maid here into his bed, willing or nay. Those who were nay willing tried to speak to her ladyship, but it got them naught but a scolding. 'Tis odd, but whene'er Sir Fergus is here, 'tis almost as if he rules and nay the Donaldsons."

"Aye, verra odd," he murmured, "as I cannae see Lady Anabel bowing to anyone."

Artan listened to Davida's litany of complaints about Lady Anabel as she scrubbed his back. The lady of the demesne obviously did little to ensure the loyalty of her maids. What Davida revealed troubled Artan. Something was not right here. If one believed Davida, Cecily was being treated as some burden, as if she were some poor kinswoman taken in so she would not starve. From what Angus had told him before he had left Glascreag, Artan had come to believe that Cecily's father had been a doting parent. It made no sense that the man would have left his daughter penniless and at the complete mercy of unkind kinsmen.

Stepping out of the bath, Artan continued to mull over the problem as Davida dried him off. Consumed by his thoughts, he was easily able to ignore the maid's many attempts to rouse his interest until she eventually gave up and began to work with brisk efficiency. He was quick to don the robe set out for him when he was dry, however. The woman seemed to have a dozen bold hands.

As Davida had the bath cleared away, Artan stood by the fire thinking on what he had learned thus far, until he finally decided there were too many questions left to ask and each one had too many possible answers. Artan knew he had to search out the truth. Even if he did not marry Cecily, he owed it to Angus to make sure his niece was being treated fairly and was happy. He did wonder why that laudable goal did not make him feel happy or even just pleased with his own nobility.

He looked at Davida, who was kneeling on the floor and mopping up water. "'Tis disappointing to think Lady Cecily is one of those women who doesnae care what happens to the maids in her household," he said with what he felt was the appropriate amount of disgust and regret.

"Oh, the lass doesnae ken anything about it, and God have mercy on any who tell her," replied Davida as she stood up and brushed off her skirts. "I think Lady Anabel fears the lass would balk at marrying Sir Fergus if she kenned what he was truly like." Davida grimaced. "Poor wee lass has her own troubles anyway, aye? She doesnae need to be weighed down with those of others. Aye, and she couldnae do aught to help in the end, which would fair break her heart."

"So this marriage isnae the lass's choice?"

"Why are ye so interested?"

"Her uncle sent me here, her *dying* uncle."

"Oh, aye. Weel, I dinnae think Lady Cecily had anything to say about it all. Dinnae think many lasses do, do they. Lady Cecily does seem to be accepting it." Davida put her hands on her well-rounded hips and frowned. "I have ne'er understood why they didnae let the poor lass go to her uncle. 'Tis clear to anyone with eyes in their head that Lady Anabel doesnae like her." Davida suddenly blushed and looked wary. "Ach, but what do I ken, eh? Ye should-nae heed me. Nay, and I spoke out of turn and all."

"I willnae be repeating it all, so dinnae fret, lass. Her uncle will want to ken the truth, and I suspi-cion I willnae get much of that from Lady Cecily's guardians or her betrothed."

"They wouldnae ken the truth of it if it bit them on the arse," Davida muttered. Then she asked, "If her uncle cares so much about the lass and how she fares, why has he ignored her all these years?"

"He hasnae. The mon wrote to her often."

Davida gave him a look of utter disbelief. "Nay, there was ne'er a word from the mon. Poor wee lass wrote to him a lot in the beginning. 'Twas enough to make ye weep when she finally realized he was ne'er going to reply or e'en come to see her. Then she just wrote to him at Michaelmas time. Nay, she kens that all she has left for family now is this lot, and isnae that right sad, eh?" Davida shook her head, sighed, and then looked Artan over, her growing smile re-vealing that her pity for Cecily was quickly being re-placed with lust for him. "Shall I help ye dress?"

"Nay, I believe I can fend for meself," he drawled.

The heavy sigh Davida released as she left the room stroked Artan's vanity and he grinned. That good humor faded quickly, however. His suspicions had been roused by all the maid had told him. It was not just the fact that Cecily had never received any of Angus's letters or gifts, either. Artan still could not believe Cecily's father had left her desti-tute, although it was possible that the man had not realized how poorly his kinsman and his wife would treat Cecily. If Cecily's father had been the only one in the family with a full purse, Anabel and Edmund could have always been on their best behavior around the man.

A lot of what Davida had told him about the situation at Dunburn could be explained away, but not the fact that Cecily had never received anything from Angus. Someone had wanted to make very sure that Cecily felt she had no choice, that she had no other place to go or anyone else to turn to. One had to ask why, and the only answers Artan could think of to that question were all bad. Even if he were not already considering Angus's suggestion that he marry Cecily and become the heir to Glascreag, he would have felt compelled to linger at Dunburn and investigate. He might have used the excuse of a dying Angus to keep Davida talking, but the implication behind that excuse was the truth. Angus *would* want to know what was happening to his niece.

It was odd that Artan felt so outraged by the mere possibility that a woman he had only just met was being mistreated or cheated; but despite that, he accepted his feelings. He had never been one to sit and examine how he felt anyway. He either accepted the feelings as reasonable or banished them. This time instinct told him there was good reason to be outraged, if only because this was Angus's niece. So he would linger at Dunburn, unwanted and uninvited, and find out just what was going on. Recalling a pair of deep green eyes, he decided there was another good reason to linger. He may well have just met his mate.

Chapter 4

Cecily glanced at Fergus. He sat across the table from her. As her betrothed, he should have been sitting next to her. Instead, he sat opposite her, scowling at the man seated on her right, the man who had somehow managed to usurp Sir Fergus's rightful place. She had the uncomfortable feeling that one reason Sir Artan sat at her side was because Sir Fergus had been too cowardly to stand firm and claim his rights. And it had all been done without a word spoken. It seemed her betrothed was not only chinless but spineless.

As covertly as she could, Cecily peeked at the man seated next to her on the bench as he selected a slice of roast goose and set it on her plate. For a leanly built man he took up a lot of room. Every time his muscular thigh had brushed against her, she had shifted away from him until she now teetered on the far edge of the bench, but his thigh was yet again pressed close to hers. Cecily briefly considered nudging against him to see if he would shift away from her, but quickly dismissed that thought. She had the oddest feeling that he would not move an inch and she would end up sitting on his lap. And why the thought of sitting on Sir Artan's lap should make her feel all warm and anxious she did not know. Deciding that might be what temptation felt like, she forced her attention to the large amount of food the man had piled onto her plate.

"Eat up, lass," said Artan. "Ye will need your strength."

Hastily chewing on a piece of meat she had put in her mouth, Cecily wondered what he meant. She frowned at the amount of food he had put on her plate and began to feel insulted. Cecily knew she was not very big, but she was no puling weakling either.

"Why do ye think I should build up my strength?" she asked.

"'Tis clear to see that this celebration is going to keep ye busy from sunrise to sunset for at least a fortnight. Aye, and then there is the wedding itself and, of course, the wedding night."

The wedding night, Cecily thought and silently cursed. That was something she had tried very hard *not* to think about. She did not thank Sir Artan for reminding her of it either. Desperately, she tried hard to think about something else, anything else, so that she could return to that comforting state of blissful ignorance.

"Is my uncle really dying?" she asked and ignored the knowing look he gave her.

"He is ill and he is carrying three score years."

Cecily frowned and wondered why that news made her eyes sting with tears. She had not seen her uncle for years, and he had shown little inclination to have anything to do with her. Over the years she had done her best to convince herself that it did not matter, that it was only to be expected for she was not a male who could become his heir. Obviously, she had failed in that endeavor, for she felt honestly grieved that her uncle may well be dead soon, that she would never have the chance to see him again.

"'Tis but natural for a mon to wish to have his loved ones close at his side when he is at the end of his life," murmured Artan, sensing her upset and hoping to take advantage of it in convincing her to leave Dunburn willingly and soon.

"Loved ones?" Her voice was so tainted with bitter anger that even Cecily winced at the sound of it. "He doesnae see me as a loved one. If he did, he would have written or e'en come to visit."

"And why are ye so sure that he hasnae written?"

"Because I have ne'er seen e'en the smallest, most crudely written letter. Nary a word. And he has certainly ne'er come to visit with me or asked me to come to him."

Artan sensed a deep hurt behind her sharp words and inwardly cursed. Unless he had proof to give her, hard proof that her guardians had kept her apart from Angus, it would be difficult to free her from their grasp. It would not be easy to get any proof. Still, he mused with an inner smile, at least searching for that proof would give him something to do while he was at Dunburn.

"'Tis odd," he murmured, "for I ken weel that he tried."

"Tried to write or tried to visit?"

"Write. I fear he wouldnae come here unless ye were on your deathbed or in grave danger. He has no liking for the Lowlands."

"So gently said. He loathes this place and has nary a kind word to say about Lowlanders."

"He liked your father, didnae he?"

"Aye," she said softly, "he did." A sudden on-slaught of cherished memories made her smile. "Uncle Angus always spoke as if Papa were of the Highlands, and thus ne'er tempered his opinion of Lowlanders. Why, I think only the English enrage him more."

"The English enrage everyone."

Cecily hastily swallowed the urge to laugh. The man spoke as if he was reciting one of God's own laws. In many ways, he sounded very like her uncle, and she suddenly wondered exactly what his relationship was to Angus MacReith. Her uncle would not send just anyone as his emissary.

"How are ye related to my uncle? Or, are ye e'en a kinsmon?" Again, Cecily was not sure why the thought that he was a very close relation should trouble her so. She should be glad to have found other family.

"I am but a distant cousin. My mother is Angus's cousin. I believe I am a step or two more distant than Malcolm."

"Malcolm?" Cecily struggled to recall a cousin named Malcolm. "I cannae really recall a Malcolm."

"Brown hair, thin, pointy wee face and little eyes? Makes one think of a weasel, a verra cowardly weasel."

Even that harsh description did not immediately rouse a memory. Cecily did her best to think through that last visit to Glascreag. She was a little surprised at how clear those memories were after so long, especially when the visit had had such a tragic ending. Slowly, a particular memory became clear. There had been a feast and other kinsmen had attended. Her uncle had intended it for these more distant relations to meet Colin, who would be his heir. Recalling that feast brought to mind a well-rounded woman and her son, both of whom had so obviously disliked the idea of Colin as heir that even she, as a child, had sensed it.

"Lady Seaton and her son."

"Aye, Malcolm Seaton. His mother was also a cousin to Angus, and she has always expected her son to be Angus's heir."

"He was, if I recall right, an irritating young mon."

"Aye, ye recall right. He still is. Sly, manipulative, weak, and dishonest."

"Oh dear. Uncle Angus must be most dismayed that such a mon will take his place as laird one day."

"Aye, ye could say that."

Artan tried to think of something else to talk about, for this topic was too close to the reasons why he was at Dunburn. If he thought for even a minute that the truth would cause her to come with him back to Glascreag, he would tell it. Instinct told him she would not take it well, however. Women tended to take offense at the thought that they were being married for the land or coin they would bring to the marriage, even though that was the way of the world. Once such knowledge was in their hands, they were reluctant to believe any protestations to the contrary. It was true that he had an eye to being made Angus's heir, but he would not marry simply because of that. Unfortunately, once Cecily found out about the arrangement with Angus, she would always question his reasons for wanting her as a wife.

Of course, he was still not absolutely certain he would do as Angus wished. Cecily was lovely, and just hearing her voice seemed to stroke him and rouse his lusts. There was more needed in a marriage than property and prettiness, however, and he was not yet completely sure he could find that with Cecily. What he needed to do was steal a kiss or two, he decided. He knew well that a man could be aroused by the look of a woman only to find a deep coldness in her arms.

Subtly glancing at Sir Fergus, Sir Edmund, and Lady Anabel, Artan suspected that it would be difficult to woo Cecily in even the smallest way. Not that he was particularly good at wooing, he mused. His best chance to draw Cecily back to Glascreag was in proving that her guardians and her betrothed were not worth her loyalty. He also needed to hold fast to Cecily's interest so that she would remain close at hand in case she continued to bow to the will of the others and he had begun to run out of time. The more he saw of these people, the more he felt sure that it would be best if Cecily went to stay with Angus. If she did not agree to go with him and the wedding drew too near for comfort, he would simply pick her up and take her away from here.

Now that he had a firm plan, Artan relaxed. He found the company poor, even annoying, except for Cecily, but the food and wine were good. Anabel sat on his right and he knew she was angry. He could almost feel her glare boring into his skin. His sisters had always accused him of being completely insensitive, but Artan decided it was probably a good thing under these circumstances. If he had any tender feelings, they would be sorely abused by lingering in a place where he was so clearly unwanted. He almost grinned as he refilled his plate with food. If these people thought he would give up and return to Glascreag liked a whipped cur just because they scowled and were rude to him, they were doomed to defeat.

"I dinnae recall ye from Glascreag," she said quietly, hoping she did not sound as suspicious as she suddenly felt.

"Weel, I wasnae at Glascreag when ye were. My brother and I fostered with Angus. At that time we had returned to Donncoill and our family as our Grandmere was ill."

"Oh, I am so sorry. 'Tis always hard when the old ones falter, e'en when ye ken it must happen. Did she recover?"

"Aye, she did, although it was a close run thing, but ye have the right of it. She is three score and ten and my grandsire is four score years. Their time is near, but one can only give thanks for each day they are still at hand and pray that when the end comes 'tis easy. 'Twill be a great loss for the clan, but they have both lived a good life."

Cecily nodded. "Kenning that can be a great comfort." She hesitated a moment, then quietly asked, "Has my uncle lived a good life?'

"He has. He is a fine, strong warrior and has held his land against all comers."

That was not quite what she had wanted to hear, but she could tell that Artan thought it was high praise indeed. Cecily realized that, as a foster son, Sir Artan would share some of the same characteristics as her uncle. Coming to know Sir Artan would be somewhat akin to coming to know her uncle.

A tickle of unease went through her as she covertly watched Sir Artan eat. He had a prodigious appetite, but his manners were excellent. The man spoke scathingly of courtiers, but in his looks and his table manners, it was evident that he could hold his own against any of them. She did not understand why she suddenly felt it might be dangerous to come to know Sir Artan well. Then he glanced at her and smiled and she felt as if something inside of her had melted. There was the danger. For the first time in her life she was truly attracted to a man. Considering how he had first entered Dunburn, a nearly unconscious man dangling from each hand, she found that astonishing.

"Do ye want some more food?" Artan asked her, wondering why she looked so stunned. Looking at her plate, Cecily was surprised to discover that she had eaten everything on it. She had never eaten so much at one sitting. Taking a meal with her kinsmen and her betrothed had always killed her appetite. Even before her betrothal, eating beneath Anabel's constant watch had always been difficult. This night she would not have need of the plate of cold meat, bread, and cheese the kindly cook always set aside for her to steal away with and eat in the private comfort of her bedchamber.

"Nay, nay. 'Twas ample." She cautiously peered around him and breathed an inner sigh of relief to find that Anabel had not noticed her gluttony. The woman had been too busy glaring at Sir Artan to notice anything else.

"An apple then?" he asked as the fruits and sweets were set out.

"Aye, that would please."

Her eyes widened slightly as he produced a gleaming knife from inside the sleeve of his shirt. He chose a large apple from the basket a small page held out. In a few swift, clean moves, he cored and sliced the apple, setting each piece upon her plate. After doing the same for himself, he returned the knife to its sheath that she suspected was strapped to his forearm. Sir Artan Murray was a well-armed man. He had also not offered to provide the same service for Anabel. Obviously, his manners were not quite as good as she had first thought. To stifle a sudden urge to giggle, Cecily quickly stuffed a piece of apple in her mouth.

"Did ye enjoy fostering with my uncle?" she asked after swallowing the piece of apple and telling herself that the intense curiosity she felt concerned her uncle and not Sir Artan.

"Och, aye. My clan doesnae often foster out their sons, ye ken. We have a bounty of lads, however, and Angus wrote to my mother asking if any of the Murray lads would be of a mind to foster with him. He preferred one of her own sons as we are blood kin to him, but said he would be pleased to take any lad. Lucas and I decided to go, as did our cousins Bennet and Uilliam, my uncle Eric's sons." He smiled faintly. "Angus was fair pleased when he found himself with four lads to train. Donncoill and my uncle's lands are a wee bit too peaceful for some lads," he drawled and winked at her.

"Can a place e'er be too peaceful?"

"Och, aye, especially when ye are a young lad who dreams of becoming some great, fearsome warrior."

Cecily had to smile. There was a touch of self-mockery in his deep voice that charmed her. Out of the corner of her eye she caught Sir Fergus glaring at her, but ignored him. Although some of the stricter rules of conduct had eased because there were so many people staying at Dunburn, it was usually considered poor manners to talk across the table. Sir Fergus had made no attempt to breach that barrier and she saw no reason why she should do so. There was also the simple fact that if Sir Fergus had wished to sit with her and speak to her, he should not have so quickly relinquished his seat.

"Aye, if I recall, Glascreag provides a suitable wild, mayhap e'en dangerous place for a lad to prove himself."

"It does, indeed."

Although a small voice in her head warned her that she would suffer for almost completely ignoring her betrothed and Anabel, Cecily kept her attention fixed upon Sir Artan. He was such a change from her usual companion at a meal that she could not help but revel in it. The way he spoke of Glascreag and Angus MacReith revealed a deep affection for both, and she wondered what it would be like to feel such a bond to the place where one lived and the people there. Once upon a time she had felt such a thing for Dunburn and its people, but that had died along with her family. No matter how hard she had tried, she had failed to regain that deep, comforting sense of belonging.

As soon as the meal was done, Cecily decided it would be best if she made her escape. She did not want to confront either Anabel or Sir Fergus. For once she was confident she had done no wrong and she did not want to listen to any lectures. If nothing else, she did not want to be made to feel she *had* erred. The sense of confidence she now felt was a rare thing and she wanted to savor it.

It did not really surprise Cecily to find herself escorted to her bedchamber by Sir Artan. She did not even attempt to figure out how the man had managed to be at her side. He had undoubtedly used the same methods he had used to usurp Sir

Fergus's place at the table. The fact that she did not have to endure a lecture from Sir Fergus or a kiss was reason enough for her to be heartily grateful for Sir Artan's guile.

At the door to her bedchamber, she turned to wish Sir Artan a good sleep, only to catch him staring at her in a very intense manner. Cecily clenched her hands into tight fists at her sides to resist the urge to check the state of her hair and gown. "I thank ye for your escort, Sir Artan. 'Twas nay necessary, but it was most appreciated."

Artan looked into her lovely eyes, saw her uncertainty, and decided he needed to do one more thing before he was absolutely sure of his next step. Placing his hands on the door on either side of her, he took a step closer until their bodies almost touched. He took the sound of a slight hitch in her breathing and the widening of her eyes as a good sign. As he slowly lowered his head, he watched her face, her rapidly changing expressions telling him that she knew what he was about to do. The fact that she made no move to halt him or flee encouraged him.

The moment Sir Artan's lips brushed over hers, Cecily felt a warmth flood through her body with such speed and fury she felt dizzy. Sir Fergus's lips had never felt so warm or soft, or so gentle. The only feeling her betrothed had ever stirred within her was one of disinterest touched with revulsion and fear. At first, the gentle prodding of his tongue against her lips puzzled her. Then he sucked on her bottom lip and she gasped over the flurry of feelings that raced through her. The moment her lips parted, he thrust his tongue into her mouth, and in but a heartbeat, she felt herself shudder beneath the strength of what his stroking tongue was making her feel.

When he started to pull away, she grasped him by the front of his shirt and tried to pull him back. His soft chuckle brought her to her senses and she quickly released him. Even as she stared at him in astonishment, he opened the door to her bed-chamber and gently nudged her into her room. Dazed, she watched as he slowly smiled.

"Good sleep, Sile," he said before closing the door.

Cecily touched her lips with her shaking fingers. Her heart beat so fast and hard she was surprised she could not see it beneath her bodice, could not see the material moving to that erratic rhythm. Kissing one man when she was betrothed to another had to be a grave sin. At that moment, with her blood afire from a riot of feelings, she simply did not care. Cecily just hoped she would not have to pay too great a penance.

Whistling softly beneath his breath, Artan headed toward the bedchamber allotted to him. The kiss he had just shared with Cecily had marked the path he would now walk and marked it very clearly. There was a fire beneath that shy beauty of hers and it had flared up quickly, stirred to bright life by his kiss. That she had stirred a similar fire within him was even better. She would be his.

When he saw Sir Fergus Ogilvey standing outside his bedchamber door, Artan almost told the man about his decision. Only the instinctive knowledge that there were secrets at Dunburn that needed un-covering held him silent. He did not think it was just his dislike of Sir Fergus that made him believe the man was part of those secrets. Artan stood in front of the man, crossed his arms over his chest, and stared down at him. The way the man's upper lip beaded with sweat gave Artan some satisfaction. The fact that Sir Fergus stood firm despite his obvious fear would have earned the man some respect if Artan had not seen two very large men lurking in the shadows just a few steps away.

"Step aside, lad," he told Sir Fergus. "I seek my bed and ye block the route to it."

"I think it would be wise if ye left Dunburn in the morning, Sir Artan," said Sir Fergus.

"Och, do ye now. And why do ye think I should do that?"

"Because Lady Cecily Donaldson is to marry me and I will tolerate no interference."

It was the very firmness of that statement that warned Artan, that and the slight sound of a booted foot sliding stealthily over the stone floor. He was ready for the men when they attacked, and it was a short fight. The men obviously had not been ready for him to anticipate the attack. Artan looked at a pale, wide-eyed Sir Fergus, who stared at his fallen men in dismay and then looked at Artan.

"Move," Artan said, and nodded in satisfaction when the men fled.

Once inside his bedchamber, Artan securely latched the door. If it had been jealousy that had stirred Sir Fergus's anger, Artan might have shrugged it aside, but he sensed that it was not. That also meant that this would not be the man's only attempt to force him to leave. Artan smiled as he got ready for bed. A woman to woo and a threat to avert. This visit to Dunburn had definitely just improved.

Chapter 5

"Do ye nay join the hunt?" Cecily asked Artan as she sat down opposite him and began to help herself to what remained of a lavish morning feast.

She was surprised to find the man in the great hall. After waiting so carefully before coming to break her fast, wanting to be sure all the guests had ridden out on the hunt, Cecily had anticipated a few moments of peace. She thought it rather contrary of her not to be annoyed that he was there. She had to forcibly quell a blush when she began to wonder if he would give her another kiss, perhaps one that lasted a great deal longer than the one he had given her last night.

"Nay," replied Artan. "I have seen such hunts before. 'Tis nay more than a wasteful slaughter. Too many of the fools cannae e'en make a clean kill. Aye, and they are often so noisy, most of the game they seek has had ample time to flee them. Better a few skilled men be sent out to bring home some meat for the table. These courtiers wouldst probably starve if they truly had to hunt for their supper."

Cecily blinked in surprise. He had delivered that

harsh denunciation of the hunters in such an amiable tone of voice, it had taken her a moment to realize just how harsh it was. It was all quite true, of course, and she had often thought the same, but she never would have expected a man to share her opinion.

"There are a few skilled hunters going along."

"Aye, to give whate'er poor beastie the fools maim the mercy blow."

She winced and nearly nodded her agreement. Only a fleeting sense that she would be insulting her guests, her kinsmen, and her betrothed with one small gesture caused her to hold back her words. A quick glance into Artan's silvery blue eyes told her that he would not be surprised to learn that this particular group of people were worse than others.

"Weel, since we are both here and dinnae wish to go hunting, mayhap ye would like to ride with me?" Artan asked her. "I have ne'er visited the Lowlands, and I doubt I shall return. I wouldnae mind being shown the lands around Dunburn by one who kens them weel."

"We shall have to stay out of the way of the hunters."

Cecily knew her words were an acceptance of his invitation and wondered what had possessed her. While it was true that it was her duty to help entertain the guests, she doubted going out riding with Sir Artan, alone, would be considered appropriate. Anabel was always most strict about her daughters and Cecily, never allowing them to be alone with a man. Cecily supposed she could ask young Peter at the stables to ride with them, but she doubted that would fully satisfy Anabel. Or Sir Fergus.

Rebellion stirred to life within her heart and she

found it a heady feeling. None of the others cared whether she was entertained or not, and not one of these guests was her friend. Soon she would be married to Sir Fergus, and Cecily doubted she would find much entertainment or many friends when she went to live with him. She had to admit that she would not be at all disappointed if her actions caused an end to the betrothal, either. For once she was going to do exactly what she wanted, and she wanted to go riding with Sir Artan. She found herself smiling at him a lot as they finished their meal.

Artan was pleased as he escorted her out of the great hall. He had feared that the uncertainty he had read in her expression would cause her to refuse to go riding with him. Then a look of determination had entered her fine eyes, and even though she had obviously startled herself by doing so, she had agreed. The lass was not fully broken to the harsh bridle Lady Anabel and Sir Fergus wished to put on her.

As they approached the stable, Artan frowned. He had that odd tingle in his spine, the one he usually felt when danger was at hand. Since the bailey was almost completely deserted, he fixed his gaze upon the stable and felt that sense of impending danger sharply increase. He turned to smile at Cecily. If there was some danger inside the stables he did not want her caught up in it.

"Wait here, lass," he said, "and I will bring ye your horse."

"I can saddle my own horse, sir, and truly, I dinnae mind doing so."

"And 'tis a good thing for a lass to ken, but my

mother trained me to be courteous and do such things for ladies."

Cecily smiled faintly and nodded. She would prefer to stay outside in the warm sun anyway. After Old Thomas the stable master had died three years ago, the cleanliness of the stables had slowly declined, and she much preferred the fresher air of the outdoors as well.

She stood enjoying the unusual warmth of the day and wondered why she was suddenly so rebellious. The way she was acting, especially since Sir Artan had arrived, was most unlike her. Cecily had thought herself resigned to the marriage her guardians had arranged, but it seemed she was not. Whenever she looked at Sir Artan Murray, a little voice in her head urged her to do as she pleased and not as she should, to remember that soon she would be married to Sir Fergus.

An odd series of thumping noises from the stables drew her out of her dark thoughts about her future as Lady Ogilvey. Cecily frowned toward the shadowy opening to the building. The noises had sounded not unlike bodies hitting something hard, a sound she had, thankfully, only heard a few times. They certainly did not sound like the kind of noises one would make while saddling two horses. Although she could not think of any danger Sir Artan might face inside the stables, she felt a little concerned for his safety and took a few steps toward the stables.

"Sir Artan?" she called. "Do ye need help?"

"Nay, lass," he called back. "Ye wait right there. I will be out in a moment."

He certainly sounded hale and hearty, she decided. Cecily did not feel particularly calmed, however.

She decided to give the man a few more moments to appear, and if he did not, she would seek him out. Keeping her gaze fixed upon the opening to the stables, she waited and tried to stir up her courage just in case she would have need of it.

Artan looked at the three unconscious men scattered around on the stable floor and shook his head. He recognized two of them from last night. Sir Fergus was obviously not going to give up on his quest to make Artan leave Dunburn. As he finished saddling the horses, Artan decided he had best work very hard at convincing Cecily to leave Dunburn with him and at uncovering whatever secrets her guardians were keeping. If Sir Fergus kept increasing the number of men he sent to attack and pummel him into an ignoble retreat, the fool might actually reach a number Artan could not defeat on his own.

Leading the horses outside to where Cecily waited, Artan returned her concerned look with an easy smile. She frowned as she looked him over, glanced again at the stables, and then met his gaze. It was obvious she was curious about the noises she must have heard coming from the stables. Fortunately, what few bruises he might have gathered in the brief fight were well hidden by his clothes.

"Shall we go?" he asked.

"What was all that noise?" she asked as he helped her mount her mare.

"What noise?" He mounted Thunderbolt and started toward the open gates.

"A thumping noise. It sounded verra much like a body hitting the wall."

"A body hitting the wall? Ye have heard that noise often, have ye?"

Instinct told her that he was trying to distract her, and Cecily told herself that was why she felt a strong urge to wipe that grin off his handsome face. "I havenae heard it that often, but often enough to ken what it sounds like."

"Much like Thunderbolt here giving his stall a wee kick in his eagerness to get out, I suspect." Artan patted his horse's neck in silent apology for that slur upon his good behavior.

Cecily found herself ready to question that answer and was appalled. She could almost hear Anabel screeching in her ear, telling her repeatedly that a woman never questioned the veracity of what a man told her. Of course, Anabel also said that that did not mean they were telling the truth, that men rarely told the truth. What appalled Cecily was that she seemed to have taken that cold advice to heart, for there was no reason for her to doubt Sir Artan's words. She promised herself she would shake free of such an unkind and unjust opinion and turned her attention to showing Sir Artan the lands her father had loved so much.

Artan studied the land Cecily spoke of with such affection and wondered how she would like the rougher, stronger beauty of the Highlands. Dunburn had good lands, he mused, despite looking a little too soft and civilized. It was not being husbanded well, however. The occasional frown he caught darkening Cecily's sweet face told him she was becoming aware of the creeping neglect of the lands. It had obviously been quite a while since she had ridden the lands of her father, and he wondered if she had been purposely kept from doing so.

When they paused by a clear, swiftly running burn Artan recalled crossing when he had come to Dunburn, he listened to Cecily describe the many hours she had spent in the shelter of a cluster of trees near the bank. Her voice carried the soft touch of fond remembrance followed by a hint of sadness as she spoke of the times she had brought her brother here with her. Artan dismounted, then helped her dismount. He followed her into the shady bower formed by the trees.

"I havenae been here for such a long time," she whispered.

"Because the memories hurt?" he asked as he put his arm around her shoulders.

"Partly. Also, Anabel doesnae allow me to ride about on my own, and when I do go for a ride, whate'er guardian she sets at my heels has obviously been given verra specific instructions as to where I am allowed to go. I think the chance of painful memories being stirred up was one reason I didnae fight the restriction much."

"We can leave if ye wish."

"Nay, it has been a long time, and e'en though memories of that happier time and poor wee Colin cause a pang, there is more joy in the memory than pain. 'Tis wrong to clutch grief close for too long or to try to dismiss all memories of lost loved ones just to save oneself the pain of thinking of them."

Artan placed two fingers beneath her chin and tilted her face up to his. He kissed her lightly, intending it to be a gesture of comfort. When she slid her arms around his neck and pressed her slim body closer to his, however, comfort was soon lost in a swiftly rising lust.

Cecily clung to Artan, parting her lips at the first touch of his tongue so that he could deepen the kiss. A shudder tore through her body as he stroked the inside of her mouth. She tentatively touched his tongue with hers and the low, almost feral, growl he gave encouraged her to be more daring, giving back as much as he gave.

It took every ounce of willpower Artan had to pull back from the heated embrace. He was delighted by the soft mew of objection she gave and the way she tried to pull him closer again, but he held firm. He would not take her here, out in the woods in the middle of the day with far too much chance of being discovered. Cecily might not know it, but that was exactly where such heated kisses would take them.

For a moment, he paused as he brushed a kiss over her forehead. If they were caught rolling about on the banks of the burn, her betrothal to Sir Fergus might be ended. It would mean he did not have to exert himself to do any wooing, simply pack her up and take her to Glascreag. Then he considered how humiliated she would be and knew he could not do it. There was also the chance she would not be cast out, even by her betrothed, but her life would undoubtedly be made very miserable indeed. Nor would he have the chance to find out exactly what was going on at Dunburn. Nay, he thought as he took another step back from the temptation of her mouth, this had to stop for now.

When he saw her start to realize what they had been doing, that realization bringing a deep blush to her cheeks and a look of shame into her eyes, he gave her his best cocksure grin. As he had suspected, it worked on her as it so often had on his sisters. The hint of shame was rapidly replaced by anger. Before she could show him just how sharp her tongue might be, Artan felt something brush

past his face. Even as he started to pull Cecily into
his arms to shield her with his body, an arrow em-
bedded itself in the tree.

"Artan!" Cecily cried, terrified that he had been
hurt or soon would be.

He did not answer but nearly threw her to the
ground and sprawled on top of her just as a second
arrow thudded into the tree. The sound of a horse
rapidly fleeing reached his ears, but he could not
see anything. After a few moments, Artan cautiously
rose to his knees, but he still kept Cecily sheltered
beneath him.

There was no doubt in Artan's mind that someone had just tried to kill him. The only thing that
really puzzled him was that they would try to do so
when Cecily was with him. He had to believe that
her presence was not expected. There was no benefit he could see to killing her; but then he had not
yet uncovered the secrets he knew her guardians
and, perhaps, even her betrothed were keeping.

As he slowly got to his feet and pulled Cecily up
alongside him, he thought about how determined
her guardians were that she marry Sir Fergus. And
although there was certainly no hint of love there,
how determined Sir Fergus was that nothing and
no one stop this marriage. He would give himself
three more days to ferret out the truth; then he
would get her away from this place whether she
agreed or not.

"The hunting party?" Cecily asked in a shaking
voice, giving in to the urge to hug Artan out of a
deep sense of relief that he was unharmed.

"Mayhap." Artan kept a close watch for any sign of
the one who had shot the arrows as he began to walk

Cecily back to their horses. "They must have realized their error when ye screeched out my name."

"I ne'er screech." The soft chuckle he gave did a lot to soothe her lingering fears. "They cannae be such poor hunters. Ye look nothing like a deer."

"We were within the wee leafy bower. It could have confused someone."

"Someone who thinks deer come to drink at the burn on horseback?"

"Weel, I didnae say that the someone couldnae be a complete idiot."

Cecily opened her mouth to say more, then quickly closed it. She simply did not believe this was a hunting accident and did not think he did either. Yet what else could it be? She had no enemies. Sir Artan might well have a few, but she doubted an enemy would follow him to Dunburn, lurk about waiting for him to venture outside the protective walls, and then shoot arrows at him. And if someone was after him, she doubted an enemy who was so persistent, so blindly determined, would miss him—twice.

Something was not right here, she decided as he swung her up onto her saddle and she took the reins into her hands. There was a hard look in Sir Artan's fine eyes that told her he felt the same. Cecily suspected he had a suspicion or two but suddenly knew he would not tell her what they were, not yet. He would not throw out unproven accusations. She was not sure how she knew that; she just did.

"Mayhap ye ought to leave Dunburn," she said quietly once they were both mounted and headed back to the keep.

He was pleased to hear the sharp reluctance in

her voice when she made that suggestion. "And miss your wedding?"

Despite the attack and all the fear it had bred, Cecily could still feel the warmth of his kiss, still taste him on her mouth. Not once since the day Anabel had informed her that she would marry Sir Fergus Ogilvey had Cecily felt such a fierce reluctance to do so. Now that she had been held in Sir Artan's strong arms, had tasted the sweet fire of his kiss, the thought of giving herself to Sir Fergus made her feel distinctly ill. Before Sir Artan had arrived, she had thought she could make herself content with her lot. Now she doubted she could ever achieve that. Since the day she had learned her fate, her marriage had loomed as a necessary duty. Now it looked as if she were marching straight into purgatory.

"Ye best tell me exactly what happened today."

Artan blinked, groped for the linen cloth on the floor by his bath, and wiped the soap from his face. He looked at the plump, middle-aged woman standing by his bath, her hands on her hips and a fierce scowl on her round, pretty face. How she had gotten into his bedchamber he did not know. He had not heard a thing. Either she was very skilled at stealth, or he had been dangerously lost in his thoughts.

"And who are ye if I may be so bold as to ask it?" he asked.

"They call me Old Meg. I was Cecily's nurse and many another thing until that she-wolf Anabel threw me out of Dunburn."

"Ye obviously didnae go far."

"When I heard that my wee lass was to be married off, I came back. I ken weel how to get in and out of this place without being seen."

"Why did Lady Anabel throw ye out?"

"I caught her thrashing the lass until the blood ran. The bitch quickly proved that she can wield the stick but cannae bravely face a taste of it herself." She nodded in approval at the look of fury on the young man's handsome face. "'Tis said old Angus MacReith sent ye."

"Aye, he did."

"Why? He hasnae had aught to do with the poor lass since her da and her brother were killed."

"Ah, now there is an odd thing. He claims he has often written to her asking her to come to him at Glascreag." There was only a moment's look of confusion on the woman's face before fury hardened her pleasant features. "Now if ye would be so kind as to turn your back for a wee moment so I can get out of this bath, dry myself, and put some clothes on, we can have ourselves a fine long talk about all of this."

By the time Artan was dressed, it was obvious by the tapping of her foot that Old Meg was losing all patience. He quickly poured them each a goblet of wine and handed her one. In between sips of the hearty wine, he told Old Meg all of his suspicions, the attacks that had been made on him, and what had happened at the burn. However, he did not tell her about the kisses and the bargain Angus had offered him. Such things had nothing to do with the trouble facing Cecily now, and he believed they should remain private, strictly between him and Cecily. The faint hint of suspicion in her dark eyes told him she knew he held something back, but to his great relief, she did not press him for more.

"It seems they dinnae want any emissary of Angus's here," Old Meg murmured. "They have done their best to see that old Angus has naught to do with the child. Ye are right to think there is something they are hiding. I have always thought so. I have ne'er believed Cecily's father would leave her with naught. He was the type of mon to leave verra careful instructions and to make sure none of his family were left at the mercy of others. Nay, and he ne'er liked or trusted Anabel and Edmund either. So what do ye plan to do?"

"Find out their secrets."

"But they mean to wed her to that worm, and e'en ye think he has had his hand in this somehow."

Artan nodded. "And Cecily willnae be marrying him."

"How can ye stop it? Ye are but one mon."

"If I have to, I will bind and gag the lass and take her to Glascreag flung o'er my saddle."

Old Meg studied him intently for a moment, then nodded. "If that is what is needed to save her, I stand ready to help ye."

Artan smiled and touched his goblet to hers in a silent toast, welcoming his new ally.

Chapter 6

"That mon simply willnae leave!"

Artan halted at the sound of Anabel's shrill voice coming out of the solar through the slightly open door. After four days of putting himself firmly at Cecily's side and doing his meager best to woo her, as well as glean as much information about her guardians as possible, it appeared that he might have finally gotten lucky. Silently inching closer to the door of the solar, he listened carefully, hoping Anabel would reveal some of the secrets he knew she clung to. Careful not to cast his shadow across the slight opening of the door, he waited for her obvious anger to make her careless.

"I have tried to get him to leave, Anabel."

Recognizing Sir Fergus's voice, Artan was not really surprised. He had suspected that the man was part of whatever scheme was brewing at Dunburn.

"It has only been four days, Anabel," said Sir Edmund. "Ye are too impatient."

"The mon is asking too many questions, Edmund," she snapped.

"And getting no answers."

"For now, but I dinnae think he is the stupid brute he would like us to think he is."

"Nay? He is a Highlander, is he not?" drawled Sir Fergus.

Artan hoped he would have the chance to grind Sir Fergus's face into the mud before he left Dunburn with Cecily. In truth, it was going to please him a great deal to rob the man of his bride.

"That Highlander appears to have the wit to escape all of your attempts to hobble him," murmured Sir Edmund. "How many men did ye send the last time ye tried to beat him into fleeing?"

After a small, tense silence, Sir Fergus muttered, "Six."

"And your fool men nearly killed Cecily when they tried to put an arrow through the mon."

"They didnae see the lass until too late and stopped the attack the moment they recognized her."

"Weel, they had better begin to take more care. She is nay use to us dead, at least nay until she has married you."

"I understand that weel enough. Ye dinnae need to fret o'er losing your fine, comfortable life. The lass will marry me, her lands and coin will soon be safe in my grasp, and ye will gain firm hold on Dunburn and much more."

"I dinnae see why ye must lay claim to so much," grumbled Anabel.

"I am nay the one with blood on my hands. And without me ye can ne'er truly lay claim to any of it, can ye? Ye are naught but the stewards of Cecily's fortune. When she passed her twenty-first saint's day ye were nay longer e'en that. My marriage to

Cecily and the contract we have signed finally makes at least part of it all legally yours."

"Her widow's portion—"

"Will be mine when I weary of her, less what has been promised to ye in the marriage contract. If her uncle had e'er discovered the truth, ye would have been left with naught. Nay, not e'en your lives. Ye cannae believe I would give ye all of it just because ye are giving me Cecily, can ye? Aye, she will keep me entertained for a few months, and I may keep her long enough to gain an heir, but I am nay besotted with the wench. This marriage is to fill my pockets. Be glad I am willing to share the bounty."

"Weel, if ye dinnae do something about Angus's mon and quickly, all we will be sharing is the gallows!"

Artan was fighting the urge to charge into the room and break a few bones when a work-worn hand suddenly grabbed him by the wrist. He glanced to his side to see a grim Old Meg there. She was definitely skilled at stealth, he decided. Yet again he had not heard or even sensed her approach. He gave her a curt nod of greeting and returned to listening to the three people he now saw as his enemies.

"He will be dealt with. Ye might try harder to keep him away from Cecily. He stays too close to her, and my men feel certain they were embracing that day at the burn. 'Tis why they didnae recognize her. Thought she was just some maid or village wench."

"Ye are her betrothed. Mayhap ye ought to be trying to keep a tighter rein on her. So far all ye seem to be able to do is cower in your boots whene'er that Highlander comes near to ye."

"I havenae seen either of ye standing firm against him," snapped Sir Fergus.

"I have nay wish to anger a mon who ne'er has less than three weapons on him," drawled Sir Edmund. "And considering he not only defeated six of your men but didnae e'en get bruised in doing so, I see only wisdom in treading warily about the mon."

"He willnae hurt a woman."

"Aye, I think ye may have the right of it, Fergus. So, m'dear wife, ye shall have to be a better shepherd to our little lamb until she is penned and sheared."

"As ye wish," said Anabel, the tone of her voice far from that of a truly submissive wife.

"Good," said Sir Fergus. "Now, I mean to go and plan another attack upon that barbarian."

"Let us hope ye are a little more successful than ye have been so far," said Sir Edmund.

Artan felt Old Meg tug on his wrist. He allowed her to lead him away from the door and they slipped into a room that adjoined the solar. As she went to the fireplace and yanked on a torch holder, Artan fought to calm the fury roiling inside of him. A small passageway was revealed as a well-hidden door opened and he followed her into it. Artan fought the urge to shiver when the door closed behind them. He had always loathed small, dark places. The candle he now held did not do much to light their way.

"We can continue to listen from here," Old Meg said, standing on her toes to whisper in his ear.

It took Artan a moment to realize Old Meg was peering through a very small crack in the thick stone wall. Even as he stepped up beside her, he snuffed the candle, not wanting to risk any chance

that Edmund or Anabel would notice the light through the crack. He knew he had heard enough of their secrets to justify anything he did to free Cecily from their grasp, but there was always the chance they would give him even more.

"I dinnae trust him," said Anabel. "I think he means to betray or cheat us in the end."

"He may try," replied Sir Edmund, sounding utterly bored. "Of course, if ye hadnae spread your legs for him, he would ne'er have gotten into your bedchamber and found those papers."

"So condemning ye sound, ye who ruts with anything in a petticoat."

"But who ne'er leaves important secrets where any fool can find them."

"Gloat if it makes ye feel better. It was an error in judgment. Most of what he holds o'er us was naught but conjecture, and ye did as poorly as I in defending yourself against that. Can we now turn our minds to what must be done about that kilted brute? He is trying to woo Cecily into leaving with him for Glascreag, ye ken."

"Then ye had best make your disapproval of the mon verra clear to Cecily. Ye have kept the girl cowed for years, done verra weel in making sure she ne'er asks questions and seeks to please ye in all things, so I ken ye can twist her to your way now. Keep yourself at her side. Mayhap cutting the mon away from our wee prize will be enough. Ye have made her hungry for approval. Let her see that having anything to do with that mon will surely lose any she might gain from her marriage."

"I could always lock her in her bedchamber."

"'Twould give rise to too many questions. So would a sound beating if that was your second choice. If ye wish to continue to live as weel as ye have for the last twelve years, keep the lass close so that Highlander cannae talk to her alone and weaken her allegiance to us."

"That will make for a verra long eleven days."

"Think of the noose awaiting each of us should ye fail. That should provide inspiration."

Artan held himself very still until he was sure Sir Edmund and Lady Anabel were gone. This time he did the leading. Careful not to be seen with Old Meg, he took her to his bedchamber. He poured them each a goblet of wine and spent several minutes going over all he just heard as he drank.

"They mean to kill the lass," said Old Meg after several moments of tense silence.

"Aye, and I believe they killed her father and brother, although that would be hard to prove after so many years," said Artan. "Did ye arrive in time to hear Sir Fergus say that at least he didnae have blood on his hands?" Old Meg nodded, her fury clear to see in her eyes. "Then there was Sir Edmund's remark about living as weel as they have for twelve years."

"But Cecily could have died in that attack."

"I suspect the fact that she did not was a hard disappointment to them. Once she returned to Dunburn they feared doing anything to be rid of her."

"And so that bitch played upon my poor wee lass's feelings and her need to have a family."

"It kept Cecily from asking questions such as why her uncle ne'er wrote and all."

"And so by keeping Cecily thinking Angus had turned aside from her, Anabel was able to tighten her grip."

"Banishing ye from Dunburn did the same, I expect."

Old Meg sighed. "I should have held fast to my temper. I am lucky I wasnae hanged for beating the woman. But, aye, taking me away from Cecily only left the poor wee child e'en more alone and in need." Old Meg cursed and shook her head. "I was no better. I ne'er asked any questions and was quick to cast aside whate'er suspicions I had in the beginning. I only briefly doubted it was just thieves who did the killing, and I fear I just cursed Angus for an old fool and assumed he had e'er only been interested in the laddie."

"Most men are. An heir and all that." He patted Old Meg's shoulder. "Dinnae chastise yourself too heartily. They obviously didnae use any Dunburn men or ye would have heard a whisper or two to set ye to thinking." He shrugged. "'Tis done and past. There is no changing it. Aye, and the ones who are really at fault are her kinsmen, the verra ones who should have cared for her."

"So what is to happen now?"

"I need to get Cecily out of here." He frowned. "I can nay longer just try to convince her to come to Glascreag with me and openly ride away with her. That would ne'er be allowed, and I cannae fight off all of the Donaldson and Ogilvey men."

"It sounds as if ye have been giving it a goodly effort."

Artan ignored that remark. "I need to get Cecily to Glascreag as quickly as possible. She can be better protected there. There isnae any chance of doing that here, as this is her enemy's home ground. Howbeit, I am nay sure how I can get her away unseen."

Old Meg crossed her arms over her chest. "Your greatest problem is how to get her to go with ye at all. Aye, we now ken that she has been cheated of what is hers by right and that her life is in danger, but she isnae going to believe it just because ye say it is so."

"What if ye tell her all we have just learned?"

"'Twill plant a few doubts in her mind, but nay enough to make her calmly walk away with ye. Wretched as these people are, Cecily sees Dunburn as her home and these people as her family. Bonnie as ye are, she has only kenned ye for a few days, so why should she believe ye o'er them? And I have ne'er liked Anabel or Edmund and have made my dislike far too clear o'er the years for her to heed me too closely."

Artan softly cursed. Old Meg was right. Cecily would be slow to believe them, if only because no one would want to accept that they had been made a fool of for years, and there was no time to convince her. He could not depend on getting her to overhear another revealing conversation by her own guardians so that she could hear the ugly truth from their own mouths. It appeared there was little chance Cecily would willingly walk away with him, at least not this soon in the game or without far more proof of the danger she was in than just his word.

"I am going to have to try to get her to meet with me somewhere outside the walls of the keep and then kidnap her," he said. "After listening to those three swine, there simply isnae any time left for convincing her that her guardians and her betrothed are a threat to her or to woo her into coming with me."

"Nay, there isnae enough time, although I cannae believe I am e'en thinking of helping ye kidnap the lass; but better she go with ye than stay here with these carrion. And what do ye mean *woo* her?"

There was a tone to Old Meg's voice that sharply reminded Artan of the one his own mother would use when she had caught him out in some mischief. To his utter dismay, he felt a guilty color burn in his cheeks. For a moment he considered several ways to wriggle out of answering that last question, but then he looked into her eyes. There was *that* look, the one he suspected all mothers gave erring sons that seemed able to pull the truth right out of them. Artan heard himself tell her all about the bargain Angus had offered him and was not really surprised that he was doing so.

Old Meg frowned and studied the young man. She did not like the idea that Cecily would be taken away from a marriage she had been forced to accept and thrown right into another that she was being lured into by pretty words and a handsome face. Neither man seemed to care much for Cecily's feelings. Then she inwardly cursed. Sir Fergus planned to kill the girl when he had taken all he wanted from her. Sir Artan might also be marrying the girl for gain, but he would keep her safe. Cecily might have her feelings hurt when she discovered exactly why this big, strong man had married her, but at least she would still be alive to complain about it. Considering Cecily would have this man in her bed instead of Sir Fergus, Old Meg decided that hurt could be quickly soothed. As soon as she could collect up the things Cecily had hidden away, Meg also decided she would take them to Glascreag herself and make sure that her lass was being treated well.

"I dinnae like the fact that Cecily is still being wed because of her dower, but better ye than that sly ferret Fergus," she said.

"I willnae marry her just to gain Glascreag," said Artan.

"Are ye trying to tell me that ye already love the lass?"

The bite in Old Meg's words was so sharp Artan almost winced. "I like her, I desire her, and I am a mon who will hold fast to vows made. She wouldnae get that from verra many other men, nay when she is so richly dowered."

"Aye, that is the sad, hard truth. So, best we start planning on when and how we can get her out of here."

"The when had best be tonight, I am thinking. Anabel may hesitate just tonight to take up her role as guard, but she *will* take it up and it will make an escape nearly impossible. I need to get Cecily alone long enough to convince her to slip away and meet me. Since we cannae guess how quickly or firmly these carrion will increase their guard on her, 'tis best if we take time to consider ways to elude them."

Artan limped through the gates of Dunburn. A few men chuckled, but most watched him with a look of fear or respect. Cecily had to be the only one at Dunburn who did not know he was being attacked at every turning. This time he had actually had to draw his sword and two men would not be returning to Dunburn. It had, however, given him a good excuse to leave Thunderbolt secured near the burn. No one would question that his horse had gotten away from him during the attack, although he found it irritating that he had to leave these fools thinking he had so little skill with his mount. It was a necessary bruise to his pride, however. Getting Cecily out of Dunburn was going to be difficult enough. The only ideas he had come up with for getting his horse out at night could all too easily have given Cecily the idea that he had left for good, and she would then think there was to be no meeting after all.

It was not just Cecily who had to leave now either. This last attack had been much more than a nuisance. Eight armed men had come at Artan, and he had been hard-pressed to even the numbers enough so that he could more easily rout the others. He was a skilled fighter, but even that could not save him if the number of men attacking him continued to increase. Although he hated to run from any fight, he would do Cecily no good if he died.

As he walked toward his bedchamber, a noise from within Sir Fergus's room caught his attention. It sounded as if someone was crying. For a minute Artan thought the fool may have already heard that his men had failed once again, but then he heard a soft feminine voice cry out. It was followed by the distinct sound of a fist hitting flesh. Stealthily entering the man's bedchamber, Artan had to fight the strong urge to immediately kill the man. Only the knowledge that if he did so he would have to fight his way out of Dunburn and that that would leave Cecily unprotected stayed his hand.

Sir Fergus had a young maid pinned to the floor. She did not look to be much older than twelve or thirteen. Her gown was torn, and her face was bruised. Artan silently closed the door behind him and walked over to the struggling couple. He grabbed Sir Fergus by the back of his jupon and threw him against the wall. The man seemed to stick there for a moment, staring at Artan in horror, but then his eyes rolled back and he slowly slipped down into a heap upon the floor.

"Get ye gone, lass," he told the girl as he helped her to her feet, "and stay far away from this swine."

"Aye, sir, I will," she said in a voice choked with tears as she fled the room.

Artan walked over to Sir Fergus. There was blood on the wall and he could see a small stream of it running down the man's neck. He checked for a pulse and was relieved to find a strong one. The man sorely deserved killing, but now was neither the time nor the place. Artan was sure, however, that there would be one less guard on Cecily tonight, for Sir Fergus would be a long time waking and would be feeling poorly when he did. He would have to be satisfied with that, Artan mused as he left the room.

Cecily found that she was actually enjoying herself. Dining in the great hall was much more pleasant without Anabel and Sir Fergus glaring at her and critically watching her every move. Both were indisposed according to Sir Edmund. Although Cecily felt a little guilty about being so pleased that neither one was at the table, for she would never wish anyone to fall ill, she could not deny what she felt. Sir Edmund was still at hand, but he mostly ignored her as was his habit. At the evening meal most of Sir Edmund's time was spent in deciding which woman he would drag to his bed for the night.

When Sir Artan placed some venison on her plate, she smiled her thanks. Cecily found it hard to believe that such a handsome man sought her company and her kisses. It was a heady thing to hold the attention of such a man, and she appeared to be the only one who did. Many of the women at Dunburn, guest and maid alike, had tried their best to catch his eye, but he showed no interest. Although Cecily found that odd, she also found it exciting.

Once the meal was done, she allowed Sir Artan to walk her to her bedchamber. Several of Sir Fergus's kinsmen scowled at her, but Sir Edmund was too busy trying to charm the plump Lady Helen to notice what his ward was doing. Cecily suspected the unusual freedom of movement she had been allowed for the past few days would shortly come to an end. She could still hear Anabel's furious lecture on the day she had taken Sir Artan on a tour of Dunburn lands. Anabel had even made it sound as if it was all Cecily's fault that some fool had nearly killed them.

"Do ye ken that no one claims to have been near the burn the day we had those arrows shot at us?" she asked Sir Artan as they halted before her bedchamber door. She hastily smothered the shocking urge to ask him to step inside with her.

"Aye," he replied, placing his hands on the door on either side of her and slowly moving his body closer to hers. "No huntsmon would e'er admit to being so poor at hunting. Since neither of us was harmed, he doesnae see any need for confession and no one else sees any need to ask too many questions."

She nodded absently, her attention fixed upon

his mouth despite all her efforts to raise her gaze to his eyes. She actually ached for his kiss. She clenched her hands against the urge to grab him and pull him into her arms. When he brushed a kiss over her forehead, she shivered with longing.

"Lass, come meet with me tonight. Midnight. At the bower near the burn."

"Creep away ye mean?"

"Aye, slip away from this crowded place, from all these curious eyes." He kissed the hollow by her ear and heard her breathing quicken. She was so responsive, so soft and warm, he had to fight the urge to pull her into her bedchamber and ease the ache she so effortlessly stirred inside of him. "We havenae been alone since the day we went riding together."

"And were verra nearly killed." She was almost panting and found it difficult to catch her breath.

"'Twill be safe this time. Come meet with me. 'Tis a warm night and the moon is full."

She was so tempted it almost frightened her. "But I am a betrothed woman."

Artan kissed her and all hesitation fled her heart and mind. She wrapped her arms around his neck and readily opened her mouth for the hot invasion of his tongue. He made her feel almost wild in so many ways. Her blood raced through her veins and her breathing grew heavy and fast. He tasted like sin, and she knew he was tempting her to commit a very big one. Then she thought of the man she would have to marry soon and no longer cared.

"Meet me, lass," he said in a husky voice as he kissed her throat.

"Aye, I will. Midnight. At the burn."

He gave her a quick kiss, opened her door, and gently nudged her inside her bedchamber. "If ye can bring some food and wine, we can share a wee meal beneath the stars."

As if he could not help himself, Artan gave her another kiss and shut the door. Cecily stared at the door and wondered why he would want her to bring food. The only meal she wished to share had nothing to do with food. *Unless I could lick it off his body,* she thought, then gasped in shock at her own thoughts.

For just a moment she considered running after him and telling him she could not do it, could not share a tryst with him by the burn, but she hastily pushed aside that burst of cowardice. It was wrong, but for once, she intended to do what *she* wanted to do. She would meet Sir Artan at the burn and take whatever he had to give her, for all too soon she would be married to Sir Fergus.

"Did ye convince her?" asked Old Meg as Artan entered his bedchamber.

Seeing the woman sitting comfortably in his bed-chamber, Artan shook his head in a mixture of amusement and exasperation. "Do ye ne'er enter a room through the proper door?"

"Anabel might discover I am here if I did that. Why? Are ye afraid I might catch ye with one of the maids? Davida, perhaps?"

"Davida is fair, fulsome, and verra friendly, but she is nay for me. Ye ken weel that one of the reasons I came here was to decide if I wanted Cecily for my wife. 'Tisnae a time to be shaking the linen with any willing maid in reach. And, aye, I have convinced Cecily to meet me at the burn, at midnight. Neither Fergus nor Anabel attended the meal tonight and Sir Edmund was ogling Lady Helen, so Sile was verra lightly guarded. Now, I ken what happened to Sir Fergus, but I am curious about what happened to Lady Anabel."

"I put a purgative in her wine."

"Cruel woman." He laughed softly but quickly grew serious again. "Do ye think ye can gather any of Cecily's clothes?"

"I already have." She pointed to a sack set near his bed. "I long ago showed her the easiest and safest way to slip out of the keep."

"Good. I will take her clothes with me when I leave." He gently grasped the woman by the hand and tugged her out of her seat. "Now, I mean to have me a wee rest, for 'tis certain I will be riding for near all the night."

Old Meg went to the hidden door she had used to slip into his bedchamber unseen, then looked back at him. "Be good to my lass, Sir Artan, or I will make ye regret ye e'er touched her."

"I will be verra good to her."

He shook his head and laughed when the woman just grunted and then slipped away. Although he would like to reassure the old woman more, he did not have the time now. There was a long journey ahead of him and instinct told him it would not be an easy one.

Chapter 7

Cecily shivered as she crept along the dark, narrow passage that would take her outside the walls of Dunburn. She was reeling from shock at her own actions, yet trembling from anticipation as well. She was both terrified and eager to see Sir Artan. This was all so very wrong, yet a little voice in her head denied that truth, telling her it was right and urging her onward. It did not care that many would think this tryst equal to an act of adultery. Obviously, Artan's kisses had given her a fever of the brain.

She shook aside that thought. This was her choice. The only thing Sir Artan had done was look so handsome it made her heart ache and kiss her until her toes curled. There had been no sweet lies and practiced flatteries, no gifts, and no seductive coaxing. She was not sure he would know how to do such things anyway, and that was one of the things that so deeply attracted her. There did not appear to be any guile in the man.

And she wanted him, badly, as she had never wanted anything else in her life. In ten days she

would kneel before a priest to bind herself forever
to a man she felt nothing for, could not even like.
She had a chance to grasp a few sweet memories
to cherish during the long, cold years ahead of her
and she was determined to do so. For a little while
she wanted to savor what it felt like to be with a man
she wanted. It was wrong and she would undoubtedly pay dearly for it, but she did not care.

When she reached the end of the tunnel she set
down the bag of supplies she had brought with her
and cautiously opened the hatch. A torrent of
debris fell on her and she grimaced as she hastily
brushed the leaves, sticks, and dirt off her. Then,
very slowly and tensed for some outcry indicating
she had been discovered, she stuck her head up
through the opening and looked around. She felt
almost dizzy with relief when she saw no one.

Grabbing the sack of food and wine she had collected, Cecily climbed out of the tunnel. She
pushed the hatch back down and spread more of
the forest's debris over the top of it. After taking
careful note of its location, she picked up her sack
and hurried toward the burn, eager to get as far
away from the walls of Dunburn as she could. If she
were caught now, she would undoubtedly spend
the remaining days before her wedding locked in
Dunburn's dungeons.

Her courage faltered a little when she came
within sight of the burn and saw Artan. He stood
idly tossing rocks into the water. The full moon
made it easy to see him, to see how tall he was, how
strong, and how broad of shoulder. Cecily was suddenly all too aware of the fact that this man could
easily kill her with but a flick of his wrist.

She quickly shook her fear aside. Not once in the

four days she had known him had he hurt her or
even shown a hint of wanting to. Even when he
held her and kissed her, she had sensed how careful he was in the way he enfolded her in his strong
arms. Yet she still felt a slight, lingering unease as
she moved closer to him. This man was a warrior
and such men could be dangerous. Cecily wondered if that was part of the reason she was so attracted to him.

Artan heard a slight rustle in the grass from behind
him. His hand on his sword, he slowly turned around
and then relaxed when he saw Cecily shyly approach-
ing him. She was no threat. At least not yet, he
mused. When she realized what he intended to do,
that could swiftly change.

He felt the pinch of guilt and hastily smothered it.
She was expecting a lover's tryst, not a kidnapping
and a hard ride to Glascreag, but he had no choice.
It might take a while for her to believe that her kinsmen and Sir Fergus were a threat to her, but when
she did, he felt sure she would forgive him for this.
She had the wit to understand that he could not
wait until she found out the truth for herself.

The thought of the other truth he hid from her,
his bargain with Angus, made him wince. That could
prove to be a far more tangled problem than stealing her away from Dunburn first and explaining why
later. Somehow between here and Glascreag he was
going to have to tell her about that bargain. The dif-
ficulty would be in explaining it in such a way that it
did not sound too mercenary. Artan was not sure
there was any way to remove the taint and he cursed
Angus for even making the offer. He would face that
problem later, he decided, stepping close to her and

relieving her of the sack of food and wine she had brought with her.

"Ye have brought us a verra grand feast, I am thinking," he said as he set the bag aside.

"Weel, I recalled that ye have shown yourself to be a mon with a verra hearty appetite." Cecily blushed a little, afraid that he might take those words as an insult, but then he smiled and she relaxed a little.

"Aye, I do," he said softly. Taking her by the hand, he tugged her into his arms.

Cecily felt her pulse immediately speed up as he enfolded her in his strong arms. This was what she needed, what she craved. The feel of his hard body pressed close to hers banished the last of her fears and doubts. She did not care that he did not speak of love or marriage. There was no future for them anyway. She was promised to another, and once wed, she would never forsake her vows no matter how wretched a husband Sir Fergus proved to be. Her time to grasp some pleasure with Artan was fleeting, and she had no intention of letting a minute of that time be wasted. She wrapped her arms around his neck, took a deep breath of his scent, and pressed her lips against his.

Artan silently cursed his weakness as he returned her kiss. He had not meant to do this, not when his plan was to forcibly take her away from her home. But as he savored the sweet heat of her mouth, he decided he could spare a little time for lovemaking. The chances of anyone discovering she was gone before daylight were very small. Perhaps if he gave her a greater taste of the passion they could share her anger over his trickery would fade more quickly.

He would not take her now, he told himself as he lowered her down onto the soft grass at the bank of the burn. Instinct told him that that would only add to whatever sense of betrayal she might feel when she realized why he had really lured her here. When he settled his body on top of hers the need that swept through him was so sharp and strong he knew he would need every scrap of his willpower to resist consummating their coming marriage right now on the bank of the burn.

An urge to make her feel the same needs he did possessed him. The fact that she was a complete innocent yet had come to him alone and in the night told him that she wanted him, but he needed more, much more. He wanted her to know that no other man could ever make her feel what he did.

As he kissed her throat he slowly unlaced her bodice. A quick glance at her face revealed that she wore a deep blush but he saw no rejection there and he tugged her bodice down, freeing her breasts from its confines. The moonlight made her skin glow as it settled over the breasts he had just revealed. He felt his breath catch as he studied the treasure he had found. Her breasts were smaller than he was accustomed to in a lover but were plump and beautifully shaped. Her areolas were large and, even in the moonlight, looked as pink and soft as a flower petal. He gently weighed her soft breasts with his hands, enflamed by the way they nestled so perfectly into his palms; the taut nipples bore into his skin and branded him in ways he doubted he would ever fully understand. He bent his head and lightly licked one impudent nipple. She gasped, shuddered, and slid her hands into his hair to hold him closer. Artan decided that was invitation enough to do as he wished and he began to feast upon her, using his fingers, lips, tongue, and even his teeth to make her grow as frenzied as he felt.

Cecily felt as if she were on fire. Artan began to suckle her and her whole body arched up to rub against his. She was trembling so much from the force of the hunger raging inside her she was astonished that her teeth were not chattering. She wanted to tear off her clothes and then tear his off so that they could be flesh to flesh. Cecily had no idea where such wild, wanton thoughts sprang from, but they did not shock her now that she was in Artan's arms. Instead, she reveled in them, let them take a firm hold on her and lead her on. Every instinct she had told her that she would never find such passion again, and certainly not in the arms of Sir Fergus.

When Artan felt Cecily's fingers tugging on the laces of his shirt, he quickly moved to help her. He threw off the drape of his plaid that went over his shoulder, then yanked off his shirt and tossed it aside. He was already panting as if he had just finished a long, hard run, but the way she looked at his bared chest only made it worse. There was an unmistakable look of appreciation and desire on her face that made him feel almost vain. When she placed her small hands upon his chest, lightly caressing his skin, he groaned.

"So smooth and hard," she whispered in a husky voice as she ran her fingers over the neat ridges of muscle on his taut stomach.

Hard, definitely hard, he thought as he returned to her delightfully welcoming arms. For once the lack of a manly covering of hair on his chest did not trouble him. Cecily seemed to like him as smooth as a lad, and that made it all right. He stilled as his chest met her breasts, his whole body going rigid as he felt her hard nipples, dampened by his greedy kisses, press against his skin.

She shifted beneath him, her breasts rubbing against him, and he growled softly as he kissed her. The feel of her hands stroking his shoulders, back, and sides had him shaking with the need to bury himself deep inside her heat, but he fought against that temptation. He was so full, so aching for release, he did not think he would need that to fulfill his need this time. It was more important to leave her maidenhead intact, to show some restraint no matter how small, so that his sins did not loom too large in her eyes when she finally understood why he had lured her here.

A cool breeze touched Cecily's legs and she realized Artan had pushed up her skirts. Only a faint hint of shock flashed through her as she felt his long, faintly calloused fingers stroke her legs. The way he feasted upon her breasts had her so dazed with need she barely twitched when he removed the small braies Old Meg had insisted she wear years ago.

The touch of his fingers on the aching place between her legs caused her to grow very still, however. This was an intimacy she had not expected. "Artan?"

"Hush, Sile," he murmured against her cheek. "Let me feel your heat, feel the tears of desire your sweet body sheds for me." He gently nudged her tensed legs farther apart with his knee. "Open for me, Sile mine. Let me take ye to paradise."

She clung to him as he stroked her with his fingers.

A gasp of shock and delight escaped her when he slipped one finger inside her. By the time he slid a second finger inside her she was past the point of caring what he did so long as he did not stop. Compelled by the demands of her body, she moved against his stroking fingers, silently begging for more of something she had no words for.

The feel of her damp heat was nearly enough to send Artan over the edge. His plan was to give her a taste of the passion that flared between them, one that might soften her anger later, but he was discovering that it was a lot fiercer and hotter than he had anticipated. Consummation was almost impossible to resist, but he managed to cling to at least one thin thread of control. That did not necessarily mean he had to leave this embrace knotted up with an unsatisfied need. Although he had not done such a thing since he was a lad of fourteen playing love games with Mattie, the blacksmith's daughter, Artan pressed his throbbing erection against Cecily's slim thigh and rubbed himself against her. It would serve, he thought, groaning as he felt her hot sheath tighten around his fingers. The last time he had done it, it was because he had feared Mattie's very large father would tear him to pieces if he took Mattie's maidenhead. This time he did it to try to save himself from Cecily's hatred. He realized he was more afraid of that fate than he had ever been of the blacksmith.

When he felt the pulse of her release begin and her slender body bow up slightly, Artan fixed his gaze on her face. She clutched his arms as she cried out his name, and he did not think he had ever seen anything as beautiful as Cecily in the throes of her release. The sound of his name upon her lips as she reached that pinnacle was sweet music to his ears. He kissed her as he moved against her thigh and found his own release, not really surprised when he slumped against her weak from the strength of it. He hoped he did not have to wait too long before he could savor that bliss while buried deep inside her lithe body. Although if he could find such pleasure just playing a lad's love games with her, full consummation would probably kill him, he thought and grinned against her neck. Then he remembered what he had to do now and his good humor swiftly fled.

Cecily came to her senses very slowly, reluctant to leave the haze of a lingering pleasure. She was astonished that the man now idly nuzzling her breasts could make her feel such incredible things, such wild pleasure. Her whole body still tingled from the waves of pure delight that had swept through her. She knew she ought to be mortally ashamed or, at the very least, embarrassed, but she was too sated to worry about what she had allowed him to do. In truth, all she could think of as she closed her eyes was just when they could do this again.

It was not until she felt Artan tug her up into a seated position that Cecily realized she had fallen asleep and she inwardly cursed. She hoped it had been only a very short sleep, for she did not want to lose any of the meager time she could steal with Sir Artan. She was disappointed to see that he had donned his shirt. He had a beautiful chest, all sleek, hard muscle and dark skin, she thought with an inner sigh of pleasure. When he tugged up her bodice and retied her laces she blushed a little, wondering just how long she had lain there with her breasts exposed. She shifted a little and realized he had also put her braies back on and she almost frowned. Had she slept so long that their tryst was already over?

Then she realized that Artan had never put himself inside her. Cecily did not know all that much about the intimacies a man and woman could share, but she did know that that long, thick part of him he had been rubbing against her thigh was supposed to go where his fingers had been. Considering all the other intimacies they had shared, she did not understand why he had not done that. She had come to the burn ready and willing to give him her innocence and gladly suffer whatever consequences there were for doing so. The fact that Artan had not taken her maidenhead did not please her as she thought it ought to. In fact, she felt a growing unease, a strengthening certainty that something was wrong.

"Artan, ye didnae finish," she said softly, and felt even more uneasy at the closed look upon his face.

"Aye, I did," he replied as he helped her stand up and tugged her into his arms.

The embrace lacked the warmth of the others they had shared and Cecily felt her anxiety increase. "Nay, ye didnae. Ye didnae put yourself inside me." She was so uneasy now that speaking so bluntly did not even bother her.

Why she was pursuing this she did not know. Considering the length and width of what he had been rubbing against her leg, she ought to be very pleased that he had not attempted to put it inside her. She was not pleased, however. She actually felt distinctly cheated.

"Ye are betrothed, lass."

"I was aware of that when I came here. As were ye when ye asked me to."

"I dinnae want ye to suffer for meeting with me."

"'Tis my choice, aye? If ye didnae want to, then why did ye ask me here?"

"Oh, lass, I want to. I want to so badly I fair ache with the need. But now isnae a good time."

"Why not?"

"Because I am about to kidnap ye."

Cecily stared at him, gaping slightly as she struggled to make sense of his words. She was so confused and stunned, she did nothing to stop him when he pulled her hands in front of her, wrapped them in a cloth until she could not even wriggle her fingers, and then tied them securely with a surprisingly soft length of rope. It was just as she gathered the breath and the wits to speak that he tied a gag on her. He gently pushed her down until she sat on the ground; then he tied her ankles together.

As he picked up the sack of food and wine she had brought and went to tie it on his saddle, Cecily stared dumbly at her bonds. A part of her wanted desperately to believe that this was all a dream, that she was actually still wrapped in his arms and resting after their lovemaking. The greater part of her, the one shaking itself free from shock and amazement, was not so deluded.

It had all been a lie, she realized. He had not drawn her here because he had any feelings for her or because he lusted after her. He had brought her here so that he could tie her up and force her to go to Glascreag. The pain that knowledge brought her was so acute, she bent over as if to shelter her body from the blow.

She had been such a fool, a witless, silly child.

The worst part was that she could not even blame it all on sweet lies and clever flatteries that had turned her head. Artan had not given her any of those. The fact that he had not, that he obviously realized she had not needed such niceties to put her at his mercy was a severe blow to her pride. Hot kisses, a handsome face, and a wretchedly mistaken belief in his honesty had lured her here.

For one brief moment she was terrified for her very life, but she wrestled that flash of panic into submission. One thing she was sure of was that this man had fostered with her uncle. Artan knew far too much about her uncle and Glascreag to have been lying about that. And despite this treachery, this betrayal, she still could not believe he was the sort of man to hurt a woman.

Clearly, he had no qualms about using a woman's passion against her, she thought angrily. Her innocent faith in the man he had pretended to be had gotten her into this mess, but she would never be fooled by him again. That determination would do her no good at the moment, but she would cling to it, for a chance to escape him might just present itself and she wanted to be ready to take it.

"Easy now, lass," Artan murmured in what he hoped was a calming voice as he lifted her up and set her on his horse.

He was speaking to her as if she were some nervous pet or ill-tempered horse, she thought crossly. She considered hurling herself off the horse, then scolded herself for even considering such a foolish idea. There was a very good chance that all she would accomplish was to hurt herself. About the only way such an action could harm Sir Artan was if she fell on him. Considering her somewhat small stature, she could not even be sure she could do that.

Artan mounted behind her. "Now we can remove these bonds," he said as he untied her ankles so that she could sit astride the horse. "Just wanted to be sure ye didnae try anything foolish like running."

It was a little late to run now, she thought crossly. The time to run had been the first time he had kissed her. In fact, she should have immediately informed her kinsmen and her betrothed about the insult. They would have tossed him out of Dunburn after beating some manners into him. But, no, she had been intrigued, delighted, and deeply stirred by his kiss, and the feeling had just grown stronger with each embrace. Just thinking of how stupid she had been made her so angry she proceeded to vilify his character, his manhood, and his ancestors.

"Now I ken that ye are a wee bit angry at this rough treatment, but 'tis only until we get away from Dunburn," Artan said as he started to ride, eager to get out of the Lowlands.

Cecily wondered if having visions of staking a man out in the dirt and slowly gutting him could really be called being *a wee bit angry*. She sincerely doubted it. She was feeling bloodthirsty and was heartily frustrated by the gag that prevented her from telling him so.

Artan could not see her eyes, but he was fairly sure that she was not simply asking for an explanation. The gag made her words impossible to understand, but the tone of them was fairly clear. For a moment after he had tied and gagged her she had looked so hurt he had almost freed her. Only the knowledge that her life was in danger kept him from doing so. Anger was better. He could deal with anger. However, just in case she was demanding why he was doing this, he decided to give her a partial explanation.

"I am taking ye to Glascreag. I couldnae wait any longer to persuade ye. Now, we have to ride hard for a while as I need to put as much distance between us and Dunburn as possible, but when we stop for a rest, I will tell ye everything."

When he spurred his horse to a greater speed, Cecily was thrown back against his chest. She did not want to go to Glascreag. She did not want a full explanation. All she wanted was to get back to her bedchamber at Dunburn and lick her wounds. When they stopped and he untied and ungagged her, she would make that very clear to him.

And then she would kill him.

Chapter 8

"Pestilent swine! Overbearing ogre! How dare ye do this to me!"

Artan looked down at the furious woman berating him so colorfully and idly wondered if he ought to put the gag back on her. Her fine green eyes sparkled with fury, her smooth cheeks were flushed with the heat of her anger, and her lovely breasts heaved as she spit out insults so quickly she could barely catch her breath. She was glorious and he felt his whole body go rigid with lust. Here was the spirit he had caught the rare glimpse of back at Dunburn. Here was his mate. He hastily bit back a smile, knowing that it would only enrage her more.

Cecily caught the glint of amusement in his eyes and felt bloodthirsty. "Are ye laughing at me?"

"Nay," he replied.

She did not believe him. "This isnae amusing. Ye will take me back to Dunburn immediately and mayhap, just mayhap, I willnae demand that they hang ye in chains from the walls to be food for the crows." When he grinned, she kicked him in the shin and felt a sharp pain go right up her leg.

"Brute!" she nearly screeched as she hopped around until the pain began to ease. "Ye are made of stone, arenae ye! Jesu, ye have crippled me!" Cecily reached out to rub her sore foot and realized her hands were still wrapped in cloth and her wrists were still tied.

Artan did not think he had ever heard a woman growl like that. It was the kind of noise that could make a whole pack of dogs tuck tail and run. He grunted softly when she hit him on the chest with her bound hands. For a moment he let her pound on him. He felt he deserved the abuse. She had come to their tryst ready to be his lover and had ended up his prisoner. If the same thing had happened to him, he would be very eager to kill someone. When he sensed her weakening, he grabbed her by the shoulders and held her away from him as he struggled to think of the best way to begin his explanations.

Cecily blew aside a lock of hair that was hanging in her face and glared at Artan. She knew hurt was part of the fuel that fed her anger, but she refused to let it show. The man had tricked her in the lowest, most despicable of ways. She had believed in his attention and his kisses and had been willing to risk so much just to be held in his arms for a while. If the depth of the hurt she felt was any indication, she had also allowed him to creep into her heart. She could not believe she had been such a blind, credulous fool.

The way he so effortlessly held her at a distance also told her she had been a fool to think she could hurt him in even the smallest of ways. Her toes hurt and her fists stung, yet he did not look to have suffered even a bruise from her assault. It was utterly humiliating.

No, she thought, what was humiliating was the fact that she had let this man touch her. Even after riding all night she could still feel the touch of his hands on her body and the warmth of his kisses on her mouth. She had allowed him to make her weak and blind with passion, while he had obviously just been waiting for the right moment to bind and gag her and toss her over the back of his horse. Hanging him from the walls of Dunburn was too gentle a punishment, she decided.

"Now, lass, there really is a good reason for what I am doing," Artan said.

"Ye have obviously taken far too many blows to the head," she snapped as she continued to glare at him.

Artan ignored that. "I am doing this to keep ye safe."

"Safe? Safe from what? The tedious chore of having to share a table with Anabel and Sir Fergus?"

"Anabel and Sir Fergus want more than to bore ye at your meal. They are all cheating you and have been for years. Nay long after ye marry that chinless fool Sir Fergus, he intends to make verra sure that ye are nay longer in the way of him, Anabel, and Sir Edmund living grandly off your inheritance."

"Dinnae be ridiculous. I dinnae have any inheritance."

"Aye, ye do, although I cannae be sure of what and how much. Whate'er your legacy is, the Donaldsons and your betrothed dinnae want ye to enjoy any of it. Never have."

"Ye are just trying to justify what ye have done."

"Nay, I heard them, all of them. Lady Anabel, Sir

Edmund, and your betrothed. They have been lying to ye from the verra start. Dunburn and whate'er coin it brings or your father had should all be yours, but they have left everyone, including ye, thinking that Sir Edmund was the heir."

"Of course he was the heir. He is the closest male relation."

"It doesnae have to be the male. Your da wasnae a laird. Aye, he has some rich lands, but he still wasnae a laird, wasnae the head of the clan. He could leave his holdings and his coin to ye if he chose. Did ye really think he would leave ye naught?"

Of course she had never thought that. It had been one reason she had been so hurt when she had been told that she was no more than a poor orphan who had to depend upon the kindness of her unkind relations. She had simply thought that her father had not made his intentions clear or had neglected to say what should happen if both he and Colin had died. Cecily felt the tickle of belief and quickly smothered it. She had accepted matters as they were for so long, she did not dare think otherwise. If nothing else, it would mean she had been the greatest of fools.

Just as she had been for Artan, she suddenly thought and scowled at him. Standing in front of her was hard proof of just how big a fool she could be. While that meant he might be telling the truth, that she had been lied to and cheated for years, it also told her that she had to be very careful about heeding anything he said.

"I think he ne'er thought that both he and Colin would die, that is what I think. Everyone kenned that Colin was his heir, but no one said who should take my brother's place if he too died. I was too young to discuss it all with Da. And there may weel have been something set down that placed Sir Edmund as my guardian if my father died. Aye, probably of Colin as weel."

"So your father liked and trusted Sir Edmund, did he?"

Cecily felt the urge to kick him for simply asking that question, but then she recalled the injury to her toes when she had kicked him earlier. She had been only a child when she had lost her father, but she felt very sure that he had never liked or trusted his cousin Edmund. Sir Edmund had no morals, and that alone would have disgusted her father. However, he might have had no choice. There were few other close Donaldson kinsmen, and someone, specifically some man, had to be named as guardian to the children in case her father died before they were old enough to care for themselves. Better a bad guardian than none at all.

"I was too young to ken exactly what my father felt about his cousins."

She was lying, Artan thought and sighed. "The way ye try to ignore the truth is just why I could-nae wait and talk to ye about it or help ye find out the truth for yourself. Once ye were married to Sir Fergus, your life would have been in imminent danger."

"If I am such a great heiress, why should my life be in danger? The mon willnae wish to kill the fatted calf."

"He will if all that calf owns then comes to him as her husband."

He nodded when she paled. It was easy to see that she was valiantly fighting that fear, pushing aside his truth for the one she had believed for so long. It was a start, however. The very fact that she felt that fear, no matter how brief, told him that she did not have complete faith in the innocence of her betrothed or her guardians. Cecily was too smart not to see that none of them was a good person, that they each lacked any true morals, and it was but a short step from that to seeing that they could indeed be plotting her demise.

Deciding to let her think on all he had said so far, Artan fetched the bag she had brought to their tryst. He spread out a blanket, then gently urged her to sit down on it. Ignoring her scowl, he tied their ankles together before he untied her hands so that she could eat and drink. Artan felt sure she would not try to attack him again, but he suspected she would still try to run if he gave her a chance. Until she accepted the danger that awaited her at the hands of her guardians and betrothed, he could not allow her too much freedom.

The silence that held while they each had something to eat and shared some wine was not a comfortable one, but he let it stand. Even if she did come to believe him about the threat from ones she had long considered her family and the man she had been about to marry, there was still the matter of how their romantic tryst by the burn had ended. It would be a while before she began to forgive him for that. He just hoped it was not too long, for just thinking about those heady moments they had shared in the moonlight had him aching for her.

Cecily was surprised she could eat anything she was so knotted up with fear, anger, and doubt. Being kidnapped obviously gave one a hearty appetite, she thought crossly, then sighed. Looking beyond her hurt over what she saw as Artan's gross betrayal, she had to admit that he had not really hurt her. If he really believed what he was saying about Anabel, Edmund, and Fergus, then he had truly been thinking only of her safety.

She inwardly shook her head. It could not be true. Not one of those three people was a particularly good person, but she could not believe they would actually steal from her for twelve long years and then want her dead. And how would Sir Fergus have become a part of all this? He had never been close friends with Edmund or Anabel, so Cecily could not believe they had suddenly taken the man into their confidence. And if they truly had been cheating her for so long, they would hardly willingly hand everything over to Fergus.

"Just how did ye happen to hear all of this?" she suddenly asked. "I cannae believe Anabel and Edmund wouldnae be verra, verra careful if they were hiding something."

"They were careful. After all, ye havenae heard anything and ye have lived with them for twelve years."

"And yet ye come to Dunburn and within four days hear and know all?"

"I dinnae ken all, but I was simply in the right place at the right time and heard them. I think Lady Anabel's voice could cut through steel," he murmured, and caught the briefest flash of amusement in Cecily's eyes. "As I passed by her solar, I heard her complaining that I wouldnae leave. Since I had been set upon several times since arriving, I was curious to hear if she spoke of any further plans to see me gone."

"What do ye mean ye were set upon?"

"From the verra beginning I have been attacked

at least once a day, most often twice. Ere we left
Dunburn, the number of men set after me had
grown to eight."

"But I ne'er saw any wounds on ye, nay e'en a
bruise or two."

"There were a few after that last attack, but, nay,
I was ne'er seriously wounded. Your uncle taught
me weel, and the men sent after me werenae verra
skilled in battle."

He sounded so arrogant it made her teeth
clench. Then Cecily recalled his entrance into the
great hall that first day and decided he may have
the right to be so arrogant about his fighting skills.
She doubted any of the Donaldson or Ogilvey men
could have gotten past all the guards and so casually held two men by their jupons, then tossed them
aside with such ease.

"But why should anyone want to attack ye, to make
ye leave? Sir Edmund invited ye to stay after all."

"That doesnae mean he meant it. I come from
your closest blood kin. It wouldnae be wise to cast
me out, to refuse to allow me to stay for the wedding. Such treatment of your uncle's emissary
would raise questions, aye? And Sir Edmund doesnae want anyone asking questions."

"I cannae see that Sir Edmund would worry
about my uncle asking questions. The mon hasnae
cared what happened to me since the day Da and
Colin were killed. 'Tis only because he is facing the
end of his life that he e'en recalled me."

"Are ye sure of that?" Artan asked softly, and
watched both doubt and hurt flicker over her face
before she controlled it. "He says he has written ye
and sent ye gifts, that he has often asked that ye be allowed to come stay with him at Glascreag. Ye say ye

have written him and sent him gifts at Michaelmas, yet he got nothing." He shrugged. "One has to wonder why when two people say they have done such things that neither of them received what was sent."

Cecily opened her mouth to say that her uncle was a liar but could not get the words out. Her memories of her uncle had always been clear, partly because they were all tied up with the tragedy of watching her brother and father killed. Every little thing about that time was etched into her memory. Angus MacReith was blunt to the point of rudeness. She simply could not believe he would lie about writing to her or not receiving her letters. The various messengers she had used had never mentioned having any trouble, but then she had never pressed any of them very hard for information.

For a moment she felt almost panicked, but she took several deep breaths to calm herself. Even if it was true that Edmund and Anabel had deceived her about her uncle, had made certain that she believed the man had forgotten about her, it did not make the rest of what Artan said the truth. It could just mean that her guardians had not wanted Angus to try to interfere in her raising in even the smallest way.

Sensing that he had hit the mark with that revelation, Artan hurried to continue, "And though it shames me to admit to it, that last attack did leave me marked." He yanked up his kilt to reveal the wound he had taken on his right thigh. "That mon willnae be abusing any more of Dunburn's guests," he said with some satisfaction. "And the attack did allow me to leave Thunderbolt at the burn, though I hated letting anyone think me fool enough to lose my horse."

Cecily stared at the wound on his thigh. There was no denying that it was a sword wound. Artan had been very lucky. It had been a shallow cut, so shallow that it had already closed, even the hard ride through the night not tearing it open.

Once the shock of seeing his wound began to fade, however, she grew fascinated by the sight of his bared leg. Despite the long, thick hair on his head and the dark shadow of an emerging beard, Artan was not a very hirsute man. The covering of hair upon his long legs was light, revealing dark skin stretched taut over hard muscle. He even had attractive knees, she mused. Her hands actually itched to stroke that long, well-shaped leg.

When he pulled his kilt back down, Cecily blinked and then had to fight back a blush. It was obviously going to take some time for her to conquer her attraction to this man. She quickly turned her thoughts to the matter of his claims concerning Angus and how he himself had been attacked several times while at Dunburn. Since she had, more or less, accepted that her guardians could have worked to keep her and Angus apart, she supposed it was also possible that they had tried hard to rid themselves of Angus's emissary. They would not want to risk her or Artan asking too many questions. It still did not mean that there was some insidious plot to cheat or murder her. After all, Artan was still alive. She quickly said as much to him.

Artan sighed but was able to push aside his annoyance over her continued disbelief. She was right. Just because her guardians might be guilty of keeping her away from Angus did not mean they plotted with Sir Fergus to kill her and keep her inheritance, one she still did not believe she had anyway.

"I ken what I heard, lass," he said. "Sir Fergus is to marry ye and he has signed marriage contracts that will allow your guardians to legally claim Dunburn and a hefty purse. For that generosity he gets ye and a small fortune. He intends that your widow's portion will also become a part of the spoils the three of them shall share. After he tires of ye he means to become a widower. I heard him say so."

"Ye cannae expect me to believe Sir Fergus is capable of cold-blooded murder."

"Just because he doesnae show much spine when confronted with a mon? E'en he could o'erpower ye, lass. Once married to him, ye wouldnae have any place to run either. And e'en if ye willnae believe the rest, believe that Sir Fergus is a brutal swine when dealing with lasses. Davida said he likes the play to be rough, and I myself caught him trying to rape a wee lass who couldnae be much past her first flux. Her gown was all torn and she was covered in bruises. 'Twas just last night ere I came down to the great hall. I threw the bastard against the wall, which was why he was *indisposed.*"

"If he goes about raping the maids, why have I heard naught about it?"

"In Anabel's household such a thing isnae seen as a crime," he said quietly, sensing her growing agitation and wondering if he had said enough for now. It would do him no good if he pushed her to accept too much too quickly. "I need to rest ere we continue on," he said as he sprawled on his back. "Dinnae think ye can wait until I am asleep and then slip free. These knots arenae easily untied, and I will ken it if ye try. As I will if ye try to help yourself to any of my weapons."

Cecily looked around and was sorely disappointed not to find a very big rock close at hand. Hitting him on the head a few times would do a lot to ease her anger. She sighed and slowly settled herself as far from his side as her rope shackle would allow. There was more he wanted to say, she was sure of it, but she was very glad he had paused to rest. Each word he said had to be weighed and considered, and she had more than enough to deal with now. She was also glad that she had spent most of last night's ride sleeping against Artan, for she suspected it would be a long time before she slept again.

It thoroughly dismayed her that she could all too easily see Sir Fergus as a man who would hit and rape women. He had barely even kissed her, so she really had no basis for that belief. Yet she had seen the way some of the maids had acted around him, as if they feared he would notice them. Since Sir Edmund carefully selected women who were free with their favors to work within the keep, Cecily knew that aversion was not due to the fact that Sir Fergus might decide he wanted one to warm his bed. She was a little surprised that there was a very young girl inside the keep, but decided it was probably because extra people had been brought in to help serve the guests.

What dismayed her the most was not that Sir Fergus was a brutal swine, but that her guardians could not be ignorant of that fact, yet continued to drag her toward the altar. That meant that they simply did not care that they were marrying her to a man who would undoubtedly shame her with his many infidelities and abuse her. Cecily knew that neither Sir Edmund nor Lady Anabel had ever cared much for her, but if Artan was telling her the truth, it was far worse than that. They liked her so little that they would blithely give her to a man who regularly beat and raped women.

It was all too much, she thought and closed her eyes. She had been betrayed by a man she had thought to take as her lover, and he wanted her to believe that she had been betrayed by her guardians for twelve long years, that they were about to make her marry a brutal man who planned to kill her when he grew tired of her. Just trying to wade her way through what might be truth and what might be lies had her head spinning. For just a minute she needed to rest her poor, beleaguered mind.

The next Cecily knew she was being nudged awake by the toe of Artan's boot. She scowled at him as she struggled to her feet. Her scowl grew into a glare when she realized she now had a rope around her waist and the other end was attached to thick leather baldric he wore. It was obviously a mistake to go to sleep around this man.

When she realized she had to relieve herself, she nearly cursed aloud. She did not even ask him if he would allow her any privacy, but just stomped off toward the shelter of the trees. Only briefly did the rope go taut, indicating his hesitation; but then she heard him come up behind her. When she reached a tree trunk wide enough to provide her some shelter, she turned to face Artan and simply pointed her finger toward another spot. The amusement that glittered in his eyes made her want to scream.

Deciding that talking might provide each of them with just a little more privacy as they tended to their personal needs, Artan said, "Ye will come to see the truth soon, lass. Ye are clever, and a wee bit of time to think will make ye see things ye have missed before now."

"Right now the only thing I am missing is my own soft bed," she muttered.

"Ye can have a nice soft bed when ye get to Glascreag."

"Did ye ne'er think that I might want to marry Sir Fergus?"

"Nay, ye proved that by coming to meet me at the burn."

"It might be best if ye dinnae speak on that. One doesnae like to be reminded too often about how big a fool she has been."

"Ye werenae a fool," he said sharply. Then before she could argue that, he continued, "Ye may be slow to heed what else I tell ye, but I could see that ye were close to believing the truth about Sir Fergus ere ye rested. 'Tis best if ye get away from Dunburn just to avoid that marriage."

"I cannae avoid it, nay unless my guardians end it. All I shall do by staying away from Dunburn is shaming the Donaldsons, mayhap e'en draw them into a feud or the like."

"'Tis nay more than they deserve."

Cecily stepped out from behind her tree, put her hands on her hips, and glared at him. "Mayhap, *if* what ye are saying about them is the truth. Of course, if what ye are saying about Sir Fergus is also the truth, then I doubt his family will take such great offense when the marriage doesnae take place. Howbeit, I only have your word that all these things are true."

He moved closer to meet her glare squarely. "Of course I speak the truth."

"So ye say."

"And so Old Meg says as weel."

"Old Meg?"

"Aye." He pointed to one of the bags hanging from Thunderbolt's saddle. "Who do ye think packed some clothes for ye?"

Old Meg had known what he was going to do and had allowed it? thought Cecily, her mind reeling in shock at the possibility. She quickly shook aside what felt like a traitorous thought. Old Meg would not agree to having her kidnapped. Then she recalled how much Old Meg disliked Edmund and Anabel and how much the woman had scorned Sir Fergus. It was possible that she had helped Sir Artan, not because she believed his accusations, but because she wanted to get Cecily away from Dunburn and Sir Fergus.

"Just because Old Meg helped ye pack a few clothes for me doesnae mean she believes all ye say. She has ne'er liked Sir Fergus, and she could have just been trying to get me out of that man's reach. Aye, especially if she kenned how he is with women."

Artan grabbed her by the arms and gave her a little shake. "At some time ye are going to have to accept the truth. I am nay lying. I heard Edmund, Anabel, and Fergus plotting how they will soon be rid of ye and how they will divide up the spoils."

"But it makes no sense. E'en if Edmund and Anabel have been lying about the inheritance and cheating me out of what is my due for years, why would they bring Sir Fergus into the fold? If they couldnae e'en share what was all mine with me, why would they share it with him? He isnae kin to them. He isnae e'en a close friend."

"He has been Anabel's lover. How much closer do ye want him to be?"

"Anabel has lovers?"

Artan found it interesting that that was the thought that would come to Cecily's mind and not the fact that her betrothed had betrayed her. "Aye, oh she is verra discreet, unlike her husband; but, aye, she has lovers. Sir Fergus was one of them, although I cannae say much for her selection. She obviously doesnae practice what she preaches."

"Has she been your lover?"

"Nay, I havenae touched a single woman at Dunburn except you."

"Davida doesnae count, is that it?"

"I ne'er touched Davida either. She was sent to me in the hope that she would make me miss the meal in the great hall that evening."

He certainly looked as if he was telling the truth, his gaze not wavering from hers at all. Cecily hastily pushed aside all thoughts of what Davida had or had not been doing with him in his bedchamber. It carried the taint of jealousy, and she did not want this man to know that she might care enough to even be jealous.

"Nay, just because Sir Fergus and Anabel once shared a bed, it doesnae mean she shared anything else. She is as good, if nay better, than Sir Edmund at keeping a secret."

"Some secrets can slip out nay matter how careful one is, e'en if it is only enough for someone else to start adding things up."

"And ye think Sir Fergus did a wee bit of adding

and came up with something that has the power to make Sir Edmund and Anabel do what he wants?"

"Aye, he has something to club them with to get what he wants."

Cecily waited a moment but Artan said nothing else, so she demanded, "Weel? If ye want me to believe all ye are saying, 'tis best if ye tell me all ye heard or think ye heard. Why would Sir Edmund and Lady Anabel do what Sir Fergus asks them to?"

"Because he discovered they had something to do with the death of your father and brother."

Every ounce of color fled Cecily's face and Artan reached for her. Just as he moved there was a noise he recognized all too well. He felt the air stirred by the arrow as it sped by just behind his neck. How had Sir Fergus found them so quickly?

Chapter 9

The arrow was still trembling when Cecily suddenly found herself scooped up into Artan's arms. Her gaze stayed fixed upon that arrow as he ran to his horse and tossed her into the saddle. Not once did she protest as he mounted behind her and kicked Thunderbolt into a gallop. She just hung on for dear life and tried to sort out her confused thoughts as Artan saw to their escape.

Despite all of her threats, she did not wish Artan to be hurt, yet it was now very clear that his life was in danger. If he had not leaned toward her just a little at that precise moment, that arrow would have buried itself in his neck instead of in the tree. She would have had to stand there and watch him die.

Cecily shivered as a chilling fear for him rushed through her. Obviously, his deceit and betrayal had not been enough to kill her feelings for him. She did not believe all he had told her about her kinsmen and Sir Fergus, but she knew that Artan meant her no real harm. He had been told to bring her to her uncle at Glascreag, and although she might deplore his methods, he did not deserve to die for it.

She decided she was left with two choices. She could get Artan to leave her behind and then run for his life, or she could stay with him until they reached Glascreag. Cecily felt almost certain she could never accomplish the former. A man like Sir Artan Murray would not run away, especially not after all he had done to entrap her into this foray. And if he truly believed all he had told her, he believed her life was in danger and he would never leave her to face her enemies alone. That meant she was headed to Glascreag. She knew she was not much of a shield, but she felt her presence should cause their pursuers to at least show some care. After all, they did not want her to die.

As soon as they stopped running she would tell Artan her decision. It would not stop the pursuit of her kinsmen and, she suspected, the Ogilveys, but it would make it easier for Artan. At least he would no longer have to worry about guarding her anymore. He could turn all of his attention to guarding his back and getting them both safely behind the walls of Glascreag. She just hoped he did not give her much of an argument when she told him that her stay there would be very short. As soon as the Donaldson and Ogilvey men arrived at her uncle's gates, she had every intention of returning to Dunburn with them.

It was dark by the time they halted. The only sound Cecily made as Artan helped her to dismount was a soft groan. Her body felt as battered as if she had been thrown down a rocky slope—several times. She could not even feel duly grateful for the fact that Artan had untied her and she was now free. Espying a lush spot of grass, she walked toward it and carefully sat down. Putting her full weight on her abused backside was more than she could bear, however, and she slowly reclined until she was flat on her back.

Glancing to her side, she watched Artan tend to his horse. The beast was well trained and had both speed and endurance. At the moment, however, she did not appreciate that as she knew she should. The fact that Artan moved around as if he had not spent the better part of two days in the saddle did not please her very much either. In the mood she was in, Cecily suspected angels could descend from heaven and offer her all she could ever desire in life and she would be hard-pressed to count her blessings.

"No fire?" she asked when Artan came and sat down beside her.

"Nay, I cannae be sure where they are, and I dinnae want e'en the faintest hint of smoke in the air to lead them to us. In truth, I was taken by surprise today. I hadnae expected them to take up the pursuit so quickly."

She frowned as she thought about that. "Nay, they shouldnae have guessed I was gone until the morning meal at the very earliest. I wonder how they kenned I had slipped away? I am verra sure no one saw me if only because, if they had, an alarum would have been called."

Artan took a drink of wine and handed the wineskin to her. He did not want to say what he was thinking. Someone had gone to his or her bedchamber and discovered they were missing. Considering what he had done to Sir Fergus, there was every chance the man had sent someone to cut his throat. It was just as possible that the man himself had tried to slip into Cecily's bedchamber and take from her what he had been denied taking from that poor wee maid. The fact that Artan had been showing Cecily some marked attention certainly would have inspired the man.

The why of their discovery did not really matter, however. All that was important was that someone was after them and would be trying to catch or kill him all the way to Glascreag. When he thought of what a poor job had been done in the various attacks on him at Dunburn, Artan was deeply concerned about Cecily's safety. She could all too easily be injured or killed, despite the fact that they would have been sent out to retrieve her. Unfortunately, she would be no safer at Dunburn, and he could think of few places he could safely hide her between Dunburn and Glascreag, not without traveling miles out of their way. Worse, until she believed him about the threat to her life, she would undoubtedly just try to return to Dunburn if he left her side.

"So 'tis just ill luck that has put them on our trail so quickly," Cecily muttered. "I seem to be having a lot of that just lately."

Artan bit back a smile. She sounded sulky and there was the definite hint of a pout in her expression. He did not remark upon her statement because he knew she would undoubtedly let him know she considered it all his fault. In one way it was. He had not planned on the pursuit starting so quickly.

"We shall rest here for the night and start our journey again just before the sun rises," he said.

"I ne'er really saw who was chasing us."

"Some of your guardian's men and some of Sir Fergus's."

"Who leads them?"

"I believe it is Sir Fergus."

Cecily could not hide her surprise. Sir Fergus did not seem to be the sort of man who would leap into the saddle to chase anyone anywhere. He certainly had never shown her the sort of attention or interest that would drive a man to do so. A little voice in her head suggested that the man was not chasing her, but chasing a fortune, and she struggled to ignore it.

"I have come to a decision," she said.

"Oh, aye? Have ye decided to believe me now?"

"Nay, not completely, and especially not about that last club ye hit me with ere we had to flee for our lives."

"Then what is your decision about?"

"I shall travel with ye to Glascreag. I willnae keep trying to run away, not that I have had much opportunity to do so. Nay, I shall agree to go to Glascreag and give ye no more trouble about it."

He sprawled on his side and rested his head on his hand as he studied her. "But nay because ye believe all I have told ye."

"Nay, but I will do it because I cannae see that ye need to die just for doing what my uncle asked ye to. 'Tis evident that the men chasing us intend ye harm and would nay hesitate to kill ye if given the chance."

"So ye think to be my shield?"

She sighed at the hint of mockery in his voice. "In a way. I ken I willnae be much of one, but I will be enough to make them at least take care. E'en if ye arenae right about Sir Fergus, he doesnae want me dead. And if ye are right, weel, he still doesnae want me dead—not yet."

Artan wanted to protest this idea she had to protect him but bit back the words. She had agreed to go to Glascreag willingly. He certainly did not want to risk her changing her mind. It would make the journey a great deal easier on both of them if she was willing, and a lot less dangerous as well.

He moved away to get them something to eat. They had enough supplies to last a few days, but then he was going to have to find them more. Hunting was a possibility, but it took time and he did not think it would be wise to lose too much time in the pursuit of food. He would have to lose Sir Fergus and his men so that he could get some more supplies from some cottager or in a village. It should not be too difficult to lose his pursuers for at least a little while, he decided. Sir Fergus might know where he was taking Cecily, but he did not know exactly how Artan would get there.

"Do ye think we can get to Glascreag without confronting Sir Fergus and his men?" Cecily asked as they shared some bread and cheese.

"There is a good chance of that. I ken this land weel. I dinnae believe Sir Fergus does."

Cecily frowned. "I dinnae think so, but I now realize that I ken verra little about the mon I am to marry."

"Ye willnae be marrying him so I wouldnae worry about it."

"If what ye have told me about him is true, then, aye, I willnae be marrying the mon. I have yet to decide that it is true, however."

"Ye are a stubborn lass," he muttered, and had a big drink of wine to still his annoyance.

"I cannae believe something just because ye tell me it is so."

"Why not? Ye can trust me."

"As I did when I went to the burn?" She held up her hand to silence his angry protests. "I ken that ye believe ye are helping me. I may e'en go so far to say that ye truly believe all ye say. Howbeit, I have lived with these people for twelve long years, and although I willnae say it has been pleasant, I cannae think of anything that happened in those years to make me believe they want me dead."

"And I think ye were kept verra sheltered from the truth."

Cecily sighed and had to acknowledge that. "Mayhap I was. I do ken that I wasnae allowed to mix with servants or go anywhere. That feast ye walked into was one of the first I have e'er been allowed to attend."

"And ye ne'er questioned why ye were being kept so close, as if ye were some secret no one should ken about?"

"I assumed it was because I was only a child and then because I was ill-mannered, something Anabel was always accusing me of being. The first thought that came into my head was not that they had had a hand in the death of my father and brother or that they planned to kill me. 'Tis still not the first thought."

Artan quelled the urge to ride back to Dunburn and strangle Anabel. "I have not made this all up in my head. I heard the three of them talking. So did Old Meg." Seeing the stubborn look on her face, he sighed. "Think on it some more, then. But think on this as weel and see if ye can come up with an answer. If Anabel and Edmund consider ye such a burden, why didnae they send ye to Angus? Why did they work so hard to keep ye and your uncle apart?"

It was not something she wanted to think about, but Cecily just nodded. "I will think about it as we ride to Glascreag. Then if I still cannae believe all ye say, I shall make a short visit with my uncle and ride away with Sir Fergus when he arrives at Glascreag. I am betrothed to be married and I cannae just walk away from that. 'Tis a bond, isnae it? And I willnae be the one to break it unless I have a verra good reason."

"I dinnae think ye were worrying much about that bond when ye came down to the burn to meet me." He could tell by the narrowing of her eyes that he might have been wiser not to remind her of that just yet.

"'Tis clear to me that I am paying a penance for that sin."

He rolled his eyes; then he collected up what was left of the food he had unpacked and returned it to the saddle pack. It was going to be a hard battle to get her to accept what he was telling her. He would be deeply insulted by her refusal to accept his word except he knew he forfeited some of her trust by kidnapping her. Until she believed what he said about Edmund, Anabel, and Fergus, she could not accept that he had good reason for such trickery.

"Do ye swear on your honor that ye willnae be trying to run away if I dinnae tie ye tonight?"

"I swear. I told ye, whate'er else I might think of your actions and what ye tell me, I dinnae think ye deserve to die for it all. If naught else, ye are just doing what my uncle asked ye to. And, mayhap, ye truly believe ye are saving my life. I will stay and travel with ye to Glascreag without any further protest."

Artan nodded and watched her walk away until

she disappeared into the shadows. He was going to have to start wooing her if he had any hope of her being receptive to the idea of marrying him by the time they reached Glascreag. Although he really did not want to use the passion they shared against her, he would. As far as he could see, it was the quickest, if not the only, way he could rid her of the anger and mistrust she now felt for him. Worse, he could not tell her about Angus's offer until he did and he did not have all that much time to find the right moment to tell her.

He winced. There was probably no good time to tell her such a thing. She would undoubtedly see him as little better than Sir Fergus, marrying her for what he could gain. It stung his pride to even think of being compared with that swine, but he could understand why she might think it. The only advantage he had beside the passion they shared was that she felt safe with him. Despite everything he had done, she obviously trusted him not to hurt her.

What he really needed to do was get her bound to him as quickly as possible, he decided as he made up a bed for them on the soft grass. The moment Cecily accepted the fact that she could not marry Sir Fergus, Artan knew he had to try to get her to marry him, and he had better have some good reasons to make her. At any point along their route to Glascreag he could handfast with her. Once they reached Glascreag and settled the problem of Sir Fergus they could have the marriage sanctioned by a priest. He felt confident that Cecily would never walk away from such a bond, and that would give him all the time he needed to soothe her hurts and her anger.

When he saw her walking back from the trees, he

breathed an inner sigh of relief. Although he had accepted her word of honor, he had obviously had a lingering doubt or two. Artan saw her glance at the bed and scowl. Taking the coward's way out, he strode off into the trees so that he did not have to answer any questions about why he had made up only one bed.

Cecily watched him leave, then glared at the bed. She supposed there was not much choice, if only because they had only two blankets. Despite the fact that it was summer, there could still be a sharp bite to the air at night. The deeper they rode into the Highlands, the more true that would be. Since she did not want to shiver all night and she doubted he would want to either, there really was not much choice.

Slipping beneath the blanket, she waited for him to return. She had never spent the night outside, and she definitely did not want to do it on her own. She would just make it very clear that she no longer sought what she had when she had met him at the burn. A warmth spread through her body, putting the lie to her words, but she ignored it.

She tensed when Artan returned and stood by their rough bed. He removed his weapons and set them within easy reach before he slipped beneath the blanket at her side. Cecily tensed when he curled his arm around her waist and pulled her close, her back tucked up snugly against his front.

"Now, lass, there is nay need to go so stiff," he murmured. "I willnae be doing anything save for sleeping."

"Ye had better not." She frowned, certain he was nuzzling her hair.

"A shame, for I thought ye rather liked what I did."

"I liked it until I realized it was all a trick to make me easier to kidnap."

"Ach, lass, that isnae how it was at all." He gently kissed the hollow by her ear. "Did ye think I could lie with my body? Didnae ye feel how I wanted ye?"

"Men's bodies can feel lust for anything in petticoats. There doesnae have to be any honesty in it."

Artan tsked and lightly bit the nape of her neck, pleased when she shivered in his arms and did not pull away from him. "Do ye now mistrust every word I say?"

Cecily wondered how he could make her feel guilty, but he did. She did not really believe she was being too harsh. If some woman had done the same thing to him, Cecily felt sure he would be out for someone's blood. She did not know why he should think she should be more forgiving of betrayal than he would be.

"Nay every word, but dinnae think that means ye can try to seduce me with false promises and flatteries."

"Now why would ye think anything I said or did that night whilst we were in each others arms was a lie?"

"Because ye needed me there and ye needed me senseless so that ye could easily kidnap me."

He sighed and slowly rubbed his hand over her belly. "I hadnae intended to do what we did. I had thought to just kiss ye and hope ye didnae notice that I was binding your wrists. Ah, but then we started kissing, and I forgot about what I was supposed to do." He could sense her doubt in the hint of tension in her body. "Sile mine, do ye really think any mon who is but using your passion to his advantage would stop ere he took your maidenhead?"

There was that to consider, she mused as she

hunched her shoulders so that he could not make her senseless with his hot, nibbling kisses on her neck. Cecily did not think any man could pretend to be as aroused as she had thought he was, yet he had not completed the act. He had known she was willing, the very fact that she had met with him had told him that, but he had not taken what she had so clearly offered. Then again, she thought she would have preferred him to knock her over the head than do what he had done.

"I have no idea how men think," she muttered.

"I will tell ye how I think. I think I cannae keep my hands off ye. I think ye taste as sweet as sun-ripe berries. I think I mean to keep ye for my own."

"Keep me for your own?"

"Aye, my own, my mate, my wife."

For a moment Cecily was so stunned she could barely breathe. If he had always wanted her for his wife, why had he not mentioned it back at the burn? A part of her wanted to get up and dance and sing, and then say aye. Another part of her wondered what game he was playing now.

"Your wife?"

"Aye, my wife."

"I am betrothed to Sir Fergus Ogilvey."

"Ye willnae be for verra long." He held her close and closed his eyes, afraid that if he did not stop kissing her and touching her, he would lose all control. "I swear to ye, lass, the mon is all I have told ye he is and nay doubt a lot worse."

"Ye will forgive me, please, for nay wanting to believe that people who have cared for me for so long would betroth me to a monster."

"And forgive me, lass, for saying that those people didnae care for ye in any way. They put ye under their boot and did everything they could to keep ye there. Aye, e'en to making the one person who truly cared for ye leave when they threw Old Meg out of Dunburn."

"Old Meg beat Lady Anabel," she murmured, a little unsettled by his sharp words. "I but thank God they didnae hang her."

"And were ye nay surprised that they didnae?"

"Aye," she answered carefully, "I was, but I had begged them for her life."

"Which they so graciously gave ye, thus making ye feel e'en more indebted to them."

She blinked as the hard truth of that hit her squarely. It had made her feel indebted to them. Whenever she had felt the stirring of anger or rebellion, she had thought of how they had let Old Meg live and she struggled to subdue such feelings. It was hard to believe that they had planned that, though. Anabel had certainly seemed very eager to see Old Meg dead.

Cecily began to see that she had not yet thought enough on all Artan had told her. She needed to search through her memories of her time beneath Lady Anabel's rule much more carefully. It was still hard to believe they would want her dead, that they had actually had a hand in the murder of her father and Colin, but it was time to stop simply refusing to even consider it. She had told Artan she would think about all he had accused Anabel, Edmund, and Fergus of, but she saw now that she had not really done so.

"Mayhap," she murmured. "Did ye e'er think that I am reluctant to believe the things ye say because it means I have been living with people who dinnae care for me at all and ne'er will, people who may actually have been wishing I was in a grave alongside the rest of my family? 'Tis nay an easy thing ye ask of me."

He sighed and kissed the top of her head. "I ken it, lass. I just dinnae want ye to ignore the possibility that I am right, because if ye do, it could mean your life. And that, my Sile, is too high a price to pay for loyalty to people who have ne'er given ye any."

She nodded slowly. He was right. He was also putting his hand on her breasts, she realized and gasped. She grabbed his hand and quickly moved it away.

"There will be none of that."

"I was just getting comfortable." He grinned when she snorted, the sound rife with mockery.

Held in his arms, Cecily realized she felt safe and warm. She did not know if she wanted to curse or weep. The man had tricked her, kidnapped her. She should not be lying in his arms thinking foolish things such as how she would like to go to sleep every night with him at her back. She was indeed a fool, a sad, besotted one. All she could do was pray that Artan did not discover just how weak her will was.

Chapter 10

Hot. She was so very hot. Cecily struggled to wake up, to shake free of dreams of a man with a lovely broad, smooth chest and kisses that made her toes curl. When she finally came to her senses, she found herself clinging to Artan and being heartily kissed. Worse, she was kissing him back—again—just as she had done last morning and the morning before that. For a moment she even had the traitorous idea of pretending she was still asleep so that she could continue to enjoy his lovemaking and not feel guilty about it, but she quickly banished that disgraceful plan and pushed against Artan's chest.

The man was driving her mad with his kisses, she thought as she met his slumberous gaze. Every chance he got he kissed her or touched her. It was bad enough they were running from Sir Fergus's dogged pursuit without Artan turning everything into a part of his continuous seduction. The fact that she spent long hours sitting in his arms as they rode toward Glascreag only made it easier for him. It was getting so that he could have her knotted up with desire with only one brief glance from his silvery blue eyes.

"There will be nay more of that," she said for what she felt must have been the hundredth time.

"Cannae a mon woo the lass he means to wed?" Artan asked as he sat up and stretched.

Out of the corner of his eye Artan caught Cecily staring at him, her gaze moving over his body with what could only be called greed. If he did not feel the same way about her lithe body, he could begin to feel quite vain. In some ways he already did, for what man would not when the woman he wanted eyed him much as a starving man eyes a meal.

He stood up and stretched a little more, mostly to give her a good eyeful of what she was denying herself. If she ever figured out what he was doing and decided to retaliate, he could be in serious trouble. Just the thought of Cecily flaunting her slender beauty in front of him was enough to make him sweat. He would have to be very careful to keep her unaware of his games, or she could find out just how easily he could be captured if she tried a few games of her own.

Cecily bit back a curse and scrambled to her feet. She winced and rubbed at her lower back. Although she was beginning to become accustomed to spending so much time on the back of a horse, sleeping on the ground made her feel like an old woman in the morning. She walked toward the shelter of some trees to tend to her needs, hoping that just walking around would ease some of the stiffness from which she was suffering.

By the time she returned to their rough camp, Artan had the horse readied and handed her an oatcake. Cecily prayed they would reach Glascreag soon. She desperately wanted a lavish hot meal, a hot bath, and a soft bed. When she realized that her vision of a big, soft bed included a big, hard Artan lying in it—naked—she almost screamed. Now she was not even free of his seduction in her own mind.

"If all goes weel, we should reach Glascreag in about three more days," Artan said as he handed her the wineskin.

She frowned, took a drink, and handed the wineskin back to him. "I can recall it taking much longer."

"Aye, but I suspicion ye were traveling at an easy pace and staying to whatever roads and trails ye could find. Old Meg took ye back to Dunburn on much the same route as we are taking, so it would have been quicker."

"I dinnae recall much about the journey with Meg," she said quietly.

"Ah, nay, ye wouldnae would ye. 'Twas a sad and frightening time."

"Verra much so." She shook off the old memories and the grief that came with them. "Aye, we traveled the roads at a much slower pace, but I also think children find such journeys tedious."

He smiled and nodded. "Despite how eager I was to get to Glascreag to start my training, I quickly found it tedious as weel. Ready?"

"To get on that horse and ride all day?"

"Aye," he replied, his voice choked with laughter. "Mayhap today we can take a longer rest when the sun is high."

"In a village?" Cecily had seen several in the distance and longed to stop in one, but Artan had ridden right past them, clinging firmly to a more hidden route.

"Nay, but there are other places that should be safe. Of course, if ye are ready to marry me I would be willing to risk entering a village. The verra next one in truth."

"That is bribery." She should be angry, Cecily told herself, not amused.

"Aye, it is, indeed."

"Why do ye keep speaking of marriage? I am nay free."

"Ye could be," he drawled and put his hand on his sword.

"Ye cannae kill Sir Fergus just because I am betrothed to the mon."

"It sounds a good reason to me," he said as he grasped her by the waist and set her in the saddle.

Cecily hid her frown as he mounted behind her and took up the reins. He had sounded perfectly serious. It would be quite a heady thing if she thought for one moment that he was so deeply jealous of Sir Fergus that he wanted the man dead, but Cecily doubted that was the case. There might be a small amount of jealousy or possessiveness behind those words, but mostly, she suspected Artan would like to kill the man for many another reason. Sir Fergus had apparently been behind the attacks on Artan at Dunburn, and Artan did seem to be convinced that the man wanted her dead.

Gazing a little absently at the country they rode through, Cecily thought yet again on everything Artan had told her. She no longer thought that he was lying to get her to go to Glascreag with him, but she was convinced that he had told her what he believed was the absolute truth. The part of her that believed him was getting stronger every day, and not just because Artan's kisses gave her a fever of the brain. He was slowly pulling out of her all manner of memories concerning her time beneath the rule of Sir Edmund and Lady Anabel, as well as what few memories she had concerning Sir Fergus.

She wanted him to stop it, to stop prodding at her memories and stop dragging forth thoughts and feelings she had buried as deep as possible. Cecily understood what he was doing, that he was trying to get her to see the truth for herself. It was getting harder and harder to deny it all as only *his* truth and nothing more. Almost everything she recalled seemed to add weight to his claims, making it increasingly difficult for her to defend or excuse her guardians or her betrothed. What was worse, however, was that it was also showing her how much she had denied, how often she had lied to herself, and how much she had forced herself to forget and ignore. It was slowly making her see just what a sad, miserable life she had been living for the past twelve years.

At times it made her very angry with him even though she knew he did not deserve that anger. The tales he told her about his life and family, tales filled with crowds of loving relations, only added to her anger and misery. Despite the loss of her mother, she had had such a life with her father and brother before it had been brutally stolen from her. She had begun to realize that even the people of Dunburn, everyone from the maids to the swineherd, had been taken from her as well. From the day Old Meg had brought her home from that tragedy, everyone had been kept from her. Old

Meg had been the last to be taken away, and after that, Cecily realized, she had been utterly alone.

There had to be a reason for that. What troubled Cecily was that she could not come up with a good one, one that explained everything so clearly it proved that Artan was wrong. More and more a little voice in her head whispered the question: Had she been living with, and bowing to, her family's murderers? It made her feel cold to the bone to think it might be true.

She leaned back against Artan and closed her eyes, smiling faintly when she felt him press a kiss to the top of her head. The anger and hurt she had felt when he had kidnapped her was almost gone, leaving only a small, lingering mistrust of his desire for her. He had, after all, used passion to capture her, and she was uneasy whenever the desire between them began to stir to life again. She grimaced as she forced herself to admit that that desire never really rested.

And just why was she denying it? she asked herself. He spoke of marriage, so even if her betrothal to Sir Fergus came to an end, she would have a husband. And a far better one than the man her guardians had chosen for her, she mused. The desire she felt for Artan was like a living thing inside her, a very hungry, demanding living thing. If Artan was right, she was in a fight for her very life. So why was she denying herself what she so badly wanted? Cecily began to wonder if she was pushing him away to punish him for what was beginning to look like a very minor sin against her. Either that or she was punishing herself for wanting a man other than the one to whom she was betrothed. Neither was really acceptable. On the other hand, she was wary of her own arguments, afraid she was just finding ways to convince herself that it was acceptable to take what she wanted.

It was time to stop playing that game, she decided. The more she thought on her life, the more she was inclined to take what *she* wanted and enjoy it to the fullest. Artan was offering to marry her, and even if she could not decide on that just yet, she could certainly help herself to everything else he offered her. It was only her word that held her to Sir Fergus, and although she did feel a pinch of guilt for betraying the promises she had made at their betrothal ceremony, it was only a pinch and she knew it would not stop her.

Letting the rhythm of the horse and the pleasure of being lightly embraced by Artan as they rode relax her, she settled herself more comfortably against his broad chest. All problems aside, this was where she wanted to be, and it was time to stop fighting him and herself. As soon as she rested a little, Cecily decided she would let the man know that she would not push him away again. Feeling a now-familiar hardness pressing up against her backside, she smiled. She suspected she would not have to do much to make him accept her change of heart.

Artan peered down at the woman sleeping in his arms and wondered why she was smiling, then decided that it might be best if he did not know. Her anger had definitely softened toward him. He was sure that she no longer thought he was lying to her even though she still had not fully accepted the truth of what he said. That contradiction did not make much sense to him, but he suspected it did to her. It was, however, one step closer to having her fully accept the cold, hard truth about the Donaldsons and Sir Fergus.

At the moment, his strongest reason for hoping she would quickly accept the truth was that it would make her cease holding fast to promises she had made to Sir Fergus. Artan loathed the idea that she might feel bound to the man in even the smallest of ways, and the man's crimes had little to do with that feeling. He admitted to himself that he simply loathed the idea of her feeling bound to anyone but him. He also wanted her to accept him as her lover, the sooner the better, as he seemed to be in a permanent state of aching need. He could wait a little longer for her to accept him as her husband, but he was not sure he could endure another night of lying beside her rigid with need but unable to slake it. Artan would not be surprised to discover that something like that could quickly turn a man into a dribbling madman.

He sighed and nudged Thunderbolt into a slightly faster pace. For a man who could go without a woman for long stretches of time, he was proving to have very little control around Cecily. Artan was not even certain that the problem would fade once he knew he could bed her any time he pleased. It could be that it was simply Cecily who kept him in a state of permanent rut, and he was not sure he liked that. If the woman ever realized the power she held in her small hands, he could find himself in dire trouble.

Shaking aside that troubling thought, Artan suddenly recalled a small loch he had paused at on his way to Dunburn. If all went well they would be passing by the place just as the sun hit its zenith. Artan decided that would be the perfect place to stop for a rest and, if he was very lucky, a little lovemaking. They could also bathe in the water. Naked. When that thought made him painfully hard, he grimaced and tried to fill his head with thoughts of the journey ahead and how to continue to avoid the men following them.

Cecily looked around as she stretched and idly rubbed the small of her back. It was a lovely place, the water of the small loch clear and bright and land surrounding it lush with flowers, mosses, and trees. She slipped off her boots and hose and approached the edge of the water. It chilled her toes as she idly trailed them through the water, but the heat of the day made that chill welcome. When Artan threw a blanket on the ground and placed a few of their dwindling food supplies on it, she smiled at him.

"'Tis a beautiful place," she said as she walked to the blanket and sat down.

"Aye," he replied, tearing off a chunk of their last bit of bread and handing it to her. "I thought that when I stopped here on the way to Dunburn." He cut the last of their cheese in half. "I spent the night here and had a fine meal of fish fresh from the cold waters of the loch." He frowned at the loch. "Mayhap I ought to try and catch a few fish now."

"By the look upon your face I must assume that ye think it would take longer than ye wish."

"It did so the last time, and I am loathe to lose any time past what is needed to rest us and Thunderbolt."

Cecily nodded and slowly chewed on the slightly stale bread. "I dinnae suppose one can catch a roasted chicken in that loch."

Artan grinned. "Nay, nor a fine apple pudding either."

"Ah, weel, 'tis still lovely e'en if it is useless. 'Tis cold, though."

"So ye willnae wish to be swimming in it, aye?" He allowed himself a fleeting moment of regret for the loss of a nice dream of them swimming naked together. Considering how chill the water was, that was probably for the best, as he would not appear at his manliest in such water.

"I cannae swim." She sighed. "Da meant to teach me when we returned to Dunburn after visiting my uncle for he had heard that I spent a great deal of time by the burn. He feared I might drown if I played too close to the water and fell in."

"I could teach ye, but nay here and nay today. When we are at Glascreag. There are several places where I can take ye to teach ye how to swim."

She looked at him and suddenly felt incredibly sad. "I may nay be staying long at Glascreag."

"Ye will be."

"And ye say I am stubborn," she muttered. "I may be leaving with the Donaldsons and Sir Fergus when they arrive at my uncle's gates."

"E'en if ye cannae believe what I say about them and their plans, why return with them? Ye dinnae like them, dinnae like Sir Fergus, and ye are nay happy at Dunburn."

"True. All of that is verra true, and I think ye will understand if I dinnae thank ye for making me see that. Howbeit, unless I accept all your talk about lies, deceptions, thievery, and plots to murder me, I must look at promises made and duty owed."

"Do ye nay owe your mother's brother a duty as weel?"

"I do and I begin to believe the Donaldsons did purposefully keep my uncle and I apart. My duty is to see that that ne'er happens again. I am nay sure what the laws are concerning guardianship, but it might cause my uncle a great deal of trouble if I did try to stay at Glascreag. I am worried enough about the trouble ye and I are about to bring to his gates, but that can be turned aside by my returning to Dunburn with the Donaldsons and Sir Fergus."

"Angus willnae care about that. He would drag himself out of his sickbed just to have a chance to fight some Lowlanders."

"Weel, I shall be sorry to deprive him of his fun, but I willnae allow it. Others are always hurt in such battles, innocent ones and ones who have no part in whate'er argument set the men at sword point with each other."

Artan had to chuckle over her dry tone of voice. She made denying Angus the chance to fight sound like she was denying a child a little treat. The rest of her argument was sound, however. Artan could agree with it even if such concerns did not always stop him from joining in a battle. His concession to such things was to do his best to make sure neither he nor any men fighting at his side were guilty of hurting the innocent caught up in the midst of a battle.

Her talk of leaving Glascreag shortly after she arrived did not trouble him much. He was confident she would see the truth by then, and if she did not, he would simply secure her somewhere within the keep until she did. Also, he could stop worrying about it altogether if she married him. Cecily would feel bound to him by the exchange of their vows and he knew she would never walk away from him then.

Not even when she discovered what secret he had been keeping from her, he thought, and silently cursed his own cowardice. They had spent hours talking about her past and his, yet he still hesitated to tell her about what Angus had offered him. There was a contrary part of him that felt it should not matter. Many men married for gain, and it made no difference to what they felt or did not feel. In this instance, it was also mostly for her that the offer was made. Angus could not leave the lairdship of Glascreag and its people to a small, bonnie lass simply because all the surrounding clans would see it as an invitation to take Glascreag. He needed to have a strong man at the head of the clan. A marriage satisfied both that need and the one that the man had to leave something to the child of his sister, one of the few remaining close kin he had. It made perfect sense and should not trouble her that it was so or make her think it lessened what Artan felt for her.

That, of course, was the way a man felt. Artan could not depend upon her feeling the same. Worse, he was not skilled enough with sweet words to convince her that he did feel something for her, something far above and quite separate from what he gained by marrying her.

He shook aside that concern. If he could not find the right moment or the courage to tell her about Angus's bargain before they reached Glascreag, he would deal with the matter when they did arrive. His only concern should be that she did not find out about it from anyone else.

Knowing they could not linger here too much

longer, Artan stood up and pulled her up to stand beside him. "We shall need to leave soon, and I intend to wash some of this dust off. Do ye feel the need to do the same? I can swim verra weel, so ye dinnae need to fear ye will drown if ye tumble in."

"That is a comfort," she murmured as she frowned toward the water, then nodded. "Aye, I think a brief wash in even that cold water will be welcome. I cannae e'en convince myself that, since we will be back on the horse and riding until the sun sets, 'tis all a bit of a waste of time."

He laughed and began to pull off his boots. It pained him to do so, but he cast aside his plan to steal a few moments for some lovemaking. There was a sense of unease growing inside of him, a warning of trouble, and he would heed it. A quick cleansing and they would be back on Thunderbolt and leaving this place. When he finished pulling off his shirt and saw that Cecily had stripped down to her shift, he almost changed his mind, but pushed aside the urge to give into temptation. He could not ignore his instincts and they were indicating that this place was not a safe place to linger for too long.

Cecily squeaked with shock when she stepped into the cold water. She had to laugh at the dramatic shudder Artan gave when he strode into the water. Despite his assurances that she was safe, that he could swim very well and could rescue her if it was needed, she stepped farther into the water very cautiously. When the water reached her knees, she stopped, unwilling to go any farther. Crouching down, she slowly washed the dust and the scent of horse from her skin. Her shift was soon soaked, but she did not care. It too needed a rinse and it would dry quickly in the heat and the sun.

"Hold your head back, lass, and I will rinse your hair for ye, if ye wish it," said Artan.

"Oh, aye, I should like that."

Artan tried not to stare while he washed her hair with the clear water of the loch, but it was hard. The water had turned her light shift so thin he could see all of her charms. The moment he finished with her hair, he strode farther out into the water and dove in. The cold of the water was so sharp it made him grit his teeth, but it did the job he intended it to do. He was no longer hard with lust.

For a little while, Cecily watched him swim. The fear she had felt when she had seen him dive into the water eased as she saw that he had not succumbed to an idle boast when he had told her he could swim very well. It was fascinating to watch his strong body move along so gracefully in the water, but the cold soon drove her back onto the bank. She was not surprised when he soon joined her there. Even he had to feel that cold after a while.

"I need to skip into the trees for a moment," she said as she used the blanket he had handed her to rub herself dry.

"Skip away, but nay too far," he said as he donned his shirt and began to pull on his boots.

Cecily threw her gown on over her damp shift, then sat down to put on her shoes and hose. She grimaced at the odd feeling of wearing damp clothes beneath dry ones as she stood up and hurried off into the trees. Uncomfortable though it was, she could tell even now that it would prove cooling for a while.

She was just straightening her clothes when a sound made her tense. Without thought, she hurried back toward Artan. The moment she cleared the trees she knew she had made a serious error. Artan was surrounded by armed men and it did not appear that the men were graciously asking for his surrender. Fergus had found them.

Taking a few steps back into the shadows, she struggled to think of what she could do to help him. About the only thing she could think of was running toward the men and drawing their attention long enough to give Artan a chance to flee. It was a mad idea and she did not have much confidence that Artan would flee, but it was the only idea she had. When Artan gave an ear-splitting bellow and attacked the men, she decided she had to do it if only to save the fool from his own idiocy. Just as she started to move, however, she was grabbed firmly from behind. Before she could act, there was a blinding pain in her head and all she knew was blackness.

Chapter 11

Someone was groaning. A moment later, Cecily realized that someone was her. Her head felt as if some little demon sat on her shoulder and was beating a brick against her head. Had she fallen out of the saddle? That would be highly embarrassing, she thought.

Then her memory returned; her mind was swamped with images she wished she could banish forever. Her last sight of Artan filled her mind's eye and made her whole body ache with grief. He had to be dead. No man could face so many men determined to kill him and survive. There had to have been a dozen swords aimed at him. Even so, a small part of her refused to give up hope. She decried it as foolish and blind, but that tiny flicker of hope remained.

Cautiously, she opened her eyes, wincing slightly as even the dim light surrounding her made her head throb. She was in a tent and a rather lavish one as well. It was as she started to sit up that she realized she was bound at the wrists, but then quickly discovered that was not the worst of it. The other end of the rope was secured to a stake stuck in the ground in the middle of the tent. She had the wild thought that there must be something in a man's character that compelled him to put a woman on a leash. Odd though it was, that thought caused her growing alarm to fade and anger took its place. That anger also pushed her fear for Artan aside, and she decided to cling to it.

Her head hurt and she was beginning to be aware of other aches and bruises indicating that her journey to this place had not been an easy one. Her clothes were torn in several places and covered in dirt. She was leashed to a stake like some beast, and she desperately needed a drink. Cecily badly wanted to kill someone or, at the very least, beat someone bloody.

Sir Fergus entered the tent at that moment and she fixed all of her fury on him. Somehow it did not surprise her that the man would travel with a tent worthy of royalty. The fact that he looked as clean as he did when he sat at the table in the great hall of Dunburn only added to her anger. Even the man's thinning hair looked well combed. When he poured himself a tankard of wine, not offering her any, and sat on a stool to watch her, Cecily suspected the pounding in her head now had less to do with the fact that someone had struck her and a great deal to do with the fury pounding through her veins.

"Might I be so impertinent as to ask why I am tied to this stake?" she asked between tightly gritted teeth.

The way his eyes widened told her that her obvious anger had surprised him. He looked at her a little more closely and appeared to be even more shocked. Cecily would not be surprised if her eyes fairly screamed her rage. It was obvious he felt as if some mouse had just grown large fangs and was leaping for his throat. That he was so astonished that she would be angry to be treated so told Cecily as much about herself as it did about him. She had clearly appeared weak and timid to him, an easy victim. It disgusted her.

"I couldnae leave ye loose, could I?" he said. "Ye might have run back to your lover."

"I have no lover," she said.

He moved faster than she could have believed possible and backhanded her across the face. Cecily sprawled back onto the ground from the force of the blow. For a moment she stayed there, sprawled gracelessly on her back. The pain of the blow made the whole side of her face throb, but the shock of the attack was worse. It was not really the shock over a man striking her either; it was the shock of knowing at that precise moment that Artan had been telling her the truth.

"Do ye think I hadnae guessed that ye had willingly met that Highlander at the burn?" he snapped and gulped down the rest of his wine. "Ye crept away like a thief in the night to rut with that mon. Ye are betrothed to me, and yet ye let that barbarian touch ye."

Warily, a little afraid that he would knock her back down again, Cecily sat up. "And just how did ye discover I was even gone, let alone where I went and with whom?"

"I had someone watching the Highlander and ye werenae in your room."

"Ye went to my bedchamber?"

"I felt it was time to remind ye that ye are betrothed to me."

That told her all too clearly why he had gone to her room, and Cecily barely suppressed a shudder of revulsion. She had always done her best not to think too much on the fact that, as her husband, Sir Fergus would have the right to share her bed, to claim her body. He had evidently decided not to wait any longer to claim those rights. Cecily suspected it had nothing to do with lust and everything to do with making a firm claim on her, one that might cause Artan to turn away from her. Recalling what Artan had told her about Sir Fergus and the young maid he had tried to rape, she also knew her willingness or lack of it would not have mattered. Worse, she was absolutely sure that her guardians would not have done anything to help her or avenge that insult.

"Weel, 'tis a good thing I wasnae there then, isnae it, seeing as I have decided that we are nay longer betrothed."

"*Ye* have decided? This has naught to do with ye, ye witless whore. Your guardians gave ye to me."

"Curious that. Nay matter how hard I think on it, I cannae understand why they chose ye. Ye dinnae gain them verra much. There were others they could have chosen who would have brought them far more gain."

"Aye, but *I* can send them to the gallows."

His smug look chilled her as much as the revelation that yet another thing Artan had told her was really true. Sir Edmund and Lady Anabel had ordered the killing of her father and poor wee Colin. If not for Old Meg and a few stalwart men, she would have died with the rest of her family. She found some comfort in the fact that Old Meg had never guessed the secret of her guardians' crimes, but only a little. A part of her felt as if she had betrayed her father and Colin by living with their killers and trying so hard to please them.

"I can see that ye ken what I mean. In payment for my silence concerning the blood on their hands, I got ye and quite a bit of the fortune your father left ye. He was a verra rich mon, ye ken, and Anabel and Edmund have lived weel off your money for long enough. 'Tis time they shared a wee bit."

"Did my father e'en name them as my guardians?"

"Nay, he chose another cousin, but that poor, kindly mon had a tragic accident and died."

"It must be a sizable fortune if ye are willing to give them Dunburn."

"Weel, weel, your barbarian did manage to uncover many a secret, didnae he. He is obviously nay as stupid as he looks." He shrugged. "It matters not. He has taken them to the grave with him. As for Dunburn, I will let those two fools enjoy it for a while longer. I cannae move against them too quickly. It would raise too many questions."

Shoving aside the fear that he was right when he said Artan had taken those secrets to the grave, Cecily forced herself to look at Fergus with scorn. "Did ye ne'er think that they might be planning the same fate for you?"

"Of course. I ne'er let myself forget that they have already killed to gain Dunburn and its wealth. It troubles me not. I am a match for them."

"Intend to rid yourself of Anabel the next time ye share her bed?" She was a little surprised by the look of distaste that crossed his face.

"She wasnae to my taste. The woman enjoys it too much."

"*It* being the occasional loving punch in the face?"

He scowled at her. "That bastard told ye about the maid, didnae he? He nearly killed me!"

Cecily snorted. "If he had wanted ye dead, then ye wouldnae be standing here acting so proud of all your crimes."

"Oh, aye? Just who has won this game, eh?"

"I wouldnae play head cock of the dunghill yet, Sir Fergus. Ye ne'er saw Artan's body."

To her amazement he paled and hurried over to the tent opening, calling over one of his men. "Have Tom and his men returned yet?"

"Nay," replied the man, "we have been waiting for them, but mayhap the fading light slows them down."

The man did not sound too sure of that, and although Cecily would not have thought it possible, Sir Fergus grew even paler before he abruptly dismissed the man. She watched as Sir Fergus poured himself another tankard of wine and gulped down the whole thing. Artan terrified him.

"See? No body yet."

"He *is* dead," Sir Fergus hissed, then kicked her in the side. "I left ten men there to see to it. He couldnae survive that."

"He survived the eight men ye sent after him last time."

Cecily hastily scrambled out of his way when he tried to kick her again. It might be gratifying to taunt him, but it was not wise. Even as she prayed that she had the right to hope, she planned how she could keep Sir Fergus from beating her too badly or raping her before Artan came for her.

Artan held his sword at the throat of the last man standing, and demanded, "Where has he taken her?"

"He is camped in a clearing about a mile from here. A mile to the north. Ye cannae miss him. He has a huge tent set up. Aye, with pennants on it."

"Pennants?"

The man nodded, but carefully, all too aware of the sword point but inches from his throat. "He had them made when he was knighted."

"What is on them?"

"Some wee blue flower and a rampant boar."

"How fitting. Now, ye are a Donaldson, aye?"

"Aye, her ladyship sent near thirty of us with Sir Fergus."

"Do ye ken that her ladyship and her rutting swine of a husband are nay the true owners of Dunburn?"

The man grimaced. "'Tis the lass, isnae it?"

"Aye, 'tis the lass, and verra soon Sir Edmund and Lady Anabel will be made to pay for their thievery and for the murder of Lady Cecily's father and brother." He nodded when the man just stared at him in shock. "I would suggest that ye slip away home. Now."

The moment the man ran away, Artan sheathed his sword and whistled for Thunderbolt. He ached all over and had a few small wounds that stung badly, but he had survived hale and strong enough to go after his woman. Hearing a groan, he quickly mounted his horse and started to ride away. Some of the men were starting to wake up and he had no wish to fight them all over again. With one man having fled, one dead, and two seriously wounded, he would only have to fight six, but he did not want to risk it. It was more important to get to Cecily as fast as he could.

He saw the pennant first and nearly laughed. There was so much white in the thing that it fairly glowed like a lantern even in the fading light caused by the increasing clouds. He suspected Sir Fergus's men were heartily cursing the man's vanity. Silently, he drew as close as he dared to the back of the tent. Dismounting, he began to move toward the tent when he espied one of the Ogilveys standing guard in front of a shepherd's shieling. Although he doubted Fergus would have put Cecily in there, he had to check.

After slamming the hilt of his sword into the man's head, Artan carefully set him on the ground. He pulled aside the oiled leather door of the shieling and found himself staring at two very young men. Despite the fact that he knew he looked like he had been in a hard fight and he held a sword in his hand, both young men smiled at him. Artan suspected it was because they were pleased to see one of their own.

"Does he have a wee lass in that tent?" he asked in Gaelic.

"He does," replied the thinner of the pair in the same language. "She was carried in, but we could see that she had a fine pelt of red hair."

"That is my bride by the sounds of it. You had better leave. I believe the man with no chin will be mad enough to kill in a few minutes."

"Ah, you intend to steal her back."

"She is to be my wife, so it is not stealing, but retrieving."

"Since you have been so kind as to free us, we will see that that fool with his tent and his banner with a rutting swine on it will not be able to follow you very soon."

"Why do you not just gut him and be done with it?" said the shorter one.

"It is a tempting thought, but it is more important to get my bride out of here."

"It is," said the tall one after jabbing his companion in the side with his elbow. "You can see the man has already been in a fight, fool. One squeal from that pig in there and he will be facing far more men than he can fight." He turned back to Artan. "Go and fetch your bride, my laird. We shall go and cut a few cinches, then make for the hills."

Artan smiled and stepped aside to let the two young men out. Cut cinches would be a very big help. He softly warned them not to cut the cinch on his mount and pointed out where the horse was. Both young men nodded and silently disappeared into the shadows. Artan suspected Sir Fergus would also find himself short two horses.

He turned his attention to the tent. Slipping up to the back, he used his dagger to cut a very small slice in the cloth and peered inside. He saw Cecily tied to a stake in the ground and felt cold with anger. When Sir Fergus suddenly kicked her, it took all of Artan's willpower not to immediately cut his way into the tent and kill the man.

It took several slow, deep breaths before he felt calm enough to continue. Sir Fergus was dangerously close to Cecily and stealth was needed, he reminded himself. Although it had not been his plan to kill the man, Artan knew he would do so now if given half a chance. The most important thing was to get Cecily safely away from Sir Fergus. Killing the man would simply be an added and unexpected pleasure. Artan slowly began to make a cut in the tent large enough for him to slip through.

Cecily swore as Sir Fergus's booted foot grazed her ribs. He was in a blind fury. She had ceased to taunt him, but that had made little difference. There was still no word from Tom or any of his men, and the mere thought that Artan might have escaped death yet again had put Sir Fergus into a rage. It was an anger bred of fear, but that did not make it any less dangerous to Cecily.

"Ye had best be careful, Sir Fergus," she said as she twisted away from him until she was facing the back of the tent. "Ye dinnae want to kill me yet."

"Ye willnae die from a little beating," he snapped.

"Oh, I might, and then ye will have nothing. Ye have to be married to me to gain my dower and then my widow's portion." She watched his eyes narrow and realized his greed had finally cut through his fury.

"Ye ken far more than ye ought to."

She sighed and was not surprised by the weariness in her voice. "What does that matter? Ye have ne'er intended for me to live verra long after the wedding, have ye?"

"Someone might listen to ye if ye choose to speak out."

"When has anyone ever listened to me?"

Even to her own ears, Cecily sounded pitiful. It seemed to calm Sir Fergus, however. She suspected it was how he expected all women to sound.

One of Sir Fergus's men stuck his head inside the

tent and dolefully announced, "There is nay sign of Tom and his men yet."

"Do not tell me again," yelled Sir Fergus. "I dinnae wish to hear another word until ye can tell me he has returned and he is holding Sir Artan Murray's head in his hands."

"Ye asked him to bring ye Artan's head?" she asked after the other man had fled and was not surprised to hear her voice trembling with horror.

Sir Fergus looked as if he badly wanted to kick her again. "They have failed time and time again. I need proof."

Cecily hastily put the coldly terrifying thought from her mind. If she thought about it too much she could go mad. She preferred to take hope in the fact that Tom and his men had not returned. The fact that they had not so frightened Sir Fergus that she found a reason to hope in that as well.

If Artan was alive, she hoped he would come soon. Sir Fergus wavered between fury and what looked to be a growing lust. Cecily wanted no part of either, although she would take a beating if she had the choice. The mere thought of Sir Fergus touching her in a lustful manner turned her stomach. She could recover from a beating, but she was not so sure she would recover from being raped by the man.

Sir Fergus moved to pour himself another tankard of wine and Cecily felt her throat tighten with the need for a drink. She hated asking the man for anything, but her thirst was so great she was willing to swallow her pride, especially if it meant she could swallow a little wine as well. After studying her leash for a moment, she realized it was too short to allow her stand upright, so she sat up as straight as she could.

"Sir Fergus, might I please have a little of that wine?" she asked in what she hoped was an appropriately meek tone.

He turned to stare at her and she wondered how she could have ever thought he had nice eyes. The color was fine enough, but there was no life in those eyes, no softness or humor. It was very much like looking at a pretty piece of glass.

For a moment she thought he was going to refuse. It would not surprise her as he seemed the sort of man to take pleasure in another's misery. Then he shrugged as if it was all a matter of complete disinterest to him and brought his tankard over to her. With her wrists tied it was a little awkward to take a drink and she loathed the idea of putting her lips on a tankard he had drunk from, but the wine soothed the aching dryness in her throat. He took it away when she had had only a few sips, but it was enough to give her the strength to silently accept the deprivation.

"Thank ye," she said, even though the words nearly gagged her and she sorely wished she could kick him when he nodded arrogantly as if he had done her some great service.

"Ye have changed," he said, frowning at her.

"Changed? I dinnae understand what ye mean."

"At Dunburn ye were always quiet, a pleasant wee shadow slipping about the halls of the place. There was ne'er any hint of a temper or a sharp tongue. I dinnae like either. Ye would be wise to control them again."

A pleasant wee shadow? she thought and grimaced. She supposed she had been. It had made life a lot easier for her if no one noticed her. Yet it pained her to think of herself like that.

He supposed he was right to say she had changed. She had begun to sense the changes in herself before she had even left Dunburn. It was being with Artan that had done it. He made her feel safe, and that allowed her to say and do what she wanted to. Little by little she had relaxed the close guard she had kept on her words and actions. It was amusing to think that he had helped her by kidnapping her, yet the farther they got from Dunburn, Lady Anabel, and Sir Edmund, the more she had relaxed, the more she had felt as if she had been freed from a prison.

"Running from people who are eager to see ye in the grave probably has something to do with that," she murmured. "Being *a pleasant wee shadow* willnae help one stay alive."

The slap he gave her was delivered almost casually. She held herself steady this time and did not sprawl in the dirt. For a moment she stared at the ground; sure she looked like a true penitent, but knowing she needed to hide the anger she felt before she looked at him again.

As she lifted her eyes she caught the glint of something at the rear of the tent. Shielding the direction of her gaze by keeping her eyelids lowered, she stared at the spot and finally located what she had seen. The very tip of a blade was ever so slowly moving down through the cloth at the rear of the tent. Someone was cutting their way inside.

Her pulse increased as hope surged in her heart. She desperately wanted to believe it was Artan coming to rescue her. Even if it was not him, the only reason someone would be attempting to enter the tent so stealthily was because they meant no good for Sir Fergus. That made whoever it was her ally. She was determined to make sure that he was not discovered until it was too late for Sir Fergus to cry for aid.

Cecily looked at Sir Fergus and made no attempt to hide her contempt for him. His eyes narrowed in fury as he recognized that look for what it was. A fleeting glance toward the rear of the tent told her that whoever it was out there would soon been trying to slip inside and she was determined to keep all of Sir Fergus's attention on her.

"Only men who are afraid that their manhood is the size of a bairn's beat on women," she said, not surprised to see his cheeks flush with the heat of his anger.

"Ye had best tread verra carefully, Cecily," he said, his voice tight with anger.

"Why? Ye mean to marry me, steal all that is mine, and then kill me so that ye can steal the rest. Why should I be careful?"

"Because I can make what time ye have left seem like a hell upon earth."

"Ye do that just by breathing the same air as I do, ye spineless cretin."

Even though she had braced herself for his attack, she was still winded by the force of it. He threw himself on top of her and put his hands around her throat. The man proved to be a lot stronger than she would have thought, and she very quickly felt robbed of precious air. She was just beginning to think she had made a serious error when he was yanked off of her and tossed into the side of the tent. He bounced off the cloth a little, unharmed, but then fell to the ground and hit his head on something hard. Cecily suspected there were a few rocks near the edge of tent and Sir Fergus had found one. She looked up at Artan and saw him frowning in the direction of Sir Fergus.

"Nay as good as a nice solid wall, is it?" Cecily said as Artan held out his hand and she grasped it firmly in hers.

"Nay, it was a wee bit disappointing."

She saw him look at the rope and could tell by the hardening of his expression that he had seen how it would not allow her to stand upright. "Just cut it and get me out of here."

"I would really like to kill him," he said as he cut her free.

Seeing how Sir Fergus was creeping toward the opening of the tent, she said, "I think that will have to wait."

Artan threw his dagger and smiled when it pinned Sir Fergus's jupon to the ground and the man squeaked. "Stay," he ordered the man and hastily collected up what food and drink he could find in the tent, putting it all in a blanket and tying the blanket into a rough bag.

"She is my betrothed wife," Sir Fergus said as he struggled to free his jupon.

"Nay, I am not," said Cecily. "I am Sir Artan Murray's wife."

Artan looked at her and quirked one brow. When she nodded, he grinned and said, "Aye, she is, and I am her husband."

Sir Fergus's eyes widened as he realized what they had done, that they had just declared themselves before a witness. "Nay! Ye cannae do this!"

"Are ye sure I cannae kill him?" Artan asked

Cecily even as he urged her toward the back of the tent.

"I dinnae think we have time and I suspect ye are a wee bit tired after fighting off ten men."

"Help! Help!" screamed Sir Fergus.

Two men stumbled into the tent and gaped at Artan. He nudged Cecily through the slit in the back of the tent as he smiled at the two men. A third man stumbled into them, pushing them even closer to him. He felt Cecily grab the back of his shirt and tug on it.

Finally freeing his jupon, Sir Fergus stumbled to his feet. "Kill him, ye fools!"

"Artan, I should really like to leave now," said Cecily.

Artan roared at the men and thrust his sword in their direction. As they all tripped over each other in an attempt to flee, he slipped out the back of the tent and, grabbing Cecily by the hand, ran for his horse. He threw her onto Thunderbolt's back, handed her the blanket sack, and mounted up behind her. Kicking his horse into a gallop, he headed away from the increasing chaos of Sir Fergus's camp.

It was two hours before he felt he could slow his horse's pace. He felt Cecily slump against him and knew she had felt as tense as he had as they had both waited to hear the sounds of a large pursuit. He wrapped one arm around her waist, held her even closer to him, and pressed a kiss to the top of her head.

"Did he hurt ye, lass?" he asked softly, sure that she would understand he was not referring to any beating.

"Nay, just a few slaps and kicks," she answered,

reaching down to lift the wineskin from where it hung on the saddle. "He also ne'er offered to give me a drink and I had to ask for one." She had herself a long drink of wine, sighed with pleasure, and replaced the wineskin.

"Ye do understand that by calling yourself my wife before a witness we are now handfasted," he said carefully.

"Aye, I ken it. I remembered Old Meg telling me about it." She cautiously looked at him over her shoulder. "Sir Fergus will ne'er say anything if ye wish to just let it be forgotten."

"Och, nay, lass, ye willnae be rid of me that easily. We will hie ourselves to the verra next village and find a witness or two who willnae be reluctant to hear our declarations."

"Do ye think there will be a place where I can have a hot bath?"

"Aye, there will be. And there will be a place with a nice big bed as well."

Cecily decided it would be wise to act as if she had not heard that.

Chapter 12

It was a few hours later and very late indeed when they rode into the village. Cecily thought the tiny inn they rode toward looked like the grandest of palaces. She knew she would find a meal and a bed, but what she really prayed for was a hot bath. She desperately wanted to wash the stench of Sir Fergus off her skin and soothe all the bruises she had collected. Glancing over her shoulder at Artan, she knew she also wanted to be clean when she shared his bed as his wife for the first time.

"Are ye certain 'tis safe for us to stop here?" she asked as he dismounted in front of the inn and helped her down.

"Aye, lass," he replied as he collected their packs and took her hand in his. "Sir Fergus willnae be going anywhere for a while, nay unless he wishes to leave a fortune in saddles behind and ride without one."

"Ah, I see. Nay, he willnae want to do that."

"Are ye sure ye are all right?" he asked quietly as they entered the inn.

She briefly tightened the grip of her hand upon

his. "Aye, I am, although a hot bath would be verra welcome, indeed."

Cecily stood very quietly by his side as he spoke to the innkeeper. She almost protested when she heard how much the man demanded for preparing her a hot bath, but Artan's next request diverted her. The innkeeper looked from Artan, to her, and back again, and then grinned before hurrying off.

"Why do ye need another witness to our handfasting?" she asked.

"Because, as ye said, Sir Fergus will ne'er admit to hearing our declaration, and the other fool who was lurking just outside the tent might nay survive the confrontation yet to come. I certainly dinnae intend for Sir Fergus to do so."

"Ye think Sir Fergus will continue on to Glascreag?"

"Oh, aye. There is a fortune to be had, and greed can give e'en a worm like him some courage."

That troubled Cecily, but she had no chance to discuss it further for the innkeeper returned with two men, a quill, some ink, and something for them to write on. Artan wrote down what was needed as they each declared themselves in a more formal way and the other men made their marks on the document. After it was done, Artan carefully stored the document in his pack, paid for some ale for each of the men, and had the innkeeper escort them to their bedchamber. Within moments she found herself alone with her bath readied and waiting for her. Cecily did not think she had ever shed her clothes so quickly. For a moment she felt guilty that she had not even asked Artan if he wanted her to hurry so that he could enjoy this luxury, too; but then she sank into the hot water, sighed with pleasure, and forgot everything but how good it felt.

Artan stood outside the door of the bedchamber he would share with Cecily and softly cursed. He felt as nervous as an untried lad. It had been a long time since he had bedded a woman, but he knew that was not the cause of his unease. He had never bedded a virgin and he had never bedded Cecily. This would mark the start of their married life, and he felt the importance of that weighing him down. Not even once in his life had he ever been so concerned about giving his partner pleasure.

Stiffening his spine, he entered the room. Seeing Cecily kneeling near the fire combing her hair dry, he quietly shut the door behind him and just watched her. She was beautiful with her long, thick hair falling in soft waves to her slim hips. Her nightgown and robe were very modest, but just seeing her readied for bed was enough to make him ache to take her there.

A rap on the door announced their meal. Artan moved to stand so that he blocked all view of Cecily before bidding the one at the door entrance. Once their meal was set out on the small table near the window, he tossed the innkeeper's son a coin, then securely locked the door after he left. Artan turned to face Cecily and bowed her toward the table.

"Oh, I fear I will be gorging myself like some wee starving piglet," she said as she sat down and smiled across the table at Artan as he sat down.

"Gorge away," he said. "I made certain the man sent us a feast."

Looking at all the food set out before her, she nodded, "'Tis indeed a feast." As she filled her plate, she said, "I must apologize, Artan. I should have believed ye."

"So, Sir Fergus confessed all, did he?" he asked as he began to eat.

Between mouthfuls of food, Cecily related what Sir Fergus had told her. "I did point out to him that Edmund and Anabel could weel be planning the same fate for him as he is planning for them."

"Without doubt." He filled her tankard with wine. "He isnae worried about that?"

"Nay, not at all. I cannae believe Anabel and Edmund murdered three people, three kinsmen and one of them only a child, and all for greed. I think that is what shocked me the most. That and the fact that I lived with the murderers of my family. Nay, not only lived with them, but struggled daily to please them."

"Ah, lass, ye were but a child. Ye cannae blame yourself."

She nodded and had a deep drink of wine to calm herself. "I do understand that, and yet there is a part of me that feels I betrayed the memory of my dear ones in some way."

"Weel, ye didnae. It just may take ye a while to accept that. Aye, and accept that ye survived."

Cecily stared at him for a moment, then smiled. "How did ye ken that that troubles me at times?"

"'Tis a common enough feeling. Men leaving loved ones behind on a battlefield whilst they walk away can suffer from the same feeling. The mon gets to thinking he was chosen by God to live and wonders why, especially when he feels unworthy of the honor. It passes."

"My father and brother were murdered twelve years ago."

"True, but I think ye have done your best to forget about it and them e'er since that day."

She sighed and nodded. Artan might be rough of speech and nature, but he had a true understanding of people. One could even call it a sympathetic nature, she mused, but was very certain he would not appreciate anyone saying so. Sometimes she got the distinct feeling that Artan liked people to think he was a barbarian whose wits were as thick as his muscles. It was rather nice to know something about him that others did not. Watching as he peeled, cored, and sliced an apple for her, she thought about how those nimble hands had worked their magic on her body and quickly turned her thoughts elsewhere.

"I am nay sure what to do about Anabel and Edmund," she said, then popped a slice of apple into her mouth.

"Make them pay for their crimes." He ate his apple and wondered if it was too soon to take her to bed. How slowly did one have to move with a virgin?

"Of course. I but wonder how. Sir Fergus kens the truth, but I dinnae think he will help me."

Looking at the bruise upon her cheek, Artan said, "Nay, for he will soon be dead."

She grimaced. "Although he had naught to do with the deaths of my family, I do think he has crimes aplenty he needs to pay for. The ones he has already committed and the ones he plans to commit."

Unable to wait any longer, Artan rose, took her by the hand, and pulled her to her feet. "I dinnae wish to speak about that swine any longer. Or about your murderous, thieving guardians. Or about the fate of Dunburn."

Although she was suddenly feeling very nervous, Cecily had to smile. "Nay? What do ye wish to speak about?"

"How sweet ye taste," he said as he removed her

robe and carried her to the bed. "How soft your skin is. How the heat of your mouth flows straight into my veins. How I am like to curl up and die if I cannae make ye mine verra, verra quickly."

Cecily welcomed him into her arms when he joined her on the bed and said very quietly, "Oh, nay too quickly I pray."

Artan grinned. Mayhap bedding this particular virgin would not be so difficult. There was a deep well of passion in Cecily and it appeared that he was the lucky man who could set it free. He kissed her and began to undo her nightgown.

Cecily felt embarrassment and shyness start to cool her desire and ruthlessly banished them. This was her wedding night, and although she doubted she would soon be skipping naked about the room in the full light of day, she should not be flinching because her husband wishes to help her disrobe. After the lovemaking they had indulged in by the burn, there was not much Artan had not seen or touched anyway.

Despite the stern lecture she had given herself, she tensed when he drew off her nightgown and tossed it aside. He crouched over her, staring at her body, and she began to feel all too aware of what she lacked. It was one thing to be naked; it was quite another to be naked and stared at. Slowly, she began to lift her hands from where she had kept them clenched at her sides, intending to cover herself as best she could.

"Nay, lass, dinnae cover yourself," Artan said as he threw off his plaid, revealing that he had nothing else on. "Dinnae hide all that soft beauty from your husband's eyes."

If there was beauty to be seen in this bedchamber

tonight, it was his, she thought. She doubted she would ever cease to be awed by the sight of his chest, but the sight of his strong body completely unclothed left her breathless. He was perfection with nothing too long, too short, too misshaped with muscle, or too soft. His legs were long and well shaped, his firm backside had a lovely curve to it, and his back was a pure delight for the eyes.

The only thing she was not sure of was the rather large protrusion at the front of his body. It was not that it was unattractive; she did, in fact, rather like the look of the thing. It was just that it was large. Cecily had not pictured it as being that impressive when Artan was pressing it against her leg.

Artan stroked her side and caught the direction of her gaze. Obviously flaunting himself in front of his still virginal wife might have been a mistake. He decided that he had left her unkissed for too long. It was probably not wise to let her desire wane at all. Once she was breeched and realized their difference in size did not matter, he would not have to be so careful.

He had to fight the urge to stare at her, to slowly and gently touch every perfect part of her. Her breasts were plump and tipped with soft pink. Her waist was small, and her hips curved enough to be womanly. Her bottom was nicely rounded and taut. She had long, slender legs and smooth, pale thighs so slender there was a gap at the top that invited a man. Her womanly secrets were hidden beneath a dainty vee of red curls. He knew her skin was smooth and soft, and all he could see was how much of its unmarred beauty was right there for him to enjoy. When she started to lift her hands to cover herself again, he kissed her.

It took a moment for Artan's kiss to banish her embarrassment, but Cecily soon fell under its spell. She wrapped her arms around his neck and returned his kiss with an increasing passion. When he began to caress her body, each stroke of his big hands seemed to smooth away her shyness. The moment his kisses reached her breasts she no longer cared what he saw or what he did; all she cared about was that the feelings he stirred within her continue.

Cecily stroked his back as he feasted upon her breasts. When she slid her hands down his spine and caressed his backside, he groaned, and his kisses and caresses grew a little fiercer. She did not even flinch when he slid his hand down between her legs and stroked her as he had done during their tryst at the burn. Cecily willingly opened herself to his touch and heard herself groan softly as her desire began to reach painful heights.

It was not until his kisses reached the lowest point on her stomach that a brief hesitation came in her growing passion. Her eyes grew so wide with shock when his mouth replaced his fingers and he kissed her there, they stung a little. By the time she recovered from her shock enough to move, she did not want to. She buried her fingers in his hair and held him there, silently asking him to continue giving her such pleasure. A tightening in her belly nudged her free of her mindless desire and she called out his name, but he ignored her. Suddenly, that tightness snapped and she cried out as waves of pleasure swept over her.

She cried out again when he was suddenly there, inside her, united with her. It took her a moment to realize he had gone very still and she gently grasped him by the hips. She was not sure what she wanted him to do, but it was not to just lie there quietly joined with her.

"Artan?" she whispered, lightly stroking his hips.

Artan prayed she was not about to ask him to pull out because it hurt too much. He did not think he had ever felt such pleasure. The feel of her tight heat all around him made him nearly dizzy with pleasure. The strain of not moving soon grew too great to ignore, however, and he brushed a soft kiss over her mouth.

"Are ye in pain, Sile mine?" he asked.

"Och, nay. I just wondered if this is how it is done. Are ye supposed to just lie there?"

He laughed softly and kissed her again. "Nay, lass, I am supposed to do this," he said quietly and began to move.

Cecily arched up to meet his gentle thrust. "Aye, that is what I needed."

It was what he needed as well, and Artan was deeply gratified when she quickly caught his rhythm and met him thrust for thrust, her body in perfect harmony with his. Just as he began to reach between their bodies to stroke the nub of flesh there and try to add to her enjoyment, he felt her tense. A heartbeat later he felt her release convulse around him and it pulled him along with her. As their cries echoed in the room, Artan decided there was something sweeter than hearing her cry out his name, and that was to hear them cry out together.

When he was finally able to move from where he had sprawled at Cecily's side, Artan fetched a scrap of cloth, dampened it in a bowl of water left for the morning, and washed them both clean of the stain of her lost innocence. He returned to the bed and pulled her into his arms. As the last of passion's haze cleared from his mind, he found himself wondering how long he needed to allow her to heal after her first time with a man. Artan prayed it would not be too long, for he was already hungry for her again.

Artan felt like patting himself on the back. He had breeched his wife and there had been no tears and no cries of pain, only of pleasure. Loving her with his mouth had been an inspiration brought on by a need to kiss every beautiful soft inch of her, to mark her in ways he had never marked a woman before, and a sudden memory of something he had once done half-heartedly when playing those love games with the blacksmith's daughter. It had worked, sending his little wife into such a state of desire she had barely flinched when he had broken her maidenhead. He began to think he had suffered more than she had.

He briefly grinned into her hair as she rested her cheek against his chest. Artan realized that he liked loving his wife that way. He especially liked the way she went wild in his arms and made soft, moaning noises. There would be more of those intimate kisses. Artan would not allow her to grow all shy and uneasy over such an intimacy. He had every intention of doing it again. It enflamed him almost as much as it did her.

"Artan?" Cecily asked a little timidly as she stroked his chest.

"Aye, wife?" He decided he liked the sound of that word.

"Am I supposed to make so much noise?"

Knowing that laughing now would hurt her feelings, he bit the inside of his cheek until the urge passed. "Ye can make as much noise as ye want. I do and I will."

"'Tis just that it isnae anything like Lady Anabel said it was supposed to be."

He did not like the idea that Lady Anabel had advised her on how to behave in the marital bed. "It is what ye make of it. Ye can have a cold bed or a verra warm one. I prefer a verra warm one, thank ye."

"Weel, I wish to do what ye like, because then ye may nay have the need of another woman."

Artan grasped her by the chin and turned her face up to his. "I am your husband. We have made promises to each other e'en if the marriage is only a handfasting. We will have our vows afore a priest as soon as can be and I will mean those vows, too. I will be faithful."

That delighted her, but she wondered if he really knew what he was promising her. "Anabel says men cannae be faithful."

"Neither can she it seems." He kissed her. "This is all I need. Men who say they need more either have a wife they loathe or are making excuses for their own inability to hold fast to a vow made before God."

"So Sir Edmund—"

"Is naught but a rutting swine. The mon killed three of his own kinsmen for the sake of money. I think that settles the matter of his morals. He doesnae have any."

"Ah, of course. I think it is going to take a wee while before the truth of that truly settles in my mind and heart. 'Tis too horrible, and I think I keep shoving it into some dark corner of my mind."

"Then mayhap I need to fill your poor wee mind with something else," he murmured as he gently pushed her onto her back and settled himself comfortably in her arms.

"And what would that be?" she asked as she looped her arms around his neck.

"Weel, it will depend upon how sore ye are?"

"Oh, the few blows dealt by Sir Fergus dinnae bother me any."

Artan touched the bruise upon her cheek. "I wasnae talking about these abominations."

"Oh." Cecily felt herself blush, but still took a minute to think about how she felt and was a little surprised to find that she did not feel much of anything at all. "Nay, nothing."

"Ah, lass, ye cannae believe how glad I am to hear that."

"I think I am rather pleased myself," she murmured, and slowly eased her hand down over his hard stomach and gently wrapped her fingers around his hardness.

Artan closed his eyes and savored the feel of her soft little hand stroking him. "I was a wee bit worried about hurting ye," he said in an increasingly husky voice.

"Nay as worried as I was," she said, and smiled when he laughed. "What do ye call it?"

"Mine," he replied, and winked at her when she giggled. "And now yours."

Artan proceeded to make love to her. The last time the fear of hurting her had lingered in his heart and mind, controlling him in some ways. Now he could simply make love to her. He quickly discovered that she, too, seemed more at ease now that that hurdle had been leapt. In far too short a time he knew he had to be inside her and sensed that she had reached that point as well.

Turning onto his back, Artan pulled her on top of him. He smiled a little at her look of confusion and then showed her what he wanted. As she eased her body down on his he was sure his face held the same delighted expression as hers did. She quickly learned the perfect way to ride her man, and it was not long before they were both shuddering from the strength of their release. He held her close as she collapsed on top of him, breathing as heavily as he was.

When he felt sleep creeping up on him, he gently set her back on the bed and fetched a cloth to clean them off. Afterward, he climbed back into bed and pulled her into his arms, her back tucked up against his front. He would not be surprised if he soon found it hard to sleep unless she was in his arms like this.

"Is our wedding night over?" she asked in a sleepy voice.

He pressed a kiss to the top of her head. "I fear so, wife. We have both had a verra busy day. Aye, and we had best be returning to our journey ere the sun finishes rising."

Cecily groaned but made no other complaint. "Aye, between ye fighting off an army and me being kidnapped by Sir Fergus and then running away as fast as we could, it has been a verra long day."

"It wasnae exactly an army, although I was hard-pressed. I fear the Donaldsons and the Ogilveys dinnae have too many well-trained fighting men."

"There isnae such a great need for them where I live."

"Weel, it worked in my favor. I am nay sure insulting Sir Fergus as ye did worked in your favor, however."

"Nay, but at first I was just so verra angry. I also thought ye might be dead and, weel, getting angry with him was better than thinking about that. After a slap and a kick, I decided it might be better to temper my words. Then I saw your knife."

"Ye saw it?"

"A wee bit of light glinted off it at first and then I lost it, but by looking verra carefully, I caught sight of it again." She sighed and stroked the arm he had wrapped around her waist to soothe the fear for him that was still too fresh. "I hoped it was ye coming to rescue me if only because it meant ye had survived Sir Fergus's attempts to kill ye yet again. But I felt that anyone trying to slip into his tent so stealthily couldnae mean him any good."

"And that made whoever it was your friend."

"Weel, at least someone who would help me. To keep Sir Fergus from seeing the knife, I kept his attention on me."

"If it hadnae been me ye could have been killed."

"I was so hoping it was ye, but I also hoped that whoever it was might be a thief, but he wouldnae just stand there and let a mon kill a woman. Truth is, I suspected him to slap me or kick me again, nay try to strangle me."

"Weel, ye did tell him that his manhood was the size of a bairn's. Tends to enrage a mon."

"I thought that was a verra good insult. I worked hard to think of that one and have been waiting to use it. I thought up the spineless cretin one right then. It has a nice flavor, so I think I will keep it."

"Ye think up insults?"

"Weel, I am too small to fight anyone and have ne'er learned to use a weapon, so I decided I needed a good supply of insults. Something to make me seem fierce and daring. I also think of them when I am angry but cannae show it. That happened a lot at Dunburn."

He could not help it, he laughed. "'Tis a strange game to play, lass, but there is nay harm in it. And ye do come up with some verra good ones as I recall from that time I took your gag off after I kidnapped ye."

She smiled faintly and closed her eyes. He had laughed but he had not ridiculed her for her somewhat peculiar game. That was a good sign.

Cecily then thought of his vow to be faithful. She desperately wanted to believe in it, and his scorn of men who break their vows made her inclined to. Yet it went against everything she had seen at Dunburn. She hoped it was the truth, that he was different from Sir Edmund and his ilk, for she knew that if he were unfaithful it would crush her.

Artan felt her body grow heavy against his and held her a little tighter. She was a lass with a lot of twists and turns and, he feared, a lot of bruises on her heart. From the things she had said about her life at Dunburn, she had been kept apart from everyone. She had come home, grief-stricken and probably terrorized after seeing her father and brother killed, and been given nothing but criticism, lies, and cold indifference from that day onward. He was surprised she had grown up to be the sweet woman she was.

And now she was his. He would have a marriage before a priest as soon as he was able to arrange it. Handfast was all right, but he wanted her bound to him as tightly as possible. Artan was not sure he understood why that was so important to him, but it was and he accepted it. Cecily Donaldson was his mate and tonight had proved it. He slid his hand up to rest it over her breast and she murmured a sound of pleasure and snuggled closer as he closed his eyes. This was how he wanted to go to sleep every night, he decided and smiled.

Chapter 13

Hot. She was so very, very hot. Cecily woke to find Artan heartily kissing her. Wrapping her arms around his neck, she proceeded to kiss him right back. The feel of his body pressed so close to hers had her trembling with desire. Even after three days of being his wife, she was still astonished by how a man so much bigger and stronger than she was could make her feel so safe and cherished even as he made her wild with need.

She pushed at his shoulders until he rolled onto his back. Cecily was a little surprised at how bold she felt as she sat astride him almost idly rubbing herself against his erection. There was the hint of the coming dawn in the sky, and before the sun rose she fully intended to live out some of the heated dreams she had enjoyed, all of them featuring a naked Artan completely at her mercy. What she wanted to do was shower praise upon that big, strong body of his from his lips all the way down to his long toes. Cecily hoped she did not shock him, but mostly, she hoped he would not try to stop her.

Artan growled softly as Cecily kissed the hollow at the base of his throat. There had been a look of determination upon her face that made him wonder what she intended to do. His little wife was proving to be a very passionate lover, and he was more than willing to let her play her games. When he realized where her kisses were headed, however, his eyes widened and his whole body tensed in anticipation.

The feel of her hair caressing his groin as she kissed her way down his leg made him shudder. By the time she began to kiss her way up his other leg, he was close to demanding that she cease playing with him and give him what he now craved. Only the chance that she was not intending to do that, that she was too innocent to even know he might like it, held him silent. In his entire life he had only been given the pleasure twice, once by Mattie and once because he had paid for it. He could not demand such a thing of his gently bred wife.

When he felt the soft warmth of her lips touch his erection, he trembled as much with relief as with passion. He threaded his hands in her thick hair to hold her there. He attempted to tell her just how much he liked what she was doing but did not think he was very coherent. When she slowly took him into her mouth, he prayed for the control to enjoy this pleasure for a long time. Hours would be nice, he thought a little wildly.

A few moments later he knew he had no control left. He grabbed her beneath her arms and pulled her up his body until she sat astride him. The flush upon her cheeks, the turbulence in her eyes, and the damp heat of her pressing against his manhood told him she had been stirred by loving him, and he wasted no more time before burying himself deep inside her.

It was a long time after their shared release before Artan found the strength to move. He lifted his head enough to look down at the woman sprawled on his chest and grinned. With everything she did Cecily ran the risk of turning him into a very vain fellow. No other woman had ever made him feel so wanted, so handsome, or so desirable. Sir Fergus was a fool. The treasure of the Donaldsons was not chests of gold or rich lands, it was little Cecily. He kissed the top of her head and gently moved her to his side, grinning at the way she blushed and was unable to meet his gaze.

"Ye shouldnae give a mon so much pleasure in the morning, wife," he said as he stood up and stretched, "especially when he must needs have the strength to ride for miles."

Cecily rolled her eyes as she hastily donned her shift, but she inwardly grinned. His words were no soft vows of love and passion, but they soothed all her fear that she had shocked or disgusted him. That pleased her, for she had discovered that feeling such a man trembling beneath her hands and her mouth had stirred her passion in a way she had every intention of enjoying again.

Hurrying away to see to her personal needs, she struggled to subdue that part of her that was disappointed over the lack of love words. It was too soon. She knew she loved Artan, had suspected it long ago, but she also suspected men like Artan were very slow to admit to such feelings. He desired her, would always protect her, spoke to her in such a way that she knew he trusted in her mind, and he made her feel safe. He had also sworn to be faithful. It was foolish to bemoan the fact that he did not proclaim undying love for her. Most women would be in the chapel every day on their knees thanking God for such a husband. Since she had left Dunburn with Artan she had felt stronger and braver. There was no need to be greedy as well.

When she returned to camp, Artan handed her some bread and cheese. She noticed that Thunderbolt was readied for the journey ahead. It suddenly occurred to her that her husband was very efficient and had shown many a skill that had made their journey easier. All part of his training, she supposed. He draped an arm around her shoulders and she looked up to find him grinning at her.

"What has amused ye?" she asked as she accepted the wineskin he offered her and had a drink.

"Nay amused actually," he replied, "just pleased. We shall reach Glascreag ere the sun sets today."

"And no sign of Sir Fergus and his men?"

"None at all; but I doubt he turned tail and ran home. He may nay have as many men with him as he did before, however." He frowned. "Unless he joins with one of the ones about here who wouldnae mind seeing Angus brought low."

"Uncle Angus has enemies, does he?"

"Aye, a few, but dinnae fret. They havenae won against him yet." He gave her a brief kiss, hooked the wineskin onto his saddle, and then lifted her up onto Thunderbolt's back. "I dinnae think any alliance Sir Fergus will make here will last long. E'en our enemies are smart enough to see what a coward and a fool that chinless knight is. It willnae be long before he discovers his allies have slipped away home and left him to his fate. And none of them are any fonder of Lowlanders than Angus is," he added as he swung up into the saddle behind her and took up the reins.

Cecily nearly cursed. "I dinnae understand why ye are all so scornful concerning Lowlanders."

"'Tis simple, wife. They are too akin to the English."

She nearly growled and decided such nonsense deserved no response, so she turned her attention to studying the lands they rode over. There was a beautiful harshness to the scenery. Cecily discovered that she felt a deep appreciation for it even though it looked as if it made the people who lived on it work very hard for their survival. She supposed one reason the Highlanders scorned the Lowlanders was because they lived in a softer, kinder land.

Settling herself comfortably against Artan's chest, Cecily began to wonder about her uncle. She had not seen the man for twelve years. Due to the need of her guardians to keep her and Angus MacReith apart, she had had no contact with him at all. It was sad that her closest kinsman should be a complete stranger to her. She should ask Artan about Angus, she thought, and she would, right after she had a little nap. Having a passionate, demanding husband was exhausting, she thought, smiling faintly as she closed her eyes.

She was smiling in her sleep again, Artan thought as he studied Cecily's face and he grinned. He was still fairly sure he did not want to know what she was smiling about, but he hoped she was having a very good, very passionate dream about him. The way she awoke in the mornings, all warm and eager, made him think she did have dreams about the passion they shared. It would certainly explain what she had done to him this morning.

He was a very lucky man, he decided. His wife made no complaint about day after tedious day of travel. She could peacefully endure long silences, not pestering him to fill every waking moment with talk. It appeared she had completely forgiven him for kidnapping her, even before she found out that he had been telling her the truth about Sir Fergus and the Donaldsons. And then there was her passion, he thought, knowing he was grinning like a very satisfied man. He had never enjoyed a passion as sweet and fierce as the one he shared with her.

There was a shadow on his happiness, however. He had yet to tell her about the bargain Angus had made with him. That was a mistake and he knew it, but he did not know how to fix it. They would be at Glascreag by the end of the day, and he was thinking it might be best to wait until they got there. Perhaps if she could see what they would share it would make it easier for her. He hoped he could think of a way to give her a few hints first, however; a little something that would settle in her mind and not make the truth such a complete shock. That required a guile he was not sure he possessed, not with her, but it was the only idea he had had and he decided to stay with it. When she woke from her nap, he would begin to gently ease her toward the truth.

"It looks a great deal bigger than I remember," Cecily murmured as she caught sight of Glascreag in the distance.

"Usually a child's eyes see things as a great deal larger than they are, and so we are often shocked to see that they arenae so big once we are grown.

Mayhap ye didnae really pay attention until ye were inside the gates."

Cecily laughed. "A verra big possibility." She frowned. "And this is to be left to Malcolm?"

"Aye, he is Angus's closest male kin."

"My memories of Malcolm are verra dim, but I just cannae see him as laird here."

Neither could Artan, and he was hoping she would remember that opinion when she found out the truth. He also hoped she would recall it when he explained that it was the thought of Malcolm becoming the laird that had made him even consider Angus's offer. Making her think of Malcolm as laird had been the only guile he had been able to think of. It was a weak ploy to win her sympathy for both him and Angus when he had to tell her about the bargain, but he had decided that a weak one was better than none at all.

It was as they rode in through the gates of Glascreag that Artan began to feel a touch of panic. A huge crowd had gathered. He would have to get Cecily to their bedchamber as quickly as possible. If he still could not spit out the truth, he would go to Angus's room and tell the man to be silent about the bargain for a little while longer. Artan prayed the old man had not told anyone else about it.

Like Malcolm, he thought as that young man moved toward them through the crowd as Artan dismounted and then helped Cecily down. By the time he had accomplished that Malcolm was standing right in front of them. He could be ignored. When he saw how Malcolm was looking at Cecily, however, he decided that his cousin should be beaten, at least just enough to wipe that lecherous smile off his face.

Just as he stepped toward Malcolm, Artan felt Cecily's hand tighten on his. He sighed and reluctantly halted. Greeting Malcolm by planting a fist in his teeth might make Artan happy, but he knew it would upset Cecily. This was her first time at Glascreag since she was a small child, twelve long years ago, and she was nervous. He would not add to that by turning this meeting with her kinsman into a brawl.

"Malcolm, this is Cecily Donaldson." Artan decided to wait to announce his marriage until he could speak to Angus. If nothing else, Angus would not like it if everyone was told about such an important event before him. "She visited here with her father and wee brother about twelve years ago. She is Angus's niece."

"Ah, aye, I remember. The Lowlander," Malcolm said.

Glancing at his wife, Artan almost laughed. Now she looked like she wanted to hit Malcolm. Cecily was proud of her father and the place where she had grown up despite all the tragedy and problems that had beset her in her own home. She knew, however, that the Highlanders considered it an insult.

"That isnae important now, Malcolm," Artan said. "Now I think Sile would like to clean off the dust of a long journey and mayhap e'en steal a wee rest ere we all gather in the great hall to dine."

"Sile would like to ken why ye introduced me as a Donaldson," she said softly.

"Angus wouldnae like it if we announced our marriage right here in the bailey. He is the laird, ye ken, *and* your uncle."

"Ah, of course. He should most certainly be told first."

Artan hoped she would be so quick to understand

later. Continuing to walk toward the keep, he ordered a man to see to his horse. A few steps later he ordered two youths to bring his saddle packs and Cecily's bag to his bedchamber. He inwardly cursed when he realized why they were grinning so widely as they ran off. As far as they knew, Cecily was just some woman he had brought back to Glascreag. Instead of a proud husband, he was now seen as a rogue. By the time he opened the door to the keep and pulled Cecily inside, it felt as if every MacReith for miles around had tried to talk to him, slowing him down every step of the way.

"I think some of those people were verra anxious to talk to ye, Artan," Cecily said, wondering why she felt Artan was trying to hide her away as quickly as possible. "It might be important. I can wait."

"Nay, lass, if 'twas truly important they would hunt me down. Ye dinnae see anyone charging into the keep after me, do ye?"

"Nay, true enough, and ye are right. If it was truly important, a matter of life and death, they would persist."

"Now, let us get ye to my bedchamber and I will see that a hot bath is readied for ye."

"That would be most welcome. At times I feel as if the dirt and dust of travel has buried itself deep into my skin. And I really should be clean ere I go to visit Uncle Angus in his sick bed."

"He isnae in his sick bed," Artan said, watching the man coming down the stairs with a wary resignation.

"Where has he gone? Oh, Artan, did someone out there tell ye that he has died?"

"Nay, lass, he isnae dead," Artan replied, ruefully admitting that, in a few minutes, he might be heartily wishing that the old man was cold in his grave. Worse, Artan feared his wife might be wishing the same fate for him.

Angus stopped a few steps from the bottom of the stairs. He stared at Cecily and a hint of moisture gleamed in his eyes. He took another step down and touched her hair.

"Ye look just like your mother, lass," he said in a quiet, husky voice. "Aye, ye are my wee Moira reborn."

"Thank ye, Uncle." Cecily could sense a true emotion in the man, a true joy to see her, and she felt a lot of her uncertainties vanish. "I have ne'er had a prettier compliment or a kinder one."

Angus suddenly hopped down and swept her into his arms. Very strong arms for a dying man, she suddenly thought. She glanced at her husband and saw that he was watching Angus with a look of amusement well combined with irritation. She suddenly recalled that Artan had said he had come to fetch her because Angus was dying. Her uncle had obviously been plotting. She knew enough about healing to recognize a strong, healthy man when she saw one.

"Angus, if I could speak to ye for a moment?" Artan asked, clinging to a rapidly dwindling hope that he could yet avoid disaster.

"Later, lad. It can wait."

"Oh, nay, it cannae. I *really* need to talk to ye."

"Ah, to plan the wedding, eh?" Angus slapped Artan on the back and smiled at Cecily.

In an attempt to startle Angus into silence, Artan snapped, "We are already married. We were handfasted in a wee village four days' ride from here.

Now, could we please go somewhere and talk about this?"

"No need to creep away. No shame in a handfast marriage, but I will see it done right, by a priest. Cannae have anyone asking questions about my heir's marriage, can I?"

Cecily frowned. "But, Uncle, Malcolm is your heir. I am married to Artan."

"Aye, I ken it, lass, and that now makes Artan my heir. He and I talked on it ere he went to fetch ye. Now I dinnae have to have Malcolm as my heir." Angus rubbed his hands together in an expression of pure delight. "This cheers an old mon's heart, that it does. I can rest easy kenning that when I am gone a good, strong mon will step into my place and keep Glascreag strong. And e'en better, the bairns ye two make will have more MacReith blood in their veins than any spawn of Malcolm's would." He frowned at Cecily. "Are ye weel, lass? Ye have gone all pale."

"Have I?" she murmured.

Cecily was a little surprised she was still standing and not lying in shards upon the floor. She felt as if she had shattered into hundreds of little sharp pieces. Finally able to move, she slowly looked at Artan. Artan her husband, her lover, her betrayer.

Artan saw the pain in Cecily's eyes and almost embraced her in a desperate attempt to ease it. Only a strong instinct for survival stopped him. "Now, Sile, I can explain this."

"Can ye? Explain what? Did ye speak to Uncle of marrying me in order to be made my uncle's heir?"

He knew there had to be something he could say to soften the hard edges of that question yet still be the truth, but all that came out of his mouth was a hoarse, "Aye."

She had not really thought it possible to hurt any more than she did already. Somehow she was not surprised that Artan found a way to prove her wrong. "And when did ye think ye might tell *me*?"

"Weel, I have been trying to think of a way since the day we left Dunburn, but I couldnae think of the right words."

"Nay, I suspicion 'tis difficult to ask a lass, 'Please marry me because I really wish to be a laird.'"

"It wasnae like that."

"Nay? Ye lied to me."

"I didnae lie. I just didnae tell ye all the truth." He could tell by the look in her eyes that that sounded as bad to her as it did to him.

Cecily leaned toward him and said quietly, "Sometimes, Sir Artan, nay telling the truth is as near to telling a lie as to make no difference at all. I believe this is one of those times." She straightened up, turned toward the stairs, and started to climb them, wondering why it felt as if she were climbing a mountain. "If ye would excuse me, I believe I shall go to *my* bedchamber to bathe and rest."

Artan did not like the sound of that *my*. "I will join ye later."

"Nay, if ye wish to sit in a laird's chair."

"I think your wee wife just threatened ye," said Angus, smiling faintly.

"Aye, she did." Artan sighed. At a complete loss as to what to do, he turned to Angus. "Ye and I need to go to the solar and talk. There is a lot ye need to know."

"Arenae ye going to go and soothe the lass?"

"I think I will give her temper some time to cool first."

Several hours had passed before Artan found the courage to go up to his bedchamber, the one that Cecily had claimed for her own. He cautiously opened the door, faintly relieved that she had not locked it against him, and called out her name. He ducked just in time to avoid being hit square in the face by a large ewer. It hit the door he crouched in front of and shattered, soaking him with the water it had held. Artan quickly retreated even as he wondered how she had managed to hurl a full ewer of water at his head and spill so little of the water. Maybe a night of sleeping alone would make Cecily willing to listen to him.

Cecily stared at the door her lying, betraying slug of a husband had just fled through. She had spent hours all alone crying until her chest hurt. Now she was angry, at him and at herself. She had been foolish enough to think he had wanted her, just her, and that there was little gain in his marrying her, and all that time he had been thinking of becoming the laird of Glascreag. Until she got her raging emotions under control, she did not want to see him or talk with him. She knew all too well how easily he could sway her back to his side, and she would not play the fool again. She needed to stay away from his silvery blue eyes and his strong body until she found the strength to treat his words and kisses with the cynicism they so richly deserved.

She also needed time to build a few more layers of ice around her poor, shattered heart.

Chapter 14

"Ye should have told her."

"I ken it," snapped Artan, glaring at Angus, who sat in the laird's chair at the head of the table and looked remarkably healthy for a man who had claimed to be dying only a few weeks ago.

"I am nay sure what she is so upset about," said Bennet as he spread a thick layer of honey on his bread. "Shouldnae she be pleased that she can bring ye such a fine dowry?"

"Ye would think so," said Artan, pleased to find that someone thought as he did. "But I had guessed that she wouldnae think that way and should have told her all about Angus's bargain days ago." Right after they had become handfasted and he had made her his, and thus could be certain she would not run away.

Barring him from their bedchamber for two days was almost as bad, he decided as he scowled up at the ceiling of the great hall. The first night he had tried to go in and talk to her, she had thrown a ewer at his head and he had quickly retreated, deciding to give her time to let her anger cool. Last night, she had thrown a rock at him, and suspecting she had slipped outside and collected a pile of them, he had retreated again. Surely after two nights alone she should have calmed down, he thought, but he was hesitant to go up the stairs and test her temper yet again.

"Mayhap ye can go up and talk to her," he said to Angus, who was filling his plate with more food than any sick man ought to be able to choke down. "Ye could put in a kind word for me ere ye return to your deathbed." He almost grinned at the guilty look that passed over Angus's face but struggled not to laugh along with his cousin Bennet.

"Ye were gone so long I had plenty of time to heal and regain my strength," muttered Angus.

"Of course. Weel? Ye are the one who was so eager for this marriage and 'tis that fool bargain ye wanted that has caused all this trouble. Why dinnae ye go and speak to her?"

"I have tried, but every time I try to speak about ye, she threatens to geld me."

When both Bennet and Angus hooted with laughter Artan fought the urge to get up and knock their heads together. It was not really Cecily's anger that troubled him so, but the hurt he knew lay beneath it. He was haunted by the look that had settled on her face when Angus had blurted out the truth. He knew she felt as if he had betrayed her again, and he needed to talk to her before that belief settled in too hard and fast.

"Just go up there, take her to bed, and soothe her feelings with a few pretty words," said Bennet.

"Before or after she knocks me cold with a rock or another ewer?" Artan shook his head. "Nay, I need to explain things and I cannae do that whilst dodging rocks and crockery. She has verra good aim, too."

"Ye sound almost proud of that."

"Aye, I am, and I ken that I deserve this anger. Recall all she has just escaped from."

"Ye would ne'er hurt her. Ye would ne'er hurt any lass."

"Oh, she kens that I am no threat to her, nay in that way. Ne'ertheless, I should have thought more on all she has been through and made better choices. Whilst I slept in my cold bed last night—"

"Should have put more peat on the fire," murmured Angus.

Artan ignored that and continued, "I thought on how I would feel if I stood in her shoes. 'Tis a hard blow to one's pride. I am nay sure how women abide it."

Angus snorted. "Do ye think women ne'er wed for fortune or land? Aye, some of them may wish to wed for love or passion, but most wed for name, bloodlines, alliances, money, or strength. And they arenae all forced to do so either. Neither of my wives were." He frowned. "I have always been of two minds about it all. 'Twould be a fine thing if everyone could just marry who they chose to or their heart told them to. Yet, 'tis also a fine thing to unite lands or clans, make alliances, and fatten one's purse. The lass kens the way of things. I think this temper is just because she thought she was chosen by the heart and nay the purse. Ye just need to remind her of these hard truths."

"Those hard truths should have been discussed long before now. By nay telling her of the bargain, I let her think there was no gain for me in this marriage and thus let her think, weel, other things. I must needs apologize for that, but I cannae e'en do that if she willnae e'en talk to me."

"Ye could always try talking to her from behind the safety of the door."

"Aye, 'tis a thought although, I dinnae like the idea of everyone being able to hear all I have to say." He grimaced. "Nay, especially when 'tis me who is in the wrong. Hard enough admitting that to one's woman." He had to smile when both men nodded vigorously in agreement.

"Better that than nay being able to say it at all."

"She cannae hold on to her anger for much longer." Artan hated that hint of doubt that crept into his voice.

Angus shrugged. "She is a stubborn lass," he said with a distinct touch of fondness in his voice.

Artan finished his wine and stood up. He was desperate enough to try it. The idea of sleeping alone again gave him the courage. It was not as if the whole clan was not already aware of this feud between him and his wife. He supposed he ought to be angry with her for that, but he was far too aware of how this was mostly his own fault. At the door of the great hall he looked back at Angus.

"Any sign of Sir Fergus yet?" he asked.

"Nay, but I am keeping a close eye out for the swine," Angus replied.

"Weel, I hope ye do a better job of that than ye did of seeing how many rocks my wife collected when ye took her for a walk yesterday." He nodded at Angus's look of guilt, his curiosity about where his wife had gathered all those rocks now satisfied.

All the way up the steep, narrow stairs Artan thought about what he could say to Cecily. He had not told Angus, but he had the suspicion that

Cecily truly cared for him, might even be coming to love him. It would explain why she had looked so utterly devastated when she had learned about his bargain with Angus. The idea that she might love him pleased him immensely, but it also meant that the blow dealt to her by what she saw as his betrayal would take a lot more than pretty words and love-making to heal. He was beginning to think he was a lot better at the latter than he had thought he was, but he knew he had absolutely no skill at the former. It might be an idea to practice some as Cecily practiced insults.

Not that she needed any more, he thought as he stopped in front of their bedchamber door and heard her yell, "Ye are midden slime! Ye are a boil on Satan's arse!"

That was followed by a thud and what sounded like pathetic whining. Artan cautiously opened the door and looked inside. He quickly stepped in and shut the door behind him, all the while watching his tiny, pretty wife beat Malcolm's head against the floor. After a moment of enjoying that sight, he noticed she had a tear at the shoulder of her gown and suddenly understood why she was beating Malcolm senseless. Fury rose in him and then just as quickly fled. Malcolm had a bloody nose and was flailing about in a weak attempt to get a tiny, furious woman off his back. Such humiliation was probably punishment enough, although Artan thought the man would be wise to leave Glascreag as soon as possible and intended to tell him so. He had no doubt that Angus would back him on that.

"When my husband finds out what ye tried to do he is going to gut ye, slowly, and feed your entrails to the swine!"

"I think we will have to let him recover a wee bit first, Sile mine," said Artan as he lifted his wife off Malcolm's back and set her at his side.

Malcolm turned over, looked up at Artan, and turned so white Artan was afraid he might swoon. "She misunderstood!" he said, staggering to his feet. "I wasnae . . . I didnae . . ."

"Leave."

When Artan shut the door behind a fleeing Malcolm and turned to face her, Cecily was suddenly all too aware of the fact that she was alone in a bedchamber with her lying, betraying slug of a husband. She was not ready for this, but she was unable to move to get anything to throw at him. Her legs were shaking and the tremor seemed to be spreading to the rest of her body. When Artan strode over to her, picked her up in his arms, and sat down in the large chair by the fire, she gave him a disgusted look before she settled herself more comfortably in his lap.

"Did he hurt ye, wife?" Artan asked as he rubbed her back, pleased to feel the trembling in her body was already easing.

"Nay, he tore my gown a wee bit 'tis all." She shuddered. "He also tried to kiss me."

"Only tried, eh? Pushed him away, did ye?"

"Nay, I rammed my knee into his—"

"Ah, aye, I understand. Ye dinnae need to tell me any more. Explains why he had an odd gait when he ran away." He began to stroke her hair, subtly undoing the thick braid. "When I realized what he had tried to do, I had thought to throw him against the wall a few times; but then I decided being pinned down by a wee lass and having your head slammed into the floor was humiliating for even a mon like

Malcolm and that was punishment enough. Howbeit, if ye wish, I could hunt him down and break a few bones."

"Verra kind of ye, but it isnae really necessary. I dinnae believe he will try that again."

Artan slowly shook his head and frowned. "I confess I am a wee bit surprised at this."

"Weel, he is a verra angry mon at the moment. He isnae the heir anymore."

"And what does that have to do with you?"

"I am the heir's wife and I will give the heir his own heirs. Malcolm had a plan to make ye suffer by getting me with child. Ye would have to claim it as your own since we are wed, and then he will have made ye lose all ye stole from him."

"He is mad."

"I believe I told him that. It didnae seem a particularly weel thought-out plan. Also told him that if he is so set on having his spawn be claimed as heir, then why didnae we just meander down to the swine pen as there was a new brood of piglets born today and he could have his pick." She grimaced while Artan laughed. "That was when he tore my dress."

"Was that one of those insults ye have been saving for just the right time?"

"Nay, I thought that one up on the spot. It appears that the more one uses insults the easier they are to think up quickly."

Cecily knew she ought to move. She was calm again. It was just this sort of thing she had been trying to avoid over the past few days. Yet, she could not find the strength to leave his arms, not even when she felt him begin to unlace her gown.

"What are ye doing?" she asked, telling herself

that enjoying the light caress of his fingers on the back of her neck was no threat to her determination to keep a distance from him, that she could walk away from him at any time.

"I thought I had best see if he left any bruises that might require a salve." Artan bit back a grin when she made a soft sound of exasperation and he knew she was rolling her eyes.

"I think I left more bruises on him."

Artan tugged on the bodice of her gown until her shoulder was bared, then kissed it. "I have missed ye," he said softly as he tugged gently on her hair until her head tilted back a little and he kissed her forehead.

"Stop it," Cecily said in a breathless voice that carried no threat of command.

"Ah, Sile, my Sile, ye dinnae mean that."

"I do. I must. Ye lied to me," she added in a tearful whisper, the ice she had tried to wrap around her heart too thin to completely smother the pain.

"Hush, sweet." Artan kissed her cheeks, cleaning away the slow tears with his kisses. "Aye, I lied. It felt better to just say I hadnae told ye the truth yet. But, ye are right, it was just a lie by another name."

"Ye married me to become Angus's heir. Ye want to be the laird of Glascreag."

"Ye would ne'er believe me if I denied wanting to the laird here." He eased her bodice down until it rested at her small waist, then began to unlace her shift. "Name me a mon who wouldnae want to be a laird, wouldnae want to hold a place like Glascreag. Howbeit, I didnae marry ye for it." He slid his hand inside her shift and pressed his cheek against the top of her head as he savored the feel of her soft breast filling his hand, the taut nipple teasing his palm.

"There, I can think better now." He was sure he heard a small choke of laughter, but he ignored it.

For a brief moment Cecily had tensed when he had put his hand on her breast. That resistance faded at the first light caress of his long fingers. She told herself she was just being accommodating because he was talking freely about the problem between them. Deep inside she had the feeling it was mostly because she had missed his touch.

Even as she cried over how he had hurt her with his lie, it was his arms she wanted to be enfolded in to seek the comfort she so badly needed. That weakness alone was enough to make her want to cry some more. The way he was holding her now with one hand lightly stroking her breast, touching soft, fleeting kisses over her face, and idly caressing her neck or shoulder with the fingers of his other hand was so gentle, so loving in so many ways, that, too, brought tears to her eyes. It seemed just about anything could make her cry lately, but she knew the real reason for the tears. No matter what reason she gave herself, they were shed for the loss of her dream, the foolish dream that this strong, handsome man had wanted her enough to marry her despite the fact that she could not say for sure if she had any dowry at all. The dream that had her believing she could trust in him, in his word, and in his passion.

"I am now going to tell ye the whole tale of this bargain from the verra beginning," he said and did.

Cecily frowned when he finished his tale at the point where he had ridden away from Glascreag. It all sounded so reasonable, and even though she had known him for only a few days, so very much like something her uncle would do. In their talks she had also become very aware that her uncle was desperate for an heir, an heir that was not Malcolm. She could see the truth in all Artan said, yet she was terrified to believe him. She could not bear the pain betrayal brought, not again.

Artan cupped her face in his hands. "Lass, it was wrong of me to keep the bargain a secret. I ken it now, and I kenned it from the beginning."

"Then why didnae ye tell me?"

"Because I didnae think ye would marry me if ye kenned the truth. I was sure ye would ne'er believe that I no intention of marrying just to be made Angus's heir. I told him that, and I swear that is the truth. Most people marry for some sort of gain, e'en if it is just a goat. I have naught. I am a second son, the last born of twins. But no one in my family weds only for gain. There is always more, if only because we believe in vows said. Since we do and we ken we will be tied body and soul to the one we wed, there has to be more. 'Tis why I tried to make it verra clear to Angus that I would have to come to ken who ye were, what ye were like, ere I would do it. If I hadnae wanted ye, I would have simply tried to get ye to come to Glascreag to see Angus."

Cecily sighed and leaned against him. It all made sense, but she remained uncertain. She suspected that would be true for quite a while. She had been surrounded by lies and secrets too much to be too trusting anymore. She knew that was not fair to Artan, but her wounded heart was not particularly interested in fairness at the moment. It was interested only in protecting itself from more pain.

"Nay, I shouldnae have assumed anything."

"I let that happen by nay telling ye the truth, and I am sorry for that. Yet, what I am trying to say is that it is not just the lairdship or Glascreag that has made me your husband, lass. Ye must ken that there is more between us than that; that more than land and e'en Angus's wishes bind us."

She nodded slowly. "Aye, how could there not be after all we have been through."

"So am I allowed back into your bed?"

"Is that one of the things that binds us, Artan?"

"Could ye think otherwise?" He tilted her face up to his and gave her a slow, gentle kiss.

"And ye think passion is enough to hold us together?"

"'Tis a verra fine beginning, and I really dinnae like sleeping all alone in a cold bed."

"Ye could always put a bit more peat on the fire." She sat up and frowned at him when he started laughing. "It wasnae that funny."

"Angus said the same thing when I complained about my cold bed."

Cecily grimaced. "Oh dear. I am nay sure I like the fact that I say the same things Angus does."

Still laughing, Artan carried her over to the bed and set her on her feet. He rapidly divested her of her clothes, ignoring her blushes. As he tossed aside the last of her clothes, she scrambled into the bed. He grinned, quickly shed all his clothes, and climbed in beside her. Taking her into his arms, he savored the feel of her soft warmth pressed close to his body and sighed with satisfaction.

"This is where ye belong, lass. This is how it should always be."

There was such sincerity in his voice, she knew she could trust in this. Artan wanted to be in her arms at night. At the end of the day, he wanted to be able to curl up with her beneath the blankets. It was a start.

Although she now held fast to a wariness that would be slow to leave her, she was willing to try again. He was right to remind her that few of their ilk married just because they wanted to. Lands, alliances, and coin were always involved. She found that she did believe that Artan would not marry her for gain alone, and she told herself she should count her blessings. No matter how she felt, there was one fact she could not argue: He was her husband and she belonged in his bed, not greeting him at the bedchamber door with ewers and rocks hurled at his head. Many another husband would feel that reason enough to beat her.

Wrapping her arms around his neck, she kissed him. Even though they had slept apart for only two nights, Cecily quickly found out that she was starved for the taste of him. He acted as if he was equally starved for the taste of her. He pushed her onto her back and crouched over her, studying her body intently as he smoothed his hands over her. She felt as if he was reacquainting himself with her body, and that only stirred her blood even more.

Their lovemaking soon grew wild, each of them acting as if they had been deprived of the other for months instead of just two nights. When they finally came together the ride was fast and furious, their cries blending in the room as they reached the heights together. The way Artan collapsed on top of her and slightly to the side so that he did not put his full weight on her made him appear to be as boneless as she felt.

"Now, do ye really think it was only Glascreag that I was thinking of when I married ye?" Artan asked as he inched his head over and let it rest more comfortably on her breasts. "I missed my pillows," he murmured.

Cecily smiled and idly ran her hand up and down his back. "Nay, I guess there were one or two other things on your mind." She frowned up at the ceiling. "'Tis odd how that happened. I had ne'er e'en been properly kissed, and yet within four days of meeting ye I am creeping out of the keep and meeting ye down at the burn."

"Ah, fine as that was, mayhap we shouldnae speak of it."

"Why not?"

"Weel, I have just gotten ye to stop hurling things at me, I am nay sure I want ye to think too much on the other time ye were angry with me."

Smiling, she kissed the top of his head. "I didnae believe ye, so of course I was angry when ye tied me up and carried me away from my home. E'en before Sir Fergus confirmed all ye had said, I had begun to believe at least some of it. I also felt sure that ye believed it all, and how could I fault ye when ye truly felt ye were keeping me safe."

"I didnae do such a grand job of it, did I. The bastard got hold of ye."

She shrugged. "And ye rescued me. What I was trying to say is that complete innocence didnae save me from ye. It or this, whatever it is, was there from the start."

"Good. I was eager from the start, too."

She giggled when he briskly nuzzled her breasts, but then sighed. "He is going to come here after me, isnae he?"

"I suspicion he will, aye. There is a heavy purse he is hungering for."

"So I will be bringing trouble right to my uncle's gates."

"It has been there before."

"Aye, but that wasnae my trouble."

"And neither is this." Artan raised himself up on his elbows and kissed her. "This is all about greed. Sir Fergus's greed. Ye didnae ask to be betrothed to the fool. Nay, everyone involved in this is just tossing ye about to get what they want."

"Ye do ken how to make a lass feel so much better about things," she drawled.

Artan gave her an exaggerated grimace. "Sorry."

"No need to be. It is just the truth."

"Why do I have the feeling that, in some ways, ye have included me in that number."

Cecily knew her face revealed the sudden guilt she felt. "I dinnae want to and I certainly dinnae think of ye as akin to them. 'Tis just that discovering I have been surrounded by lies and deceit for so long and didnae have the wit to see it has made me question everything."

"As it should." He smiled when she looked at him in surprise. "I take no insult, lass. 'Tis my own fault that I dinnae have your full trust. Nay, I am just made determined to see that ye come to trust me again."

That should not make her nervous, Cecily told herself; then Artan kissed her and she found it hard to think. The fact that he could do that to her was one reason she knew she ought to be cautious. But as she wrapped her arms around him, she decided that in this there was some truth. He could no more hide his desire than she could, and although they were still new lovers, she had already learned that she had as much power over him as he did over her.

Chapter 15

Artan held Cecily closer, nuzzled her neck, and tried to ignore the banging on the bedchamber door. He had Cecily back where she belonged and he was eager for some morning delight. He slid his hand up her ribs and caressed her breast, grinning when she murmured huskily and rubbed her lovely backside against his groin. This was how a man should always greet the new day.

"Curse it, Artan!" yelled Bennet. "Get your arse out of bed! They are here!"

It took Artan a minute to understand the importance of that statement. Then, with a curse, he leaped out of bed and started to dress. A quick glance at the bed revealed that Cecily had already gotten out of bed and donned her shift. She looked pale and a little frightened and he tried to think of something comforting to say as he finished dressing.

"Does he have any Highlanders with him?" he asked Bennet, waiting until Cecily had her gown on before he opened the door.

"The MacIvors," Bennet answered even as Artan opened the door.

Cursing softly, Artan buckled on his sword. When Cecily stepped up beside him, he yanked her into his arms and kissed her. The fact that Sir Fergus had ruined his morning pleasure only made Artan even more eager to kill the fool. He set Cecily away from him, saw the fear still lingering in her eyes, and lightly stroked her cheek with his fingers.

"The MacIvors are enemies of Angus's?" she asked.

"Aye," replied Artan, "but Sir Fergus willnae find them verra good allies. They dinnae truly hate Angus, ye ken, but they do covet Glascreag. I suspicion they think they might use these Lowlanders to help them get these lands."

"They will soon find out they have made a verra poor choice," said Bennet.

"Aye, that they will. Do ye ken who Crooked Cat is, lass?"

Cecily nodded, "Angus has introduced me to nearly everyone in the keep."

"Go to her. She is the one who will be readying the women to do their part."

"Aye, I will find her. Ye will be careful, willnae ye, Artan?" she asked softly, fighting the urge to cling to him.

"Wheesht, this wee scuffle will be o'er and done ere the sun sets." He gave her a quick, hard kiss and strode out of the room to make his way to the walls with Bennet.

As Cecily finished dressing and braided her hair, she told herself to be brave. Artan was a warrior. It was why Angus wanted him to follow him as laird of Glascreag. The wife of a warrior had to be strong and support her husband, not weigh him down with tears and fear. She could not give in to the urge to crawl beneath the bedcovers and pray until the fighting was over. Cecily was determined not to shame Artan with any show of weakness.

She found Crooked Cat in the kitchens barking out orders to the women gathered there. It took a moment for the old woman to see that Cecily was standing there. After she looked Cecily over carefully, her rheumy eyes surprisingly sharp, she ordered Cecily to a table set in the far corner of the kitchen.

"Ye are to cut these into bandages," she ordered, setting a pile of old linens on the table along with a very sharp knife. "And when ye are done with these I have some herbs for ye to grind up."

"Are ye sure this is all ye wish me to do?" It was not a very exacting chore, not something Cecily thought a warrior's wife should do.

Crooked Cat leaned closer and lightly patted Cecily's cheek with her somewhat gnarled, calloused hand. "Ye are a new wife, lassie."

"Aye," she agreed, unable to hide her confusion, "although I dinnae ken why that matters."

"It matters. Ye havenae been hardened to the way of it all yet."

"Oh." She sighed. "I am nay sure I will e'er be hardened to the fact that men seem compelled to swing swords at each other."

The old woman laughed. "Aye, fools that they are, but e'en if they set down their swords, some other fools would quickly pick them up and probably take a swing at the ones who put them down. Our men do it to protect Glascreag and us, and that is no small thing, aye?"

"Aye," Cecily agreed and picked up some of the linen. "I will do this then, but I do have a skill at healing, ye ken. 'Tis the one thing I was taught to do and I am good at it."

After glancing around to make sure everyone was doing as they had been told, Crooked Cat looked back at Cecily and asked, "What do ye mean it was the only thing ye were taught?"

"My guardians didnae really teach me how to run a household for reasons I am nay sure I will e'er be told or understand. Howbeit, Lady Anabel considered the healing arts a lowly thing, fit only for peasants to learn."

"Ah, I see. She thought to shame ye."

Cecily found she could actually smile about it. "Aye, so I was always verra careful to ne'er let her ken how much I enjoyed it all. So, if ye need help tending to any wounds——"

"I will send for ye right quick."

After the woman hurried away, Cecily began to cut the linen into strips fit for bandages. At the moment, tucked away in the corner of the kitchens was probably the best place for her. It meant she could not see the men preparing for battle or see what force confronted them. She had told Crooked Cat the truth. She doubted she would ever be truly hardened to the fact that Artan would be facing men who sought to kill him, now and all the other times he might have to go to battle. She could only pray that she could hide her fear and thank God that Angus had taught him well.

Artan stood on the walls between Angus and Bennet and scowled down at the men gathered before the walls of Glascreag. He noticed some of the MacIvors arguing vigorously with some of the

Ogilveys. The way some of the men kept pointing in the direction of the village told him they were arguing its fate. He suspected the MacIvors were arguing against burning it since it was their hope that they would soon take Glascreag and they would not want to have to rebuild too much. Since all the villagers and a great deal of their livestock were already within Glascreag's walls, Artan was not terribly concerned. They had rebuilt the village before and could do it again if they needed to.

"I would guess that old MacIvor has left his lands verra lightly guarded," drawled Angus.

"Mayhap we should try to send out a runner to inform the Duffs," said Artan.

Angus laughed. "Aye, 'twould serve Old MacIvor weel to stagger home after trying to steal my lands only to find he has lost his own to Ian Duff. Is that fool on the white horse Sir Fergus?"

Looking at the man riding toward them on a big white horse, Artan nodded. "'Tis him, and from what I can see he was in sore need of the MacIvors, as it appears that nearly half of the Donaldsons have deserted him."

After glaring down at the man reining in near the wall, Angus grumbled. "He has no chin. What fool thought to wed a MacReith lass to a mon whose neck seems to start at his mouth?"

Recalling Cecily saying much the same about Sir Fergus, Artan laughed softly. Angus may have had nothing to do with the raising of Cecily, but there was a strong hint of the man in her. He suspected Angus recognized that strong touch of MacReith blood in her and was heartily pleased.

It pleased Artan, too. Cecily might well have been raised in the Lowlands by a pair of thieving, murdering wretches, but she had the soul and spirit of a true Highland lass. She was also completely untainted by Anabel and Edmund's complete lack of morals, their selfishness and cruelty. In keeping Cecily so apart from their family and friends, the Donaldsons had actually done Cecily a great service. Recalling the faint scars on Cecily's slim back, however, Artan still wanted to see them hang.

"I have come to collect my betrothed bride," Sir Fergus called up to them.

"I dinnae suppose we can just kill him here and have done with it," muttered Angus.

"Dinnae tempt me." Artan glared down at the man he so ached to kill. "Ye have no bride here, so I suggest ye turn about and ride on home ere someone hurts ye."

"Cecily Donaldson is promised to me and ye stole her from me, right on the eve of her wedding!"

"Actually, I believe it was ten days before her wedding. But let us nay quibble o'er such things as how many days and whether or nay ye are the rutting swine your banners proclaim. There is but one truth that should concern us: Cecily is my wife. Ye yourself heard us declare it."

"I heard no such thing."

"I feared ye might say that, so we handfasted again in a wee village before three witnesses who have put their mark on a document. So, dry your tears and trot home."

"Nay, Cecily Donaldson was promised to me and I mean to have her. If ye havenae the sense and honor to send her out to me, her betrothed husband, then we shall kick down these gates and drag her out."

"Kick away," called Angus.

"Is that really a rutting swine on those banners?" Bennet asked as he joined Artan in watching an obviously furious Sir Fergus ride away.

"A rampant boar actually," replied Artan as he wondered if they would have a battle or be trapped for days just staring at each other and occasionally trading insults over the walls.

Artan was abruptly pulled from his dark thoughts about the tediousness of a siege by the sounds of pigs. It took him a moment to realize it was coming from the Glascreag men gathered on the walls. Bennet had obviously spread the word of what was on Sir Fergus's banner. It was a good taunt, he decided.

It did not take long for Artan to see just what a good taunt it was. An enraged Sir Fergus decided to plunge right into battle. Or, more specifically, order his men to plunge into battle while he sat at a safe distance on his big white horse shouting commands and ordering them to try harder. It soon became clear that Laird MacIvor did not approve of this abrupt attack and had given his men permission to hold back or join in the fight if they chose to. Few chose to fight in what was clearly an ill-planned assault on well-defended walls. As Artan threw himself into the hard work of sheltering from volleys of arrows and defending Glascreag's walls, he wondered just how long it would be before Sir Fergus's own men decided their was no honor in dying for a fool and a coward, a man who recklessly wasted their lives, and turned on the man.

"M'lady, Crooked Cat says to come and show her just how good ye are at healing," called a young girl from the door of the kitchen.

Before Cecily could respond the girl was gone. She set aside the herbs she had been preparing and hurried to the great hall that had already been prepared for tending to whatever wounded there were. Even in the far corner of the kitchen she had heard when the battle began. The cold fear that had flooded her body was still there. It was impossible not to think of how her husband and her uncle were out there on the walls in the way of arrows and swords.

She was horrified when she first stepped into the great hall. There was the scent of blood and sweat in the air, and there were a lot of men already gathered there waiting to have their wounds tended to. By the time she reached Crooked Cat's side, however, Cecily had begun to see that most of the wounds were small ones caused primarily by protecting oneself from a shower of arrows or being grazed by them. A few men had more serious wounds, but only two of them looked as if they might not recover from their hurts.

"Just how good at healing are ye, lass?" Crooked Cat asked Cecily.

"The wise woman in our village said I was very good, mayhap e'en better than she," Cecily replied, blushing for she sounded rather vain.

"And she was good was she?"

"Aye, people would travel miles just to see her."

"Weel, then, ye best come with me."

The moment they reached the young man stretched out on one of the tables lining the great hall, Cecily heartily wished she had not boasted of her skills. He had three arrow wounds and one looked to have just missed his heart. One arrow remained in his body, sticking out of his thigh. She recognized the work of the Donaldson fletcher.

"I am a wee bit afeared of taking that one out," confessed Crooked Cat, speaking quietly so that others nearby could not overhear her. "He could bleed to death, aye?"

Cecily carefully studied the placement of the arrow. It was high up on the youth's thigh and had gone all the way through. The young man was tall and almost too lean, and she was glad of that even if he probably was not. It meant, however, that she would not have to push the arrow all the way through, a necessity sometimes, but one she hated. It did look as if it was near a place where it could make a man *bleed out,* as Tall Lorna had called it.

"I would think that if that arrow had struck the place where the blood can flow as swiftly as it does from a cut throat, he would already be dead," she told Crooked Cat in a soft voice.

"Aye, ye may be right." Crooked Cat reached for the arrow to pull it out, then looked at Cecily in surprise when the younger woman stopped her. "I thought ye meant that the arrow could come out now."

"It can, but the head of it needs to be cut off or whate'er damage it did going in will be dangerously added to as it comes out."

For a moment Crooked Cat leaned over the young man to study the part of the arrow tip sticking out of him. "Aye, I can see it now. Makes sense. Suspicion ye could e'en risk hitting something it missed as it went in. So, now what do we do?"

After hastily washing her hands, Cecily showed her. She had a big, broad-shouldered woman called Mags hold the youth still as she pushed the arrow in until the point was completely clear of the body, then cut it off. Careful to clean the area around the shaft of all cloth and dirt, she then had Crooked Cat yank the shaft back out. To her relief, although the wound bled freely, it was not the pulsing flood that could so quickly drain the life from a man. With Crooked Cat's help, she stitched and bandaged the wound and then checked his other wounds to be certain that they, too, were clean. As they left him in the care of a young girl who was obviously infatuated with the boy, Cecily paused to wash her hands again before they reached the next man who needed his wounds tended.

"Why do ye keep washing?" Crooked Cat asked.

"Trying to keep your hands and the wounds clean seems to help in the healing."

"Is that what your wise woman told ye?"

"Aye, she was teaching me that no good healer e'er ignores what others say about healing. She told me that she used to, that she would decide they were all fools and she would do things just as her mother had taught her. Then she heard about how keeping her hands and the wounds clean might help hold back fevers and infections. She scoffed at that; but then something happened to make her think it might just do that e'en if no one could tell her why.

"She was called to aid a woman who was giving birth. 'Twas just after she had had the bath she takes every month." Cecily ignored the way Crooked Cat shook her head and muttered her astonishment over anyone taking a bath so often. "As she told me, she was oftimes verra concerned about getting dirt on herself for a few days after her bath, and when she arrived at this woman's house, she carefully scrubbed off the dirt that had gotten on her hands from hurriedly collecting a few herbs. The woman having the bairn was complaining bitterly about the bairn deciding to come right then, right after she had bathed and cleaned her house and all her linens. It seems an important member of her family was about to come to visit."

"So they were both verra clean; but women have bairns all the time and many dinnae die of the birthing fever."

"True, but this particular woman proved to be having a verra difficult birth. The bairn needed turning." She nodded when Crooked Cat gasped. "Tall Lorna said both she and the woman kenned the possibility of the woman getting the birthing fever or worse and dying from what needed to be done, and that there were healers and others who say ye shouldnae try to turn the bairn in the womb, that women arenae sheep or mares, but Tall Lorna says they are fools. She did it and the woman had a fine son."

"And the woman?"

"Lived. There was ne'er a problem, ne'er a hint of fever. Tall Lorna decided she would try a few more births and healings whilst being careful to keep herself, her hands, the wounds, and all as clean as she could."

"And?"

"Her fame spread, for her successes increased tenfold or more."

Crooked Cat stared at her hands and frowned. "Do ye ken those Murray lads are always clean and willnae let me tend their hurts until I have washed my hands. A lot of the women in their clan are gifted healers, too." She nodded to a big, heavily bearded man sitting on a bench and holding a rag to a wound in his arm. "There is an easy one to tend to. I will be right back."

By the time Crooked Cat returned to her side Cecily was tying a bandage over the man's stitched and cleaned wound and Crooked Cat's hands had been vigorously scrubbed clean. It was not until a little while later that Cecily realized the woman had ordered the other women to keep their hands clean, as well as the wounds they tended to. The men who returned to the walls not only had clean wounds and a clean bandage, but quite often a wide clean patch of skin on an otherwise dirty body.

As the day dragged on, Cecily caught only fleeting glimpses of Artan. Once, she saw her uncle and Artan standing shoulder to shoulder on the wall deep in discussion. The sight eased the last of her hurt over Angus's bargain with Artan, over how her marriage to Artan would make him Angus's heir. Artan may have only a little MacReith blood in his veins, but he was Angus's son in many ways, including in his love for Glascreag. All her marriage did was make him fully acceptable to those who might offer a complaint about Angus's choice and silence any who might be moved to support Malcolm's claim. She should have been told of the bargain, but the fact that she had not been was no great crime. In truth, watching Angus and Artan work together to defend Glascreag made her feel that it had righted a wrong and put the right man at Angus's side as the heir to all he had built.

Something Sir Fergus was trying to destroy, she thought angrily. The fact that this was all happening because Sir Fergus was a greedy man who wanted part of a wealth that he had no rights to made her even angrier at him. The man had no feeling for her. She did not know why Sir Fergus did not just return to Dunburn and use his knowledge to bleed Anabel and Edmund of a fortune. He was acting like a spoiled child who did not really care about what he had been denied, only that someone had said *nay*.

She went to see how the youth with the three arrow wounds was doing and was pleased to see that he had not yet grown feverish. That was a very good sign. In fact, despite Glascreag being vigorously attacked twice, only two men had died. Cecily moved on to tend to a gash a young boy had gained when shoved against a wall by his father just as another torrent of arrows fell into the bailey. As Crooked Cat fed the boy a sweet, Cecily bathed his wound and prayed that this would all end soon and end with Sir Fergus dead and his men fleeing for home as fast as they could.

"The mon is verra weel supplied," said Angus as he wiped the sweat from his face with a wet rag.

"I suspicion some of that is due to allying himself with Laird MacIvor, but, aye, he *is* weel supplied. There is one thing he will soon grow verra short of if he doesnae change his ways, and that is men."

"And MacIvor willnae give him many of his if the fool refuses to change the way he fights."

Frowning down at the people collecting the arrows shot over the walls by Sir Fergus's army, Artan was surprised that the number of dead was so low. There was, however, a lot of wounded. Soon the spaces upon the walls would be hard to keep filled. The way Sir Fergus was fighting this battle was wasteful of men and supplies, but it could well win the day for him. Artan looked back toward Sir Fergus, Laird MacIvor, and all of their camped men.

"We need to do something about all those supplies he is using against us," Artan murmured.

"Oh, aye? Such as what? Ask him to share?" Angus scowled toward Sir Fergus's tent.

"Something like that."

"Oh, nay. Nay, ye arenae going out there."

"We cannae keep crouching here hoping he runs out of arrows. 'Tis costing us too much. After the first attack the man does seem have to grown a wee bit more careful with the lives of his men. So now we are the ones losing men to Sir Fergus's archers. Do we just sit here waiting for who ends up the weakest first?"

Angus cursed and dragged his hands through his hair. "Do ye think ye can destroy his supplies?"

"I have been watching them closely every time I dared stand up and I ken where their supplies are." He nodded when Angus's eyes narrowed, knowing he had caught the man's interest. "Five men to go with me as soon as the sun sets."

"And ye are back here ere the man can curse over the loss of those supplies."

"He will ne'er e'en ken I am there ere I am gone," Artan boasted.

"Ready yourself then."

By the time Artan was slipping out of Glascreag he was still wondering if he should have told his wife what he planned to do instead of leaving Angus the chore. It was too late to do anything about that now, he told himself firmly. Despite his boasts to Angus, Artan knew this was a very risky thing to do, but he felt he had no choice. He had picked out men he knew could disappear into the smallest shadow and move across the rough ground without making a sound. It was the best he could do to improve their chances of success.

They found the supplies, silenced the guards, and set fire to the carts holding them before Artan really began to feel confident of success. That confidence faded abruptly as, during their escape, they stumbled across five Ogilvey men laughing as two of their number wrestled two young girls to the ground. When Ian the Fair crept up to his side and softly cursed, Artan inwardly sighed. He had not been sure of the identity of the two girls, but it appeared that Ian the Fair was, and that meant they were of Glascreag. He knew he could not turn his back on the girls, probably could not have even if they had not been Angus's people. The fact that they were only made his need to help them that much stronger.

"Those lasses are the daughters of the blacksmith," whispered Ian.

"Why arenae they inside Glascreag's walls?"

"The mon said they were off visiting their grandsire and wouldnae be back until the morrow. Ah, poor lassies. This will sore grieve their father."

"Be ready to run."

"Five of them; six of us. No running."

Glancing behind him, Artan saw the others crouched there, their swords at the ready. "It must be done quietly."

Although he regretted the killing, Artan had to admire how swiftly and quietly his men had done their gruesome work. However, the girls screamed like banshees. It did not surprise Artan to hear more men running their way. For just a moment, he thought they would escape, but their lead on their pursuers was lost when one of the girls stumbled and fell. The cries escaping her before Ian the Fair told her rather bluntly and crudely to be quiet led their pursuers right to them.

Seeing how many men were running toward them, Artan knew he and his men had no chance of escaping unless the pursuit was delayed. Even a few minutes' delay would be enough. With a sharp jerk of his head, he silently ordered his men to grab the girls and keep running, pleased by how quickly they obeyed him. Unsheathing his broadsword, Artan faced his enemies. There were at least two dozen of them, and Artan decided that Sir Fergus might finally have discovered how many of his men were needed to bring down Sir Artan Murray.

With a roar, he charged them, swinging his broadsword wildly and causing a brief panic amongst the men. A few men actually stumbled to a halt, gaped at him, and then turned and fled. Artan held to the attack, his huge sword and furious fighting causing a few more men to back off. For one brief, glorious moment, Artan thought he might actually win or at the very least be able to escape. Then something slammed into the back of his head. He had the wild thought that he really should have told Cecily what he had planned to do; then he sank into blackness.

Chapter 16

"He did what?" Cecily stared at Angus and then at the five men standing behind her uncle. "He went *outside* the walls right into the camp of the enemy?" All six men nodded as they watched her warily. "I cannae believe it! If he gets out of this alive, I will kill him myself."

She knew she was yelling if only because she could see that Angus could actually hear what she was saying over the piercing wails of the two girls Artan had sacrificed so much to save. She was just about to scream at the two girls to be quiet when there was the sound of an open hand striking flesh, twice, followed by a blessed silence. Cecily looked over her shoulder to see Crooked Cat standing watch over the girls.

"Thank ye," she said to the woman.

"My pleasure. They were making my head ache."

Taking a deep breath to steady herself, Cecily turned back to face Angus and the other men. "He has been captured?" She could not even think of the other possibility, let alone speak of it.

The man Angus had called Ian the Fair nodded

his bald head. "I held back to see what happened, kenning that the laird would want to hear it all. Sir Artan had them all shaking in their boots. I think he might have e'en beat them and made an escape, but ere I could act, some coward crept up behind him and hit him with verra big stick. Then the cry came up about the supply carts burning and they dragged Sir Artan away."

Some of the fear inside of her eased just a little. "What do ye think they will do with him?"

"Try to make a trade," replied Angus. "Ye for him."

Although the mere thought of returning to Sir Fergus and Dunburn made her feel ill, Cecily nodded, "All right."

"Wheesht, lass, dinnae stand there looking as if ye are about to be hanged. We willnae give ye to the fool."

"If that is what they ask for to spare Artan's life, then I shall pay the price."

"Nay, Sir Chinless wants to marry ye to get whate'er wealth might be left after the hellish pair ye call your guardians have been spending it for so long. He cannae let your husband live. If he hasnae reasoned that out yet, he soon will. Nay, ye will *act* as if ye mean to pay the price." He slung his arm around her shoulders and began to lead her out of the great hall. "I suspicion that fool will soon strut up to the wall to make his bargain. Ye will listen, mayhap plead and insult him a wee bit, and then ye will tell him that ye will accept it. The trade has to be Artan's life for your return, nay just a retreat." When she nodded, he continued, "That is all ye have to do. Just play along as if ye are going to do exactly as he says. Me and the lads will do the rest."

"The rest being that ye will rescue Artan?"

"That is the plan. And, nay, I willnae tell ye what the plan is, only your part of it. Here is how ye will do it so that it will have the best chance of all going as we want it to."

As they made their way to the top of the walls surrounding the keep, Angus told her what she had to do. She was to do all she could to keep Sir Fergus's attention fixed solely on her, and that would give Angus and his men the time to get to Artan and free him. Angus made it all sound so easy, but Cecily knew there were all kinds of things that could go wrong. She pushed those thoughts aside and promised herself that she would believe wholeheartedly in her uncle and his skills. It was the only way she could cling to her sanity.

"Cecily Donaldson, I have your lover!"

For a moment Cecily almost swooned, but Angus's grip on her arm kept her upright and gave her strength. She stepped nearer to the wall and looked down at Sir Fergus. His horse did not look so white now and his fine clothes were not so clean either. She suspected that annoyed him.

"'Tis Cecily Murray now, Sir Fergus," she called back. "The mon is my husband nay my lover, so I am Lady Cecily Murray, wife to the future laird of Glascreag."

"Aha, that has set Old MacIvor to thinking just as I had hoped it would," murmured Angus.

"Why should that trouble him?" Cecily asked Angus.

"Old MacIvor is a cautious fellow. He is always aware that he hasnae won against us yet. He willnae be wanting to kill my heir until he is sitting in my chair in my great hall drinking my ale." He frowned at her. "Dinnae ye faint, lass."

"Then cease talking about people killing Artan."

"Fair enough. Here, pay attention. Lord Chinless is ignoring Old MacIvor and wants to say something to ye."

"I could just spit on him," she muttered and ignored her uncle's grin.

"Ye were betrothed to me!" Sir Fergus yelled. "Ye took vows and contracts were signed."

"I declared them all null and void when I discovered that ye planned to kill me and keep my widow's portion," she yelled back. "I would say that ye broke all of your vows first. That didnae sound much like cherishing and protecting to me. And ye bedded Lady Anabel. I want no adulterer for a husband."

"Ah, good one, lass. Old MacIvor is a pious fellow for all his rough ways. He frowns on adultery," Angus said.

Looking at the huge, hairy man sitting on a horse just behind Sir Fergus, his heavily muscled body bristling with gleaming weapons, Cecily found it a little difficult to think of him as pious. She was also finding it difficult to remain calm and play this game with Sir Fergus. Angus had assured her, however, that this was how it should be done and she had complete faith in his knowledge of such things.

"Ye cannae just decide ye dinnae want to be betrothed anymore," said Sir Fergus after casting a narrow glance at the large, scowling Laird MacIvor behind him. "Now, here is what ye will do if ye want Sir Artan Murray returned to ye alive. Ye will come to me in two hours and put yourself in my care. Then and only then will I allow Sir Artan to return to Glascreag. If ye dinnae come to me in two hours, then for every ten minutes I have to wait, I will send ye a piece of him."

"If he keeps talking like that I am going to be violently ill," Cecily told her uncle, her voice shaking.

"Just be sure to lean o'er the wall and aim for that fool," Angus said as he awkwardly rubbed her back.

"What promise do I have that ye will keep your word?" she called down.

"Ye have my word as a king's knight."

Cecily was about to tell him just how little she thought that was worth when Laird MacIvor called out, "Ye have *my* word. Did ye hear me, Angus MacReith?"

"Aye, I heard ye and I accept," Angus called back.

After watching Laird MacIvor and Sir Fergus ride away, Cecily looked at her uncle. "There was a message there, wasnae there? Laird MacIvor was telling ye something."

"Aye," agreed Angus as he escorted Cecily off the walls. "He was telling me that he already kens that Sir Fergus's word isnae worth warm spit. And if that chinless fool e'en starts to think of breaking his word, old MacIvor will make sure he is dead before he finishes the thought."

"So, Laird MacIvor isnae really a bad mon?"

"Och, nay. Most of the time he isnae any trouble. 'Tis just that he has always wanted Glascreag, as have most of the lairds that came before him. He couldnae resist the chance that this wee trouble might be enough to let him inside the gates."

The moment they reached the ground Crooked Cat ran over and hugged Cecily. For a little while Cecily allowed herself to be comforted; but then she took a deep breath and stood back a little, although she kept a tight grip on Crooked Cat's hand for a little while longer. She was terrified for Artan, and

even knowing that, in an odd way, Laird MacIvor
was protecting him did not ease that chilling fear by
very much.

"'Tis clear that Sir Fergus doesnae ken that new
wives are to be tucked in the corner of the kitchen
until the battle is o'er," Cecily said, and was surprised to feel herself smile a little when Crooked
Cat laughed.

"There is my brave wee lass." Crooked Cat took
Cecily by the arm and tugged her toward the keep.
"Now we must get ye ready."

"Exactly what does that mean?"

"Weel, I think we shall dress ye as a widow. That
should be a sound slap in that fool's face. And we
have to make sure we hide all your weapons."

"I have ne'er used a weapon," Cecily felt compelled to confess.

"Wheesht, dinnae fret about it. That fool willnae
expect ye have any, aye? Ye willnae be needing any
skill. All ye will have to do is get close enough to the
chinless bastard to stick a wee knife or two into
him."

Cecily looked at her uncle who just grinned. "Ye
do have a plan, aye?"

"Aye, I do, lass," he replied. "Dinnae worry. All ye
need to do is make Sir Fergus the Chinless think he
has won this game. Keep him from thinking too
much on how ye may be part of a fine trick on him,
eh? I just wish I could have thought of a way to warn
MacIvor."

"Why would ye want to warn MacIvor? He is Sir
Fergus's ally."

"Nay, MacIvor is his own ally and, as I said, he
isnae a bad fellow. Just as he kens hurting Artan willnae gain him anything but grief, I ken that hurting

him will do me little good, e'en if he has put himself in the way." He shrugged. "Ah, weel, my lads ken that as weel as I do, and MacIvor isnae as stupid as he looks. I think he will quickly guess what is about to happen and disappear or, at the verra least, have his men do so. Now, off ye go with Crooked Cat and get yourself ready to do your part."

Artan winced and shifted his body slightly in a vain attempt to find a more comfortable position upon the ground. It had taken a lot of men to bring him down and he could be proud of that, but it had cost him. He had several wounds that had bled freely, leaving him weak. They needed to be tended to and soon or they could easily become fatal wounds. Infection and fever had killed more men than any sword or arrow.

The abuse he had suffered at Sir Fergus's hands had not helped. Once he had been tied head and foot and leashed to the same stake Cecily had been tied to, Sir Fergus had become brave enough to attack him. Only Laird MacIvor's intervention had stopped the man from beating him to death.

When both Sir Fergus and Laird MacIvor walked into the tent, Artan just stared at Sir Fergus. The look of distaste that crossed MacIvor's heavily bearded face gave Artan his first hint of hope. Despite his attempts to gain hold of Glascreag, the man was not without a sense of honor. The way Sir Fergus had dealt with a fellow knight obviously troubled the Highlander. That did not mean the man would rescue him, but Artan suspected there would be no more beating of a wounded and securely bound prisoner, at least not while Laird MacIvor was near at hand.

"Ye had best do just as ye have promised," Laird MacIvor said to a scowling Sir Fergus.

"I gave my word, didnae I?" Sir Fergus snapped.

MacIvor spat at Sir Fergus's feet. "That for your word, laddie. There is a lot about this that ye have ne'er told us. That lass isnae some Lowland wench who ran off with a bonnie face, is she? For a moment I thought I was seeing an angel on old Angus's walls, mayhap e'en a ghostie. Then I remembered that Moira MacReith wed herself to a Lowlander, some gentle, scholarly fellow. That lass is Angus's niece."

"Who is betrothed to me!"

"Did old Angus sign the papers? Did he e'en ken she was being given to ye? Nay, I think not."

"That doesnae matter. Her guardians gave her o'er to me. They are the cousins of her father. Her father's wishes take precedence over those of some Highland laird."

"Angus is her uncle and her laird. I ken that for a fact. I dinnae ken these Lowland cousins. And their word doesnae mean her father would have betrothed her to ye. Aye, and I only have your word that she is your betrothed." The tone in MacIvor's voice made it very clear that he held Sir Fergus's word on that as lightly as he did on everything else.

"She admitted it just now. Ye heard her."

"I also heard her say she had cast aside those promises for what seem verra sound reasons."

"Such as the fact that she is my wife," said Artan, who cursed when Sir Fergus kicked him. His eyes widened when MacIvor immediately held a sword against Sir Fergus's throat.

"Just what do ye think ye are doing?" squeaked Sir Fergus. "We are allies."

"Sad to say we are, indeed, as I gave my word and I keep my word. Howbeit, there will be no more kicking a wounded mon who is bound up like a pig for the spit. This mon is a knight and he is the heir to Glascreag. And I doubt ye will ken the importance of this since ye are a Lowlander, but he is also a Murray. I have no wish to find myself on the wrong side of them and all their allies."

Sir Fergus glared down at Artan and then strode over to a small table and poured himself a drink. "Weel, there is no need for ye to linger here, m'laird," he finally said. "I will nay abuse the mon again, and he will soon be gone, aye? Once Cecily arrives, we can send this mon back to Glascreag and I shall return to Dunburn and have my wedding."

Laird MacIvor frowned. "How can ye have a wedding? The lass is wed to this mon."

"Kidnapped and then handfasted with him. It can easily be set aside."

"Kidnapped, handfasted, and vigorously bedded," said Artan. "It willnae be so easy to set that aside. And with all that vigorous bedding I have probably already set a bairn in her belly."

"Ye may want to temper your words a wee bit," murmured Laird MacIvor to Artan as he watched Sir Fergus go white with fury.

"I am nay concerned about any bairn ye may have set in her," said Sir Fergus, but his lingering fury was clear to hear in his voice.

Recalling that the man's plan was to rid himself of his reluctant bride after a suitable amount of time and then claim her widow's portion, Artan felt his anger grow. He could not believe Angus would hand Cecily to this Lowlander, not after all Artan had told him. He suddenly felt a small flicker of hope spring to life in his chest. He knew Angus would not give Cecily to Sir Fergus, yet the man felt sure she was coming. That had to mean that Angus had a plan.

Glancing at Laird MacIvor, Artan wondered if he could make use of the distaste and distrust the man already had for Sir Fergus. If he could make Laird MacIvor so disgusted with his ally that he utterly regretted allying himself to the man, then MacIvor and his men would leave. It seemed the laird was already at that point, but he could still feel bound by his word and he was very determined in his wish to gain and hold Glascreag. Still, it was worth a try as MacIvor's defection would aid Angus in whatever he was planning.

"Ah, of course," he murmured. "I was forgetting your plans for the lass. Ye mean to allow her to live for a few months and then ye will be rid of her so that ye can collect her verra handsome widow's portion. How long do ye plan to let Anabel and Edmund live ere ye do what ye must to claim Dunburn in your poor late wife's name?"

"Ye are mad," Sir Fergus said, then gave a frowning Laird MacIvor a sickly smile. "He would say anything to ensure that he can keep the woman promised to me and her dower."

"Ye are eager for her dower as weel, I suspect," said MacIvor. "Only reason I can see for working so hard to fetch back a lass who doesnae want ye."

"Of course her dower is important, but ye saw the lass. What mon wouldnae want her for a bride?"

MacIvor shrugged, then strode over to the table where Sir Fergus stood and poured himself some wine. After studying an increasingly nervous Sir Fergus for a moment, MacIvor pulled a stool over to the table and sat down. Artan was disappointed that the man had not left, but the look of dislike MacIvor made no secret of as he stared at Sir Fergus was enough to give Artan a little bit of hope. It seemed that Sir Fergus had just lost his ally. Now, since the man had not left, Artan just had to wonder how complete the cut was.

He tried again to get comfortable on the ground. It was impossible to plan anything himself as he was too weak. If he could just rest a moment, he thought, then hastily pushed that temptation away. He needed to stay alert so he could help his rescuers when they arrived, and he was sure they would soon. Artan just wished Cecily was not part of the plan.

"In about an hour we shall see just how much your bride cares for you," Sir Fergus said as he moved a little closer.

"And how do ye plan to see that?"

"She will come to trade herself for you. She will put herself under my command so that ye may live. If she cares, that is."

"I am too weary to play this game, laddie," Artan said, knowing the contempt in his voice enraged Sir Fergus. "Whether the lass cares for me or nay isnae what matters in this."

"Oh? And what does matter?"

"Whether she is fool enough to think ye will e'er keep your promises."

Artan could see how badly the man wanted to kick him again. He did not understand why such remarks angered the man so much. Sir Fergus's rage was no act to fool MacIvor, although it should be.

Sir Fergus knew he was lying, but he might yet hope that MacIvor did not, and he needed that ally until he could get safely away from Glascreag. Artan just did not think Sir Fergus was that good a player.

Glancing at his wounds, Artan saw that the bleeding had finally stopped. It had been a very slow sort of bleeding, but even a slow loss from several wounds could be dangerous if it was slow to stop. He hoped his rescue came soon, as it was increasingly difficult to keep his wits about him, and that was a very bad sign. He felt very tired and cold, another very bad sign.

"So old Angus has named ye his heir, has he?" asked MacIvor.

It took Artan a moment to focus on the man. There was an intent look on MacIvor's face that made Artan think MacIvor knew exactly what he was feeling. It was just possible that MacIvor sought to help him in his efforts to cling to consciousness. If the man wanted to help, he would help him to a more comfortable place and give him a drink, Artan thought angrily, but he kept his anger out of his voice as he talked to the man.

"Aye," Artan replied, "ye ken that he had to call Malcolm that for a wee while since Malcolm has a closer blood tie to Angus."

"Ha! How it must have galled Old Angus to claim that whining ferret as his heir. Blood ties are important, though. Of course yours are much stronger now that ye have married the lass."

"Aye, much stronger. She is his niece after all."

"A fine way to secure it all and be rid of a spineless little cur like Malcolm. I suspicion ye dinnae have any complaints about it all, eh?"

"Nay, none at all." Artan tried to hide his surprise

when the man picked up the jug of wine, poured a tankard full, and brought it over to him.

"What are ye doing?" demanded Sir Fergus as MacIvor helped Artan drink.

"Making sure the laddie doesnae die too quickly. A wounded mon needs drink."

Artan, pained by the way he had needed to be held upright a little to drink, could only manage a grunt as his expression of gratitude, but it seemed to please MacIvor. As he struggled to recover from the man's help, a young MacIvor man came into the tent. After a look at Artan followed by a glare at Sir Fergus, the young mon had a quick word with MacIvor. Artan could not even guess at the words the two men exchanged, but a few moments later, the young man left without even a word or a bow of courtesy to Sir Fergus. The contempt for the man they found themselves allied with obviously went through the whole clan.

"So, ye were told about the niece and asked to wed her?" MacIvor said as he returned to his seat at the small table. "Find her, wed her, and become Angus's heir?

"Aye, something like that," Artan replied. "Angus wanted me to believe he was on his deathbed."

"It wasnae all that long ago ye left and Angus looked as hale as he e'er has."

"He recovered." Artan smiled fleetingly when MacIvor snorted with laughter.

"Is any of this important?" asked Sir Fergus in a sharp, angry voice.

"To me. I will nay be running to the Lowlands when this is o'er. Nay, I must needs stay here on my lands, which border the MacReith land," replied MacIvor. "'Tis wise to understand the ones who live so close to ye, especially when a lot of them are verra weel-armed men."

"Have your wee gossip then. Once I have Cecily back I will be gone from this place and your little intrigues willnae matter to me."

Artan had the feeling that MacIvor was doing more than gossiping. Instinct told him that MacIvor was trying to make a decision and wanted as much information as possible. What decision that might be and how it might help him was not something he had the wit left to untangle, however, so he simply answered MacIvor's questions, using what few wits he had to make sure that he did not tell the man more than what Sir Fergus called gossip. By the end of the conversation, however, Artan knew that MacIvor had learned a great deal about Cecily's connection to Angus and how much Angus had wanted Cecily and Artan's marriage; he just could not think of why it should matter to the man and he had neither the strength nor the privacy needed to find out.

One of Sir Fergus's men cautiously entered the tent, frequently glancing back over his shoulder. "Sir Fergus, Lady Cecily is coming," he said.

"Good. Ye may go." Sir Fergus turned to speak to MacIvor only to hear the Ogilvey man cough and draw his attention back to him. "Go."

"But, sir, I think, weel, I need to speak to ye. Privately."

"Later."

"Er, later willnae help, sir. I really think—"

"I dinnae require ye to think! Get out of here!"

When the man still hesitated Sir Fergus threw a tankard at him and he finally retreated. Sir Fergus forced himself to be calm and fussily brushed the front of his jupon with his hands. Artan could not see MacIvor's expression for the man was intently staring into his tankard. There was something happening, something Sir Fergus was unaware of, but Artan could not seem to collect his thoughts enough to even guess what it was. He was rapidly becoming too weak to care about any intrigues, and that worried him. Looking toward the door, he waited for Cecily, hoping that she had not really come here alone.

Chapter 17

"Why are all the MacIvors sitting outside the camp?" Cecily asked Bennet, who was escorting her to Sir Fergus's tent.

"'Tis a puzzle, lass," replied Bennet; then he grinned. "Howbeit, I think whate'er game they play it is to our advantage."

"I pray ye are right. I dinnae ken what my uncle's plan is, but I suspect any advantage will aid him in carrying it out." She frowned when, at the opening to the tent, two Ogilvey men stopped Bennet and relieved him of his weapons—but still held him back. "He is disarmed now, so why willnae ye let him come in?"

"Only you," said the shorter of the two men.

"Go on in, lass," said Bennet. "'Tis no matter. We didnae really think they would let me step inside with ye."

Heartily wishing yet again that Angus had told her what his plan was, Cecily stepped inside the tent. It took a moment for her eyes to accustom themselves to the darker interior, but when they did, she immediately sought out Artan. Her first sight of him made her fear that she would actually swoon and ruin all of Angus's plans. He was tied hand and foot and leashed. Even in the position he was in, half curled up on his side, she could see that he suffered from several sword wounds and had been badly beaten. She started to move toward him but a faint shake of his head brought her to her senses.

She turned her attention to Sir Fergus and caught him watching her very intently. Instinct told her that if she had rushed to Artan's side as she had wished to and exclaimed over his injuries, it could have cost Artan dearly. It would have accomplished what Angus wanted, keeping Sir Fergus's attention fixed firmly on her, but she suspected using Artan to accomplish that was not what Angus would want.

"I see that your hospitality to a guest is as gracious as ever," she drawled, and was sure she heard MacIvor snort with laughter, but she did not dare take her gaze from Sir Fergus to see for herself.

"The mon is nay a guest, but a prisoner," snapped Sir Fergus.

"A prisoner ye said ye would release as soon as I came to ye. Weel, here I am, so release him."

"I am nay sure I ought to do that. Nay, at least not until we are off the MacReith lands."

It had been a fleeting hope that he would not only hold to his word but do so without trying any tricks. "Do ye mean to go back on your word?"

"Of course not," he said so quickly she knew he was lying. "I said I would release him, but I ne'er said when."

Cecily chanced a fleeting glance toward Laird MacIvor and saw him nod to himself as if he had just had a question answered or some decision con-

firmed. "That, sir, is naught but a base trickery, for
ye ken weel that the immediate release of Sir Artan
was what ye had agreed to."

"'Tis nay my fault that Laird Angus didnae have
the wit to make it more specific."

"Actually, I believe the lass here is the one ye
made the agreement with," murmured Laird
MacIvor, standing up and idly leaning against the
edge of the table.

"Fine then," snapped Sir Fergus. "Then 'tis she
who lacked the wit to be most specific." He glared
at Cecily. "And why are ye dressed as if someone has
died?"

"Nay someone but something. I dress in mourn-
ing for all my lost dreams," she said in a soft, unsteady voice and sighed a little.

"Ye would be wise to nay try to anger me."

"Sir Fergus, there appears to be verra little
anyone can do that doesnae anger ye."

Cecily could see that she could, indeed, hold his
attention on her. Angering him did that very efficiently. She hoped Angus was quick to arrive, however, for angering Sir Fergus Ogilvey was the surest
way to get struck down, and she could not be sure
that Laird MacIvor would do anything to stop him.
While his beating her would certainly keep him oc-
cupied, Cecily would greatly prefer it if Angus arrived first.

"It would appear that MacIvor has decided he has
had enough of Sir Chinless," murmured Angus as
he looked around at all the MacIvor men now
camping outside of Sir Fergus's camp.

Ian the Fair nodded as he also looked around.

"Aye, and I ken weel that they ken we are here, and yet they do naught."

"But where is MacIvor?"

"Still in the camp? He did give ye his word that Artan willnae be killed. Mayhap he stays near at hand to be sure that promise is kept."

"Ah, aye. I suspicion that is just what he is doing. And it would seem that he has also figured out we mean to come and get Artan ourselves, hence putting all his men out of the way."

"Weel, that is a fine thing, but it still leaves us all of those Lowlanders to deal with."

"But there are holes in the defenses now, lad. 'Twill be easier to slip in and get Artan and Cecily out of there."

"Aye, I could see that the lass didnae want to get near that bastard Sir Fergus, but she wasnae going to let Artan come to harm. She has spine."

"Aye, she does."

"Laird, what are ye doing?" Ian asked in shock, grabbing Angus by the arm when he started walking straight for the five MacIvors they had been watching.

"Trust me, lad. They willnae do anything to stop us. I ken old MacIvor weel. Been adversaries for years, havenae we. He wants naught to do with this, but he kens we are coming after the lad. How to stay out of that tussle yet appear to be keeping his word? I suspicion he has set his men here and told them to ignore us. After all, if by some miracle Sir Idiot wins the day, there will be questions asked, aye? And the MacIvors will say that they ne'er saw us."

"Sly, verra sly. But are ye sure that is what this is all about?"

"Sure enough to walk right through that camp

and save myself a great deal of slipping through the shadows."

Angus bit back a grin when Ian muttered a curse even as he fell into step at his side. The moment he and Ian stepped out into the open, all five MacIvors sitting around a little fire dipped their heads and stared firmly at the ground. He was impressed by the sly trick MacIvor had devised. Even the men who were poor liars could look anyone straight in the eye and claim they had seen no MacReiths. He strode right through the middle of the camp, Ian at his side just staring at men sitting there with their heads bowed.

"I cannae believe it," muttered Ian as they reached the other side of the camp and all the MacIvors lifted their heads but were careful not to look to the left or the right.

"'Tis verra clever. I ne'er would have thought MacIvor had that clever a mind. I have underestimated the poor fellow."

"That poor fellow has been trying to get Glascreag for his whole life and is probably teaching his sons to crave it, too."

"Aye, I suspicion he is, but that has been the way of it since MacIvors and MacReiths first set out their hearthstones in these hills."

As they approached the tent, Angus caught sight of Bennet just standing there chatting with two of the Ogilveys and inwardly shook his head. Bennet could make friends with Satan himself, he thought a little crossly. Just as he thought he was going to have to do something to remind the lad of his part in this plan, Bennet moved to the side of the tent. Angus was not sure what the young man was saying, but it was good enough to draw his two guards around the corner with him.

He was getting too old for this, he mused as he waited for Bennet to reappear. His patience for this game was gone and he was going to be more than happy to hand such duties over to Artan soon. Angus was actually starting to move to go and see what had happened to Bennet when the young man and another MacReith, both wearing the jupons the guards had had on, came back around the corner.

It was then that Angus noticed a small hole in his plan. The guards had been standing guard on a MacReith and now it looked as if they had lost their prisoner. A quick look around the camp showed him that no one was paying any attention and he breathed a quick sigh of relief. He felt a need to act quickly now, however, for there was a chance there were other holes he had not considered and he wanted Cecily and Artan back inside the walls of Glascreag before someone did notice.

Staying to the shadows, Angus and Ian crept up close enough for Angus to whisper to Bennet, "Who is in the tent?"

"Artan, Cecily, Sir Fergus, and Laird MacIvor," Bennet answered in an equally soft voice.

"Weel, that should make things interesting," Angus said; Bennet laughed softly. "When ye hear my whistle . . ." he began.

"Get out of here. Aye, I remember. Artan may need help getting back to Glascreag."

"He is wounded?"

"Aye, although the brief glance I got inside the tent wasnae enough to tell me where or how badly. He is also bound hand and foot and leashed to a stake in the ground."

"I cannae wait to kill that bastard."

"Good luck."

Cecily glanced over at Artan, not liking his color or the way he seemed to be more unconscious than conscious. "Ye have done naught to tend his wounds. Most people would treat a dog better."

"He can wait. He will be back at Glascreag ere they worsen and he will be past caring then."

That was an ominous statement, and out of the corner of her eye Cecily saw MacIvor tense. Fergus did not seem to grasp the need to take care in what he said. Laird MacIvor had given his word to Angus that Artan would be returned to Glascreag quickly and alive. Fergus's cold words strongly implied that not only would Artan not be returned quickly, he would be returned dead. Unlike Fergus, Laird MacIvor was a man of his word, and hearing Sir Fergus, his ally, strongly imply that he had no intention of honoring that word had to enrage him.

"Ye would have been treated better by the Mac-Reiths, Sir Fergus, and ye ken it weel," she said.

"That doesnae mean I have to be as foolish as they are. This mon has wronged me!"

"Oh, and ye havenae wronged me? Ye who intended to wed me for my dower, bed me until ye tired of me, and then kill me for all the rest my father left me? Who kenned weel that my own guardians had my father and brother killed and had expected, e'en fervently desired, that I should die with them? Yet ye said naught to me? Ye kenned about my inheritance as weel and ye said naught."

"Ye are but a woman. Ye didnae have any need to ken any of it."

"'Tis all mine and ye were silent because ye wanted as much of it for yourself as ye could get. But let us say that, as a woman, I should have naught to do with such concerns about my own inheritance and which carrion get to feast upon it. Our betrothal wasnae a long one, sir, and yet ye couldnae e'en be faithful to me. Worse, ye broke your vows to me in my own home."

"Faithful? What mon is e'er faithful, ye daft wench."

"My husband has promised to be faithful."

"Pretty words to lift your skirts is all."

"Nay, Artan isnae a mon much skilled in the saying of pretty words. He means it. He willnae be rutting with a maid within mine own home. Nay, nor will he commit adultery with a kinswoman of mine, although I have few of them sad to say. And one thing he will ne'er and would ne'er do is try to rape a lass barely past her first flux."

"She was willing and she looks younger than she is."

"And the bruises ye gave her were naught but wee love taps, aye?" She shook her head. "I cannae believe I almost married you. I thought ye might actually have a few attractive attributes, somewhere, buried deeply. What a fool I was. I ne'er suspected that ye were quite the thoroughly rotten bastard that ye are. Nay, I just thought ye were a tedious bore."

She heard a now-familiar snort of laughter and realized it had come from behind her. Laird MacIvor had somehow managed to slip around the room until he was standing near to Artan. She did not understand what the man was doing but, after a brief flash of alarm, felt certain he was no threat to Artan.

Sir Fergus, however, was, she thought as she turned her attention back to that man.

Where was Angus, she wondered. It seemed as if she had been standing here trading insults with Sir Fergus for hours. Although she knew stealth would be needed for whatever Angus had to do and that such stealth took time, she was beginning to get nervous.

Another fleeting glance at Artan only added to her tension. He was looking poorly. Although he was watching her, there was a slightly glazed look in his eyes that frightened her. His silence also bothered her. It made sense that he would not want to show too much interest in her or give Sir Fergus the satisfaction that this apparent victory of his might cause either of them any real distress; he had not even insulted the man once since she had entered the tent.

Looking more closely, she saw what looked to be blood on the ground around his body and she felt chilled with fear for him. His wounds had been left untended for a long time and it was clear that no one had even tried to stop the bleeding. Artan had probably lost a lot of blood, which did not bode well for his chances of recovery. She hastily stilled the worst of her fears by reminding herself of how strong and healthy he was. All he needed was to get back to Glascreag, get his wounds tended to, and be cared for, she told herself firmly.

"If ye mean to honor your word, Sir Fergus, ye should either allow Artan to go back to Glascreag now or tend his wounds."

After staring at Artan for a moment, Sir Fergus looked back at her and shrugged. "He still breathes, which is more than can be said for the five men he killed ere we caught him."

"Those five men were trying to rape two young girls."

"Peasant wenches. Lusty, the whole lot of them. They like to protest in the hope of gaining a wee bit more coin for their favors. Ye have been sheltered at Dunburn and dinnae understand the ways of the world. Aye, and yon knight was a fool to let himself be caught because of two little whores who feared they would have to give it away for free."

"Ye, Sir Fergus, are indeed the rutting swine your banner declares ye to be."

"'Tis a rampant boar!" he yelled.

Obviously that particular taunt had begun to sorely anger the man. "I see little difference."

"As do I, lass."

The sound of Angus's voice was such a relief Cecily was astonished she did not fall to the ground at that very moment. She did obey the little quirk of his finger, however, and hurry over to stand at his side. Her heart ached to go to Artan's side, but Angus did not need to have to keep a watch on two people as he confronted Sir Fergus. The only thing she could do was sidle along until she was on Angus's far side, nearest to Artan but still protected by Angus. The moment he took care of the threat Sir Fergus presented, she would be able to reach Artan in only a few steps.

She suddenly recalled Laird MacIvor and saw him standing close to Artan, his sword in his hand, and her blood chilled. Cecily looked at her uncle and knew he was aware of Laird MacIvor, but Angus did not look at all worried about where the man was and what he was holding. She tried very hard to share his calm.

"Ye are a fool to come here, MacReith," said Sir Fergus. "Ye may have been able to slip in past my guards, but ye will ne'er be able to slip out. Nay, especially since ye will have to carry Sir Artan."

"Aye, I can see that ye have done him hard," agreed Angus. "Ye have become a real irritant, ye have."

"All I sought was that which was mine—Cecily Donaldson."

"She isnae yours, laddie. I am thinking she ne'er was and ne'er would have been. Ye and those two scum back at Dunburn have stolen enough from my poor wee lass, and it will end here."

"Oh, do ye mean to fight me for her, old mon?"

Sir Fergus did not have the brain of a flea, thought Cecily as she winced over his mocking tone of voice and the remark about Angus's age. If the man would just open his eyes, he would see that her uncle was still strong, probably stronger than Sir Fergus, and more than capable of fighting the fool. Sir Fergus should be afraid, not standing there feeling so superior and safe.

"He just called ye an old mon, Angus," murmured Laird MacIvor.

"Aye, I ken it, but I have heard worse."

"Going to kill him?"

"I am fair hungering to do so."

"Aye, he is a sad waste of a knighthood, that is for certain."

Sir Fergus stared at Laird MacIvor in shock. "Have ye gone to his side then? Is there naught but betrayal in these lands? I thought ye were a mon of your word. Ye have certainly deafened me with the claiming of it for hours."

"I am on my side, laddie. Ye are the one who had no intention of keeping his word. Did ye nay listen at the walls? I gave Angus my word that Sir Artan would be returned alive. I mean to keep it. If that means I step aside from ye, weel, so be it."

Sir Fergus took a step toward the opening of his tent only to find Ian standing there. "Nay, laddie. Ye will find no aid there. Two of ours stand guard."

Now Cecily could see the fear creep over Sir Fergus. He realized he had no ally and was trapped in his own tent by Sir Angus and his men. If he had not been planning to murder her to satisfy his greed and kill Artan to satisfy his anger, she just might have felt sorry for him. Cecily did not like the idea of seeing him killed, however, but in some ways, she was just as trapped as he was. Well, she thought, she was the wife of a Highland warrior and she would undoubtedly see men killed from time to time. Best to get the first shock of it over and done with.

"So, ye mean to murder me, do ye?" Sir Fergus said.

"Och, nay, laddie," said Angus. "Now, I would like naught better than to kill ye for what ye have done to my lad here and what ye planned to do to my niece, but I really just wish to get my lad and his lass back to Glascreag as quickly as possible."

"She isnae his lass. She is mine!"

"Ye havenae got the sense to ken when ye have lost, do ye? Leave it be, lad. Keep your life and go home. The money isnae worth it."

"'Tis a fortune, ye old fool, and this wench has to

pay for humiliating me by running away with that Highlander during our wedding celebration."

"Ye cannae spend a fortune if your corpse is rotting away in these lands, now can ye."

"Nay, I cannae let him win. I cannae let her win. I had this all carefully planned."

"Go home, Sir Fergus," Cecily said. "If 'tis a fortune ye hunger for, then pry it out of my guardian's hands. They were willing to give me to ye as weel as a near fortune just to shut ye up. Ye can still play that game with them. Just leave me out of it."

"Nay, nay." He shook his head and Cecily feared he had lost his mind, if only briefly. "I was humiliated. I willnae let that barbarian beat me!"

He lunged toward Artan even as he drew his sword. Angus, Ian, and Cecily all moved at once, which only impeded them all. By the time Angus broke free of the tangle, Sir Fergus was lifting his sword over Artan, who seemed too dazed to get out of the way. Cecily could neither move nor speak, terrified that she was about to see her husband murdered right in front of her eyes.

Then, suddenly, Laird MacIvor moved and swiftly settled the problem.

Chapter 18

Sir Fergus's head landed right at her feet. Cecily stared down into his wide eyes and thought how surprised he looked. She wondered why she was not retching and decided she must be in shock. One minute it had looked as if Sir Fergus was going to succeed in killing Artan and none of them would be able to stop him. In the very next moment, Laird MacIvor was standing there with a bloodied sword in his hand and Sir Fergus's head was touching the tips of her shoes while his body was sprawled out next to Artan.

"It is touching my shoes," she whispered.

Angus picked her up and set her down again several feet away. "There now, lass. Just take a few deep breaths and ye will be fine."

She did as he told her to and watched as he and Ian moved Sir Fergus's body away from Artan and began to untie her husband. When Laird MacIvor calmly cleaned his sword off on Sir Fergus's jupon, apparently unconcerned that that jupon was on a headless body, Cecily decided that she would probably never understand men. Sir Fergus deserved to die. She felt no remorse or sorrow about that. It was just the quick, cold way that it was done and how none of the men were troubled by having the body—both parts—right there in the tent with them.

"How are ye going to explain Sir Fergus's death?" Angus asked Laird MacIvor.

"Weel, if I have to explain it at all, I will say that ye did it," the man replied.

"Fair enough. I was certainly ready to do it. But what do ye mean by *if*?"

"I dinnae intend to be here when his men discover the fool's body."

Angus nodded. "I had wondered on that. All your men sitting outside the camp made me think ye were planning to slip away. 'Tis the first step to leaving, isnae it?"

"Aye, I should have left earlier, but I gave ye my word that the lad would come home alive and I meant to keep it. That fool let me ken that he didnae intend to keep his word. He was a bad one."

"He was. Somehow I dinnae think his men will be crying for vengeance. Or his family."

"Nay, do ye ken one of his men tried to tell him about how all of my men had moved out of the camp, but the fool wouldnae listen, wouldnae e'en hear what the mon had to say. Threw a tankard at his head and the man finally gave up. Mayhap if Fergus had learned to listen to others he wouldnae be dead now. Has me thinking hard, though."

"Oh? On what?"

"On the way me and all the MacIvor lairds afore me have had covetous eyes on Glascreag." He shook his head. "Look what I joined forces with just to get a chance to take it from you. I begin to think it has become a sickness with us, and truth tell, I cannae e'en remember why we think we have any right to it."

"Didnae ken ye needed one."

"Ah, but there's the wrong in it, aye? Weel, get the lad home. He needs tending. That bastard nay only refused to treat his wounds or e'en give him water, but I caught him beating on the lad whilst he was tied up like that. Put a stop to that and gave your lad a drink. The man is a fine warrior and he will make a far better laird than that weasel Malcolm. Wasnae right to treat him as if he was some common thief."

Artan groaned with pain as Ian hefted him up across his shoulders. Cecily grabbed a blanket from the bed. As soon as there were other men to help, they could carry Artan in the blanket. Being carried over Ian's shoulder like that could start Artan's wounds bleeding again, and she could see that he had already lost enough to make him dangerously weak.

To her surprise, the cut that Artan had made in the tent when he had rescued her was still there, simply laced shut. Angus held it open as wide as he could for Ian to get through, then slipped out after him. Cecily was just about to follow the men when she suddenly realized that all MacIvor had gotten as thanks was a grunt from Angus. She turned and started because he was standing right behind her.

"Thank ye, m'laird," she said, and stood on tiptoe to give him a kiss on the tiny part of his cheek that was not covered in beard just as she heard Angus's whistle, the signal to the others to make for home.

Looking bemused, Laird MacIvor said, "Tell that old fool I will give him five minutes."

She nodded and started out of the tent only to have Angus reach in, grab her by the arm, and yank her out. "I had to say thank ye to Laird MacIvor."

"Ye can write him a pretty note."

"He said he can give ye five minutes." Seeing that Bennet and another young man had joined them, she handed Angus the blanket. "Ye can use this to carry him home. 'Twould be better, I think."

"Aye," agreed Angus. With the help of the others, he immediately started getting Artan moved from Ian's shoulders and onto the blanket. "Ye will have a lot of work to do to fix this, lass."

"I fear so," she whispered, then followed the four men as they carried Artan in the blanket. When she saw the shadowy form of the others heading toward Glascreag she realized that Angus had brought quite a large force of men with him. "Why so many men, Uncle?"

"In case there was a fight."

"Do ye think there will be any retaliation for Sir Fergus's death?"

"Nay, MacIvor will blame me if he has to, but he will let it be widely kenned that Sir Fergus died because he tried to kill a mon, an already wounded mon who was bound hand and foot and leashed to a stake. And think on this, lass. Considering the sort of mon he was, do ye really think there will be many mourners?"

She sighed. "Nay, I have met some of his kinsmen. All there will be is a hard scramble to see who can grab the most of whatever he has left behind."

"A mon reaps what he sows."

That sounded heartless, but it was also true, she mused as she did her best to keep up with the men. When she was sure five minutes had passed, she tensed and waited for some sign of an outcry. None came and Cecily thought that was even sadder. She felt no grief for Sir Fergus Ogilvey, only for the sad waste of a life, and the waste had been mostly of Sir Fergus's own making. The man had had several chances to step down a different path right up until the end, but he had not taken up any of them.

The moment they were inside Glascreag's walls, Cecily took command. She quickly had Artan settled in his bedchamber. Crooked Cat helped her undress him and wash the dirt from his body. She almost wept like a bairn when she saw the damage done to his big, strong body. It also troubled her to see him so weak and insensible, but she was glad of it as she began to clean his wounds.

He had three sword cuts; all needed stitches, but only one of them was a truly serious wound. His capture and Sir Fergus's beating had left Artan bruised from head to toe. Cecily was astonished that nothing was broken, although she suspected his ribs had taken a lot of punishment, so she wrapped them tightly. With Crooked Cat's help she even managed to get some hearty broth down his throat.

"That is a verra fine-looking mon ye have there, lass," said Crooked Cat as she collected up all the rags they had used to clean him off.

"I certainly think so, but if ye dinnae keep your eyes averted next time, I may have to kill ye." She smiled when Crooked Cat laughed. "His color isnae good."

"Nay, it isnae. I think he lost a lot of blood and 'tis ne'er good to leave wounds untended for too long."

Cecily slowly nodded in agreement. She wanted

to stay at his side, but at Crooked Cat's insistence she hurried away to wash, change her clothes, and go and have something to eat. The woman was right to say that Artan was insensible right now, but also clean and comfortable. Now was the time for her to see to her own needs before she settled in at Artan's bedside for what could prove to be a long, harrowing night, if not many of them.

"How is the lad?" Angus asked the minute Cecily sat down at the head table in the great hall.

"He remained unconscious throughout all the stitching, cleaning, and bandaging," she replied as she filled her plate. "While I am most grateful he wasnae sensible as I tended his wounds, I cannae like it. It seems he should have stirred a little. I but pray that it is a natural sleep, that Artan heals himself in that way. Crooked Cat is sitting with him now."

Bennet frowned. "The few times Artan has been ill or badly wounded he did sleep a lot and slept verra deeply. And nay with the help of any potions."

"That is good then. There are few cures which are better than a lot of rest," Cecily said, struggling to convince herself as much as she tried to convince the men. "It can e'en help ye recover from losing too much blood." She looked at Angus. "Only one of the sword cuts, one on his back that curls around to his side, was a serious one, but 'tis clean and it bleeds no more. The beating Sir Fergus gave him left him covered in bruises, livid ones. But there are no broken bones; nay, not e'en his ribs, although I wrapped them as weel." She noticed Bennet grinning, and asked, "What do ye find so amusing?"

"Ye are a healer, arenae ye?" he asked.

"Weel, aye, I suppose I am. 'Tis all I was e'er trained in and I was allowed it, I think, simply because I convinced Anabel that I hated it and she felt it was demeaning. Peasant's work, she claimed." She suddenly felt concern grip her heart. "Are ye thinking Artan willnae like it? Crooked Cat said a lot of women in your clan are healers."

"They are, and Artan will think it a fine thing. What amused me was thinking on how far afield he went and yet he ends up with a lass who will have much in common with all the lasses he grew up with."

"Crooked Cat sings your praises, lass," said Angus. "And young Robbie's mother is like to build a shrine to ye."

"Was he the lad with the three arrow wounds?"

"Aye, and he is still weak and all, but there is no sign of fever or infection. Aye, and e'en the mother, who isnae a healer, could see how close two of those wounds were to killing her only child. But the best is that wee Nell, the lass who stayed at his side, has finally convinced her doting father of her devotion to the lad and they will be married as soon as Robbie is completely healed. She is a verra rich prize for a poor mon at arms. She will have her father's wee farm in the end as weel as the stock, a full chest of linens, and ten shillings." Angus winked. "E'en better, they have been sweet on each other since he was eight and she was a lass of but four summers stumbling after him everywhere he went."

Cecily had to smile. Her uncle acted as if he somehow had a hand in the match that was, indeed, a very good one for a poor man. She suspected Robbie's work in the defending of Glascreag and the serious wounds he had endured helped sway the girl's father as well. Cecily had thought the youth looked like a boy. No doubt Nell's father did, too.

There was nothing quite like being in a battle and enduring wounds to make other men begin to see that the boy has become a man. Men seemed able to ignore the fact that anyone can be pierced by an arrow or cut by a sword and bleed fulsomely, including a woman. Saying so to her uncle, however, would probably start an argument she did not have time to enjoy.

"We need to decide what to do about that Sir Edmund and Lady Anabel," Angus said quietly.

"I ken it, Uncle. I am just nay sure what. Fergus didnae tell me much about how he learned about their crimes. Something Anabel did or said gave him the idea and she wasnae quick enough to deny it believably. They may think themselves safe now, but they may also flee. And although I was ne'er close to Anabel's daughters, was ne'er allowed to be, they have done me no wrongs. All I ken right now is that they shouldnae be enjoying what is mine, if only because it would grieve my father. The trouble is, how do I prove it is mine?"

"There has to be something written down somewhere, lass. That is what we need. With that in hand, we could move against them, burn those leeches right off your back."

"There is a thought I wish ye hadnae stuck in my head." She shuddered and then grinned at Bennet, who laughed. "I shall have to think hard on who my father's friends were and all. Old Meg might ken something and she should be here soon," Cecily said almost to herself.

"Meg? My Moira's friend and companion? That Meg?"

"Aye, she became my nurse. Colin's too."

"A fine woman if I recall correctly. But why *Old* Meg? She cannae be e'en fifty yet."

Suddenly recalling that her uncle was sixty, Cecily refrained from pointing out that fifty was considered a great age by many people. "She is called Old Meg because there were already three Megs at Dunburn when we arrived and she was the eldest. For years we had Old Meg, Young Meg, Red Meg, and Lame Meg. Oh, and ere I go up to sit with Artan, could ye please tell me why a mon with no hair is called Ian the Fair?"

Bennet laughed and Cecily yet again felt almost compelled to smile, for his laughter was a merry sound. He was also startlingly handsome with long, thick golden hair imbued with red and a pair of brilliant blue eyes. It was no wonder that she often saw him surrounded by women.

"Stop ogling Bennet," said Angus. "Ye are a married woman."

When she did not even blush, just rolled her eyes at a grinning Bennet, Cecily realized she was already accustomed to her uncle's blunt, often completely tactless ways. "I was just thinking about what a bonnie lad he is. The Murrays must be one of those clans where ye could spend hours just sitting and enjoying the view."

"Wretched lass, ye have put poor Bennet to the blush." Angus grinned, enjoying the young man's discomfort. "Now, I will tell ye how Ian the Fair got his name only the once. We dinnae talk about it much for it puts the man to the blush."

"The mon is so huge, Uncle, surely he ne'er blushes."

"He does and 'tisnae a pretty sight. Nay, Ian isnae really bald. He shaves his head." Angus nodded at her look of astonishment, obviously savoring the chance to tell the tale. "When he was younger, he had long, flowing fair hair, hair any woman would envy. E'en had some curl to it. Weel, the lasses loved it, loved him being such a big, braw fellow with pretty hair they did. Ian mistook one lass's attentions, thought she really cared for him. She was just enjoying the fact that she held his attention and the others didnae. He heard her say so herself."

"Oh dear."

"Aye, found out she was just toying with him whilst having every intention of wedding up with the cooper in the spring. Good mon the cooper, with work that pays weel and a neat wee cottage. Ian's tender feelings were hurt."

The thought of the man who could carry Artan over his shoulder having tender feelings was a bit difficult to grasp, but Cecily could feel a great sympathy for anyone who was tricked in love. "So he shaved his head?"

Angus nodded. "He said he wouldnae grow his hair again until he found a lass with a true heart."

"In other words, one who will care for him when his head is as smooth and shiny as an egg."

"Exactly."

"He doesnae look to be even thirty yet. Doesnae he ken that most people here must recall when he had hair and just how fine it was?"

"I did say about that to the lad, but he isnae exactly sensible on the matter."

"Er, nay, I dinnae suppose he is. He did, after all, shave his head because of a youthful heartbreak, and it cannae be easy to keep it shaved." She had to bite back a smile when both men winced faintly and lightly touched their hair. "Weel, I hope he finds what he is looking for, although one can only wonder what will happen when he finds his true heart, lets his hair grow again, and the lass expresses her admiration."

When Angus just began to frown Cecily finished her meal and tried to ready herself to return to Artan's bedside. She was reluctant to go and find him still insensible yet she preferred it to finding him suffering from a fever or a putrefying wound. Nevertheless, she admitted to herself that she found disturbing the sight of Artan just lying there, his strength still visible in the lines of his body, yet no sign of it appearing in any other way. To have Artan not move or speak as she bathed his open wounds and stitched his wounds gave her the shivers, so deep and cold was her fear for him.

Sitting and talking with Angus and Bennet helped her let go of some of her fear. She could talk, even laugh a little, and think of Artan as just sleeping, something that was only good and healing. In such a surrounding it was easy to think only of having had a victory over Sir Fergus and bringing Artan home alive.

The touch of a calloused hand on hers told her that her thoughts had not been as private as she had hoped them to be. She gave her uncle a faint smile. Suddenly, she thought of how Edmund and Anabel had deprived her of the company of this man, her mother's brother. Anger swept through her at the thought of all the lost years, years during which she had hungered for a kind touch or a shoulder she could spend her grief upon. Angus would have provided such things without hesitation, and she felt decidedly bloodthirsty. It took all of her willpower not to demand that they immediately ride to Dunburn, armed and ready to fight, and slaughter her guardians.

"Ah, now ye look better, lass," Angus said. "Just had a good thought, didnae ye. For a moment ye look afeared of something."

"I was thinking of how I would like to ride to Dunburn and slaughter Edmund and Anabel."

"Just as I said, a verra fine thought, indeed. The perfect thought to cheer ye."

Cecily laughed and stood up, then bent to kiss his cheek. "I had best go and sit with Artan. Thinking on that was why I had grown pale. I just dinnae like to see him lying so still. He is nay a still mon."

"Nay, he isnae. He will be weel, lass. He is young and strong."

She just nodded and headed for the bedchamber she shared with Artan. Her uncle was kind to give her such encouraging words, but they both knew that being young and strong did not always matter. Young and strong men died every day.

The mere thought of Artan dying caused her to stumble on the stairs. She stood very still and took several deep breaths to calm herself. Except for the unsettling stillness, there were no signs that Artan was suffering unduly from his wounds. All he needed was to be kept warm, given plenty of healthy broths, and kept clean. She had the skills to do that and more, as well as the patience to keep caring for him until he opened those beautiful silvery blue eyes of his and smiled at her.

"It doesnae look encouraging, does it?" Angus murmured after Cecily left the great hall.

"Nay, not really," Bennet agreed in an equally soft

voice. "I dinnae think I have e'er seen a mon beaten so badly before."

"Nay alive leastwise, eh? I hadnae gotten a close look at Artan until Sir Fergus was dead, or I would-nae have tried to convince the little swine to just give up and go home. I would have killed the bas-tard right there, right then. There was nay need to beat the lad so."

"Sir Fergus thought so. He had been trying to rid himself of Artan from the moment my cousin walked into the great hall of Dunburn. Each time he failed he grew more enraged. The fool prob-ably thought Artan was the reason all his great plans for wealth were falling apart. I think the man was one of those who could ne'er be wrong. If something wasnae going as he thought it should, it had to be because someone was ruin-ing it."

"And Artan was that one. Aye, I ken what ye mean."

"He will recover. I have seen him this still before. 'Tis a little frightening, but 'tis his way to heal. And he has a lot to live for, aye?"

"The lass, ye mean?"

"Aye, the lass."

"So ye think he cares for her?"

"Oh, aye. I think he cares for her verra much indeed."

"Good, good. I didnae want to think I had pushed them both into something they didnae really want."

Bennet shook his head. "Artan wanted it. They may take a while to see what I can, but 'tis there. They are a good pairing."

"They will give me some verra fine grandbabies." Angus just smiled when Bennet laughed.

* * *

Cecily sat in a chair by the bed after Crooked Cat had taken her leave. Artan had not moved. She leaned forward to check if he still breathed, then told herself not to be a fool. His breathing might be somewhat shallow, but his chest very clearly moved in a steady rhythm.

Resting her elbows on the edge of the bed, she took his hand in both of hers. It felt warm, but it lay limp in her grasp. She idly rubbed it with her fingers, but there was no sign that he felt it. For a brief moment, she was tempted to fetch a needle and poke him with it, but she quickly pushed that idea aside. It would hardly make any more impression than the way she had to sew his flesh together on his wounds a few hours ago. Again and again, the needle had pierced his flesh, but he had shown no sign of feeling it.

This sort of utter stillness was beyond her ken as a healer, and that worried her. From the way Crooked Cat talked to her, Cecily knew she was the most skillful healer they had ever had in Glascreag or anywhere nearby. Unfortunately, that meant Artan had to depend on her to pull him out of this, and she simply did not feel up to the task. She had only ever had Tall Lorna for a teacher, and that woman had never spoken of what to do for a man whose spirit seemed to have fled his body.

"Artan," she whispered, and kissed his lips only to quickly pull back when there was not even a hint that he felt her mouth moving against his.

"Ah, Artan, where have ye gone? Ye cannae leave me." She stroked his forehead, felt no hint of fever, and knew she should be pleased, yet, in some ways, it would be a sign that this was not some empty shell they had brought back to Glascreag.

"Mayhap I should have Bennet seek out one of those famed healers in your family."

She let that thought settle into her mind and actually found comfort in the knowledge that there were others to whom she could turn. They were some distance away, but she knew they would come if she sent word. She would speak to Bennet in the morning and together they would decide when they should send word to the Murrays. It was no promise of some miracle cure, but she felt calmed by the mere fact that she had a plan.

Climbing up onto the bed, she settled herself next to him. She rested her head on his chest, comforted even more by the steady beat of his heart, and wrapped her arm around his waist. Despite the warmth of his body and the sound of his heartbeat, Cecily felt very alone despite being so close to him. The spirit that made Artan the man she loved more than life was not there.

It was there, she told herself firmly. She would know if it had somehow fled his body completely. Thinking back to that time in Sir Fergus's tent, she felt sure she knew when Artan had begun to sink into this sleep. She had seen the almost dreamy look in his beautiful eyes and he had not participated in his rescue in even the smallest of ways. The groan of pain he had made, when Ian the Fair had slung him over his broad shoulders had been the last sound Artan had made, but she did not think Ian's actions had done this. Artan was already escaping the pain of his body by then.

And who could blame him for that, she thought. There was not a part of him that was not bruised or stitched together. Many men would have been screaming from the pain.

"I am nay sure what to do, Artan," she whispered. "Frightening though this is, I can see how it is best for ye. Ye would suffer so if ye were aware of the pain ye are in. This sleep takes that away, doesnae it? Nay, it takes ye away from the pain.

"Weel, for a little while I shall just leave ye be and let ye sleep this deep sleep. I will care for this poor battered body until ye come back to it. That willnae be such a hardship, it being such a fine body e'en covered in bruises as it is." She touched a kiss to his lips. "But I warn ye, I cannae let it go on for too long and nay just because I miss ye already. There is only so much I can do to tend your body ere it starts to weaken.

"And therein lies the danger, my love. Each day that ye sleep your body heals but also weakens. Soon the flesh begins to leave your bones for ye cannae live weel on just broth and 'tis all I shall be able to feed ye. So we shall do this and I shall let ye rest in whatever hiding place ye have found in there. But when I see that the flesh is slipping off your bones, I will send for a healer from your clan to come and help wake ye up so that ye may eat and drink proper food and regain your strength."

She settled her cheek against his chest again and sighed. Cecily knew that the chances he could hear her were very small, but she felt better for having told him her plan. She wondered if she should don her nightgown. The thought had barely finished passing through her mind when she realized she was already so near to sleep she doubted she could get up and undress. She closed her eyes and prayed that it would not be long before she could feel her husband's arms wrap around her once again.

Chapter 19

"Where is she? Where is my wee lass?"

Angus stopped in his descent of the stairs to look at the woman who had just entered his keep. He recognized her almost immediately as Meg, his sister's companion and Cecily's nurse. A few extra pounds on her lush body, a few lines on her round, pretty face, and some gray in her hair, but it was definitely Meg. Suddenly smiling despite the grief he was struggling with, he hurried the rest of the way down the stairs to greet her, feeling the first touch of happiness he had felt in six long days, ever since Artan was carried home to Glascreag.

"Hello, Meg," he said, pleased when he saw the recognition in her dark eyes.

"Angus?" she said, stepping closer.

"Aye, 'tis Angus. A little older, a little battered, but definitely Angus."

"I heard ye were dying."

"Nay, I was ill, but it didnae take me."

"Aye, weel, I can see that, old mon. So, where is Cecily?"

Still as tart as a green apple, he thought, and nearly grinned. "She is sitting with her husband."

"Ah, so he did marry the lass. Good. I thought he was a good lad, was telling me the truth, but as soon as they were gone, I started to fret about her."

"If Artan told ye he would marry her, he meant it. And it wasnae just to become my heir."

Meg smiled. "I ken it. I ne'er really thought it would be. So, where is she? Where are they sitting?"

"Come in here," he said as he took her by the arm and started to lead her into the great hall, "and have a wee bite to eat and a drink. Ye need to ken a few things ere ye go to Cecily."

By the time Angus had finished telling Meg everything that he knew had happened to Cecily and Artan since leaving Dunburn, she had grown a little pale. He realized that the woman truly cared for Cecily and was not calling the girl *my Cecily* in just mild affection for a child she had nursed. "The danger is past," he assured her.

"Nay, it isnae, is it. The laddie is caught in a deep sleep from what ye have just told me. Mayhap it is his way to heal and mayhap it isnae. Cecily is a good wee healer and she kens it weel, for all she doesnae have confidence in anything else she does. She also kens weel that some sleeps can be verra dangerous things. Poor wee lass must be terrified."

"Then I am certain ye will be a great comfort to her."

"I mean to be. She cannae bear another loss, Angus." Meg grimaced. "Weel, that isnae really true. She is a strong lass e'en if she doesnae ken it. She *will* bear it, but I darenst think of how grieved she will be. She may nay have admitted it yet, but she loves that braw lad. I think she has from the beginning."

"I think she has, too, and whatever doubts I held about how she felt about Artan have faded over these last six days. Howbeit, she needs to rest, Meg. Crooked Cat has managed to make her rest for short periods of time now and again, but she needs to rest. She lies down with him at night and I made the mistake of thinking she slept until I looked in on her t'other night. She was wide awake with her ear resting against his chest and her hand placed upon his neck.

"I heard her talking to him, too. 'Tis as if she is trying to convince him to stay. Bennet, Artan's cousin, has ridden off to his kinswomen to see if they have any advice. They are all said to be excellent healers."

"Will one come back with him?"

"Probably not. He means to tell them that our Cecily is a gifted healer, too. He says they will send medicines that might help or advice. Howbeit, he is nay hopeful that they will ken what to do any better than Cecily does."

Meg nodded. "It sounds as if the problem lies in his head or his spirit, and e'en the best of healers have trouble with those ailments."

Angus rubbed his chin. "Cecily thinks his spirit has retreated to get away from the pain that wracks his body."

"And what do ye think?"

"I actually think that makes sense."

"Aye," Meg agreed and smiled faintly, "it does, and 'tis such as that that makes wee Cecily a gifted healer."

"Because she can think such things out and understand them?"

"Aye and nay." Meg chuckled at the disgusted

look upon Angus's face. "Some she feels. That is it. She feels it. Some she thinks out. This, weel, this I think she is feeling. It would explain why she crawls abed with a mon who must have all the warmth of a corpse at the moment."

"If that." Angus sighed and dragged his hand through his hair. "His body is there, but he isnae, Meg. I stand there watching him breathe and I want to shake him, to do something to get a response out of him. Cecily bathed and stitched three sword wounds on him when he first came home and he didnae e'en twitch."

"Ye fear that the next time ye stand by the bed ye will be watching him take that final step away from the living," she said quietly and reached across the table to pat his hand.

"'Tis exactly the way of it. I think it is what Cecily fears, too."

"Nay doubt. Such a nightmare. The fact that he is such a fine-looking mon, strong and young, only makes it harder to bear. Ones like him arenae supposed to just fade away."

"Ye have the right of it. They are supposed to stride through life knocking aside all opponents. This slow dying, this giving up seems, weel, cowardly."

"Nay, not at all. Just because a mon is young and strong doesnae mean he will have any better control of his body than if he is an old mon whose bones creak. Ye say he was beaten and kicked. How can ye tell what was hurt? There are many injuries that can cause this."

"'Tis what Cecily says." Watching as Meg stood up, Angus asked, "Do ye ken what ye may be able to do to help the poor lass?"

"Nay yet, but I will do by the time I reach whate'er room she is in."

Angus stood up and took her by the arm to lead her to Artan and Cecily's bedchamber. "I hope the lad comes back to us and nay just for my sake. A mon in the village had a brother who acted like this after he feel off a roof. He has told us what to watch for to ken when to send for Artan's family so that they can be here for his last days. It seems that, since we can get some food and drink into him, he could last this way for a verra long time. This poor mon's brother lasted two years and then one night he was gone."

"That would be too sad if it happened to Sir Artan."

There was little Angus could say to that hard truth, and so he only nodded. At the door to the bedchamber he paused, hating to show her the sad scene. Each time he went in it felt more and more as if he was just there to say faretheeweel.

"One more thing," he said, then grimaced. "I may be a foolish old man with a more superstitious nature than I kenned I had, but she talks to the lad."

"How so?"

"Sometimes it is as if she carries on whole conversations with him, and the way she speaks and pauses, weel, 'tis as if there really is someone there."

"Ah, poor Angus. 'Tis but the game of a lonely child, one who doesnae have anyone to play with. She used to do it at Dunburn when she was a small child, but she would use some rag or the like as her toy. I fear she now uses the poor insensible Sir Artan. Ye ne'er can tell, Angus. It might finally reach him."

"One can but pray for that. See if ye can get her to eat or drink something. Crooked Cat left her something."

"I will. She hasnae got any pounds on her to waste." Meg shooed him aside. "Tend to your business, Angus, and let me tend to mine. Oh, there are two carts of belongings set out in the bailey. I gathered up what few things Cecily and I could gather from things Anabel threw away. I will explain later, but right now I must see how my wee lass fares."

The moment Angus walked away Meg slipped inside the bedchamber. She needed a minute to see clearly in the heavily shadowed bedchamber, but when she finally saw her Cecily she thought she might have to slip away for a few minutes to weep. Cecily lay curled up at Sir Artan's side. One small hand was on his neck and her ear was obviously placed so that she could hear his heartbeat.

Meg studied the man lying so still in the bed and could understand what Cecily was doing. He seemed dead, lying stiller than anyone she had ever seen. Meg suspected she would feel compelled to keep an ear cocked to his heartbeat as well. Then she became aware of the soft whispers from the bed and cautiously moved closer. Although she felt guilty for listening in to what might well be private words Cecily would much rather keep secret, Meg also knew something might be said that could show her the way to help Cecily.

"'Twill be a sennight tomorrow, Artan," Cecily said, idly stroking the side of his neck. "I think your wounds dinnae pain ye as much as they did. An aching instead of an agony. As I have told ye, ye didnae break anything. Rather that chinless bastard didnae break anything when he beat on a wounded mon bound up tightly and leashed to a stake."

Meg decided that anger at the man who had done such a thing was a good sign.

"Ye are worrying Angus, ye ken. Oh, he tries nay to show it, but 'tis easy to see. He stands there by the bed and stares at ye as if he would like to see inside your head to find what keeps ye asleep and kill it. I suspicion that may be a monly feeling. Ye cannae fight this with a sword or a strong punch in the eye so it angers ye."

For a lass who had never had anything to do with men, Cecily had a good understanding of them, Meg thought, fighting the urge to say so out loud.

Cecily sighed and gently kissed Artan's chest just above his heart. "It has been a sennight since ye made me screech like a banshee. I dinnae ken if I can endure sleeping alone too much longer. I shall have to leave ye from time to time soon so that I can find someone to, er, make me hum."

Rising up on her forearms, Cecily studied his face, and then cursed softly. Not even the twitch of an eyelid. Mayhap she should dance naked about the room, she thought, then shook her head. He was unconscious. He would not notice and she would get cold for no reason. There was always the possibility of making love to him, she mused, and even started to reach for the blanket when she heard the soft sound of a woman's skirts brush the floor.

Blinking slowly, Cecily finally managed to see clearly enough to recognize who was standing only a foot or so away from the bed. "Oh, Meg," she whispered even as she stumbled off of the bed and hurried toward the woman. "I was so hoping ye would come."

Meg caught the smaller Cecily in her arms and held her close. She was not surprised to feel the damp of tears begin to seep through her bodice. For a little while she would let Cecily cry and they would sit down and discuss what had been done for Sir Murray and what needed to be done next. Keeping her arm around Cecily's shoulders, Meg led her to a little table near the fireplace and urged her down into a seat. Meg then sat right across from her.

"What have ye done for him beside keeping his body comfortable, clean, and fed? Oh, and threatening to go out and find a mon." She almost grinned at the look of dismay and guilt that crossed Cecily's face.

"I was rather hoping that, if he is still in there, he might hear that and wake up just to stop me," Cecily replied.

"Ah, possessive, is he?"

"I think he may be. But how did ye get here?"

"Brought two carts of goods. Ones ye kept to the side and ones I kept to the side. Of course, it now looks as if it will soon all be coming to ye."

"Nay, maybe not. We have no document proclaiming me heir to it all."

"The priest has it."

Cecily nearly gaped at Meg. "What priest?"

"The priest but a few miles from where we were attacked. Your father gave it to me ere we left Angus's and told me to put it someplace safe if we were attacked. We were and I did. I couldnae read then, ye ken, and I have only just realized what I must have been giving the priest."

"If we can find that we can get rid of Anabel and Edmund."

Meg put her hands over her face and shook her head. "I cannae believe I ne'er thought on the importance of that paper."

Cecily reached over and patted Meg on the arm. "Ye couldnae read and we were all running for our lives at the time. Handing a piece of paper to a priest probably was the last thing ye recall from that day."

"Nay, true enough. If the memory e'er crept up on me it was poor wee Colin I thought of and I shoved it right out of my mind."

"Aye, I did the same. It hurt too much."

"It hurt me, too, lass, but it also twisted me up with guilt each and every time. I grabbed ye and ran, love. I ne'er thought of anything else. I didnae e'en look to see if I could have reached the boy; so, nay, I didnae think of that time much and pushed the memories from my mind.

"Colin died first," Cecily said quietly and nodded when Meg looked at her, shock clear to read on her face. "Ye held me so that I was looking back. Colin was dead ere ye e'en started running, Meg." She took a deep breath to steady herself for saying out loud what she had seen in her nightmares for so many years. "He took an arrow in the eye. I can still see it, still see Papa looking at his bairn dead at his feet, and then hurling himself right at all those armed men, one sword against ten. He did do one thing ere he did that." She frowned as she forced the memory to linger for a moment. "He kissed Colin, then looked to see us running away. I can still see the tears on his face, but he smiled then, tapped his forehead as he liked to do in greeting or faretheweel, and then he ran straight at all those men."

"Have ye always recalled it so clearly, Cecily?"

"Nay, and I didnae want to, did I."

"Then why now?"

"Weel, I have been talking for near a sennight, havenae I? I have talked and talked and one time that just all poured out of me. He saw us live, Meg. That is what I decided. At the last moment he saw that one of his bairns was going to live."

Meg dragged a piece of linen from her pocket and wiped the tears from her eyes. "Oh my, this is nay what I came in here for."

Cecily smiled faintly. "Ye were sent in by my uncle, were ye?"

"Och, nay, I came and asked for ye ere he told me of all that has happened to ye." She looked at the bed. "So ye married your Highlander, eh?"

"Weel, handfasted, but 'twill be a priest when he is better."

Hearing the unsteadiness in Cecily's voice, Meg reached out and clasped the girl's hand in hers. "He will be better soon."

"It has been a verra long time, Meg, and there still isnae e'en the smallest sign that he kens anyone is here. I have pinched him, stuck him with a needle, and all sorts of things in an attempt to get a twitch, just a wee twitch. Naught. I really do begin to fear that he isnae in there anymore."

"He is alive, so he is in there. He is just verra deep inside."

"I looked for some wound on his head to explain this, but there really wasnae anything big, no great swelling. He looks better than he did, the bruises and swellings all fading, so why doesnae he wake up?"

"Who can say, lass? Ye must leave it in God's hands."

Cecily closed her eyes for a moment. "I ken it, but this frightens me so and I grow angry. That does nay good."

"Nay, it doesnae. Ye love him, dinnae ye?"

"Och, aye. So much."

When Cecily began to cry, Meg quickly moved to hold her in her arms. "We shall see this through, lass. We shall. And we shall find a way to bring your braw laddie back to ye."

"What did ye think of him then?" Angus asked Meg as they shared some wine in the solar long after others had sought their beds.

"I think it isnae hopeless, but that is all I think," replied Meg as she stretched her feet out, placing them a little closer to the fire. "Nay, I also think my poor lass is going to lose her voice if he doesnae rouse soon."

"She is talking a lot. Crooked Cat keeps bringing her a honey mix to soothe her throat for 'tis sore by the end of the day."

"The mon is missing a lot of her secrets. He will be sorry for that."

"If he has missed them, how can he ken he has and then be sorry?"

"Dinnae be so clever. 'Tis annoying." She hid her smile by sipping her wine.

"I want him back, too. I thought I had picked him for my heir because he has some MacReith blood in him and he is a strong laddie, but thinking he might be gone forever soon has made me see it was far more than that."

"He is the son ye ne'er had."

"Aye, him more so than his twin, although Lucas is a good lad. His heart is at Donncoill, though. And there was always that standing between us."

"Weel, I have no gift of seeing or the like, but I just cannae see the lad dying."

"I will go and sit with the lass in a wee bit. Give her voice a rest."

"She said she has begun to repeat herself, so ye could save her that shame." She exchanged a brief grin with him, but concern for Artan hung so heavy in the air the good humor was quickly smothered. "I just keep trying to think of things that might break through the wall he seems to be hiding behind, but the lass has tried them all already."

"So," Angus began after a moment's silence that was not completely comfortable, "how is your husband?"

"Dead. How is your wife?"

"Dead. Both of them."

"Twice married?"

"And twice widowed and nary a bairn to show for it."

"Weel, I suspicion that lad and my lass will be filling these old halls with the sounds of children ere too long has passed."

"'Tis a sound that has been missing for too long. Laughter, too. I thought that when the lads returned and then Artan arrived with Cecily. Ye do ken that I wrote—to her and to the ones who call themselves her guardians?"

"When I wasnae cursing ye for a heartless swine who turned his back on his own blood, aye, I felt that something wasnae right. Nay way for me to find out what was happening, howbeit. The lass and I were kept apart from the others and then I got thrown out."

"For what?"

"Ripping the cane Anabel was whipping Cecily with out of the bitch's hands and whipping Anabel with it."

"Thank ye."

"Ye are welcome, and it did feel good, but it left the lass truly alone in the end, and that wasnae good." Meg sighed. "If I am wrong and this lad does slip away, I fear Cecily will feel deeply alone and with the sort of aloneness an old nursemaid cannae heal."

Cecily finished combing her hair dry and then braided her hair. The hot bath had felt good, and she was ready to face yet another night of trying to get Artan to come home, as she had begun to think of it. In the back of her mind still dangled the thought of making love to him to see if that feeling cut through to the Artan hiding inside this too-still body. Since the thought would not go away, she decided to consider the possibilities a bit more. And the how of it, she mused. She had not had the experience with Artan yet to be able to do it all on her own. The few times she had taken the lead, he had been right there with her, occasionally steering her in the right direction.

Moving to sit on the edge of the bed, she picked up the small tankard of wine she had put there earlier and had a sip. He looked so peaceful, she thought as she watched his face, something else she did regularly in her constant search for some sign of returning life. He looked so handsome, and yet, without that spark of life in his features, they were merely good, well-cut lines placed well and no more. It was that spark of life that turned well-cut lines into real beauty, and she missed it sorely.

She tried to think of something she could talk about that she had not talked about before and then tensed. Turning her full attention back to his face, she waited, knowing she had seen something there, some twitch in his cheek or flicker behind his eyelid. Setting her wine back down on the table by the bed, she straddled his body and stared at his face, trying to will the movement back so that she could see it and judge its worth. Her whole body soon began to ache with tension, but she was so sure she had seen something she did not dare to turn away for one minute.

"Please, Artan," she whispered. "Please come back. I ken ye were there a minute ago. Dinnae flee."

When several more minutes passed and nothing happened, Cecily decided to try pleading to a higher power. "Please, God, please. I will become the perfect wife for him. I will follow all the rules and bow to him in all things. Just please give him back. I ken he started to come home, but he slipped away again. I will learn all those things good wives should ken and be his perfect lady of Glascreag. I will e'en learn how to weave tapestries. Just a twitch?"

She slowly lowered her forehead to his, her neck too sore to hold it up any longer. It must have been a false vision born of hopes that she should not still be cherishing. Sitting up again, she was just about to get off the bed when she saw his nose twitch every so faintly as if he was idly deciding not to sneeze after all. Again, again, she silently commanded, and scowled in frustration. She knew she had seen it, but she needed to be sure before she raised everyone's hopes.

"Why are ye staring at my nose?"

The voice was hoarse and soft, but it was achingly familiar, and Cecily looked up to find Artan staring at her. His silvery blue eyes appeared magic to her. There was life there again. She choked back a sob of relief as she grabbed her tankard of wine and helped him drink from it.

"Better," he rasped, lightly rubbing his throat. "Old Fergus tried to choke me, did he?"

"Nay, he tried to beat ye to death a sennight ago." She nodded when he stared at her in shock. "Ye have been senseless for a sennight. We have tried everything and there wasnae so much as a twitch out of ye until tonight. I think your nose itched."

"I can recall ye coming into the tent," he said.

"I was to keep Sir Fergus's attention fixed on me so that Angus and his men could get closer and then rescue ye." She held up his hand and pointed to his still-healing wrists. "He beat ye while ye were wounded and tied."

"What happened to Sir Fergus?"

"He was about to kill ye in a fit of rage and Sir MacIvor took off his head."

"It rolled to ye and it touched the toes of your slippers." He frowned. "I cannae remember anything else."

"Ye might not for a while."

She flung herself against his chest and began to weep. Angus chose that moment to enter the bedchamber. Artan could tell by the look on the old man's face that he really cared for him and he was touched. He then tried to lift his hand from the bed to either wave at Angus or stroke a weeping Cecily, but he was too weak to even lift his hand, which seemed to confirm what Cecily had just told him. A minute later, Angus was at his bedside grasping that hand tightly and occasionally shaking it.

"We really thought we had lost ye, that all we could do for ye was keep ye warm, clean, and weel fed."

"So I could rot in this bed for years?"

Sure the sudden temper was not really aimed at Angus, Cecily decided now was a good time to start with seeing to his needs far more completely. She started ordering people around, startled when they heeded her, even Angus. By the time she slipped into the bedchamber, Artan had been bathed and shaved and his bed linens had been changed. The dampness around his head told her that he had had his hair washed, which she thought was foolishly unnecessary but decided to ignore.

"Bed," he said, lifting the covers about an inch, which seemed to take all of his strength.

Cecily wasted no time in accepting the invitation. She curled up in his arms, not caring that he could barely move them. His strength would return and she would soon be sleeping wrapped in his arms again. For that she was more than willing to fulfill her promise to God. She would become the perfect wife just as soon as she figured out all the rules.

"Sile?"

She lifted her head to look at him. "What, Artan?"

"Thank ye."

"For what?"

"Talking to me."

"Ye could hear me?" Cecily tried to think of what she had said and knew it was practically everything she had in her head and in her heart.

"I couldnae understand the words, only one here and there, but I could often hear your voice."

"Oh, I had so hoped ye would. I was trying to bring ye back. I was so sure ye were in there, and I thought if I kept talking to ye, ye wouldnae keep slipping further and further away, ye would start to come home."

"Aye, I did, because I wanted to say something to ye."

"What is that, Artan?"

"Hush."

For a minute she was utterly shocked; then she was torn between being deeply hurt and wanting to berate him for his utter ingratitude. Then she saw it. That spark that told her he was but teasing her and was waiting to see what she would do. The quiet heartfelt thanks at the start of the conversation was where his true feelings lay.

She leaned over him and brushed a kiss over his mouth, "Welcome back, Artan."

Chapter 20

"Married?"

Cecily almost dropped the tray of food she had been carrying toward the table by the bed. She quickly set it down before Artan could say anything else. Even though he had been awake now for a fortnight, she still found it difficult to believe. Every time he had gone to sleep at night after his miraculous awakening, she had held him close, listening to his heart all night and waiting almost desperately for that first sign of wakefulness in the morning.

"We are already married, Artan," she said.

"Nay by a priest," he replied, standing up and moving the tray of food to the table near the fire.

It felt good to be walking, although Artan still did not feel quite as strong as he would like. After seating Cecily in the chair opposite him, he sat down, set some bread and cheese on a plate for her, and then served himself. He watched her closely as he ate, pleased to see her begin to eat the food he had given her. She had lost a little weight and, as delicate as she was, he did not think that was a good thing.

"Ye want us to be married by a priest?" she asked as she idly cut herself a small piece of cold mutton.

"I do. I always have. 'Tis just that we have had to deal with Sir Fergus and then with my wee sleep."

Wee sleep, he called it. Cecily doubted she could ever explain the terror she had felt, constantly, over the week and sometime after. To hear his heart beat and watch him breathe yet see no other sign of life was an ordeal she hoped she never had to go through again.

"When shall we do it, then?" she asked.

"On the morrow. I have already arranged matters with Angus and Meg."

Pushing aside the annoyance she felt over the fact that no one had consulted her, Cecily just nodded. Being a good wife was far more difficult than she had imagined. It was times like these when Artan was at his most arrogant that she had to wrestle her bad self into submission. A good wife bowed to her husband's wishes, she reminded herself.

Artan chewed on his honey-coated chunk of bread and idly wondered if shaking his wife would wake the old Cecily back up as he had been roused from his little sleep by her voice. He was growing heartily sick of all this sweetness, this meek, obedient nature she had assumed. Each day he could see a little more of the spark he loved disappear.

He blinked and stared down at his meal. Had he just thought the word *love*? He had, he decided. It had slipped through his mind as if it belonged there and would not be refused entrance again. It appeared that at some time since he had met Cecily he had fallen in love with her, deeply and fiercely in love. Having never experienced the emotion before, he had been slow to recognize it. Artan supposed he ought to have guessed at the state of his emotions. From the first time they had kissed he had been thinking of her as his mate.

It was not a revelation he was pleased to be having at the moment. Artan knew it would prey on him, distract him, and make him need to know how his wife felt about him. It was important, but right now he had to marry his Sile with the blessings of the church and then find out what game she was playing.

Slowly but surely she was changing, turning into a woman he did not know, and that worried him. She may be cosseting him because of his wounds and the illness that had kept her at his side for a sennight, but he did not really think so. He was not sure what questions he needed to ask to get the answers he needed, either.

What troubled him the most was that she was turning shy and retreating from him in the bedchamber. He supposed she could have fallen back into her virginal ways as they had not been lovers very long before his injuries had incapacitated him. He had reached for her exactly one week after he had woken up, even knowing that he was still a little too weak for such activity. It had relieved his frustration, but something had been missing and he knew it was not just because he had not been at his best.

Something had been missing in the way his wife responded to his touch. At one point he could have sworn that she had been gritting her teeth as if to silence herself, but he had no idea why she should do such a thing. It was as if the fire they shared was slowly flickering out inside of her, and that alarmed him. It was also one reason he had decided to get married to her with a priest's blessing. Perhaps once their union was sanctified by the church this strange reticence would leave Cecily and his Sile would return. Intending to be at full strength for that reunion, he had decided to wait to make love again until they were married in the eyes of the church.

"Weel, then, 'tis all settled. We wed on the morrow," he said as he stood up and gave her a very chaste kiss on the cheek. "I am sure ye will want to find Meg so that the two of ye can plan the feast."

Cecily watched her husband as he left their bedchamber. It was going to take her a while to push aside her annoyance, don her sweet smile, and become the good wife again. Although she knew one of the rules for being a good wife was to bow to one's husband's wishes, she had not realized that meant she should be ordered around like a child. It was not going to be easy to adjust to that. Artan had a way of giving her a command that made her want to hunt down something big and heavy to throw at his head.

Feeling she was calm once again, she finished off the cheese and went to find Meg. That woman was in the kitchen discussing the morrow's feast with Crooked Cat. After nearly twenty minutes of being ignored, or ordered about and not consulted, or of having every decision made for her, as well as what few decisions she made for herself gently but firmly discarded, Cecily decided she would go and find what she might wear to her wedding.

Crooked Cat peeked into the great hall, then turned back to face Meg. "She looked fit to spit."

"Good," said Meg. "She was being so polite and

so respectful to her elders, it was either chase her away or throw her into the laundry tub."

"Why is she being so sweet? Isnae that her nature? She seemed a good lass to me."

"Oh, she is a verra good lass, and she is sweet in her own way and with a verra big heart. 'Tis that awful always-willing, may-I-do-anything-for-ye type of sweetness I dinnae like. That is what Anabel tried to make Cecily into. There were times when I thought Cecily would smile and ask the hangmon if he needed help putting the rope around her neck." Meg smiled when Crooked Cat laughed.

"But what is the nature of the lesson ye are trying to give her?"

"To be what she is, to let her feelings lead her, nay rules set down by some woman like Lady Anabel who seems to want the whole world to be just as miserable as she is."

"Ah, the kind of woman who always offers to tell a lass what to expect on her wedding night and, after dispensing their great wisdom, leave behind an absolutely terrified bride."

"Aye, exactly that kind of woman."

"Weel, do ye think what we did just now will make Cecily stop playing that too-sweet lass?"

"Nay, not yet. That was just for putting another log on the fire, so to speak, to burn all that nonsense away."

"Why, Meg, that was, weel, poetical, if I do say so myself."

"Ye may." She laughed along with Crooked Cat.

Cecily frowned at her dresses. They were laid out on top of every available piece of furniture. Her

uncle had been very generous, especially with all
the gowns left by each of his late wives. Most of them
would require a great deal of reworking and could
not be done in time for the wedding. That left her
with few choices once she removed the few gowns
that no one would wear to their own wedding.

Finally, she chose a simple green one, set it aside,
and put the others back in the chest. It was going to
be difficult to look as if she was a cherished or particularly important bride in that simple gown, but
since she was neither, it did not matter. It was a
shame that she did not have her trousseau from
Dunburn, but wearing the clothes bought for her
marriage to another man might be one of those
things that was considered bad luck. The very last
thing she needed was bad luck.

Glancing at the small box Artan's mother had
sent back with Bennet, she wondered if wearing the
dark garnet pendant the woman sent her as a
bridal gift would be acceptable. She had been
touched by the woman's generosity. It made her
eager to meet Artan's family even as it made her
terrified to do so. Everything Artan had told her
about his family indicated that it was large, boister-
ous, and friendly. After a great deal of thought,
Cecily admitted she did not know how to deal with
such people. In truth, she knew very little about
dealing with any people, having been kept very iso-
lated at Dunburn.

Opening the little box, she took out the pendant
to admire it and to try to come to some decision.
Cecily also admitted to herself that some of her fascination was due to the fact that it *was* a gift. She
had never had one before. Suddenly, she noticed
that under the little velvet patch lining the box was

a piece of parchment. She cautiously opened it and read it, then had to sit down. Artan's mother had written her a very cheerful welcoming note filled with odd motherly details about Artan and not all of them flattering. Cecily could almost hear the woman chatting with her as if they had known each other for years.

Wiping the tears from her eyes, she quickly put the letter back in the box. The letter had decided the matter of whether or not to wear the pendant tomorrow. She would honor Artan's mother by wearing the woman's gift proudly. She just hoped she could do the woman's son proud, too.

"I dinnae think I ought to wear my hair down, Crooked Cat." Cecily sat, wincing a little as Crooked Cat fought a little roughly with a stubborn snarl.

"Ye were a virgin when ye married, werenae ye?"

"Of course."

"Nay of course about, lass. Fewer are than ye would think."

"That still doesnae mean I should break with tradition."

"Ye were virgin for your handfast wedding. This is the proper church one. 'Tis just the same thing with a more important fellow telling ye are wed." Crooked Cat studied Cecily very closely. "Are ye laughing?"

"Nay, of course not. Have it as ye will then. I will wear my hair down."

"It will go so fine with the green gown and that garnet."

Meg arrived and Cecily gave up all hope of having a say in what she should wear at her own wedding. She did admit, however, that she looked beautiful when they were done with her. She was no longer concerned about the rightness of wearing her hair down, either. She felt it was perfect that way for a wedding, even if it was a second one.

Suddenly, she sharply missed her father. Colin had been too young to be a big part of her life, and her mother had been gone before her father. Cecily wished he could see her as a bride and that he could be alive to hand her to her husband.

She had Angus, she told herself, and he was a very good uncle. In truth, although she was too old for a father, Angus had slowly eased into that place in all but name and she did not mind. Cecily knew that her father would have welcomed her and Angus making a family. Angus had a lot of cousins, but no direct family. It was the same for her in many ways. Angus was her closest relative and she was his.

When Angus entered the great hall and started walking toward her, Cecily had to smile. Angus was a big, strong man, and even some of the much younger women in the room watched him. When Artan walked into the great hall and every female in the room, as well as several peering in through the doors, watched him stride over to her, she did not find that so amusing. Cecily decided then and there that someone needed to make a rule that said women do not ogle the groom at a wedding. The next rule should be that, if they do, they are then subject to whatever punishment the bride chooses, such as a box full of spiders—on their head.

Feeling better at that thought, Cecily turned to smile at Artan. He did look as handsome as any man had a right to be. She was suddenly all too aware of the fact that this was a man any woman would want and far too many would not consider the fact that he had a little red-haired freckled wife an impediment. He had said he would be faithful and she saw no sign that he was a man who had to look or smile at every pretty woman he saw, but they looked at him a lot. At his age, he had to be fully aware of the temptations flung his way, but had he accepted or rejected most of them, and if he had accepted a lot, could he now refuse them? It was something she did not really want to think of on her wedding day, but since he had never offered her any words of love, she could not shake the sudden fear that gripped her so tightly.

"Ye look beautiful, Sile mine," he said as he took her hand in his and actually kissed her palm with everyone watching.

Cecily leaned a little closer to him, and said softly, "Ye are looking rather beautiful yourself." The smile he gave her took her breath away. Cecily so badly wanted this man to love her she feared she could easily make an utter fool of herself. For one brief moment she actually considered running, out of the great hall and out of the keep and out of the gates of Glascreag. She quickly stiffened her spine. If nothing else, she would not humiliate her uncle in such a way.

"Come, lass," he said, holding her hand near his hip as he tugged her toward the dais table where the priest waited for them. "Time to get the church's blessings."

The priest was a very young man and was nervous. Surreptitiously looking around as she knelt beside Artan, Cecily decided she really did not blame the man. The great hall was crowded with

MacReith warriors, and warriors seemed unable to go anywhere without a weapon. If an enemy was foolish enough to think it was safe to attack because of this solemn occasion, he would quickly and fatally find out otherwise.

When it was done, Artan gently pulled her to her feet and kissed her. The hoots and random, somewhat crude suggestions were deafening. Even more deafening was her uncle bellowing orders to watch their tongues. The occasional hooting and foot stomping continued, but Cecily was pleased that advice on what she and Artan should do in their bedchamber had almost completely disappeared. The ones who felt compelled to say something did so quietly.

"Been a mon's keep too long, lass," her uncle said to her as he took his seat at the head of the table. He nodded at Meg, who was seated on his left to Cecily's surprise, and Meg's by the look of it.

"I think there is much the same at all weddings," she said. "I havenae been to any, but I have heard the talk about them afterward."

"Why didnae ye e'er go to a wedding?"

"I was rarely taken anywhere, Uncle," she said very quietly, hoping not too many people overheard her words.

"Weel, looking at ye all done up bonnie like that, I cannae see why."

"Why, thank ye, Uncle. That was a lovely compliment." She smiled even more when he blushed a little, suddenly discomforted by uttering flatteries. "Ye do have an impressive group of men under your command. So impressive I think the priest was a little nervous."

"Ah, aye, I noticed that. He is a Lowland laddie,

so we have to be understanding. Our ways have ne'er been his and he needs to learn them."

"Ye couldnae get a Highland priest?"

"There arenae that many that go into it, I suspicion."

Just as Cecily opened her mouth to ask, Artan whispered in her ear, "I wouldnae ask that question if I were ye."

When she looked at her uncle she suddenly recognized the glint in his eye. "Tsk, Uncle," she murmured. "And on my wedding day. Have ye no shame."

"Nay, none at all," he said cheerfully and grinned at Meg, who was laughing.

There was a jovial air to the feast that made it so much more enjoyable than the few she had endured at Dunburn, Cecily wondered how Artan had endured those meals. It had all been made even worse by the fact that few had made any secret that they considered Artan little better than some animal. Cecily was not fool enough to think she would have been treated quite so kindly by everyone if she had just been a Lowlander. It was her connection to the laird and Meg's as well that kept them from feeling like complete misfits.

When it was late enough to escape without attracting the shocked attention of everyone, Artan signaled Meg and Crooked Cat to take Cecily upstairs. She had done him proud tonight. Her manners and her sweetness would have been acceptable at a king's table. There had been an odd reserve in her manner, however. It was as if she played some game or feared a misstep so much that she took each one with supreme care. This was his wedding night, but it was hardly their first, and he was beginning to need an answer to the puzzle that had

become his wife more than he needed to leap right
into bed with his bride. By the time Artan got to
their bedchamber he had honed his curiosity to a
fine edge. He wanted answers and he wanted them
now.

Meg slipped into the seat next to Angus and murmured a thank you when the page poured her
some wine. "She certainly looked pretty."

"Aye, she did, and sometimes she seemed at ease.
But other times, weel, 'twas looking and listening to
a stranger." Angus shook his head. "Over the last
few weeks that has happened more and more."

"I fear Anabel has a verra long reach," muttered
Meg.

"What do ye mean?"

"Anabel had a heavy hand when she taught
Cecily all that young ladies are supposed to know.
One reason I accepted Artan and trusted him was
because he wasnae like the courtiers cluttering up
the house then. But Anabel and Edmund are. That
is what ye saw here tonight. For reasons only she
can understand, Cecily has decided to try to be a
perfect lady. I sensed it shortly after Artan got
better. If I didnae ken better, I would think she
made a promise to God that she would be a good
wife and a perfect lady if He just let Artan live."

"And then the laddie opened his eyes."

"It would be just that girl's luck. She makes a
promise to be something she hates and all the fates
turn round and make sure she has to."

"Weel, it wasnae so bad. Just a bit of a surprise."

"Just wait, Angus. Just wait. It willnae be long
before one of ye wishes to strangle her."

"If being a lady has rules that make it all so objectionable to people, then why do any of them do it?"

Meg grinned. "It is objectionable when it takes a good lass like Cecily and turns her into a person ye dinnae ken and probably cannae get to know. It is certainly objectionable if 'tis Anabel doing the teaching, for she is the worst of the lot."

"I will, but then it isnae really my problem, is it?" Angus grinned and sat back to sip his wine and watch his guests.

Artan opened the door to their bedchamber, ready and eager to question his bride. He took one look at her in her thin linen gown with her long red hair hanging loose down her back and he forgot every question he had had ready. He just wanted to rip his clothes off and then rip hers off and they would proceed to the next step with speed and vigor.

He took a deep breath to calm himself. In many ways, his wife was still very innocent. A man did not rush an innocent. The very last thing he needed was to scare Cecily so badly she ran from the room. With the sort of luck he had had lately, he would be willing to bet that half of their wedding guests would be in just the perfect place at just the right time to see the future laird of Glascreag chasing the future lady of Glascreag through the halls of the keep. Glancing down at himself, he realized he had already removed half his clothes and decided they would quickly be telling everyone that he had been chasing his bride through the halls while naked.

He stepped up to Cecily, thinking that she looked more determined than anxious. Then again, he mused, she was Angus's niece. He suspected it would take more than a naked Highlander in pursuit to scare her.

"I thought ye looked lovely in your wedding gown," he murmured, then lightly fingered the fine linen lace trimming the placket of the night dress, "but in this ye look like an angel."

This was going to be a lot more difficult than she had thought if he was going to be complimenting her and looking so interested. It was easy enough to remain only dutiful for a man who simply says it is time to try for an heir, or so it had been implied, but this was so much different. This was heat and want, and everything inside of her was answering that call.

Artan pulled her into his arms and kissed her. He could feel the heat through his shirt and he still wanted all their clothes gone now. It was not long, however, before he got his wish.

Cecily was not sure who was the first one to rip something, but it ended the problem of being ever so careful. They were both naked and on the bed in minutes. Cecily tried one more time to rein in all those unladylike desires, but Artan started to suckle on her breasts and she was lost. The next she knew she was wrestling for the right to be on top.

Sprawled out on the bed beside each other was a good way to end the night, Artan thought. He wanted to hold his church-blessed bride, however. Summoning up all the energy he could, he rolled over and embraced his wife. She seemed a little tense considering what they had just enjoyed, and he lifted his head high enough to see her face. Her cheeks were still flushed with passion and her lips swollen with his kisses, but there was a troubled look in her eyes.

"What is the matter, Sile mine?"

"I acted like an animal," she whispered, strangely ashamed and excited at the same time.

"Nay, ye acted just like a wife should," Artan said, feeling a little drunk on the satisfaction he had just been blessed with. He just wanted to hold her close until he got his strength back.

"I did? It seemed a little, weel, loud."

"Aye, nice and loud. I think one of my ears is still ringing."

"And ye find that amusing?"

"Weel, aye, nay, not amusing exactly."

"'Tis nay the way a genteel lady would behave."

"Who the hell wants a lady in the bedchamber? I want my wife."

As Artan pulled her into his arms and started to make love to her again, Cecily fought all of her own inclinations. She knew she had still gasped and moaned a little, but retraining herself to practice some restraint was not going to be easy. It was worth it, however, to prove to Artan that she was a lady and a lady could also be wife. She had promised God to be a good wife and perfect lady and she would not, could not, back down.

Artan opened one eye and looked down at the woman sleeping in his arms. There was definitely some strange thoughts leaping about in her clever little mind. All that talk about ladies and calling her passionate lovemaking acting like an animal. He had said something stupid then and he knew it, but he could not seem to remember what it was.

She had, however. There had been a difference when they had made love the second time. There was still a fine passion in her, but he could feel her trying to control it, control herself. He needed to sleep, but first thing tomorrow he was going to sort this out. He would find out what stupid thing he had said and what odd idea she had in her head. Then he would apologize profusely for the former and do his best to talk to her of the latter.

Chapter 21

"Angus, I am going to strangle your niece."

Angus looked up from the carving he was working on and scowled at Artan. "She isnae just *my* niece now. She is also your *wife*. Howbeit, I will hold her still for ye is ye wish it."

"Nay, I believe I can manage it on my own. She isnae verra big." Artan sat down on the chest set beneath the window. "Just why are ye willing to help?"

"Might make her get her senses back. Seems to have lost them."

"Aha! So ye are finding her an irritant, too."

"Like a splinter under one's fingernail. If I hear any more sweetness, any more *May I help ye, Uncle? Shall I fetch ye some wine, Uncle? Are ye certain ye are warm enough, Uncle?* and the like, I willnae wait for ye to see to the problem, I will do it myself. What did ye do to the lass?"

"Me? I didnae do anything to her." Artan got to his feet and began to pace the room, ignoring Angus's grumbled command to have a care for his rug. "I thought all of this sweetness, humility, and care was because I was recovering from those scratches I took freeing her from that fool's grasp, but when she kept right on being so sweet it makes a mon's teeth ache e'en after I was healed, I began to wonder what was wrong. I e'en purposely said and did a few things to annoy her."

"Only a few?" Angus muttered, feigning astonishment.

Artan ignored him. "She did naught. Nary a flush upon her cheeks or a spark in her eyes. She didnae e'en toss out one those insults she likes to plan out. She acted as if I was right and told me she would try e'en harder to make sure I had no complaint in the future. The daft lass is wearying herself to the verra bone now. All that spirit she had is long gone. All her spark has disappeared. E'en in the bedchamber," he grumbled.

"Ach! I dinnae want to hear about *that*."

"Ye didnae think those bairns ye are hoping for will be found under the heather blooms, did ye? Best ye help me find out what is ailing my wife, or all those wee playthings ye are carving willnae be used. My fiery wee wife now has all the spark of a dead fish in the bedchamber. 'Tis near enough to wither a mon. If I had more experience I might be able to rekindle that fire, but . . ." Artan caught Angus gaping at him and he blushed, even though he was not sure why he should feel embarrassed. "I wasnae a virgin if that is what ye are thinking."

"Nay! But, weel, ye are a braw, handsome lad."

"And what does that have to do with it? Think a wee moment, Angus. I dinnae play the game with any of the lasses who work at the keeps I live in or where my kinsmen live, or lasses who are betrothed, or who are still maids, and I have only bedded another mon's wife once and that was in a good cause.

Lucas bedded her, too, and we did a penance together. That leaves me with widows and whores. Ye may get a wee bit of skill shaking the linen with a widow, but a whore is just a lass ye pay to give ye some ease. Truth tell, so are a lot of widows." He shrugged. "Lessons taught me by my mother and they have held fast."

Even though he was frowning, Angus slowly nodded in agreement. "Good, wise lessons. Ne'er gave it all much thought, but such rules can help a lad stay out of a lot of trouble. I wish someone had advised me thus. Had to learn that hard truth all on my own."

"Weel, we can discuss your past amours some other day," drawled Artan. "I need to get my wife back."

"Then ye should have made the lass ken weel that ye liked her just the way she was."

They turned toward the voice coming from the doorway of Angus's bedchamber so fast Artan was not surprised to hear his and Angus's necks crack softly. The smile on Old Meg's face told him that she had enjoyed startling them so thoroughly. He joined Angus in scowling at the woman. She ignored them both, walked over to the table, and placing her hands on her well-rounded hips, slowly shook her head. Her feminine disgust was so clear Artan nearly winced.

"Cannae ye see it, ye great fools? The poor wee lass is trying to be a good wife," said Old Meg.

"She was a good wife before. All fire and a sharp tongue," Artan added quietly, sighing a little in fond remembrance.

"And did ye let her ken weel that ye liked her that way? Nay, I dinnae think so."

"I married her and I bedded her. With vigor. That should be enough to tell a lass I like her."

"Ah, so ye *liked* those whores and widows ye tussled with, too, did ye?"

Artan glared at her. "I didnae bed them with vigor."

"Will ye get your wee mind out of the bedchamber for a moment?" snapped Angus.

"I cannae help it," said Artan. "'Tis where the changes in my wee wife pinch the sharpest."

"Aye, so it would," agreed Old Meg.

Angus snorted. "And what would ye ken about it, eh? Ye were married to that weak fool Lewis. Ow! Curse ye, woman," he muttered, and rubbed the ear she had just sharply twisted.

"Dinnae ye speak poorly of my late husband, Angus MacReith," said Old Meg. "He may nay have been the lusty swine ye were, but he gave me three fine sons and a bonnie lass, all who lived and are now having bairns of their own."

"If ye two could pause in your wooing for a wee while," drawled Artan, "I need some help getting my wife back." He had to bite back a laugh when both Angus and Old Meg blushed even as they glared at him, but his good humor fled quickly. "'Tis as if the spirit of some other lass has taken her o'er, a meek, puling lass who thinks she is more slave than wife."

"She is trying to be the perfect wife," said Old Meg.

"She was perfect for me just the way she was."

"As I have been saying, ye obviously didnae make that verra clear. Heed me, ever since her father and brother were killed, Cecily has tried to become a true part of a family, to win some hint of affection, respect, and acceptance from those Donaldsons. She ne'er really understood that naught she could e'er do would gain her that. Weel, she didnae ken the whole truth about them, did she? She always struggled to be what she thought Anabel wanted her to be. 'Tis why she was gong to marry that swine Fergus, aye? And from the moment that was arranged, Anabel lectured the lass on what a perfect wife should be, not that Anabel followed such foolish rules herself, mind you." Old Meg smiled sadly. "I fear my poor wee lass is e'en more determined to be perfect now."

"That is just daft," grumbled Angus. "Of course she is accepted here. She is blood, isnae she?"

"So were the Donaldsons," said Artan, beginning to understand what Old Meg was saying.

"The lass cannae be thinking we would harm her!"

"Nay, ye old fool," snapped Meg, "although one couldnae really blame her for being wary after all that has happened and all the hard truths she has had to face. The child had her whole family taken away, and the ones who should have taken her to their hearts ne'er did *and* were the verra ones who had destroyed all she loved. But, ye see, Cecily *needs* to be part of a family. With every failure to become a true part of the Donaldson family that need grew. She is blindly determined not to fail this time."

"So I need to show her that she *is* part of this family and that she doesnae have to be anything more than she is," said Artan, frowning over what he began to see as a daunting chore. "I could have some of the Murray lasses come here to meet her. She would soon see that having some spirit and a sharp tongue isnae going to trouble me at all. Ah, but that could take weeks, and I want my wife back now."

"Then ye are going to have to have a verra serious talk with her, let her ken exactly how ye feel about it all. And dinnae look so horrified. It willnae hurt. Ye have been talking to us about it, havenae ye?"

"Ye arenae my Sile."

"'Tis what ye have to do. She can be a stubborn lass, and now that she has decided this is what she must do to win her place here, she will stay on that path e'en if it kills her." Old Meg sat at the table in the chair facing Angus. "I have tried to talk to her, but she doesnae really heed me. She kens I love her like my own and thinks I but cosset her." She looked at Artan. "Ye speaking to her may help as I dinnae believe ye cosset her."

"She doesnae need any cosseting. She is a strong lass. Or was." He sighed. "Aye, I had best talk to her ere she buries her spirit so deep there is nay uncovering it again."

Old Meg nodded. "'Tis what I fear. With the Donaldsons it was ne'er so bad as this. That spirit was ne'er completely cowed. What she felt for them was mostly a sense of duty. 'Tis verra different now. Her heart's involved." She grinned at the sharp look of interest Artan gave her. "What? Didnae ye ken it?"

"How would I ken it? She has ne'er said so."

"Oh, aye, I suspicion she had told ye, just nay with words. She has told ye in those ways that have ye so eager for her spirit to be revived."

"Lust."

"Ach, nay more talk about *that*," muttered Angus, but Artan and Old Meg ignored him.

"That lass had ne'er e'en been properly kissed ere ye stomped into her life," Old Meg told Artan.

"She wouldnae have understood lust. Nay, she would have run from the fire in innocent confusion, especially if she didnae have any true feelings for ye. But she didnae run, did she? Nay, she jumped right into that fire with both feet. Of course she has feelings for ye, fool, and 'tis why she is so desperate to be a perfect wife for ye. As I watch Cecily now, I can almost hear the lectures Anabel gave her. Talks of duty, submissiveness, and all of that. Near every day the woman lectured the poor lass."

"Mayhap I should return to Dunburn now and get some retributions," Artan said, his voice hard and low.

"'Twould take weeks," said Angus, "and ye need to do something about our Sile now."

Artan nodded even though he had no idea what to say to his wife. He had no skill at discussing feelings, certainly not his own, and he suspected he would need to talk about how he felt as well. He was strongly tempted to wait and see if Cecily pulled out of this strange mood on her own or call upon his sisters for help. Inwardly, he shook aside those ideas. They were born of cowardice. They would also not work as well as a little honesty between him and Sile. He just wished he had some skill at wooing and speaking the sort of soft words a woman liked.

"I wish ye would cease looking as if I had just asked ye to cut off your own leg," muttered Old Meg.

"That might be less painful," he drawled, and briefly grinned at the look of feminine disgust she gave him. "I will do it, Meg, dinnae fear about that. I just cannae be sure I will do it verra weel. I have little skill at wooing." He felt himself blush faintly beneath the intent look she gave him.

"Nay, I suspicion ye havenae needed any."

"'Twould sound vain if I were to agree with ye."

Old Meg shrugged. "'Tis just the truth. All that doesnae matter. Cecily isnae like one of those lasses ye took your ease with in the past. Best ye start thinking of what ye can say that will make her understand that she doesnae need to be anything but what she truly is."

Artan nodded and left the room. He needed to go for a ride, a hard, fast ride. He always thought better when he rode, and he needed to do a lot of hard thinking now. It would not be easy to get his Sile back, and he was far too aware of the fact that he lacked the proper skills to fight this battle. He wished his sister and her husband lived nearer to Glascreag. Liam Cameron was a man who knew well how to woo a lady. Sweet words tripped off the man's tongue with ease. Artan had not really envied that skill until now.

Once on the back of Thunderbolt, Artan gave the horse its head. He rode hard for several miles, letting the wind and the rhythm of his steed clear his mind. When he finally reined in, coaxing the horse into a slower pace, Artan looked around to mark where he was and realized he was nearly at the eastern border of Glascreag lands. He smiled and idly patted his mount's neck. Thunderbolt might be getting old, but he still had the ability to take a man far and fast.

"Good mon," he murmured, turning the horse and letting the animal amble back in the direction of the keep and the warm stables. "Take your time, lad. I need to think. If only a woman could be as simple to ken as a good horse." He laughed softly when Thunderbolt snorted and shook his head. "Aye, I ken that I would soon tire of that."

Artan was halfway back to the keep but no closer to having a plan when he espied his cousin Bennet. The man hailed him and rode up to him to fall in at his side. At first Artan resented this intrusion, but then decided it could prove useful. With his golden hair and blue eyes, Bennet never lacked for a woman's attention. Although Artan had never noticed that the man had any great skill with soft words and flatteries, Bennet had to be doing something right to make so many women smile.

"What are ye doing riding about all alone and somber when ye have such a bonnie wife at home?" asked Bennet.

"'Tis my bonnie wife who has caused me to be out here ambling along like an old mon."

"Ah, ye have made her angry, have ye?"

"Nay, not for days, and therein lies the problem."

Bennet frowned in confusion. "I must be particularly witless today for I dinnae see the problem. Ye dinnae like the fact that your wife isnae angry at you?"

"I am nay an easy mon to live with." Artan waited patiently for his cousin to stop laughing before he continued, "For my wife to be all sweet and smiling for so long just isnae right. She is too sweet, too obedient, too virtuous. She obeys my every command and rushes to see to my every need."

"Most men would be on their knees thanking God for the gift of such a wife, especially a virtuous one."

"Weel, I didnae mean I thought she ought to be smiling a welcome to every mon she sees," Artan snapped.

Bennet nodded. "Ye mean too virtuous in that she has all the fire and life of a dead herring."

Artan knew he was blushing for he could feel the faint heat of it in his cheeks. Even though he would like nothing better than to wipe that big grin off his cousin's face, swiftly and violently, he ignored it. He needed to get his Sile back, and despite all Old Meg had advised, he still had no real idea of how to do that. It galled him to admit it, but he needed help. A lot of help.

"Sile has turned herself into the perfect wife, or what that bitch Anabel told her a perfect wife should be."

"Why would Sile heed anything that woman ever said?"

"Just because the woman turned out to be a conniving bitch who cared naught for the child in her care doesnae mean every word she uttered was a lie. And we both ken how some training can get a deep hold on a person. Old Meg says this is all because Sile needs to part of a family."

"She *is* part of a family. Our family."

"I didnae say it made any sense. Old Meg says Sile is doing this because I didnae make it clear that I liked my lass just as she was—all spit and fire. Sile is wearing herself to the bone trying to make herself perfect."

Bennet nodded. "Aye, she has looked weary of late. So tell her ye like her as she is."

"I dinnae like her this way."

"I meant as she *was*."

Artan dragged his hand through his hair. "I am nay sure of the best way to do that, to make her believe me and stop this nonsense. I tried to make her angry, but that didnae work. All she did was apologize and promise to try harder to be a good wife."

"That doesnae sound like our Sile."

"*My* Sile and, nay, it doesnae. Seems Lady Anabel deafened the lass for years with lectures on how a lady should act and what a proper wife should do and say and she enforced her opinions with beatings. Now Sile has decided to obey each and every rule." Artan nodded when Bennet cursed, pleased that his cousin finally understood his problem. "I am going to have to *talk* to her."

"I see the problem now. By talk ye mean telling her how ye feel and all that. Difficult."

"Impossible. I am nay a mon of sweet words and I have no skill at flatteries."

"Er, nay. Nay, ye dinnae. 'Tisnae something I can teach ye in but a few hours either, Artan."

That was not what Artan wanted to hear. He suddenly wondered if being skilled with flatteries and sweet words did not necessarily mean you were truly good with women, or understood them any more than any other man, or could solve a problem that arose between you and the woman of your choice. It only meant that you could draw them into your bed or make them blush and smile. It might get one a wife, but it did not mean that one could keep her happy.

"Nay, I suppose ye cannae," he agreed and sighed. "And e'en if ye did, it wouldnae sound right when I said words ye had given me to say. Sile would ken they werenae my words. Just tell me what ye would do."

Bennet grimaced and scratched his chin. "I dinnae really ken. Tell her how ye feel, I suppose.

Tell her ye liked her when she stood firm against ye and called ye an oaf when ye were acting like one."

"Actually, she called me an overbearing ogre who grunts more than he talks." Artan smiled faintly in remembrance as Bennet laughed. "Oh, and a wart on Satan's nose. I told her she needed to think harder on that one as it wasnae one of her best insults."

"She thinks up insults?"

"Aye, she claims 'tis because she is too small to physically defend herself so she wants a quiverful of insults to fling at any foe."

"I dinnae think it was her insults that left Malcolm looking so poorly."

Artan nodded, feeling proud of how his wife had dealt with Malcolm. "*That* is the Sile I want. Nay this sweet, puling little weakling of a lass. When I kidnapped her the first time and I set her back on her feet and took that gag off, she spit out insults that could make your hair curl and was practically hopping up and down she was so angry. I kenned then that I had found my mate."

"Aye, she sounds perfect for ye," drawled Bennet, and chuckled when Artan nodded in all seriousness. "So tell her that."

"Tell her I thought she was adorable when she kicked me in the shins, then cursed me for making her toes hurt? That I get as hard as a rock when her eyes spark with fury and she pokes me in the chest as she scolds me? Doesnae sound like sweet words or flattery to me."

"But it is and of the most sincere kind. 'Tis how ye can make her see that ye truly want her just as she was, that 'twas that lass ye wed and wanted as your wife, as the mother of your bairns."

Artan stared at Bennet and frowned. "Shouldnae

I be telling her how bonnie she is or something about how her hair shines or her eyes are like some flower?"

"'Tisnae her looks she is trying to change or is worried about."

Revelation came hard and fast and Artan cursed softly. Bennet had hit the mark squarely and dead center. Although Cecily did not seem to believe she was as bonnie as she was, she was also not terribly concerned about it. Only the occasional hint of jealousy revealed that she thought she was not pretty enough for a man she had declared was beautiful. Foolish lass, he thought fondly. He would have to make her see that she was beautiful, but not just yet. Now he had to make her understand that it was her spirit he married, her courage and pride, and even her temper.

"Of course ye could always just tell her that ye love her," murmured Bennet.

"And why should I be doing that?" Artan was sorely tempted to remove that smug, knowing look from Bennet's face, preferably by grinding it into the mud.

"Because ye do. Saw it the first day ye arrived, when ye realized that she had been hurt by the knowledge of your bargain with Angus."

"Weel, it may be true, but a mon has his pride. She hasnae said she loves me, ye ken. Dinnae see why I should be the first."

"Mayhap she hasnae said it in words, but she has in so many other ways that 'tis clear to everyone at Glascreag. Aye, and why else would she be trying so hard to be a perfect wife for ye?"

Artan stared blindly at the keep as he and Bennet approached the gates. His heart was pounding hard and fast in his chest at the mere thought that his Sile might love him. He had told himself that her passion, respect, and caring were enough, but now knew that he had lied to himself. There had remained an unease in his heart, a nameless craving. He now knew what that craving was for. He needed Cecily to love him because she was his life, his mate, his love. It was not enough to have Bennet say it was so either. Artan needed Cecily to say the words. The urge to race to their bedchamber and demand she say the words was fierce, but he wrestled it into submission. In her current humor she could well say the words just because he had demanded them of her. He wanted to hear them only if she truly meant them.

As he and Bennet dismounted in the bailey, Artan struggled to prepare himself for the confrontation with his wife. It could not be delayed any longer if only because waiting was not going to give him any better idea of what to say to her. Realizing he was cowering at the thought of having a serious discussion with a tiny green-eyed woman, Artan suddenly found his courage again. If he had to, he could face an army armed only with his bare hands and make a good accounting of himself. He could certainly face a discussion of feelings with his wife without flinching. Artan set his shoulders and walked purposefully toward the doors of the keep.

"Good luck!" called Bennet.

Artan only grunted in reply for he knew he was going to need every scrap of good fortune he could grab hold of. Never had so much depended on his ability to speak clearly about what he felt, and never had he been so fully aware of how little skill he had for such a mission.

Chapter 22

Cecily looked at the shirt she was sewing for Artan. A good wife was efficient with a needle. A good wife wove tapestries, made cushions and altar clothes. A good wife could sew a straight line of neat little stitches. Looking at the shirt again, Cecily decided no one could ever say that those seams were straight or her stitches neat.

She would have to pull out all her stitches and start all over again. Cecily took a slow, deep breath, but it did little to ease the anger building inside of her. It made no sense that she should be feeling so angry over nothing more than a badly sewn shirt, but she was. For several days, the anger had lurked inside her, but until now, she had been able to push it aside. She just wished she could discover where it was all coming from.

Plucking at the stitching, she wondered why it was all going so horribly wrong. She was doing what she should. Cecily had been very careful about which of Anabel's thousands of rules she would heed now, weeding out the ones she felt had been imposed upon her just to make her miserable.

What had been left were the sort of rules most ladies were taught. As a result of following those rules she should be happy, Artan should be happy, her uncle should be happy, and they should all be living in a happy home.

Instead, she was utterly and completely wretched. Her body ached from trying to be a good wife in the bedchamber, as it took a great deal of effort to be a lady when Artan kissed and caressed her. Artan was starting to look as angry as she felt, as well as confused. Her uncle occasionally looked at her as if he were sorely tempted to shove one of his carvings down her throat. Old Meg looked as if she wanted to shake her until her teeth rattled. Glascreag had not changed much, but some of the MacReiths were starting to look at her as if they thought she had been hit on the head once too often. She had failed and she had failed miserably.

She suddenly threw the shirt on the floor. Muttering every curse she could think of, she stomped on it repeatedly. She was just thinking that she should have done this earlier, that the knot of anger inside of her was rapidly loosening, when she abruptly realized that she was no longer alone.

Artan silently closed the door behind him and stared at his wife. She was doing a strange sort of dance on top of a piece of linen and muttering some very creative curses. One thing he had never considered concerning the odd humor she had been in lately was that she might be suffering from some sort of madness or a brain fever.

He quickly shook aside that alarming and foolish thought. There was not a thing wrong with Cecily's mind except that it could be too quick for a man's comfort. At times she also got some strange ideas stuck in that clever mind of hers. He suspected there was one there now.

When she looked up and saw him, Artan felt as if someone had just reached inside his chest and squeezed his heart. His Sile looked so lost, so forlorn, he quickly strode across the room and pulled her into his arms. His little wife had been through a great deal of turmoil and change just lately. She had faced some hard, ugly truths and survived. She had thus far survived marriage to a man like him and having Angus for her uncle. It was not surprising that she should be feeling emotional from time to time, especially when the people who should have cared for her had spent the last twelve years doing everything in their power to crush her spirit, to enslave her to their will.

Which, he daily thanked God, they had failed to do. His Sile had all the spirit and passion he could have ever hoped to find in his wife. It had just been waiting there inside her for someone to pull it free again. He just wished she would cease trying to bury it again, which she did from time to time. Anabel's grasp on Cecily's spirit was still tight and choking and he desperately needed to find a way to break it permanently. Artan listened closely to what Cecily was muttering against his chest, selecting what words he could understand and felt might be useful. He also waited patiently for her to stop crying on his shirt and tell him what was wrong.

Hearing a little voice in her head telling her that this was not how a good wife would behave, Cecily tried to step back, but Artan tightened his grip. "Is there something ye want, Artan?" she asked.

"Aye, I want ye to tell me why ye were dancing on that piece of linen," he replied.

Cecily looked down at the crumpled remains of the shirt she had been trying to make and felt like crying some more. "I wasnae doing a dance. I was stomping on it."

"And just what is it."

"Was. It was a shirt. I was trying to make ye a shirt." She nodded when he frowned down at it, certain that he was seeing exactly what a poor job she had done. "'Tis ruined. S'truth it was weel ruined ere I threw it on the floor and started stomping on it and cursing it. I failed. Miserably. I think someone could threaten to cut off all my toes one by one and I still couldnae sew a straight seam. All good wives are skilled with a needle. But nay me. Do ye see any cushions in here?"

"Ah, weel, nay. No cushions."

"Of course ye dinnae see any. I havenae made any. I have failed at that, too."

"I dinnae mind that there are no cushions in here, and if I need a new shirt, weel, there are plenty of women about who can sew a fine stitch and would be pleased to earn a coin or two for making me one."

Artan began to feel a little desperate. He could tell by the look on her face that he was not saying the right things. She looked even more upset now than she had before he tried to soothe her.

"So ye failed to make a shirt for me and cushions for our bedchamber. It doesnae matter," he said firmly; then frustration over being unable to talk freely to the woman she had become and his inability to bring his ewer-tossing Sile back seized hold of him. "Do ye really want to ken what I want?"

Cecily heard the faint hint of a growl in his voice and eyed him warily. "Aye, of course. A good wife—"

"I want *my* wife back," he snapped, interrupting what he felt was going to be an irritating list of all the truly stupid things Anabel had said.

"But I am trying to give ye a wife, to get back to what I was ere we left Dunburn."

"Nay, it isnae what ye are doing. E'en at Dunburn ye werenae like ye have been these last few days. Ye have been acting verra odd."

"Odd? I havenae been acting odd. I have been trying to learn how to be a good wife to ye and—"

"Curse it, ye *have* been a good wife, a verra good wife."

"Artan, I threw a ewer at your head."

He nodded and kissed the tip of her nose. "Aye, and your aim was true. I would have been trying to explain a blackened eye or broken nose if I hadnae ducked. Ye have a fine aim with a rock, too."

"Artan"—she grasped him by the upper part of his arms and stared into his eyes—"when ye were dying—"

"I wasnae dying."

"Ye were as close to it as I e'er want to see," she snapped, then drew a deep breath to calm herself. "When I thought ye were dying, I made a vow to God."

"Not to be celibate, I hope."

A good wife should not want to hit her husband with a thick stick, she told herself, and sighed out her annoyance. "I vowed that I would be the perfect wife, that that was what ye deserved."

"What I deserved? Just what is a perfect wife?"

"She can sew and weave and run a household. She does all she can to ensure her husband's comfort and cares for all the elderly kin who live with her."

"Dinnae let Angus hear ye call him elderly," he muttered and ignored her glare.

"A good wife is always gentle and kind, polite and weel-behaved, soft of voice and mild of temper. A good wife—" She peered over the top of his hand when he put it over her mouth.

"And just where did ye learn all of this?" he asked as he slowly removed his hand. "From the woman who had a hand in the murder of your family and was hoping ye would be killed along with them? The one who made your life a misery for so long? The one who has been living off of money and lands that should have been yours? Made ye feel like the poor kinswoman she so kindly raised, when 'tis truly she who is the one who is penniless? If ye are still heeding anything that woman said, then mayhap I was wrong and ye are suffering from a fever of the brain."

Cecily gasped and glared at him. "There is nay need to be insulting." She suddenly found herself with nothing to say, being at a complete loss as to how to defend herself for he was right. "Others abide by most of these rules. These are the sort of rules women teach to their daughters."

"Ye had best nay teach our daughter such nonsense."

"'Tisnae nonsense." She inwardly cursed, for she was feeling like crying again and she was not sure why. "'Tis how a wife should act."

"Why dinnae ye just be yourself?"

"Because I couldnae abide it if ye pushed me away," she whispered, then clapped a hand over her mouth as she realized what she had just said.

Artan almost smiled, touched by her words for they indicated that she did care for him, but he forced himself to keep all of his attention on what they were discussing. He was beginning to see the problem more clearly. It was as Old Meg had suspected. Cecily was trying to win his approval. Just as she had done when she had been a lonely child forced to sit apart from the family she so badly needed, she was trying to do all she could to win his approval, ne'er realizing that she had had it and so much more from the very first day they met.

"I will ne'er push ye away, Sile mine," he said quietly. "In some ways, 'tis ye who have been pushing me away these last few days."

"I would ne'er do that."

"Oh, and why wouldnae ye? Do ye perhaps care for me a wee bit?"

"Dinnae be such an idiot. Care? Of course I care. I love ye."

The moment those words left her mouth, Cecily desperately wanted to find a hole to crawl into. When she suddenly found herself being fiercely kissed by Artan, she felt her embarrassment ease. A man could not kiss a woman like this if he had just been told something he did not want to hear. There was no awkwardness or hesitation here, but a hearty welcome. Cecily suddenly felt better than she had in a long time, although she knew this acceptance of her love did not mean he returned it.

"Say it again," he whispered against her ear.

"I love ye," she whispered back and cried out softly in surprise when he picked her up and carried her to their bed.

They were naked and in each other's arms so quickly it made her as dazed as his kisses did. She tried to pull forth the ladylike coolness she had only recently achieved, but it was nowhere to be found.

Her emotions were so raw and his lovemaking so fierce that she had no time to collect herself. It took but a few kisses and she was as wild and greedy as he was. She fought with him to see which of them could drive the other more mad with desire, giving him back all he gave her, caress for caress and kiss for kiss. When he thrust into her, she cried out both in welcome and in disappointment that this wild mating would soon be over.

Still trembling and panting from the fierce release they had shared, Cecily cautiously eyed the man sprawled in her arms. Although she had much preferred this sort of lovemaking to the restrained sort she had been trying to achieve, it was not what could be considered ladylike, and she suddenly felt uneasy. It would appear that this was yet another thing she would fail to be perfect at.

"I am sorry," she heard herself say and then sighed, wondering if she sounded as pathetic as she thought she did.

"Sorry? For what? Making your mon so satisfied he will probably need a good hour ere he can even walk?" He lifted his head to give her a soft kiss and then frowned as he saw how troubled she was. "Does our lovemaking nay please ye?" He knew it did, but something troubled her and he was determined to find out what as he would not allow her to return to the cold, stiff woman he had found in his bed for the last few nights.

"Did I nay caress ye in the right places? Give ye pleasure? Kiss ye where ye wanted to be kissed?"

"Nay, it isnae your fault. Ye are all that is wonderful and ye please me more than I can say. 'Tis just that I cannae seem to behave as a lady should when ye are kissing me."

"A lady? Sile mine, the woman I have found in my bed these last few nights may have looked like my wife, but she wasnae, and she wasnae a lady either. She was a corpse. Aye, she had all the life and warmth of a dead herring."

"Artan!"

He took her face in his hands and looked squarely in her eyes, ignoring her blushes. "If someone has told ye that a lady must lie beneath her mon like a body ready for a winding sheet, they were wrong. I would e'en wonder if their aim was a cruel one, for I cannae think of much else that would more quickly send a mon out seeking a pair of warmer arms."

Cecily blinked as she realized that the anger she had sensed in him lately came from the fact that he had believed she had turned cold toward him. "But 'tis said a mon doesnae respect a lass who is too, weel, warm."

"If 'tis his own sweet wife who leaves scratches on his back and her cries of pleasure still ringing in his ears for hours later, he nay only respects her, he craves her. At least this mon does." He eased down her body a little and began to kiss and caress her breasts. "He likes to hear those soft kitten sounds she makes when he feasts upon her bonnie breasts." He slid his hand down her body and began to stroke her intimately. "Aye, and that soft keening sound when he caresses her here is sweet music to his ears."

Seeing how a returning desire had darkened her eyes, he began to kiss his way down her body. He had sorely missed the fire they shared, and he was determined to make her see that he did crave it and had no intention of letting her keep it from him again. If he had to make love to her until he could not walk, well, he mused and grinned, he was willing to make the sacrifice.

"He likes to feel how her sweet body lifts to his every kiss and caress." He used his shoulders to nudge her legs apart and open her for his kiss. "And he loves to feel her writhe with delight when he does this."

Cecily cried out softly when he began to love her with his mouth. Embarrassment and hesitation over such an intimacy came and went in the space of a heartbeat. She tried to fight her own passion, but this time it was so she could savor the pleasure he gave her for a long time. Too soon she knew her release was rushing through her and she struggled to pull him into her arms. He ignored her, taking her to pleasure's heights with his kiss. She was still crying out with the force of her release when he thrust inside of her and joined her in that blissful place.

It was several moments before she could find the strength to speak. "So, I am to cease trying to be a corpse in the bedchamber?"

Artan laughed and forced his sated body to shift a little to the side. He lifted his head enough to give her a lazy kiss, then drew her up close to his body. "Aye, ne'er bring that woman back here. I fair to froze my parts off trying to warm her."

"Oh, weel, that settles it then. I shall ne'er invite her back. The verra last thing I wish to do is damage your parts."

He grinned briefly, then grew serious. "Ye dinnae have to be any more than ye are, Sile. That insult-spitting, rock-throwing, shin-kicking lass is the one I married, the one I wanted to marry. I dinnae care if ye can make cushions or shirts or sew a straight stitch on anything other than a wound. I dinnae need those things. I need the lass who rode from Dunburn to Glascreag without a complaint, the one who tells me I am an idiot when I deserve it, and, aye, the one who throws ewers at my head when I have been a fool and hurt her feelings."

"I shouldnae have done that, Artan. I could have really hurt ye."

"And I deserved to be hurt for I hurt ye." He pressed his lips to her forehead and said quietly, "I cannae say I will ne'er do so again either, for men can be louts who dinnae think ere they act or speak. But I will do my best, for I cannae bear to see that look of pain in your eyes. I would rather cut off my own leg. Just remember that ye are my wife, my mate, my heart, aye, and my love." He felt her tense in his arms and wondered what he had said wrong now.

"Your heart? Your love? Do ye love me, Artan?" she asked in a somewhat small, unsteady voice.

"Aye, I do." He sighed and held her a little tighter when he felt the damp of tears on his chest. "That makes ye cry?"

"With happiness. Only with happiness. I ne'er thought ye would, ye see, e'en though I have loved ye for so long."

"Weel, I cannae say exactly how long I have kenned that I love ye, but I have been acting like an idiot since I met ye, so I suspicion it has been nearly from the start. Once I kissed ye, I kenned that ye were my mate and my poor mon's mind got stuck on that word." He grinned when she laughed and then, grasping her by the chin, turned her face up to him. "I love ye, Sile mine. Ne'er forget that. I love ye as ye are. Ye dinnae have to try to turn yourself into someone else to win my approval or respect or love. Ye have that. Always."

Cecily touched a kiss to his lips and lightly stroked his cheek with her fingers. She found it hard to believe that this man loved her and that he obviously understood her very well. The fact that he loved her despite or perhaps because she was a little rough at times soothed a lot of wounds, and she loved him all the more for that.

"Just as I am?"

"Aye, just as ye are. I saw that spirit peeking out of ye at Dunburn. The further away from that place we got the more that spirit showed itself and the more I wanted ye. I dinnae need excellent manners, dainty cushions, and lush tapestries. I need ye." He smiled slightly when she hugged him, hard. "I had feared that I had lost ye, lass."

There was a strong hint of grief in his voice and she pressed a kiss to his chest. "Never. And I will ne'er again try to make myself into something I think ye want."

"Good, for ye were driving all of us mad."

"All of ye?"

"Aye, your uncle e'en offered to help me strangle some sense into ye. We agreed that ye had become so sweet and so pleasant our teeth hurt and something had to be done."

"I was driving myself a wee bit mad as weel," she admitted. "I was making myself very angry."

"Ah, and that is why ye were stomping on that shirt."

"I fear so. So, I shall be happy now by being who I am, and if I try to slip back, try to do something that isnae like me just to make someone else happy—"

"I will beat ye."

"A strong word will suffice, thank ye."

"Fair enough. We will be happy, lass. Dinnae fret o'er that. How can we nay be when we love each other?"

"Verra true, Highlander."

"Ye are one, too, ye ken."

"Why, so I am. How wonderful."

He yawned. "Weel, it appears I am going to have to take a wee rest ere I love ye again. Ye have worn your mon out, wife."

"Ye do ken how to flatter a lass, husband. But I dinnae wish ye to exhaust yourself. We have our whole lives." She sighed, liking the sound of that.

"Aye that we do, but Angus is eager for a grandchild, 'weel, a grandnephew although he doesnae call it that. Ye have noticed that all his carvings are toys, havenae ye?"

He frowned when she tensed and slowly sat up. Not allowing himself to become distracted by the sight of her lovely breasts peeping out through the long waves of her hair, he studied her expression. She did not look angry or upset or even afraid, all things the mention of begetting a child might stir in a woman if she was not ready for one. She looked stunned and he felt his heart skip with a sudden hope. He waited tensely as she counted on her fingers, but his patience ran out very quickly.

"Sile?"

Blinking, she stared at Artan. "I think we may have already made one. I am, weel, I havenae," she grimaced, cursed softly, and tried again. "I am late."

"How late?"

"A fortnight."

"Is that unusual?"

"Verra unusual, and I cannae understand why I didnae notice."

Artan whooped and pulled her back into his arms, kissing her with all the joy he felt. "My sweet wee Sile, ye have made me verra happy. Nay, I was verra happy. Now I am exhultant."

"Who would have thought that we would have all this when ye first stepped into Dunburn with a Donaldson guard hanging from each hand?"

"I believe I felt the touch of fate's hand the minute I looked into your eyes, my heart."

"Oh, Artan, ye are becoming verra good with sweet words." She lifted her head and brushed her lips over his. "Verra good, indeed."

"For a barbarian, ye mean."

"Aye, for a handsome, strong, kind barbarian. My barbarian."

"Always yours." He touched his lips to hers and whispered, "But let us keep the *kind* to ourselves, shall we?"

She was still laughing when he kissed her.

Epilogue

Dunburn
Three years later

"What are ye doing?" demanded Cecily as Artan finished binding her wrists together and then reached for a strip of linen.

"Kidnapping ye," he said just before he gagged her.

Artan grinned as he tossed her over his shoulder, walked out of their bedchamber, and started down the stairs. His loving wife was obviously vilifying his character very creatively behind that gag. He paused to share a grin with Angus, who stood with a grandnephew on either side of him. Even at the tender age of two the twins looked a lot like him, so they looked a lot like Angus as well. Right down to the scowls they wore.

"Where Maman?" demanded Aiden.

"I am just going to take her for a wee walk," replied Artan.

"Fine," said Eric; then he turned and walked back into the great hall.

Meg peered at him from around Angus and scowled at him, although her eyes were alight with laughter. "She doesnae sound like she wants to go."

"She will change her mind when we get there," Artan said, tightening his grip on wife when she thrashed a little in protest to the arrogance.

"I hope so, or ye will soon have to be explaining to your wee lads how their da got a broken nose."

Artan just laughed and strode out of the keep, leaving his sons in the loving and capable hands of their grandparents. It was marriage to Meg that had softened Angus enough for them all to make the trip to Dunburn, his son Eric's legacy. Meg wanted to see her children and their families who lived nearby. She badly wanted them to meet Angus. Artan had the suspicion that she also wished to see their faces when she introduced little Meghan to them. Her miracle child she called Meghan, for Meg had been near the end of her rapidly fading days of her childbearing years. It had been a hard birth, and Artan knew Meg and Angus were being very cautious now, seeing no need to risk her life in the bearing of a child they did not need. Meghan was being raised like a sister to the twins, for no one could ignore the fact that there was a good chance that Angus and Meg would not live to see their daughter grow up.

Artan, on the other hand, did not have to worry. The twins were two years old, nearly completely weaned, and his Sile was more than ready for another child. He was the one who had insisted upon waiting, wanting to be sure that there was no chance she could be weakened by bearing children too close together. Neither of them held any real, deep fears, however. Even the midwife, with Crooked Cat and Meg standing close by her side, had expressed astonishment over the ease with which Cecily had birthed the twins, who were both of a sturdy size at birth.

All the women had declared Cecily one of those very fortunate women who could bear children with as much ease as that arduous miracle would allow. He had his bonnie black-haired sons. Now he wanted a sprightly little girl with sharp green eyes and dark red hair, a little girl filled with the same fire and spirit that made her mother his heart's delight.

The moment he set Cecily on her feet her eyes widened. As Artan struggled to undo the bonds on his wife's wrists, Cecily stood very still. She was not sure what game he played and had no inclination to do anything that might stop him.

"Here we are wife," he announced before removing her gag.

"If ye are waiting for some curses, I fear the walk over here caused me to lose most of them."

"Fell out your earhole, eh?"

Cecily ignored that and looked around the leafy bower by the burn where her journey had begun. She had been hinting that she wanted to come here since they had arrived at Dunburn a week ago and been heartily ignored. That had obviously been done because he had known they would be coming here, he had just wanted to change the moment. Food and wine were set out beneath the large group of trees that formed the bower she had so loved to play in.

"A tryst, my fine Highland knight?" she asked, smiling at him.

"Aye, a tryst," he said as he took her by the hand and

drew her under the trees. "There were a few things I didnae do the last time we were here."

"Those being?"

"Take your maidenhead."

"Long gone and good riddance, say I."

"Your heart?"

"Secure in your grasp long before the tryst."

He laughed and gently lowered her onto the thick plaid he had spread over the ground earlier. They made love slowly in the late-afternoon sun. Artan found the passion between them still as hot and sweet as it had been all those years ago when he had lured her to this place. After three years of marriage and two bright sons, he still could not get enough of her. The way she returned his every kiss and caress, the way she tried to make him as wild with need as he tried to make her, told him that she felt the same magic they had briefly shared in this same spot before he had spoiled it.

Still trembling from the strength of his release and the sweetness of sharing it with her, Artan rolled over onto his back and tugged her into his arms. She gave him the smile she always did after they had made love, the soft, satisfied one that still held the glint of a lingering pleasure. It was a smile that always made him feel as if he was the greatest lover in the land.

Cecily kissed the tip of his nose and murmured, "Ye are watching me as if ye expect me to leap up and dance about this leafy bower."

"Oh, would ye?"

"Artan, is something troubling ye?"

"Nay, love, not now. Ye see, I have always felt a wee bit guilty for what happened that night. Ye were right to feel betrayed. I brought ye out here to kidnap ye, and yet I was too weak a mon to refuse to steal a wee bit of delight first. Oh, aye, I had plans to marry ye, as in my arrogance I had decided ye would suit me and it wouldnae be a hardship to be married to ye to gain Glascreag."

It was hard not to laugh for he was not telling her anything she had not figured out a long time ago. The fact that it had troubled him for so long was, however, very touching. Cecily wondered how she had ever gotten so lucky as to have such a good man love her.

"True, that was definitely an astonishing display of arrogance. But, Artan, ye are the only one who is still troubled by what happened here. If ye had whispered a few sweet words to me, I probably wouldnae have gotten as angry as I did. But ye saved my life that night. It took me a wee while to ken it, but 'tis true. And that matters far more to me than the fact that ye trysted with me when ye had really only intended to get me away from the danger at Dunburn. In truth, if I hadnae been such a sheltered innocent, I would have been aware that a mon cannae make love to me as ye did then and nay feel something for the woman."

He kissed her. "I wanted to banish any bad memories."

"Weel, ye have, although there were only a few, and mostly due to the fact that I was so sure I was unworthy of anyone's attention, the problem being mine not yours." She slid her hand down his taut stomach. "Most of the memories are quite nice, thank ye. A sheltered lass who has been convinced that she is worthless gets to come to this beautiful spot, in the moonlight, and have the handsomest mon she has e'er seen not only make love to her but steal her away because she is in danger."

"I sound a verra daring, gallant sort of fellow in your version of the tale," he said, his last word ending on a soft groan as she stroked him with her small hand.

"Verra daring and verra gallant." She replaced her hand with her mouth. "And tasty."

Reaching down, Artan grabbed her by the legs and turned her so that he could return the pleasure she was giving him. They toyed with and tormented each other until, at the same moment, their control broke. Their cries of pleasure were still in the air when they crawled around and collapsed in each other's arms.

"Ye do ken that this was but one reason I brought ye here to Dunburn, dinnae ye?" he asked when he finally had the energy to speak.

"Aye, ye wanted me to see that they are really gone," she said quietly before sitting up and tugging on her shift. "Ye were right. In my head I kenned that they had finally paid for their crimes, e'en felt bad that their daughters were marked by the fact that their parents were hanged for murder and theft, but there were a few places that still believed they could somehow come back and ruin my life. I did need to banish the ghosts."

Tossing on his plaid, he also sat up and lightly draped his arm around her. "Good. Now I can be sure I will ne'er see the good wife again."

Cecily laughed. "Nay." She brushed a kiss over his lips. "As for the memories of this place? Ah, husband, there is one that I shall ne'er forget."

"Ah, my lovemaking."

"And verra nice it was, too. Nay, sorry, Artan, it

isnae the lovemaking. For all ye may have done wrong that night, ye did one thing that I shall never forget and for which I shall always be grateful."

"And what was that."

"Ye set me free, Artan. E'en better, ye set me free to be me and to be your Sile."

"And dragged ye into my life."

"Where I hope ye shall keep me."

"Aye, lass, for always."

New York Times *bestselling author Hannah Howell returns to the fateful realms of the Scottish Highlands, where a man's destiny lies in the heart of the woman who once betrayed him . . .*

Beaten and left for dead, Sir Lucas Murray is a man wounded in body and soul. He has brought himself back to becoming the warrior he once was—except for his ruined leg and the grief he feels over the death of the woman he once loved . . . the same woman who led him into enemies' hands.

Dressed as a masked reiver, it is Katerina Haldane who saves Lucas as he battles for his life—and for revenge. Shocked that she still lives, Lucas becomes desperate to ignore the desire raging through his body. And Katerina becomes desperate to regain his trust, trying to convince him of her half-sister's role in his beating. Lucas is reluctant to let down his guard, but his resistance melts once Katerina is back in his arms . . . and his bed. Now he must learn to trust his instincts—in battle and in love . . .

Please turn the page for an exciting sneak peek at Hannah Howell's HIGHLAND SAVAGE, now available!

Scotland
Spring, 1481

His robes itched. Lucas gritted his teeth against the urge to throw them off and vigorously scratch every inch of his body he could reach. He did not know how his cousin Matthew endured wearing the things day in and day out. Since the man had happily dedicated his life to the service of God, Lucas did not think Matthew deserved such an excruciating penance. A mon willing to sacrifice so much for God ought to able to do so in more comfortable garb.

"This may have been a bad idea, Eachann," Lucas murmured to his mount as he paused on a small rise to stare down at the village of Dunlochan.

His big brown gelding snorted and began to graze on the grass at his hooves.

"Weel, there is nay turning back now. Nay, I am but suffering a moment of uncertainty and it shames me. I have just ne'er been verra skilled in subterfuge, aye? 'Tis a blunt mon I am and this shall require me to be subtle and sly. But, 'tis nay a worry for I have been practicing."

Lucas frowned at his horse and sternly told himself that the animal only sounded as if it had just snickered. On the other hand, if the animal could understand what he said, snickering would probably be an appropriate response. Yet, he had no choice. He needed revenge. It was a hunger inside him that demanded feeding. It was not something he could ask his family to risk themselves for, either, although they had been more than willing to do so. That willingness was one reason he had had to slip away under the cover of night, telling no one where he was going, not even his twin.

This was his fight and his alone. Surrounded by the strong, skilled fighting men of his clan, he knew he would feel deprived of satisfying the other need he had. He needed to prove to himself that his injuries had not left him incapable of being the warrior he had been before he had been beaten. He needed to defeat the men who had tried to destroy him and defeat them all by himself. His family had not fully understood that need. They had not fully understood his need to work so hard, so continuously, to regain his skills after he had recovered from the beating, either. He knew the praise they had given him as he had slowly progressed from invalid to fighting man had, in part, been an attempt to stop him from striving so hard to regain his former abilities, to overcome the stiffness and pain in his leg. He desperately needed to see that he was as good as he had been, that he had not been robbed of the one true strength he had. He had to prove himself worthy of being the heir to Donncoill.

"Artan would understand," he said, stroking

Eachann's strong neck as he slowly rode down the hill toward the village.

He felt a pang of lingering grief. His twin had his own life now, one separate from the one they had shared since the womb. Artan had a wife, his own lands, and a family of his own. Lucas was happy for his twin yet he was still grieved by the loss of the other half of himself. In his heart Lucas knew he and Artan could never be fully separated but now Artan shared himself with others as he had only ever shared himself with Lucas. It would take some getting used to.

"And I have no one."

Lucas grimaced. He sounded like a small sulky child, yet that feeling of being completely alone was one he could not shake. It disgusted him, but he knew part of it was that he had lost not only Artan; he had lost Katerina. She had betrayed him and did not deserve his grief, yet it lingered. No other woman could banish the emptiness left by her loss. No other woman could ease the coldness left by her vicious betrayal. He could still see her watching as he was beaten nigh unto death. She had made no sound, no move to save him. She had not even shed a tear.

He shook aside those dark memories and the pain they still brought him. Lucas decided that once he had proven to himself that he was the man he used to be, he would find himself a woman and rut himself blind. He would exhaust himself in soft, welcoming arms and sweat out the poison of Katerina. Even though it was not fully a fidelity to Katerina that had kept him almost celibate, he knew a lingering hunger for her, for the passion they had shared, was one reason he found it difficult to satisfy his needs elsewhere. In his mind he was done with her, but it was obvious his heart and body were still enslaved. He would overcome his reluctance to reveal his scars and occasional awkwardness to a woman and find himself a lover when he returned to Donncoill. Maybe even a wife, he mused as he reined in before the small inn in the heart of the village. All too clearly recalling Katerina's dark blue eyes and honeyblond hair, he decided that woman would be dark. It was time to make the cut sharp and complete.

Dismounting, Lucas gave the care of Eachann over to a bone thin youth who quickly appeared at his side. The lad stared at him with wide blue eyes, looking much as if he had just seen a ghost and that look made Lucas uneasy. Subtly he checked to make certain that his cowl still covered the hair he had been unable to cut. Although he had told himself he would need the cowl up at all times to shadow his far too recognizable face, Lucas knew it was vanity that had made him reluctant to cut off his long black hair and his warrior braids. Deciding the boy might just be a little simple, Lucas collected his saddle-packs then gave the lad a coin before making his way into the inn.

After taking only two steps into the building, Lucas felt the chill of fear speed down his spine and stopped to look around. This was where he had been captured, dragged away to be savagely beaten and then left for dead. Despite the nightmares he still suffered on occasion, he had thought he had conquered the unreasonable fear his beating had left him with.

Annoyance over such a weakness helped him quell that fear. Standing straighter he made his way to a table set in a shadowy corner at the back of the room. He had barely sat down when a buxom fair-haired maid hurried over to greet him. If he recalled right, her name was Annie.

"Father," she began.

"Nay, my child. I am nay tonsured yet," Lucas said, hoping such a tale would help explain away any mistakes he might make. "I am on pilgrimage ere I return to the monastery and take my final vows."

"Oh." Annie sighed. "I was hoping ye were looking for a place to serve God's will." She briefly glared at the men drinking ale near the large fireplace. "We could certainly use a holy mon here. Dunlochan has become steeped in sin and evil."

"I will be certain to tell my brothers of your need when I return to them, child."

"Thank ye, Father. Ah, I mean, sir. How can I serve ye?"

"Food, ale, and a bed for the night, lass."

In but moments Lucas was enjoying a rich ale, a hearty mutton stew, and thick warm bread. The good food served by the inn was one reason he had lingered in Dunlochan long enough to meet Katerina. His stomach had certainly led him astray that day, he thought sourly. In truth, his stomach may have kept him at Dunlochan long enough to meet Katerina, but it was another heedless part of him that had truly led him astray. One look at her lithe body, her long thick hair the color of sweet clover honey, and her wide deep blue eyes and all his wits had sunk right down into his groin. He had thought he had met his mate and all he had found was betrayal and pain.

Lucas cursed silently. The woman would not get out of his life, out of his mind or out of his heart.

That would not stop him from getting his revenge on her, however. He was not quite sure how he would accomplish that yet, but he would. First the men who had tried to kill him and then the woman who had given the order.

Another casualty of that dark night was his trust in people, in his ability to judge them as friend or foe. Lucas had believed Katerina was his mate, the woman he had been born to be with. Instead she had nearly been his death. It was hard to trust his own judgment after such a near fatal error and an ability to discern whom to trust was important to a warrior. How could he ever be a good laird to the people of Donncoill if he could not even tell friend from foe?

He sipped his ale and studied the men near the fireplace. Lucas was sure that at least one of them had been there that night, but the shadows cast by the fire made it difficult to see the man clearly. One of the things he recalled clearly was that few of the men had been fair like most of the Haldanes were. It had puzzled him that Katerina would hire mercenaries, but, perhaps, her own people would never have obeyed such an order from her. If those men were no more than hired swords it would make the killing of them easier for few would call out for vengeance when they died.

Six men suddenly entered the inn and Lucas stiffened. No shadows hid their faces and he recognized each one. It was hard to control the urge to immediately draw his sword and set after them. He shuddered faintly, the memory of the beating flaring crisp and clear in his mind and body. Lucas rubbed his left leg, the ache of shattered bones sharpened by those dark memories. His right hand throbbed as if it recalled each and every slam of a boot on it. The scar that now ran raggedly over his right cheek itched and Lucas could almost feel the pain of the knife's blade cutting through the flesh there.

He drew in a deep breath and let it out slowly. Lucas knew he needed to push those memories aside if he was to think clearly. The revenge he hungered for could not be accomplished if he acted too quickly or if he gave into the fierce urge to immediately draw his sword and attack these men. When he realized part of his ability to hold back was because he did not think he could defeat the six men with a direct attack, he silently cursed again. His confidence in his newly regained battle skills was obviously not as strong as he had thought it was.

"Annie!" bellowed one of the men as he and his companions sat down. "Get your arse o'er here and pour us some ale, wench!"

There was an obvious caution in Annie's steps as she approached the men with tankards and an ewer of ale. "Hush, Ranald," she said. "I saw ye come in and was ready. There is nay need to bellow so."

Lucas watched as the young woman did her best to pour each man a tankard of ale even as she tried to avoid their grasping hands. Unlike many another lass who worked in such a place, Annie was no whore easily gained by a coin or two, but the men treated her as if she was. By the time she was able to get away from their table, she was flushed with anger and her eyes were shining with tears of shame. Lucas had to take a deep drink of the strong ale to quell the urge to leap to her defense. He gave her a small smile when she paused by his table to refill his tankard and wondered why that made her eyes narrow and caused a frown to tighten her full mouth.

"Have ye been here before, sir?" she asked as she suddenly sat down across the scarred table from him.

"Nay, why should ye think so, child?" he asked.

"There was something about your smile," she said then shrugged. "'Twas familiar."

Lucas had no idea how a smile could be familiar but told himself to remember to be more cautious about doing so again. "Mayhap ye just see too few, aye?"

"Certainly too few that show me such fine, white teeth."

"A blessing I got from my family and God. That and cleaning them regularly."

She nodded. "The Lady Katerina taught me the value of cleaning my teeth."

"A good and Godly woman is she?"

"She was, aye."

"Was?"

"Aye, she died last Spring, poor wee lass." She glared at the men who had treated her so badly. "They and the ladies at the keep say my lady killed herself, but I dinnae believe it. She would ne'er have done such a thing. Aye, and the lovely mon who was courting her disappeared on the verra same day. No one has an answer for where he went." She suddenly looked straight at Lucas. "That is who your smile reminded me of, I am thinking. A bonnie lad he was. He did make my lady happy, he did."

Lucas was too shocked to do more than nod. He could not even think of something to say to turn aside the dangerous comparison Annie had just made. Katerina was dead. The news hit him like a sound blow to the chest and it took him a moment to catch his breath. He told himself that the sharp grief that swept over him was born of the fact that he had lost all chance to exact his revenge upon the woman for her betrayal, but a small voice in his mind scoffed at that explanation. He ruthlessly silenced it.

"Is it a sin to visit her grave e'en though she is buried in unconsecrated ground?" Annie asked.

"Nay, lass," he replied, his voice a little hoarse from the feelings he was fighting. "Her soul needs your prayers e'en more than another's, aye?"

The thought of Katerina resting in the cold ground was more than Lucas could bear and he hastily pushed it aside. He also ignored the questions swirling in his mind, ones that demanded answers. He could not believe Katerina would kill herself either, but this was not the time to solve that puzzle. As he sought his revenge on the men who had beaten him he could ask a few questions, but that revenge had to be the first thing on his mind for now. When that was done he would discover the truth about Katerina's death. No matter what she had done to him, he knew he would never be able to rest easy with the thought of her lovely body rotting in unconsecrated soil.

"Do ye think ye could pray for her, sir? Would that be a sin?"

Lucas had no idea and fumbled for an answer. "'Tis my duty to pray for lost souls, child."

"I could take ye to where she is buried," Annie began and then scowled when Ranald and two of his companions came up to the table. "If ye want more ale, ye just needed to ask."

"I came to see why ye are sitting and talking so cozily with this monk," said Ranald.

"What business is it of yours, eh?"

"Ye waste your time wooing a monk, lass. If ye are hungry for a mon, I am more than willing to see to your needs." He grinned when his companions laughed.

"I but wished to talk to someone who has traveled beyond the boundaries of Haldane land," she snapped. "Someone who doesnae smell or curse or try to lift my skirts." Annie suddenly blushed and looked at Lucas. "Pardon me for speaking so, sir."

"'Tis nay ye who must beg pardon, child, but the men who compel ye to speak so," Lucas said, watching Ranald closely.

"Here now, I but woo the lass," said Ranald, glaring at Lucas.

"Is that what ye call it?"

"What would ye ken about it, eh? Ye have given it all up for God, aye? Or have ye? Are ye one of those who says vows to God out of one side of his mouth whilst wooing the lasses out the other?"

"Ye insult my honor," Lucas said coldly, wishing the man would leave for the urge to make him pay now, and pay dearly, for every twinge of pain Lucas had suffered over the last year was growing too strong to ignore. "I but question your skill at wooing."

"Do ye now. And just what are ye doing in Dunlochan? There is no monastery near here."

"He is on a pilgrimage ere he takes his vows," said Annie. "Leave him be and go back to your friends and your ale."

"Ye defend him most prettily, lass. I have to

wonder why." Ranald scowled at Lucas. "What is he hiding under those robes?"

Even as Lucas became aware of the sudden danger he was in, Ranald yanked back his cowl and exposed the hair Lucas had been too vain to cut. For a brief moment, everyone just stared at Lucas, their eyes wide and their mouths gaping. Lucas actually considered attacking the man Ranald immediately but good sense intervened. The man's friends were already rising from their seats and inching closer.

Taking advantage of everyone's shock at seeing what they thought was a ghost, Lucas leapt to his feet, grabbed his saddlepacks, and bolted for the door. He gained the outside and turned toward the stable only to stumble to a halt as someone grabbed his robe from behind. Cursing, he turned and kicked the man in the face. Knowing he would not make it to his horse in time, Lucas tossed aside his saddle packs and yanked off his robes. By the time Ranald and his friends had finished stumbling out of the inn, Lucas was facing them with a sword in one hand and a dagger in the other.

"So, it *is* ye," said Ranald as he drew his sword and he and his companions moved to stand facing Lucas. "Ye are supposed to be dead. We threw ye off the cliff and saw ye just lying there."

"And ye ne'er went back to see if I stayed there, did ye," Lucas said, his scorn clear to hear in his voice.

"Why trouble ourselves? We had beaten ye soundly, ye were bleeding from several wounds and we threw ye off a cliff."

Lucas shrugged. "I got up and went home," he said, knowing his family would groan to hear him describe the many travails he had gone through to return to Donncoill in such simple terms.

"Weel, ye willnae be crawling home this time, laddie."

"Nay, I intend to ride home in triumph, leaving your bodies behind me to rot in the dirt."

"I dinnae think so." Ranald sneered as he glanced at Lucas's left leg. "I watched ye run out of the inn and ye limp and stumble like an old mon. We left ye a cripple, didnae we."

Lucas fought down the rage that threatened to consume him. He had to exact his revenge coldly, had to fight with a clear head and think out every move he made. It was this man's fault that Lucas could no longer move with the speed and grace he had before, and it was hard not to just lunge at the man and cut him down. Before the beating he would have not been all that concerned about the other men, knowing he could turn on them with an equal speed and have a good chance of defeating them all. Now, because of these men, he had to weigh his every move carefully if he had any hope of coming out of this alive.

"E'en that wee wound willnae stop me from killing ye," Lucas said, his voice almost cheerful even as he noted with a twinge of dismay how the men began to slowly encircle him.

"Still arrogant," said Ranald, grinning as he shook his head. "Weel, soon ye will be joining your wee whore in the cold clay."

"So, Annie spoke true when she said Lady Katerina was dead."

"Aye, she joined ye or so we thought. Tossed her right o'er the cliff and into the water with ye."

That made no sense to Lucas, but he pushed his

sudden confusion and all the questions it raised aside. How and why Katerina had died was of no importance at the moment. Staying alive had to be his only priority. A quick glance toward the inn revealed a white-faced Annie and several other Haldanes watching and listening. Lucas had to hope that, if he failed to win this fight, they would find out what happened to Katerina, although why he should care about that was just another puzzle he had no time to solve.

"I dinnae suppose ye have the courage to face me mon to mon, without all your men to protect your worthless hide," Lucas said as he braced himself for the battle to come.

"Are ye calling me a coward?" Ranald snarled.

"Ye needed near a dozen men to capture me, beat me nigh unto death and toss me off a cliff, and then ye murdered a wee unarmed lass. Aye, I believe I am calling ye a coward and weel do ye deserve the name."

"'Twill be a joy to kill ye, fool."

Glancing around at the men encircling him, Lucas had the sinking feeling that it would also be a quick killing, but then he stiffened his backbone. He had been in such tight spots before and come out nearly unscathed. All he needed to do was regain that arrogance Ranald found so irritating. Lucas was a little concerned that he would fail at that. It seemed his heart was beating so hard and fast that he could actually hear it. Telling himself he was imagining things, he readied himself to win and, failing that, to take as many of these men with him as he could. This time, killing him was going to cost them dearly.

About the Author

Born and raised in Massachusetts, her family's home since the 1630s, Hannah Howell is the author of over thirty Zebra historical romances. Her love of history prompts the choice of venue, and also her dragging her husband, Stephen, to every historical site she can get to. Her fascination with the past makes research as much a pleasure as a necessity. It was a thrill for her to turn her love of history and writing into a career, one that allows her to share those loves with others. Readers can visit her website at www.hannahhowell.com.

Connect with

Visit us online at
KensingtonBooks.com
to read more from your favorite authors, see books
by series, view reading group guides, and more.

Join us on social media

for sneak peeks, chances to win books and prize packs,
and to share your thoughts with other readers.

facebook.com/kensingtonpublishing
twitter.com/kensingtonbooks

Tell us what you think!

To share your thoughts, submit a review,
or sign up for our eNewsletters, please visit:
KensingtonBooks.com/TellUs.

More by Bestselling Author
Hannah Howell

__Highland Angel	978-1-4201-0864-4	$6.99US/$8.99CAN
__If He's Sinful	978-1-4201-0461-5	$6.99US/$8.99CAN
__Wild Conquest	978-1-4201-0464-6	$6.99US/$8.99CAN
__If He's Wicked	978-1-4201-0460-8	$6.99US/$8.49CAN
__My Lady Captor	978-0-8217-7430-4	$6.99US/$8.49CAN
__Highland Sinner	978-0-8217-8001-5	$6.99US/$8.49CAN
__Highland Captive	978-0-8217-8003-9	$6.99US/$8.49CAN
__Nature of the Beast	978-1-4201-0435-6	$6.99US/$8.49CAN
__Highland Fire	978-0-8217-7429-8	$6.99US/$8.49CAN
__Silver Flame	978-1-4201-0107-2	$6.99US/$8.49CAN
__Highland Wolf	978-0-8217-8000-8	$6.99US/$9.99CAN
__Highland Wedding	978-0-8217-8002-2	$4.99US/$6.99CAN
__Highland Destiny	978-1-4201-0259-8	$4.99US/$6.99CAN
__Only for You	978-0-8217-8151-7	$6.99US/$8.99CAN
__Highland Promise	978-1-4201-0261-1	$4.99US/$6.99CAN
__Highland Vow	978-1-4201-0260-4	$4.99US/$6.99CAN
__Highland Savage	978-0-8217-7999-6	$6.99US/$9.99CAN
__Beauty and the Beast	978-0-8217-8004-6	$4.99US/$6.99CAN
__Unconquered	978-0-8217-8088-6	$4.99US/$6.99CAN
__Highland Barbarian	978-0-8217-7998-9	$6.99US/$9.99CAN
__Highland Conqueror	978-0-8217-8148-7	$6.99US/$9.99CAN
__Conqueror's Kiss	978-0-8217-8005-3	$4.99US/$6.99CAN
__A Stockingful of Joy	978-1-4201-0018-1	$4.99US/$6.99CAN
__Highland Bride	978-0-8217-7995-8	$4.99US/$6.99CAN
__Highland Lover	978-0-8217-7759-6	$6.99US/$9.99CAN

Available Wherever Books Are Sold!

Check out our website at
http://www.kensingtonbooks.com